FINAL
SETTLEMENT

ALSO BY VICKI DOUDERA

A House to Die For

Killer Listing

Deadly Offer

FINAL SETTLEMENT

A Darby Farr Mystery

Vicki Doudera

FIRST EDITION
First Printing, 2013

Book design by Donna Burch
Cover design by Lisa Novak
Cover illustration by Dominick Finelle/The July Group
Edited by Connie Hill

Midnight Ink, an imprint of Llewellyn Worldwide Ltd.

Library of Congress Cataloging-in-Publication Data

Doudera, Vicki, 1961–
Final settlement : a Darby Farr mystery / Vicki Doudera. — First edition.
p. cm.
ISBN 978-0-7387-3428-6
1. Women real estate agents—Fiction. 2. Murder—Investigation—Fiction. I. Title.
PS3604.O895F57 2013
813'.6—dc23

Midnight Ink
Llewellyn Worldwide Ltd.
2143 Wooddale Drive
Woodbury, MN 55125-2989
www.midnightinkbooks.com

Printed in the United States of America

DEDICATION

For Matthew, Nathan, and Alexandra,
with warm memories of Maine winters.

ACKNOWLEDGMENTS

I'm thankful for the assistance of many who helped with *Final Settlement.*

First, a big thank you to my faithful manuscript readers Lynda Chilton and Ed Doudera, whose comments and careful edits are so appreciated, and to Jane LaFleur and Jane Babbitt for proofreading.

Thank you to Nick Kava and Toby Wincklhofer for their advice on lobster fishing, as well as the Lobster Institute at the University of Maine at Orono.

I'm grateful for the support of the real Alison Dyer, a Darby Fan and Habitat Volunteer Extraordinaire, as well as all the volunteers who work to keep the Rockland Breakwater safe and beautiful.

Thank you to the Professor and Chair of the University of Maine's Department of Physics and Astronomy, David Batuski, for his assistance.

Once again, the experience of Aikido expert Sensei Gordon Muller of the New Jersey Police Academy has been very helpful, as has the assistance of the Public Affairs Office at the Federal Bureau of Investigation.

Much appreciation to my fellow real estate agents around the country and in Maine, above all, Scott Horty and the team at Camden Real Estate Company, including the trio always willing to lend a hand: Christopher Brown, Jeanne Fullilove, and Brenda Stearns.

Thank you to my literary agent, Tris Coburn, and to all the good people at Midnight Ink, including editors Terri Bischoff and Connie Hill; publicists Marissa Pederson and Courtney Colton;

and book designers Donna Burch and Lisa Novak. Thanks to illustrator Dominick Finelle for a chillingly beautiful cover.

Finally, nothing I do would be possible without the support of my husband, Ed. Thank you from the bottom of my heart!

Author's Note: Although the history of Unit 731 is all too real, the synthetic waterborne bacterium described in this story is a product of my imagination. (I hope.)

PROLOGUE

LORRAINE DELVECCHIO SMELLED THE carcass before she saw it.

The dusky stench of decaying marine life, mingled with seaweed, rotting mussels, and kelp—there was no mistaking the odor of death on the beach. She scanned the sand, quickly spotting the source: a seal the size of a toddler, with mottled brown fur and black, staring eyes. The dead mammal's whiskers stood stiffly at attention, coated in ice like pine boughs after a bout of freezing rain.

Lorraine gave the poor thing wide berth. This was the fifth seal washed up on the little beach, along with an assortment of lifeless gulls, flaccid fish, and once, a rare thresher shark. She never knew what she'd find when she made her daily walk to the Manatuck lighthouse and back, but so far, nothing, no matter how gruesome, had been enough to stop her.

Lorraine fumbled in her thick gloves, turning up her parka's collar against the cold north wind. She crossed the pebbly beach and approached the rough granite blocks of the Manatuck Breakwater, a man-made promontory jutting into the wide mouth of Manatuck

Harbor. The blocks were covered in a thin sheen of ice, but even that could not deter the determined walker. Her fur-lined hiking boots with their Italian-made soles would grip the slick surface perfectly, and without hesitation she hoisted herself onto the glistening blocks and began her brisk pace toward the lighthouse.

A weak sun struggled against scudding gray clouds, its rays powerless against the single-digit temperatures, but Lorraine was prepared for the bone-chilling cold. A thick fleece scarf wound around her neck and up over her nostrils, and her fur cap, purchased on a Christmas visit to Montreal, fit snugly over her head and ears. Swaddled in her fleeces and a long down parka, she was as comfortable as possible on a bleak February day on the coast of Maine.

A few gulls circled overhead, eyeing the solitary figure before winging off to more promising parts of the harbor. Lorraine watched the birds, white as alabaster against the dull pewter sky, hearing their shrieks over the crashing waves. She shivered as a brutal blast of wind hit her full on, chilling her lungs as she struggled to breathe. Lorraine coughed into the fleece scarf. Cold did not begin to describe the temperatures. Grimly she began pumping her arms in a swinging motion, determined to warm her muscles with her own exertion.

Last year, on this same day, it had been snowing. She recalled a thick, relentless snowfall that began at 11:15 that morning and did not let up until the middle of the night. The year before had been sunny and mild—a January thaw that had hit the coast in February. Lorraine gave a quick grin underneath her fleece. There certainly was neither rhyme nor reason to the weather patterns for February 11ths, although if she went back far enough, she doubtless could make some sort of correlation.

She glanced back down the Breakwater, toward the parking lot and her car. Not a soul in sight. Lorraine felt a pang of excitement. How many times had she taken this walk and been completely alone? Her mind sifted through the data. Sixty-two times. Sixty-two times in three years of walking.

By now, Lorraine was feeling warm enough to peel her scarf down from her nose. Her heart was pumping, her feet moving briskly over the granite blocks, and her mind slowly clearing of the endless data that cluttered it like knicknacks on a table. She took a deep breath, savoring the tang of the sea air, and smiled. *Dr. Hotchkiss would approve.* Her former employer, an elderly physician who'd practiced for years on the nearby island of Hurricane Harbor, was fond of prescribing a good, brisk walk for just about any ailment. Lorraine stooped to pick up a mussel shell that had washed onto the rocks. She held it up with a gloved hand, admiring the iridescent purple of the shiny interior, and stuffed it in her coat pocket. Perhaps the old man had been right.

A small cairn on her left indicated the midway point of the Breakwater. Lorraine herself had constructed it, both to give herself a reference and to provide one for the tourists, many of whom stopped her to inquire whether they were nearly finished. Lorraine always found this puzzling since the Breakwater stretched off without an obstacle, and they could easily see where they were headed, but she'd learned to reply cheerfully that the stone cairn (sometimes she had to explain what a cairn was) marked the midway, or half a mile.

There were rarely any tourists in January or February, unless it was a sparkling, sunny day with higher than normal temperatures. Before she could stop herself, Lorraine computed the number of

January and February days when she'd encountered people whom she'd judged to be tourists. Twenty-five. She paused. And the number of them who'd asked her a question? Seventeen.

She shook her head and tried to make her thoughts clear once more. It was a challenge, taming this monster that was her mind, but she found it necessary to try to disconnect once a day if she was going to keep what she called the screaming jeebies away. She'd sampled meditation and yoga, but found what worked best was walking the mile-long Breakwater, every day, rain or shine, at exactly the same time. The predictability of it was soothing, and the pace seemed to make it easier to relax. Was there a connection between the daily exercise and her sanity? She didn't know, but she knew the discipline worked. *It makes me more human*, she thought.

She had a sudden memory of a time before she'd started her ritual walks. She was lying on her living room couch, curled in a fetal position, with *Wheel of Fortune* playing on the television. She remembered the contestant, a chunky car salesman from St. Louis, winning one hundred thousand dollars, only to land on bankrupt with his next spin. His wife, sitting in the audience, gasped and covered her face with her hands.

Lorraine saw herself, a motionless figure on the couch, wearing a ripped flannel shirt and stretched-out exercise pants, the kind they used to call a track suit. There was a blister on her right thumb. The date was March 23, 2003.

She licked her lips, tasting salt water from the spray. Her mind flipped back to the twenty-third of every month before that, presenting image after image in excruciating detail, filling her head with memory after memory, until she stopped, dead in her tracks.

Enough! She picked up a small rock and tossed it into the waves, watching the splash. She imagined taking all of the disjointed millions of memories, and heaving them into the water, just as she had the stone. *Please God, enough*...

She took a deep breath and looked toward the lighthouse. Calm was replacing the recollections, spreading across her in a soothing puddle, much like maple syrup down a stack of pancakes. *I can control this,* she thought. *I can be just like other people. Normal people.* She took another deep breath of cold winter air, rubbed her gloved hands together, and resumed walking.

Lorraine strode the Manatuck Breakwater in every season, but winter was the time she considered the most special. She was almost always alone, for one. Out of habit she glanced back toward the shore and her silver Subaru, noting that her vehicle was still the sole car in the lot. Along with the solitude, winter brought a kind of frozen tableau in which she was one of the few creatures alive. Outside of a gull or the occasional duck, Lorraine was the only living thing for what seemed like miles.

She stepped resolutely over the thick granite blocks. Quarried from the city of Manatuck, as well as Hurricane Harbor and some of the surrounding islands, the speckled stone seawall was assembled in the late 1800s to afford some protection to the harbor. Lorraine knew that the Breakwater had been an instant tourist destination. She'd seen photos of men and women coming to the jetty to picnic, dressed in old-fashioned garb, the women sporting bonnets and carrying parasols and wicker baskets. How quaint it all seemed, and yet, here she was, more than a century later, enjoying the same view and activity.

She paused for a moment to readjust her scarf. The wind was calmer now, and Lorraine was feeling quite comfortable with all her layers. She pulled a tube of lip balm out of her parka's pocket and coated her lips with a quick swipe. She shoved it back in her pocket and looked up.

The lighthouse loomed ahead. In the last few decades, the structure had fallen into disrepair; the paint sloughing off the weathered clapboards in great flakes, like a burn victim's blistered skin. Complaints reached the Manatuck Police Station of teens partying in the wood-framed "keeper's house," leaving beer cans, cigarette butts, and busted windows in their wake. Lorraine leaned close to one of the windows now, her breath frosty on the jagged glass. The charred remains of a small fire scarred the old wooden planks.

Lorraine left the window and turned toward the attached tower, craning upward to see all twenty-five feet. Once the brick structure had cradled an expensive Fresnel lens, but now it was crumbling. She thought about the Coast Guard's plans to demolish the tower, and the resulting outcry from local residents. A small sign tacked on the brick announced the formation of "Friends of the Manatuck Breakwater," as well as a campaign to rehabilitate the historic 1903 lighthouse.

That's all well and good, thought Lorraine. There were certainly plenty of people in the area with enough money to save the lighthouse. They were really preserving a symbol: a beacon of hope and of safety, a welcome glow on a stormy night to sailors lost at sea. Of course, she knew that a lighthouse could also represent danger, giving a vessel no time to change course, until the flashing light became synonymous with certain death …

Lorraine shivered and pulled her fleece scarf back over her mouth. The air was becoming colder, and her heated body was beginning to cool down. She shivered again, stomping her boots against the rough granite. It was too cold to contemplate anything. *Time to finish up and walk back to the warmth of the car.*

It was also growing darker. A storm was not predicted until the weekend, but quick snow squalls could crop up without much notice. She sighed. There was just one thing to do, one thing to complete her ritual, before turning around.

Lorraine clutched the iron railing of the lighthouse tower and hoisted herself up onto the large boulder at the jetty's very end. Gingerly, she tested it for slipperiness. Her boots gripped the slick rocks, giving her assurance that she was in no danger of falling.

Slowly she eased herself out to the edge of the rock where it met the sea. The raw power of the ocean threatened to wash her away, and yet she felt completely safe. She took a deep cleansing breath, closing her eyes, waiting only seconds for the familiar calming sensation. She opened her eyes, took in the slate gray water, the pewter sky, and the clean, crisp air. *This is my peace*, she thought. *Thank you, thank you.* She turned slowly and carefully around, ready to depart.

A bulky figure stood before her, wearing a black ski mask, puffy black jacket, and sunglasses.

Lorraine screamed.

The person—for she couldn't discern whether it was male or female—raised a black gloved finger to its mouth, as if to say they shared a secret, and took a step forward.

Lorraine jerked her head to the right and the left. There was no space on the boulder for her to maneuver past. "Back up," she yelled. "There's not enough room!"

The bulky figure said nothing. Slowly it took another step closer.

"Back up!" Lorraine screeched, glancing behind her. There were only inches between her body and the boulder's edge. What was this maniac doing?

"Let me get past you!"

An instant after yelling the words, her mind flashed to the possibility that she was in danger. She lunged to the figure's left, grazing the side of the puffy black parka with her shoulder. In the air, leaping, Lorraine was a creature in flight, hoping to propel herself beyond the person and to safety.

She felt a hard shove. She flailed her arms, grabbed at emptiness, and then spun toward the water.

The sole of her hiking boot grazed, and then caught, on a rock. Somehow she used the strength of her leg muscles to hold on. She craned her neck and met the sunglass-covered eyes of the bulky figure, imploring him or her to reach out and help as she dangled over the edge.

The figure came forward and held out a hand.

Lorraine felt a rush of gratitude as she struggled to stretch. *Just an inch or two,* she thought… and then she felt another shove. She hurtled backward, her body sailing through space. A second later, she slammed into the ocean.

Dark, icy seawater engulfed her entirely. A moment passed and she bobbed back to the surface, the water streaming over her hat and down her face. Lorraine gasped, her lungs already seeming to freeze with the shock of inhalation. She thrust her arms upward in a survival position, feeling the current surging her toward the jetty.

Lorraine's weakened limbs groped for something, *anything*. Her body was heavy, heavy, a sodden mass of wet winter clothing, but somehow she managed to hit the edge of a boulder and grab on.

A wheezing sound broke the silence as Lorraine gulped for air. Her extremities were numb, as was her face, and she sensed that extreme hypothermia would soon set in. Already her thoughts bobbed about, unmoored and dangerously cloudy. The shiny black parka and the threat it represented was a distant memory—she focused only on survival.

Get out of the water, she told herself. Her torso convulsed and her grip on the rock nearly slipped. Using her last remaining ounce of strength, she pushed up with pulsing arms until her hips were level with the boulder, and then wriggled onto the jetty, gasping with pain.

A siren wailed in the distance, growing more insistent as the seconds passed. Lorraine lifted her head, the effort sending shoots of pain up her spine. A feeling of fatigue was poised to swamp her like a rogue wave, and she was nearly ready to surrender.

Out of the corner of her eye a black shape moved toward her head. Before she could react, the object connected with her skull, thrusting her whole body back toward the frigid bay as if she were a rag doll. She was airborne, and then she hit the ocean, the momentum of the blow driving her down, down, into the inky depths.

Lorraine gasped for air. Her lungs filled with icy water, and she gasped again, tasting brine and bile. *So this will be my last memory.* Darkness swirled inside her brain, then all was black as she descended toward the rock-strewn bottom and her death.

ONE

His body insulated against the cold in layer upon layer of thermal clothing, Donny Pease forced his stiff fingers to untie the line tethering his boat to the Manatuck City dock. Quickly he pulled his gloves back on and shifted into gear. He heard the engine's thunk of protest, and then a steady chugging sound as he steered the boat away from land.

He gave a rapid scan of the sky, a habit that was as much a part of him as his daily bowl of lumpy oatmeal. Even though he was only headed across the harbor on this brisk Thursday morning, more to keep his boat in use than anything else, Donny assessed the weather, noting steely gray clouds clumped like wet wool in the distance. Snow on the way—but not for a day or two, he predicted. He stomped his feet and steered toward the *Curtis T*, a red lobster boat bobbing just past the Breakwater.

Donny slowed the motor as the *Curtis T* came in sight. A short, plump figure dressed in orange waders peered up from the boat's transom, frowning, a long hooked stick called a gaff clutched in her hands.

"What the hell you doing here, Pease?" The woman barking out the question had the wizened brown face of someone who'd spent decades exposed to the sun, salt, and sea breezes, all of which had combined to transform her skin into something resembling ancient leather. "Thought I told you to leave me alone."

Donny gave an easy grin. "Now Carlene, you know I'm out here anyway." Donny ran a water taxi, mostly in the good weather months, managed several island properties for absentee owners, and worked as a general handyman for the Hurricane Harbor Inn.

"Thought I'd see if you needed a hand."

"I don't need a hand, and I most certainly don't want yours." She spat off the side of the *Curtis T* for emphasis. "I wouldn't trust a Pease if my life depended on it. You just want to see what I'm bringing over the rail is all." Her grandfather, Moses Ross, and Donny's great-uncle, Thaddeus Pease, had fought over a piece of land on Hurricane Harbor forty years earlier, and Carlene Ross was in no way ready to call a truce. She narrowed her beady black eyes and shook the gaff at him. "Go on home to your skinny bitch of a bride, Pease!"

Donny nearly chuckled at Carlene's description of Tina, his fiancée, who was indeed on the thin side and known to have her grumpy spells. Instead he kept his face expressionless, watching as his distant cousin reached over the side of the boat with the gaff. He slid his boat into neutral.

Carlene hooked the line of a striped red and black lobster buoy—her unique color scheme—and pulled it toward the boat. She held tight to the line and began hauling it up, her stout body surprisingly strong for its size.

Unlike the other lobstermen in the harbor, Carlene rejected the ease of modern hydraulics. She was just stubborn enough to prefer the old method of hauling traps by hand. Donny saw the rusty square metal cage lurch to the surface, streaming with water, before Carlene hoisted it up and into the boat. It landed with a thump on the deck, the pungent odor of bait filling the air.

A grunt of satisfaction escaped Carlene's chapped lips. She opened the trap and extracted two squirming lobsters, both of which she carefully measured. Nodding, she secured rubber bands to their claws and placed them gently into a live-tank. Checking the trap for bait, she closed it and heaved it once more over the side.

"Go on, now, get away from my boat." Her voice was quieter, her relief at capturing a few crustaceans having cooled her anger. She tugged on her wool hat with two hands, jerking it down over her reddened ears. "Let's hope you got better things to do than spending your Thursday watching me fish."

Donny shrugged. "Hoping I can get you to catch some for me for tomorrow's supper," he said. "We need ten or so."

She looked up at him with annoyance, but Donny thought he detected a bit of interest as well. "Let's see what I find in the next trap before I go promising anything," she muttered.

Carlene slammed the *Curtis T* into gear and sped 100 yards away toward another red and black buoy. Donny followed at a slower pace. He came alongside the weathered lobster boat and tied a loose line to keep the vessels together.

Carlene bent over the side of the *Curtis T*. Donny saw her powerful body grasp the line and tug to bring up the trap. She yanked once more on the line and snorted in anger.

"Damn thing." She heaved hard on the line, yielding nothing.

Donny checked to be sure he was idling before hopping over the side of his boat and into Carlene's. "Lemme help."

She scowled but allowed him to grab the line as well. Together they pulled on the thick rope, but again it did not budge.

"Ledge, most likely," muttered Carlene. Donny realized it was the first thing she'd ever said to him that was not an epithet.

"Put her in gear and ease forward," he suggested. "I'll hang on and jerk it free."

Carlene gave a curt nod and shuffled in her waders to the controls. The engine clunked as she coaxed it to move slowly, her eyes on Donny as he yanked on the line.

"It's free," he shouted. "Put 'er back in neutral and come back and help me haul."

Another thunk of the engine and Carlene was back at his side, heaving the line toward the surface.

"Good Lord in heaven but it's heavy," Carlene huffed. "What in the blazes is down there?" Her face was red, the future color of the captured crustaceans, scrabbling now with their banded claws against the sides of the tank in an effort to escape.

Donny took a quick look around to be sure their boats were not drifting. They were closer to the mammoth granite blocks of the Manatuck Breakwater than he would prefer, but whatever was down there was acting as an anchor for the *Curtis T*. He gave a good yank on the line and felt the weight finally move.

"Okay, pull!" Donny instructed.

Hauling the line with Carlene's help, he saw the corner of the rusted trap lurch toward the surface, along with something that looked a lot like somebody's winter boot.

"What in God's good name..."

Carlene screamed and let go of the line. It took all of Donny's strength to hang on himself, and then even more muscle to heave the trap upward once more. The boot they had spotted was now in plain sight. Donny noted the laces, the rugged rubber sole, and the waterlogged leg that was wearing it.

A leg.

Donny swallowed, his horror mounting, as he continued to pull on the rope. Who was this poor sonofabitch, and why was he tangled in the trap?

A torso came to the surface. A torso, wearing winter outerwear, connected to a bloated face and head. The head rotated, almost as if it was turning to say something, and Donny choked back a scream. He saw a face, a thin face, framed by strands of dark, wet hair, a face that had once been moderately attractive and was now twisted in a permanent sneer of pain.

"Christ—I know her," Carlene whispered, her voice sounding as if it would break completely. "It's that girl, the one who used to work for Doc Hotchkiss." She turned away and Donny had to strain to hear her strangled hiss. "It's one of the Delvecchio girls." She shoved her hands inside her orange overalls. "Dead, ain't she?"

Donny secured the line to a cleat, taking his time so that the knot held, and forced his eyes to look once more at the misshapen face. He felt nausea rising like a tide in his gut but refused to give into it. Carlene was right; he had seen that face when he'd fractured his ulna after falling from a ladder four years ago last March. The woman had worked in the doctor's office, answering the phone and making the patients' appointments. Donny recalled that she'd snapped her gum while she wrote out those little reminder cards. What in heck was her name?

"She's dead alright," he affirmed, his voice sounding a lot stronger than he felt.

He reached for Carlene's radio, prepared to call in their grisly catch. The harbormaster would come out in the city's boat, no doubt bringing the Manatuck police as well. It would be in the papers, and he'd have to tell the story to everyone at his favorite bar, The Eye of the Storm, again and again and again. He switched on the radio, just as his memory tossed up the missing piece of the woman's identity.

"Lorraine," he intoned in the stout woman's direction. His eyes flitted back to the waterlogged corpse, draped over the lobster trap like a bulky old overcoat. "This poor soul's Lorraine Delvecchio."

TWO

Two-twenty Cove Road was a low white farmhouse with a wide front porch framed by twin sugar maples, their limbs now bare and gray against the gunmetal sky. Darby Farr pulled into the driveway behind a new SUV, hearing the crunch of her rented Jeep Liberty's tires on the hard-packed ice. She'd caught the red eye from San Diego, rented a car to drive up the coast, and then taken the ferry from Manatuck to Hurricane Harbor. Although most people would be exhausted from hours spent traveling, Darby Farr was energized to be back on the Maine island where she'd been raised.

She turned off the ignition. The old farmhouse was her childhood home, the sugar maples the same ones she'd tapped for syrup more than a decade earlier. The place looked abandoned in the dull afternoon light, until a worried face topped by curly red hair popped into one of the farmhouse door's sidelights. A moment later, tall, thin, Tina Ames bounded out of the house, slid perilously on the ice, and yanked open the Jeep's door.

"I can't believe you're here," she blurted, giving the twenty-eight-year-old a vice-like hug. Darby embraced her right back, feeling the redhead's ribs dig into her own, despite the fact that they were both wearing thick winter coats.

"Of course I'm here. Did you think I'd miss your wedding?"

A shy grin broke out on Tina's face. "No one would have blamed you if you did. I know how busy you are, Darby. And yet you came clear across the country, into freezing cold temperatures." Her face clouded. "Thank goodness."

"What's up, girl? Don't tell me you are one of those nervous brides."

Tina fluttered her cherry-red fingernails in a dismissive gesture. "Heck, no! It's not that. I'm thrilled to pieces to finally get to the altar." She patted her red curls and sniffed. "Especially at my age."

Darby slammed the door of the Jeep. "So you're not anxious about the wedding. What's the problem?"

"It's Donny. He's gone and done it again."

"Has he had an accident?"

"No, not an accident. Not exactly." She looked down at her cuticles, frowning at one that was snagged. "How was your flight?"

"Now don't go changing the subject on me, Tina. Tell me what Donny has done to get you in such a state."

The tall woman grimaced. "Heck, he's found another body—another dead body, that is, although luckily *this* one wasn't a bloody mess."

The mutilated corpse of Dr. Emerson Phipps flashed before Darby's eyes and she grimaced. Poor Donny Pease had nearly tripped on him months earlier in the garden cottage at Fairview, the estate where he'd worked as caretaker, and it had taken him days to recover from the shock.

"Tina," she said firmly, looking into the bride-to-be's puckered face. "Tell me what's happened."

Tina gave a tremulous sigh. She hugged her voluminous winter coat closer to her thin body and blew on her bare hands for warmth. "Let's get out of this darn cold air first, okay?"

"Fine." Darby opened the Jeep's lift gate and grabbed a small suitcase. Seconds later she was following Tina up the icy walkway to the rambling farmhouse's side door. As Tina turned the knob, Darby shot a glance across the street to the postcard-perfect cove of her childhood.

Dark spruces stood like sentinels beside the tiny curving beach where she had once darted into the cold water, dug moats for sand castles, and caught tiny hermit crabs. Darby gave a painful swallow. *I'm home.*

Tina fiddled with the side door lock and made an exasperated sound. "Dang thing! Thought I'd left it open. Even with a key it's tricky."

"Allow me." Darby fished in her pocketbook for the key, jiggled it expertly in the lock, and pushed open the door.

"Not bad," Tina teased. "Almost like you used to live here."

"Some things you don't forget." *Like waiting for your parents in an empty house, only to discover they are missing at sea.* Darby shook off the dark memory, willing herself to put it out of her mind. *You dealt with your grief last visit, remember?*

A welcome blast of warm air and the sound of hissing logs met the two women as they entered. "The fire feels great. Do I have you to thank for that?"

"No, Donny. He got it going before he headed over to Manatuck." Tina frowned. "He goes over in that boat of his just about every day, running errands and whatnot. He doesn't have to do it, and certainly not in this kind of weather. I think he just likes to be on the water, no matter how low the temperature drops." She opened a vintage wooden cupboard. "Got some tea if you'd like a cup?"

"Sure." Darby watched as Tina flicked on a burner and plunked the tarnished tea kettle on to boil. It was all very familiar—the steamy kitchen's small rectangular table, the painted cupboards with cheerful red-checked vinyl lining the drawers, the warmth from the adjoining living room's crackling fireplace. She brought a shaky hand to her face.

Tina's chatter continued.

"Anyway, Donny helps that old witch Carlene Ross pull her traps. Why he even gives her the time of day, I'll never know." Tina shook her head, causing her red curls to jiggle. "They're supposedly cousins if you go way back, but who the heck cares. Carlene is about the most unpleasant person you'd ever want to meet." She took two ceramic mugs out of the cabinet and fished two tea bags from a box. "Constant Comment. I remember that was your favorite."

Darby smiled. Actually, it had been her Japanese mother, Jada Farr's, tea of choice, but it was sweet of Tina just the same.

"I do love this tea. Now tell me the rest of the story. Did something happen to Carlene?"

"Nah, nothing bad ever happens to the real ornery types." She carried the cups to the table and plunked them down. "You notice that? The real grumpy curmudgeons live on and on, making the rest of us miserable. They don't get cancer, or have heart attacks. Too mean to die." Settling into one of the wooden chairs, she dropped her voice to a conspiratorial whisper. "Here's the scoop. Carlene's in her boat, pulling up her traps, and she goes to yank up this one and it won't budge. She's hauling and hauling, and nothing is happening. The line's obviously stuck on something, and stuck hard." She dunked her tea bag into the water several times and continued.

"So Donny rafts up alongside and climbs into her boat to help. They're tugging on the line and pulling it up when—"

The ring of a phone interrupted Tina midsentence.

"Crap, that's my cell." She yanked it out of her coat pocket and glanced at the display. "Alcott Bridges. Sorry, but I've got to take this." She switched on her phone, said a brisk hello, and then walked out of the kitchen wearing an intent look on her face.

Darby blew on her tea. Tina was a brand-new real estate agent, working for the small company in which Darby was a part owner. The driven redhead managed the Maine office of Near & Farr Realty, while an old family friend, Helen Near, ran the South Florida branch. It was a very different setup than Pacific Coast Realty, the giant Southern California firm where Darby herself worked, and yet the two small offices sold a fair amount of property, including some multi-million dollar estates.

"Wahoo," Tina sang as she sashayed back into the kitchen, her narrow hips swinging, a big grin on her face. "Alcott wants me to list his house, and it's a real beauty."

"Is he the artist?" Darby dimly recalled the painter, an eccentric recluse who lived on Manatuck Harbor.

Tina grinned. "I sent him a letter last month. Looks like my timing was perfect." She typed rapidly on her phone with her red nails.

"Tomorrow, two in the afternoon," she said out loud. She tossed her phone on the table. "Now where was I?"

"Donny and Carlene were pulling traps. Hey—isn't your wedding on Saturday? Are you sure you want to have a listing appointment the afternoon before?"

Tina puffed air out of her mouth. "You kidding me? Of course I do. I'm not letting some other agent like that awful Babette get in to see Alcott Bridges, that's for sure. He's right on Manatuck Harbor, with that amazing wraparound porch and private pebbly beach. I'll get that house on the system as soon as he signs with us."

A chuckle escaped Darby's lips. "You're worse than I am, Tina Ames, and that's saying something. Who's this Babette?"

"Babette Applebaum. She moved up here from New Jersey last August after being a summer visitor for years and years. Hung up her shingle with some hotshot broker from southern Maine, and started getting listings. She's a royal pain in my neck, I'll tell you that."

Darby was used to competition for listings but knew her friend Tina was not. "You're a great agent Tina, plus you're a local. I'm sure you're doing fine." She patted the chair beside her. "Continue with the story. I'm dying to know how Donny found a body."

Tina sunk back into the kitchen chair. "She was wrapped up in the trap line, that's what happened. One of her legs was tangled tighter than a trussed-up turkey."

"Who?"

"Well, that's the weird thing. Remember your last trip to Maine, when you saw Chief Dupont?"

Darby nodded. Hurricane Harbor's Chief of Police had been less than helpful at the start of her visit, but by the time she'd departed her dislike of the man had mellowed, and they'd become colleagues, if not friends.

"Yes, I remember."

"There was a classmate of yours working for him—Lorraine Delvecchio. About a month ago she went to work for the Manatuck Police Department, doing about the same thing she did for the Chief." Tina paused. "She's the one they found, Darby. Somehow Lorraine Delvecchio got herself wrapped around that lobster trap line and drowned."

Darby flashed on the glimpse she'd had of the thin, furtive Lorraine. She barely remembered her as a high school student, but it was strange to think that she was now dead. "Poor thing."

Tina Ames lifted her mug of tea, sending the scents of clove and orange floating toward Darby. "Poor Donny is what I say." She took a sip of the steaming liquid and shook her head. "I swear—that guy's got the absolute worst luck when it comes to finding bodies."

Darby felt a twinge of something akin to excitement. She cradled her mug, feeling the warmth of the liquid radiating through the ceramic. *A dead body in the harbor.* Suddenly her visit back to Maine seemed a lot more interesting.

Every inch of the old farmhouse held a memory for Darby. The soapstone sink where she now rinsed the mugs was the same place Jada Farr had stood, night after night, washing the family's supper dishes. The scent of smoke from the living room fireplace, the hiss of the logs as they burned in the grate—these simple things stirred her senses in a way that was comforting and familiar. She dried her hands on a dishtowel, feeling as if she were in some sort of dream. Tina had departed in her tricked-out SUV and Darby was alone with her past.

The ring of her phone jarred her back to the present and she glanced at the display. A local call.

"Darby?" The voice was gruff. "It's Charles Dupont. I heard you were on the island." He hesitated. "Welcome back."

"Thanks, Chief. What's up?"

"I'd like to discuss a couple of things, if you've got time."

"Definitely."

"First, I need to list my house, and I'm hoping that Near & Farr Realty will be interested."

"Tina Ames will be thrilled, I'm sure. She's taking all the new listings but I can work with her while I'm here to get it underway." She wondered at his plans but didn't ask.

"Good." He paused. "The second thing is kind of tricky. Did you by any chance hear about what happened to Lorraine Delvecchio? Your classmate from Hurricane High?"

"Tina told me as soon as I arrived. I'm sorry, Chief. I know she worked for you."

"Yeah. She left me last month for a position with the Manatuck department. No hard feelings or anything, in fact I recommended her for the job. I knew she was sick of taking the ferry back and forth all the time. She lived in Manatuck, and I guess she decided after all these years that it made sense for her to work there, too."

"I see." Darby wasn't sure why Chief Dupont had called to talk about his former employee, but she knew from dealing with her California clients that sometimes people just needed a listening ear.

A few seconds passed before the Chief resumed speaking. When he did, his voice took on a more urgent tone. "Listen, can I come by for a quick visit? I need to run something by you."

"Sure. I'm at my parents' old house, on the cove."

"You don't need to tell me where it is, Darby. I'll be right there."

Donny Pease logged on to the computer, the spanking new one that was reserved for patrons of the Hurricane Harbor Library, and typed in the address he'd long ago memorized. An image popped up and he leaned back, a sigh of contentment escaping his lips.

There she was. He gazed in dazed satisfaction at her welcoming features, the perfect white sand in the background, the palm trees shading her front. *Beach Lady.* Was she still available? Or had he waited too long? The familiar stab of panic struck him with such force he almost gasped.

With trembling fingers he dialed the number on the screen, keeping his cell phone hidden so the librarian wouldn't see. A man answered, and Donny voiced his fear.

"Still available?" The guy had a slight southern accent. "Sure, you can get Beach Lady for the whole month of March, if you want. I'll put down your name. Just send me a deposit within a day or two and she's yours."

Donny hung up and gazed at Beach Lady. He ran a hand through his sparse gray hair. He knew Tina would think this was just a reaction to finding Lorraine's body, but hell, he didn't care. He wanted what he saw on the screen and all that she promised, dammit, whether his new wife agreed or not.

A rap on the farmhouse's side door brought Darby back into the cozy kitchen. She opened the weathered door, expecting the bulky figure of Charles Dupont, and exclaimed in surprise at the man before her.

"Chief, you're a shadow of yourself! Come on in."

He gave a sheepish smile and entered the kitchen, stomping his boots as Darby closed the door behind him.

"Yeah, I went on a diet after you left the island. Damn thing worked and I had to go and buy all new clothes." He shrugged. "Think I just may be feeling the cold a little more this winter, without all that extra insulation I was carting around."

Darby pointed at the coffee machine.

"Cup of coffee? I can brew some. Or I have tea."

"Nah, I'm fine." He pulled off his jacket and draped it over the back of a chair. "I can still see her here, you know that? Standing there at the sink with her checkered apron…" He noted Darby's demeanor and narrowed his eyes. "You don't like it when I mention your mother."

"It isn't that."

"What is it then?"

She paused. Chief Dupont had hinted about some sort of relationship during Darby's last visit. *What did he mean to my mother? Do I really want to know?*

"I never knew that you and she were…"

"Friends. That's all it was, Darby. I may have wanted it to be more, but Jada wasn't like that. Besides, she was head over heels for your father." He sighed. "You resemble her so much. Your face… the way you walk…"

Darby tucked her glossy hair behind an ear. "Thanks." She waved a hand around the kitchen, taking in the old-fashioned cupboards with their chipped paint, and the faded floral wallpaper above the sink. "She spent a lot of time in here, that's for sure."

"Yeah. Making wonderful French dishes. Remember those delicate pies with the slices of apple?"

She nodded. "*Tarte aux Pommes.*"

"I suppose it wasn't good for my waistline, but I did love your mother's cooking." A few seconds passed and the Chief cleared his throat. "Well. You're here for the big Valentine's Day shindig, eh? Tina and Donny, tying the knot?"

"Wouldn't miss it for the world."

"Miles coming out?"

Darby gave a quick nod. "For a few days." She felt her face color at the very thought of the handsome Miles Porter, an investigative journalist who'd become more than just a friend. "I'm also going to do some work while I'm here. Paint a room, replace some furniture, that kind of thing."

"You thinking of coming back here to live?"

"No. I'm going to rent the house seasonally. That way I can reserve myself a week or two in the summer."

"Smart idea, but then you always had your thinking cap on, Darby Farr." He slid a file folder across the table. "Speaking of houses, I brought along some information on mine for you and Tina. I'm still cleaning it out, so I don't want her to worry about it until after the wedding. Those two taking a trip anywhere?"

"Not that I know of," said Darby. "Tina's focused on the business, but I'm trying to encourage her to live a little, too."

The Chief nodded. "I hear you on that one." His tone seemed to indicate there was more to the simple statement than he was letting on. He lifted his eyes, gave her a direct look. "Darby, in addition to getting my house listed, I need a favor."

"I'm happy to help if I can."

"That's nice of you to say, especially when you don't know what I'm going to ask." He paused. "It has to do with Lorraine Delvecchio's death."

Darby's senses sharpened. "Yes?"

"I don't know if you knew her habits, but Lorraine was a devoted walker, and I mean devoted. Every day on her lunch hour, she drove over to the Manatuck Breakwater and walked to the end and back. I'm talking every single day, rain or shine, whether she felt terrific or lousy. She did it when she worked for me, and she did it when she transferred to the Manatuck department. Heck, I bet she even did it when she worked for old Dr. Hotchkiss."

"And I take it she had walked the Breakwater yesterday, as well?"

"Her Subaru was found in the lot, and her colleagues at the station confirmed she'd stuck to her routine. Incidentally, at least a few of them think she was nuts."

"Did you?"

"What, think Lorraine was nuts?" He shook his head. "No. She was obsessive, but not crazy. She had her reasons for doing that daily walk." He looked around the kitchen as if thinking about his words. "I'm finding it hard to believe that she walked those rocks for the last time yesterday. Even though I have told so many people throughout my career that their friends and loved ones were dead, when it happens to you, it's different, you know?"

Darby nodded. She saw him glance to the side, obviously troubled by his former employee's demise.

He shifted in his chair. "The Manatuck police are saying that Lorraine slipped on the icy rocks at the end of the Breakwater and drowned. Her body sank, and then drifted with the outgoing tide, snagging on one of Carlene Ross's trap lines." He bit the inside of his cheek. "That's what they're saying."

"Were the injuries on her body consistent with their theory?"

He shrugged. "I guess so. I can't go muscling in there to take a look myself, but the state medical examiner will inspect the body, probably later on today."

"But you aren't happy with what the Manatuck police have concluded."

He raised his eyes and met Darby's face. "No, I'm not satisfied at all. I knew that woman and I know there is no chance in hell that she slipped. We're talking about someone who did this every stinking day, in weather way worse than this. She wore the right kind of clothes, heavy boots with good soles. She didn't slip, Darby. I know that. It's ridiculous to even suggest it."

"Could she have jumped?"

He shook his head. "Not Lorraine. She was not suicidal, not in the least."

Darby made her voice gentle. "Things could have changed since she worked for you, Chief. Even in just a month. Perhaps she wasn't the same person that you knew…"

"I saw her on Monday at the supermarket! We chatted at the deli counter for Chrissake. She was fine. Listen, Lorraine Delvecchio was not a depressed person."

"So you're saying she was pushed?"

"Yeah, that's what I'm saying. Someone took that walk with her and gave her a shove at the end. That water was so cold she didn't have a chance. She drowned, got snagged on the line, and that was it."

Darby imagined the shock of the icy cold water and shivered. "Do you have any idea why anyone would try to kill Lorraine?"

The Chief looked away for a moment, and then back at Darby. "I might. I want to flesh it out first."

"Where do I come in?"

"I need you to do some sniffing around for me. I can't exactly do any investigating myself, because it would look like I'm questioning the Manatuck department's findings. But if you helped me..."

"I could talk to potential witnesses; maybe find out who was with her."

"Exactly." He looked down at his hands. "You don't need to believe what I've said, but if you can ask some questions..."

Darby put her hand on Chief Dupont's beefy one. "I'll be honest with you, Chief. I didn't know Lorraine, and what little I saw of her I didn't like."

He raised a haggard face. The lines worn by time were more visible now that he was thinner. "Yeah, I know. She wasn't exactly warm and fuzzy."

"Still, I'm having a hard time thinking someone hated her enough to want her dead."

He nodded. "I agree. But nothing else makes sense."

Questions raced through Darby's mind. Had someone pushed Lorraine Delvecchio off the Manatuck Breakwater? Was any of the Chief's reasoning correct? She didn't have the answers, and yet it didn't matter at this point. A friend was asking for a favor. That was the real issue.

Not to mention, said a little voice in Darby's head, *you're intrigued by the possibility of a murder.*

She ran a finger along the table, considering Charles Dupont's request. He'd been kind to her parents, especially her mother, and had helped during Darby's last visit to the island. She wondered whether he was nearing retirement as Hurricane Harbor's Chief of Police. As if reading her mind, her companion raised the subject himself.

"I'm sixty-four, Darby, and this is my last year in law enforcement. I'm hoping I can sell my house, retire someplace warm, and get out of this cold once and for all." He paused and she heard emotion thickening his words. "But first I need to know who in God's good name killed Lorraine."

THREE

THE ELDERLY MAN GULPED the shot of whiskey, feeling the burn as it rushed down his throat. The familiar warming sensation spread from his gut and he sighed. He put the glass on the kitchen counter, shivering, wishing the chill of being outdoors would leave his body.

He shuffled through the living room, cluttered with newspapers, magazines, and a large upright piano, toward the bathroom and the antique clawfoot tub. A bath, that's what he needed. A hot soak to melt the coldness that had permeated every pore. Alcott Bridges leaned over the tub's chipped porcelain and turned on the water.

A noise from the kitchen startled him. A high-pitched screech, almost like the sound he'd heard as a boy emanating from the factories in his Ohio hometown. He paused, remembering the smokestacks and the waves of men who would exit the long buildings, hurrying home to their wives and children.

It was the teakettle whistling, letting him know that his water had boiled. He made his way back to the kitchen and fixed a cup of strong black Oolong. He uncapped the whiskey, smelled its bitter scent, and added a splash to the steaming liquid.

Clutching the mug and moving slowly, Alcott Bridges stumbled toward a closed door. He opened it, and peered inside his studio.

The space was chilly. The old man entered anyway, lurching past completed paintings until he reached a wide easel holding his work in progress. To the untrained eye, it was a jumble of blocks, painted various hues of gray. Upon closer inspection, one could see that the blocks composed a pier with an aging lighthouse at the end. *The Manatuck Breakwater*. Alcott Bridges gazed at it and gave a small nod. It wasn't quite finished, but he knew already it was one of his finest works.

He pulled his attention from the painting and shuffled out of the studio, continuing through the kitchen and toward the bathroom. Once there, he turned off the water, slid out of his clothes, and eased into the tub. When his tea cooled a little he would sip it, and while the warm water soaked the harbor chill from his bones, the whiskey would help him forget.

Darby watched Chief Dupont climb into his police car and back slowly out of the driveway. She checked her watch, wondering if the Hurricane Harbor Library's hours were the same as when she'd lived here as a child. If that were true, she had a half hour until closing time. *A half-hour to research on the Internet until I get my own connection,* she thought. She grabbed her laptop, a pad of paper and pen, and headed out the door.

Once at the library, she accessed the city of Manatuck's website, quickly finding a map showing both the Manatuck Breakwater and its nearby neighbors. Along the shore facing the jetty were a number of homes, as well as a small condominium development with several oceanfront units. Within minutes Darby had jotted down the property owners' names and addresses. In the local phone book, she found all but one number, and that property was a piece of vacant land.

Back at the farmhouse, she began calling the numbers. She'd decided to say she was putting together some data on the lighthouse, and ask people whether they favored its restoration or not. She figured that once they began talking about the lighthouse, the question of whether or not each owner could see the end of the Breakwater could naturally be raised.

Darby hoped to find someone with a clear view, someone who had seen something strange happen at noon the day before.

Her first call was to a pleasant woman with a Boston-accented voice who said that she greatly supported the lighthouse restoration, and had sent in a generous check only two weeks prior. Darby quickly thanked her and then inquired innocently whether she had a nice view of the lighthouse from her antique Cape.

"No," the woman said, a hint of regret in her voice. "Years ago, I suppose whomever lived here had an excellent view, but now those tall cedars block it, even in the winter." She paused. "My one consolation is that those same cedars give me privacy, and they're so pretty when they're snow-covered." A long sigh. "That's something, I guess."

Darby called another number. A man with a gruff tone said yes indeed, he could see the Breakwater and the lighthouse just perfectly.

Darby felt her pulse quicken. "Did you happen to see anyone walking the Breakwater yesterday at noon?"

"Noon? No. I meet some of the fellows at the coffee shop on Main Street for lunch every day." He paused. "Damn shame about the Delvecchio girl. Must've slipped on the ice is what I figure."

Darby thanked him for his time and hung up. She'd called everyone on the list, except one number, and no one had been looking out their windows when Lorraine Delvecchio had taken her fateful walk.

She sighed and pondered her next move. *Maybe actually going to the Breakwater would help,* she thought. She glanced outside at the gray afternoon, slowly becoming dusk. It would be cold on the ferry…

Stop it, she chided herself. *You're becoming one of those wimpy Californians who're afraid of a little chill in the air*. She reached in her suitcase and pulled a warm sweater out and over her head. *I'll make this last call and then head to the harbor.*

Blonde Bitsy Carmichael rolled her mascara-accented eyes, drumming her pudgy fingers on the taxicab's window.

"We there yet?" Her voice was high, almost singsong-y, as if she were auditioning for a musical part that she wasn't going to get. The cabbie, a tall Ethiopian immigrant whose command of English was still improving, wiggled a shaggy head. Bitsy exhaled in disgust. He'd been nodding gleefully at everything and anything she said, all the way from Portland.

I could tell you it was friggin' eighty degrees outside and sunny and you'd nod your foolish noggin, she thought. She frowned out the window.

The sky was a battleship gray color, and everything had that hunkered-down look she remembered of Maine winters. Not much snow to speak of—Bitsy had expected more—and what there was lay scattered in frozen patches on the iron-hard ground.

The cab whizzed by a diner with a black and red neon sign from the 1950s and Bitsy had a stab of recognition. *Miller's*, the place with the rude waitresses, sinful fruit pies, and impossibly long lines come summer. She allowed herself to smile. It had been a favorite destination for her and Chuck. The ferry from the island, and then the ride to Miller's. Maybe a stop or two at some antiques shops, and then the comfortable drive and ferry ride back home. Such a simple way to spend an afternoon, and yet it had been so satisfying.

When had those outings turned from delightful to deadly? Bitsy couldn't pinpoint the moment. It had been a gradual creeping of dissatisfaction, like a coastal fog, that had insinuated its way into their marriage. *Well, maybe not the marriage*, Bitsy admitted. *Just me.*

She glanced at her watch, a tiny diamond-encrusted face on a thin gold band. Four o' clock. She'd just make the ferry, if the driver hustled. And if he didn't, she'd be sitting for another hour in Manatuck. She pulled a twenty dollar bill from her wallet and waved it in his rearview mirror. "Faster," she urged him, jiggling the bill as an enticement.

He smiled and bobbed his head. A reassuring increase in the cab's speed gave Bitsy hope. Perhaps this time her eager driver had understood.

The village of Hurricane Harbor consisted of a tiny shingled office that sold tickets for the ferry, a café, a bar, and the impressive Hurricane Harbor Inn, an old wooden structure with wide porches and, in the summer, rocking chairs that invited guests to pause and relax. The bar's weathered sign read The Eye of the Storm, but locals just called it "The Eye." Likewise, the Hurricane Harbor Café, which sold flavored coffee and pastries, sandwiches and potato chips, was known simply as "the Café."

Darby walked briskly by these familiar landmarks, intent on catching the ferry and keeping warm at the same time. She met the eyes of the ticket seller, who waved her toward the waiting boat. "Buy your ticket over to the other side," he yelled, opening the door but a crack. "I'm already closed up for the day."

Darby stepped on the slick walkway and climbed gingerly onto the ferry. Unlike the warmer months, when the outside seating areas were full of camera-toting tourists, the decks in February were bare of riders. Two ferry workers scurried about, untying lines and stowing fenders, while the captain waited patiently to begin backing up the vessel. Darby did not envy them their jobs in the frigid cold. She hurried inside to the heated cabin and took a seat by a window.

A mother and a baby sat across from her, the baby so bundled it looked like a plump fleece sausage. The woman smiled at Darby, a quick smile of pride, and continued rocking the child and humming a tuneless little song.

The boat gave a small lurch and began backing away from the dock. Darby remembered countless rides on this ferry—trips to go school shopping with her mother, journeys to the Manatuck boatyard with her dad. She remembered, too, the night she stole her Aunt Jane Farr's truck and drove it onto the ferry to Manatuck, beginning a painful solo ride to the West Coast and a new life.

She closed her eyes. The events of the past few months—coming back to Hurricane Harbor and facing Jane just before she died; meeting Tina, who had been her aunt's capable assistant; and making peace with her parents' disappearance in a sailing accident—all this had happened so recently that Darby had not yet adjusted. Just when she'd thought the difficult work was behind her, she'd discovered information regarding her Japanese grandfather and his involvement in World War II atrocities. None of it had been easy.

She opened her eyes and regarded her reflection in the boat's window. Long, straight black hair, parted simply down the middle, and a heart-shaped face with a little bow mouth. According to Chief Dupont, she resembled her mother, Jada Farr. Darby sighed, wondering when she would see wrinkles around her gently curved eyes, and tried to remember her mother's lovely face. *But she had died so young…*

Darby shook off the sadness and thought about the task at hand. The ferry would dock in Manatuck a good mile from the Breakwater. She'd grab a taxi, ask the driver to return in an hour's time, and canvass the Breakwater neighborhood. Perhaps someone would know something about Lorraine Delvecchio's last walk.

Fifteen minutes later, the ferry docked in Manatuck, and Darby emerged into the dim light. The gray-shingled ferry terminal was surrounded by a jaunty white picket fence, although the effect was not as cheery as in warmer weather. Darby knew that her Aunt Jane had helped fund the building's construction, which had once been little more than a shack.

A yellow taxicab pulled up before the terminal and a sturdy blonde in a white mink stepped out. Darby watched as the driver removed two enormous zebra-printed suitcases from the trunk. The blonde woman paid him, and turned to wheel her luggage toward the ferry. Darby flagged the driver and asked if he was free to take a new passenger. The cabbie, a tall dark man with a big smile, nodded enthusiastically and Darby climbed in.

Half an hour later, Donny Pease glanced up from his beer and out one of the bar's grimy windows and did a double-take. Marching past Hurricane Harbor's local hangout was a short woman with platinum blonde hair, pulling two large suitcases behind her. The wheels on her luggage were slipping on the road's icy surface, and Donny expected that at any moment the woman would slide as well. Although only five o' clock, the sky was rapidly darkening and slick spots would be difficult to see. He groaned and fished several dollars out of his pocket.

"Where you headed?" asked Earl, the new bartender at The Eye.

Donny jerked his head in the direction of the window. "Some fool's out there trying to walk up to the Inn with her luggage," he said. "Figure I'll jump on my white horse and go rescue her before she falls and gets her fur coat all dirty."

Earl wiped a beer glass and snorted. "Is Tina aware you're rescuing damsels in distress?"

"Nah. She's Little Miss Real Estate Agent now. Too busy to know what I'm doing." It came out harsher than he intended, but Earl didn't seem to notice.

"Tell her I'm looking for some land when you get a chance. Woods, maybe with a little farm pond. Course I don't have much to spend…"

Donny nodded, knowing he'd forget to give Tina this hot lead. He grabbed his jacket off the adjacent barstool. "See you later."

"Saturday, right? For the big day?"

Again Donny nodded. He still wasn't sure just who Tina had invited to their wedding. *Guess I'll find out when I get there,* he thought.

Outside, the temperature was dropping, and Donny zipped up his jacket as he hopped into his truck. He scanned the street and spotted the woman and her bulky striped bags. He started the engine and turned the heat on full blast.

"Care for a ride to the Inn?" He'd slowed down and lowered the window, hoping the woman didn't think he was a stalker or something.

"I'm not going to the Inn," she snapped, keeping her eyes on the icy road.

"Well, where are you going? I'd be happy to give you a lift."

She slid her eyes toward the truck suspiciously. "Yeah, I'm sure you would."

Donny felt the color rise to his cheeks. Of all the nerve! "Listen lady, I was just trying to be nice. Have it your way. Hoof it to wherever the heck you're going, and slip on that ice to boot."

He was about to rev the motor and speed down the street when he heard an ungodly squeal, like the sound a pig makes when it starts to panic.

"Don-eee?"

The sound was coming from the blonde woman, and it sounded a lot like his name.

"Donny Pease, is that you?"

He turned his eyes toward the shrieks and threw the truck into park. "How do you know my name?"

"It's me! Bitsy Carmichael. Don't tell me you don't remember me, Donny!" She'd stopped and turned to face the truck, her white fur reminding him of the polar bears he saw on the Nature Channel. "Bitsy, from Quarry Road." She gave a naughty chuckle. "And the homecoming dance?"

Christ Almighty. Donny inhaled sharply and peered at the blonde's reddened face. Was this truly the youngest, shortest, and most obnoxious of the seven Carmichael girls? The one named "Betsy" but always called "Bitsy" because of her stature?

"Bitsy! What in the world brings you back to Hurricane Harbor?"

She threw a penetrating stare in his direction. "Why, this is my home, Donny." She shivered and looked at the truck with longing. "I'm freezing my butt off. Give me a lift to my house?"

He opened his cab door and trotted around the truck, minding the ice as he did so. She stood with her hands on her hips, making little stomping movements in an attempt to generate warmth. Her blonde hair looked brittle up close, as if it would crack like a bunch of skinny icicles between his fingers.

"Bitsy." Donny stood awkwardly. Did he hug her? Kiss her? What exactly did one do in situations like this? He hefted the two zebra-striped suitcases up and placed them in the bed of the truck.

"Why, you picked up those bags like they were nothing," she gushed. "Looks like I brought a lot, but I am planning on staying, maybe for good."

Donny felt his mouth grow dry. This was a turning point in the island's history, he just knew it. Later, he would look back and see that this moment, when he decided to give Bitsy Carmichael a ride, was significant. But what could he do right now, standing here like a fool in the single-digit temperatures? He couldn't exactly dump her in the harbor, now could he? The image of Lorraine Delvecchio's sodden corpse came to mind, giving him a sick sensation in his gut. He swallowed and yanked open the truck's passenger door.

Bitsy looked at the truck's floor and back at her little stomping feet. Donny's stomach tightened. *She can't climb in without a boost.* Not with those little legs, even with the ridiculously high-heeled boots she was trying to walk in. This was never a problem for Tina, who was long-legged and strong as a man, not to mention stubborn. Even if Tina were a short gal, she'd find a way to climb in herself, he was sure of that.

Not Bitsy.

"Now, don't be bashful, Donny. Give me a push right on the rear end."

He frowned. *Just keep your hands on her sides*, he told himself. *You're safe if you stay on the sides...*

Donny licked his lips and rested his hands lightly on her hips. She had a deep, musky scent—not unpleasant, but noticeable. Taking a breath, he shoved the fur-clad figure forward, maybe a tad too forcefully. Bitsy squealed and popped into the cab like a cork. Before she could utter a word, he'd slammed her door shut and marched around the vehicle to the driver's side.

"Thank God it's warm in here," Bitsy Carmichael breathed as he settled into his seat. "I'm not used to the cold anymore."

Donny gave a vague nod. Two days before his wedding and he was with the girl who'd been his first love. He felt that sick, sinking feeling again. *Please God, don't let her bring it up.*

He concentrated on where he was headed with Bitsy. "N-no Carmichaels live on Quarry Road these days," he stuttered. In fact, did any Carmichaels live anywhere on Hurricane Harbor?

"I know that, silly," she said softly. "Most of my sisters are dead, and the two that aren't live out of state." She gave him a bright smile. "I'm going home, to *my* house."

Suddenly he recognized the real danger of Bitsy Carmichael's reappearance. How could he have been so stupid, focusing only on that part of her past history that involved him? *Because you're a sixty-year-old fool,* he chastised himself. *You've got an ego the size of Baxter State Park.*

"Middle Road." Her voice had a brittle edge to it. "Before it's absolutely pitch black, if you don't mind."

Donny crept forward, up the hill and past the Hurricane Harbor Inn, his stomach churning with anxiety. "Does he know?" he asked carefully. "Does the …"

"He'll find out." The clipped words showed no trace of the coy tone she'd used earlier. Donny drove on, hoping he would not need to pull over and lose his lunch.

FOUR

DARBY WALKED UP THE path to a tidy little cape. A new home, it had been constructed on a small patch of land that Darby remembered as an empty, weedy lot. Inside, twinkling indoor lights cast a welcoming glow, despite the cold and darkness.

She turned to see the view from the front of the house. The Breakwater was visible, but it was too far to see much of anything. Why had the woman who'd answered her last phone call invited Darby to visit? *Probably just looking for company*, Darby thought.

She sighed and knocked on the door. Jet lag was beginning to take its toll.

A tall woman wearing a cabled sweater in a soft blue color answered immediately. She peered at Darby through round glasses and then smiled.

"You must be Darby. Come in, come in. I'm Alison Dyer. Welcome to my home."

"Thank you for seeing me so quickly." Darby entered, then removed her boots and looked around. The home was snug, furnished in a relaxed country style with a fire crackling in the hearth. Darby moved instinctively toward its warmth. "This is a lovely little place."

"Thank you. Please, sit down." Alison indicated a wing-backed chair by the fireplace. "May I offer you a cup of tea? I've just brewed some, and I'm afraid I don't drink anything stronger than that."

"Tea would be wonderful."

Darby glanced up at the fireplace mantel where a painting of several ornate townhouses, reminiscent of the French Quarter in New Orleans, graced the wall. Looking around Darby noted another painting, this one of a jazz band, and another depicting a sleepy bayou.

Alison Dyer bustled into the room with a black tray holding a small teapot, two china cups, and a plate of sugar cookies. She set it on a small table and took a seat.

"I'm pouring you an unusual tea that has become one of my favorites," Alison said, as the steaming liquid flowed from the teapot into the cups. Darby inhaled and caught the scents of hibiscus, apple, and orange.

"It smells heavenly." She picked up the cup and sniffed. *Rosehips.* A taste revealed another surprise—the flavor of rhubarb cream. She took another tiny sip. "Delicious."

"I love this particular tea." Alison lifted her cup and drank. "Although technically it isn't a tea, but a tisane." She smiled. "It's definitely one of my favorite kinds, and it has an interesting name."

Darby's next taste gave her the final clue. "It's Blue Eyes, isn't it?"

"Why yes." Alison put down her china cup and looked at Darby, astonished. "I'm surprised that you know it. You've had it before, then?"

"Only once, with a British friend." She thought quickly of Miles and felt her cheeks grow warm again. "The taste that I remembered as being so distinctive is the cornflower, and of course that's partly where the tea gets its name."

"Of course."

Alison was clearly startled by her identification of the herbal tea, not knowing Darby possessed an unusual gift: a remarkable palate memory. She stared intently, until the young woman felt compelled to change the subject.

"Did you purchase the tea on one of your trips to New Orleans?"

"Ah, my artwork has given me away. Yes, there is a wonderful tearoom in the French Quarter called Royal Blend Coffee and Tea House. I make it a point to visit there and stock up whenever I'm in New Orleans."

"You go there often, then?"

Alison nodded. "I'm involved with a group helping to build low-income housing. I head down to Louisiana probably four or five times a year." She took a sip. "It was one of the two big things I wanted to do in my retirement. I'm a former college professor—English literature." She smiled. "The shelves of books in my den would have revealed that part of my past, I'm afraid."

Darby grinned. "Tell me about your other passion. You said you had two."

"Come with me and I'll show you. Bring your tea if you'd like."

She led Darby into the kitchen of the cape, a small but functional space with the usual appliances and a large picture window overlooking a yard dotted with birdfeeders. A round café-style table was placed in front of the window, two chairs on either side. In the distance, Darby could dimly make out the shape of the jutting Manatuck Breakwater.

"This is my baby," Alison said, pointing to a device that looked like a small telescope. It lay on a wooden table in the corner by the window. She picked it up reverently.

"It's a spotting scope, made by Zeiss," she whispered. "I waited two years before I'd let myself spend the money and get it." She gave a wicked grin. "It cost thousands of dollars, but it's worth every darn penny, I'll tell you that."

"It must be amazing for bird watching," Darby said, wishing it weren't dark so she could test the spotting scope herself.

"You wouldn't believe it!" Alison set the instrument down. "I take it with me on my birding excursions, but it's also great to look at the wildlife right here." Behind the round glasses, her blue eyes were keen. "And of course, keep track of the action on the Breakwater."

Darby gazed into the darkness, feeling her heart beat a little faster. "Tell me more. Did you see something unusual yesterday?"

Alison lifted her eyebrows. "This is where I have lunch," she said, indicating the round table with a sweep of her arm. "I make myself something and sit down at 11:45 on the dot." She pointed to a clock hanging above the table. "I'm a punctual person, and I like to keep my schedule the same whenever possible."

Darby nodded. She loved people who had strict routines.

Alison touched one of the chairs. "I sit right here, facing the Breakwater, and I watch for the Walking Lady to appear at noon." She smiled, a little sadly. "That's what I called her, the Walking Lady. I never knew her name, but she showed up every day like clockwork. Not today, though. Now I know it was that poor girl, Lorraine

Delvecchio." She looked down at her hands. "What a terrible accident."

"Did you see Lorraine yesterday?"

"Yes, same as usual. I was waiting for my bowl of minestrone to cool, so I picked up my scope, and I watched her climb up onto the blocks and start off. By now I know her walking style, too. She kind of swings her arms a little, to get her heart pumping, you know?" Alison swung her arms forcefully to demonstrate. "And she takes fairly long strides, for a woman."

Darby nodded. "Did you see her when she reached the end of the Breakwater? When she slipped?"

"Of course not! If I had, I would have called someone to rescue her." Alison's indignant attitude gave way to regret. "Although I don't suppose it would have mattered, that water is so darn cold." She sighed. "No, I didn't see her get to the end of the seawall, because my phone rang and I got up to answer it. Some telemarketer, trying to get me to go see a time share in Bar Harbor. By the time I returned, she was walking back."

"Walking back?" Darby's tone was sharp.

"Well, I assumed it was Lorraine. Whoever it was wore black clothes, just like Lorraine—but I did think it was strange."

"What?"

"She wasn't moving the same way. Her steps were much shorter, and her arms weren't swinging. They were like this, kind of close and tight to her body." Alison held her arms bent at the elbow in a 45 degree angle, almost like a boxer or runner would. "I thought it was odd, so I looked through the scope."

Darby's heart was pounding. Could this be the clue the Chief was looking for?

"And what did you see, Alison?"

"One of those creepy masks, the kind people put on to rob banks. Ski masks, I think they're called."

"Had you ever noticed Lorraine wearing something like that?"

She shook her head. "No." A moment passed while Alison seemed to be composing her words. "There is something else that's kind of odd. When I sat down here at 11:45 with my bowl of soup, there was already someone on the Breakwater. They were about halfway down." She paused. "They were also dressed in black."

"Did you see a ski mask?"

"I'm not sure. There might have been one. I couldn't tell because they weren't facing me." She glanced at Darby, her countenance showing concern. "I didn't think anything about this at the time, but now I'm wondering if I should talk to the police."

Darby put her hand on Alison's arm and gave a light squeeze. "Yes, I think you should speak with them as soon as possible. I think they'll find your information helpful." She thought of the implications of what Alison Dyer had seen—someone else on the Breakwater, someone who had perhaps hidden by the lighthouse, waiting for Lorraine Delvecchio to arrive.

She gave the older woman a quick hug. "I'm afraid I need to go, but I thank you for your time, and for the wonderful Blue Eyes tea."

"Anytime, anytime," Alison said, as Darby pulled on her boots. At the door, Darby paused.

"Alison, how long were you on the phone with the telemarketer?"

"A couple of minutes. And then I went to the powder room, so that was a few minutes more."

Darby thanked her and headed into the chill of the night.

Donny Pease pulled his truck up before a white house. His companion peered into the darkness at the lonely looking modular on the sparse wooded lot.

"Home sweet home," she sang. She pulled her gaze from the house to his face. "Well? I need some help getting out of here, you know?"

Donny hustled out of the truck and around to aid Bitsy Carmichael in her leap to the ground. He slammed the door behind her and heard her little huff of disapproval.

"My bags?"

Donny nearly rolled his eyes as he grabbed the two suitcases and plunked them on the frozen ground. "There you are." He'd be damned if he was going to take them to the house.

"Well, c'mon then, let's go say hi." She began strutting to the front door, the white fur receding into the darkness like a giant snowshoe hare seeking shelter.

Donny exhaled and lifted the bags. He was a doormat, that's what he was, not just for Tina but for this platinum blonde as well. He was fuming as he plunked the bags on the granite front step, nearly forgetting where he was or who was about to answer Bitsy Carmichael's determined knock.

The door opened with a forceful whoosh. Donny Pease wanted to shrink into the frozen earth. He tried to keep his eyes cast downward, but could not resist looking up at the sound of Bitsy's singsong-y voice.

"Hello, Chuckie." She tilted her head to the side in a way that was probably supposed to be cute. "I'm home, honey."

Donny looked at the guy. He stood frozen in the doorway, his mouth wearing a round O of surprise, his eyes wide unblinking circles of disbelief. A textbook example of a man shocked to his very core.

Charles Dupont, Hurricane Harbor's Chief of Police, wavered on his thickset legs, looking for all the world as if he were seeing a blonde ghost.

Tina Ames was waiting for Darby in the farmhouse's driveway. She popped out of her SUV holding a brown paper bag and was at Darby's car door before she could take off her seat belt.

"I've been waiting on you to get home!" Her face was flushed with excitement. "You will never guess what happened to Donny today."

"Not another dead body." Despite herself, Darby heard the note of alarm in her voice.

"Nah. More like someone returned from the grave."

"Who?" Darby stopped and turned to look at her friend.

"Chief Dupont's wife, the one who ran off to Vegas. Donny saw her walking up the hill toward the Inn and he offered to give her a ride. He had no idea she was Bitsy Carmichael."

"Carmichael—I think I remember that name." She opened the door and they entered the kitchen, removing their boots and heavy coats.

Tina nodded. "Whole bunch of girls, all of them wild, and Bitsy was the youngest and craziest. Charles Dupont fell for her and hard. They got married and she lasted a few years, then she up and took off. That must have been fourteen, fifteen years ago."

"Did they have kids?" Darby put on the kettle for tea, but Tina jerked her head toward a bottle of wine that had mysteriously appeared on the counter. She opened a drawer and pulled out an opener.

"Chief Dupont had two kids when he married Bitsy, so I guess she was their stepmom. Their real mom—his first wife—died when the kids were in middle school. Don't you remember? They're probably about your age."

"I don't remember any Dupont kids." She watched Tina pour the wine. "What's made Bitsy come back here, after all these years?"

"What makes anyone come back to Hurricane Harbor?" Tina gave a sly look. "Real estate." She picked up the two glasses. "Let's sit in your parlor."

Darby smiled. Her friend was obviously looking to share some gossip, and although it wasn't Darby's favorite pastime, she followed Tina into the living room obediently.

"So this Bitsy comes back after all this time because the Chief is going to list his house?" Darby stirred the glowing embers in the fireplace and added a few slender logs. She took a seat on the faded loveseat, wondering if she'd need to replace it—or at least recover it—for summer renters.

"How did you know the Chief was selling?" Tina's question was sharp.

"Tina, relax. We're on the same team, remember? The Chief told me this morning and I dropped off those papers to you. Geez!"

"Sorry." Tina's voice was contrite. "Anyway, yeah, I suppose that's right. Donny said she referred to the house as "home" and said she brought these two enormous suitcases because she planned to stay." Tina grinned. "I only wish I had seen the look on Charles Dupont's face. Donny said he was absolutely flummoxed."

"Now there's a word you don't hear every day."

"It means confused, bewildered, surprised, and you gotta imagine the Chief was all of those things." She tucked her legs under her, reminding Darby of a tall stork trying to get comfy. "Poor guy. First Lorraine Delvecchio and now this. He's had enough for two days, maybe a whole week, that's for sure. Anyway, here's to us." She raised her glass and grinned.

Darby followed suit and then took a sip of the wine, a smoky Merlot that was perfect with the cold weather. "Surely Bitsy Carmichael can't think she has any claim to the house. After all, she and the Chief divorced years ago."

Tina shook her head. "That's just it. They didn't divorce. When I looked up the deed to the property, I saw her name right there with his. Anita Betsy Carmichael Dupont."

"Say that three times fast."

"No kidding. She's ABCD, the whole friggin alphabet."

Darby chuckled and then turned thoughtful. "Her reappearance certainly complicates things for the Chief. I wonder how they'll resolve it?"

Tina took another long drink, drained her glass, and poured another. "I don't know, but he'd better not bring her to the wedding." Her tone was ominous. "Owning property sure can muddy the waters." She thought a moment, and then her face brightened. "Speaking of owning property, did I tell you I got an offer on my house?"

"That's great news." Darby knew that Tina was planning to move into Donny's old farmhouse right after the wedding. "Are you happy with the price?"

Tina scrunched up her nose. "I'd like more money, of course—who wouldn't? But it's a nice young couple with an adorable baby." She took another sip of wine. "Final settlement is on the last day of the month."

"Congrats."

They sipped in silence for a moment. Darby put down her own goblet and regarded her friend. "Tina, do you know a woman named Alison Dyer? She lives over by the Breakwater."

Tina shrugged. "Yes, I've met her once or twice. She gives talks about birds at the library." Her eyes widened. "Why, is she looking to sell?"

Darby nearly laughed. "No, I don't think so. I went over there to speak with her because she saw something strange." She paused. "On the Breakwater." Quickly she recounted Alison's description of the ski-mask-wearing walker.

"Crap!" said Tina. She leaned forward, placing her red-painted fingernails against her temples. "Darby—that means Lorraine may have been murdered! Shoved by someone with a ski mask off that Breakwater, and then fished out by poor Donny and that crazy Carlene." She shuddered, thought a moment, and then shook her head several times. "Nah, that can't be right. Who in the world would want to hurt Lorraine? She was one of those mousy, harmless people. You know, the kind who never say a peep." Tina grinned. "Not like yours truly, who likes to shoot her mouth off right and left."

Darby took another sip of the wine, thinking about Tina's comment. By all accounts, Lorraine Delvecchio had been a loyal employee, leading an uneventful life. Those who'd known Lorraine described her as shy and retiring.

She shifted on the loveseat, feeling an uneasy twinge of insight. Sometimes the quietest people, the ones who seemed to stay safely in the shadows, were the ones who could be the most dangerous.

Once Tina had finished her second glass of wine, pulled on her boots, and headed back into the cold, Darby fixed herself a simple salad and prepared to call Chief Dupont. She wasn't sure whether he'd want to talk, given his errant wife's sudden arrival, but she felt she owed it to him to relay Alison Dyer's information. Now, finished with her dinner and wearing comfortable clothes, Darby stoked the fire and settled into the old loveseat to call the Chief.

"Hello?" A high-pitched voice answered and Darby was temporarily speechless. "I'm looking for Chief Dupont," she explained.

"Chuck-ee! Phone call for you!" Darby heard low murmuring and then the gruff voice of Charles Dupont.

"Yeah?" He sounded exhausted, like a man who'd run about a million miles and had many more to go.

"It's Darby. I hope I'm not calling at a bad time, but I wanted to tell you what I found out today."

Immediately his tone changed. "No, no, you're fine, Darby. Appreciate the call. What's up?"

She described meeting Alison Dyer, seeing her spotting scope, and then related the amateur birder's account of what she'd seen on the Breakwater. "Alison asked me if she should speak with the police, and I told her absolutely."

The Chief was silent for a few moments. "Good. If she tells them what she saw, they'll open an investigation." She heard him blow air out through his mouth in a sigh. "This is what I suspected, but now that we have proof, I'm sick about it. Someone killed that poor girl. They waited by the lighthouse and pushed her hard. Imagine how scared she must have been, Darby. Imagine what that must have felt like…" His voice trailed off. "Okay, the thing now is to catch the creep and put him away. The guys over at Manatuck are a smart bunch—they'll follow through. Lorraine was one of their own, after all. She hadn't worked there long, but they'll make the extra effort to get this case solved quickly." He sighed again. "Thanks for the good work, Darby."

"Sure."

His voice lowered to a whisper. "You must have heard what's happened here. My—er—wife is back. Bitsy."

"I did hear about that, Chief."

"Yeah, well I'm not sure what's going to happen with the house now that she's back. She, uh, well she wants to live here for some reason." His voice was tight, strangled sounding.

"Are you okay?"

"Darby, I'm the Chief of Police of this damn island, of course I'm okay!" He made an exasperated noise. "I'm not in any *danger*, thank you very much. I'm just—well, I'm just extremely surprised. Let's leave it at that." He gave a grunt. "I gotta go. Thanks again for what you did today. I know that Lorraine would be very grateful."

Darby hung up the phone. There was one thing left to do before she got some rest. She pulled on her boots and the long down coat and headed into the cold.

Donny fidgeted, watching Tina as she scrutinized the photograph. He'd come to her house in a sudden burst of courage, explaining that he had something important to show her. Did he dare hope that she would even consider his idea? He waited, his eyes on her face, nails digging into his palms, hoping she would see the beauty of Beach Lady as he did.

Finally she put down the image and shook her red curls. "It's a cute little cabana, but I don't see how we can do it, Donny. Not this year."

Donny felt something dropping inside him. "Why not?" he mumbled. "I've got money saved. Let me spend it on a vacation for us. It will be like a long honeymoon."

"Donny, did you forget that I just got my real estate license? I'm building my client base, is what I'm doing, and I can hardly afford to go anywhere now. Why, I can't leave town for a week, much less a month! March could end up to be a super busy time for me—the spring market and all. I'm sorry, but we can't do it."

He tried to keep his hands from shaking. "What happened to what you told me when we got engaged, Tina? That you were ready to have some adventures?" His face colored and his voice dropped to a whisper. "Adventures with me?"

"That was before I became an agent, Donny!"

"Why does that have to change things?"

"Now I'm busy. I'm making money—real money—for the first time in my life. I have a career, an office, a whole new life." Her lips were set in a thin red line, her brilliant blue eyes blazing.

Donny rose slowly to his feet. He reached for the photograph of Beach Lady and tucked it carefully under his arm. His legs felt like they were weighted with heavy chains. Making them move was going to be difficult.

“You have a whole new life,” he said, his voice stony. “And a whole new way of looking at things, too. Since you got your real estate license, all you ever talk about are your deals. Well, I tell you what. You can make a deal to get married to some other fellow, ’cause I’ve changed my mind.” He grabbed his coat and stalked out the door, leaving Tina frowning behind him.

Alcott Bridges could not sleep. He pulled the covers off his bed and grabbed a worn flannel bathrobe. Pulling it over his thin frame, he made his way out of the small bedroom and into the kitchen.

He flicked on a light and checked the coffeepot. Empty. Carefully he measured out some dark brown grounds, added water, and started the machine. He took a chipped mug out of the sink, rinsed it, and poured a generous amount of whiskey into the bottom.

The coffeemaker hissed and sputtered, the rich scent of the beverage filling the room. Alcott put his mug under the dripping liquid. As soon as it was full, he took it and replaced the coffeepot. Cradling the mug, he shuffled into his studio.

Alcott was eighty years old, white-haired, with a pointed chin and watery blue eyes. His nose had a slight hook, making him appear birdlike, and his wiry frame and quick movements added to the comparison. He was arthritic, but the whiskey helped mask the constant pain. It helped with other things, too.

Like memories of Gracie.

He gazed at her portrait, hanging on the wall of his studio, and recalled one of the days she’d posed for him on the porch. He’d arranged some faded red pillows on the white wicker couch, and told her to sit there and relax. She'd complied, laughing, asking him how she could relax when she knew he was scrutinizing her every pore?

And yet she had relaxed, he thought now. She'd become almost dreamy, her thoughts a million miles away from their porch overlooking the bay. She had worn her hair to her shoulders then, and Alcott recalled that it curled in soft waves around her face. He'd managed to capture those waves in the painting, using light strokes to show the fine wisps that would not be tamed, no matter how many times she used her heavy wooden hairbrush with the special bristles. She'd been wearing a crisp white blouse, with a blue bandana tied jauntily around her neck, and the effect of the colors—red, white, and blue—had given the finished work a look of Americana, as if the artist had set out to paint something patriotic.

Alcott gazed at Gracie's smile. Guileless, as if she hadn't a care in the world, as if she knew her future would always be rosy, her heart as young and strong as it had been on that September day.

He felt his lower lip tremble and he put a shaking finger up to touch it, spilling his coffee in the process. He swore and grabbed a painting rag to mop up the mess. Guilt and shame, his ever-present companions, rose up as if revived by the hot coffee. He swallowed, and backed slowly out of the studio.

The cove was nearly silent under the cold night sky.

Darby strained her ears to hear the gentle lap of the water, as faint as a caress against the smooth sand. No breeze stirred the tall spruces, no gong of a bell buoy, nor cry of a gull, marred the stillness.

The air was bracing, chilling Darby's nose, lips, and cheeks. She shoved her hands deeper into the down coat's pockets and lifted her head to the heavens.

There it was.

The constellation Cepheus, a box-like array of stars with a triangle on top. "King Cepheus, the promise breaker," she heard her father whisper. Darby imagined, as she had so many times as a child, the proud Ethiopian ruler seated on his throne. She recalled the story of his downfall, of how Cepheus had betrayed the hero Perseus by breaking a promise, and how the king and his beautiful wife Cassiopeia had perished at Perseus's hand, turned to stone by the ugly Medusa's head.

Promises. Did they all turn out to be hollow? She thought of her parents, of their blithe assertion that they would come home from their sail on that beautiful August day. And yet they had never returned.

Minutes later Darby was back in the snug farmhouse. She made the bed in her old room with brushed flannel sheets and spread a heavy down comforter on top. She changed into her pajamas, brushed her teeth, and checked the time. Nearly eleven p.m.—the perfect hour to call the West Coast.

The phone rang at her assistant Enrique Tomas Gomez's house and an answering machine with his smooth voice picked up. Darby left a message telling him she'd arrived in Maine safely, and said she'd call again soon with a quick update. "I know I've left everything in good hands," she said, thinking about the various deals she had underway in Southern California, "but you know me—I like to keep in touch." She then phoned the man who kept causing her to blush—Miles Porter.

He answered in his clipped British accent. “Hallo?”

Darby pictured him with his rugged face, dark brown hair, and ready smile. Her pulse quickened. “Miles, it’s me. I’m here on the island and thought I’d check in.”

“Darby!” His voice sounded genuinely pleased. “I was just packing my rucksack with a warm Irish knit sweater from a consignment shop downtown. I figured it would keep me cozy, that is, when I’m not snuggling with you.”

A flush went up her face. “Your visit’s sounding more and more appealing all the time. Are you sure you don’t want me to pick you up in Portland?”

“Positive. You’ll have all kinds of wedding-y things to do with Tina. I’ll just get myself a car and drive up. I remember the way.”

“That’s good to know. Be sure to tell me when your flight lands, okay? There’s supposed to be a little snow coming.”

“Will do. Meanwhile, how does it feel to be back on Hurricane Harbor?”

“Not as strange as it did last summer,” she confessed, realizing as she said it that it was true. “I’ve seen Tina, and spoken to Chief Dupont.” She stopped, remembering the awful fact of Lorraine Delvecchio’s death. “Miles, something terrible happened yesterday, on the Manatuck Breakwater.” She described Donny’s discovery and then her conversations with both the Chief and Alison Dyer.

Miles whistled under his breath. “Is this Alison a trusty source?”

“I think so. She doesn’t seem to have any reason to fabricate the story.”

“So what happens now?”

"The Chief thinks the Manatuck police will get right on it." She then told him about Bitsy Carmichael's arrival, and this time Miles laughed.

"The poor bloke! After fifteen years she comes back to grab her share of the house? Bloody hell!" He chuckled again. "For a small island, that place has more going on than San Francisco. You be sure to be careful, Darby."

"Careful?"

"Yes. You always want to help your friends. Sometimes that big heart of yours blinds you to danger, my dear."

"The only thing I have to watch out for is Tina making me into some big-haired bridesmaid." Now it was her turn to giggle. "Miles, I think I'm getting punchy from lack of sleep." She paused, punctuating her observation with an unintentional yawn. "I'll see you tomorrow. I can't wait."

"Me neither." His voice was throaty. "Pleasant dreams."

Darby climbed under the flannel sheets and warm down comforter. She turned off the light and thought of Miles's admonition to be careful. *He's sweet to worry about me*, she thought, *but this time I can throw caution to the proverbial wind.*

She rolled on her side and let her body relax, blissfully unaware of what was to come.

A knock on the door at seven a.m. brought Darby down the stairs and to the kitchen with an inquisitive look on her face. She was dressed and ready to tackle a house project, so the unexpected visitor was a surprise.

She peered out the window and saw Tina, bundled up in a bright pink coat with enormous black buttons. She was holding a paper bag and an oversized turquoise pocketbook.

"Good morning," Darby said, pulling open the door. "How's the bride-to-be today?"

Tina grunted and came into the warm kitchen. "Sorry to bug you so early, but I need to talk." She thrust the paper bag at Darby. "I brought coffee and muffins."

Darby regarded her friend with concern. "Thanks. Let me get us some plates."

Tina pulled off her coat and black scarf and plunked down at the kitchen table. She grasped the plate of muffins from Darby, chose one, and took a big bite. After she had chewed for a few minutes, she fixed Darby with a steady look.

"Donny has called off the wedding."

"What?" Darby pulled the lid off one of the coffees and inhaled the fresh-brewed aroma. "Why in the world would Donny do that? He's crazy about you!"

"Apparently not. At least not the new me, the one that earns decent money at her new career. I think he's jealous."

"Tell me what happened." She lifted a lemon poppy seed muffin and broke it in half. The scent of citrus mingled with the aroma of the coffee. "What exactly did he say?"

"He said that since I became an agent, all I think about is making deals. He doesn't want to marry me anymore." Her voice lost its bluster and she turned a troubled face to Darby. "I thought he would be back to normal today, so I went by his house a little while ago. He said that he'd thought about it some more, and that he knew it was for the best. He said—" Her voice broke. "He said that I've become a different person." Her blue eyes filled with tears. "Do you think that's true, Darby?"

"You're the same person, Tina—kind, funny, and hardworking." She paused. Tact was needed here: extreme tact. She made her voice gentle. "You have become kind of fixated on getting new listings. Could that be what Donny was talking about?"

"Fixated? What do you mean?"

"Obsessed." Darby hated to be blunt, but there it was. Tina had turned into a real estate monster, the kind of agent people shun like a shark. She looked at her friend's face. The redhead was mulling over the label.

"Donny showed me a picture of a cute beach cottage with a thatched roof in Mexico. He wants to rent it and go for the month of March. I told him no way, that March could be busy."

"Since when is mud season in Maine ever busy?"

"Well, it could be," Tina sounded defensive. "It's a good month to line up spring listings, right?"

Darby put down her muffin and gave her friend a frank look. "Listen, Tina, life is short. You could stay here and maybe sign up a listing or two, but you might never get the chance to take this trip again. That man loves you and wants to take you somewhere warm, and fun, and different. Why in the world would you turn him down?"

"I don't know!" She sighed, her face twisted in misery. "I guess I'm afraid that I won't like it, or that I'll miss Maine. Or that I'll regret not making money."

"Making money isn't everything. And those other things boil down to fear. Going somewhere new is always a gamble, but if you approach it with the right attitude, it's an adventure. Something the two of you will share."

"That's what he said." Her voice was small. "He wants us to have an adventure."

Darby smiled. "Well then, why not?"

Tina licked her cherry red lips. "This will sound dumb, but here goes. I've never been on an airplane."

Darby wasn't completely surprised by her friend's revelation. "I'm sure you're not the only islander in that situation. Does Donny know?"

"Nope."

"Why not tell him? You guys are embarking on a new life together. You can trust him."

"Yeah." Tina thought a moment, and then gave a defiant toss of her red curls. "Okay, well as long as we're talking about trust, tell me why is it you keep that nice Miles Porter at arm's length?"

"We're not discussing my love life." Darby took a sip of her coffee.

"Why not? Seems to me you should take your own advice."

Darby frowned. Was it fear that kept her from letting Miles get too close? *Am I afraid I'll lose him?* She pictured her parents, felt the pang of their loss, and wondered if Tina was right.

"I promise I'll be a bit braver this time."

Tina smiled. "Okay, then. I'm off to find Donny. He's not getting out of this as easy as he thinks." She pulled on her coat and took her coffee. "I'll bring him a muffin or two as a peace offering."

"Good idea." Darby patted her friend on the shoulder. "Go get 'em, tiger."

"You know I will." She paused. "Thanks. You're a real friend."

Darby smiled as she pulled the door closed. It felt surprisingly nice to hear those words.

Hurricane Harbor's Chief of Police slammed down the receiver of the phone, making Bitsy Carmichael jump. It was still early in the morning, by her book, and she had a touch of jetlag from yesterday's flight.

"What the heck, Chuck! Whatever has gotten into you?"

Charles Dupont glowered at Bitsy and her flowered robe, pink puffy slippers, and matching pink lipstick. *You!* He felt like saying. *You've gotten into me.*

He grabbed his mug of coffee and took a long swig. At least she made good coffee, he'd give her that.

"Is it work related? Or something else? I'm happy to help you."

Then get the heck back on a plane to Las Vegas.

"Can you share the details with me? I watch a lot of crime shows, especially *CSI*. Did you know there's a *CSI* that's filmed right in Vegas? I know all of the places they show—Mandalay Bay, Glitter Gulch ..." She had found a file in the pocket of her robe and was now rasping it against her nails with vigor. "Some of the scenes can turn your stomach, like when they show the dead bodies with blood oozing out and stuff. You'd be sick, I tell you. But they end up catching the bad guys. Just like you, right, Chuck?"

Yeah, just like me, he thought. The words of the Manatuck detective still rang in his ears: Lorraine Delvecchio's death was being ruled an accident. If Alison Dyer had indeed seen someone on the Breakwater, it had been an innocent walker, nothing to do with Lorraine. He wanted to challenge the guy, call him an idiot;

anything but what he'd done, which was to thank him for the information and hang up. He turned to Bitsy, all the fight gone out of him.

"I wish you'd stop calling me Chuck," he said, his voice weary. "Can't you just call me Charles, like everyone else?"

"But you've always been my Chuckie!" She pouted, put the nail file down, and crossed the kitchen to where he sat at the table with his coffee. He caught the scent of her perfume as she perched on the chair next to him and gave a naughty smile.

"Don't tell me you've forgotten how I used to say, 'Chuckie, wuckie,' to you, at the same time that I—"

"I haven't forgotten," he sputtered, his face a deepening red. "It's just that—ah, heck, Bitsy, I don't get it. What are you doing here? You took off fifteen years ago, without even a postcard to tell me you were still alive. And now you waltz back in this house like you own the place?"

"Well, I sort of do own the place. Half of it anyway." She stood up, all five-feet-two inches of her. Had she really been that short when she was younger? Charles remembered her as being taller, but then she probably remembered him as thinner, stronger, and younger looking, too.

"Look, if I could, believe me, I'd settle up with you right now." He sighed, took a gulp of coffee. It was times like this that he missed his old golden retriever the most.

She went to the coffeepot, turned, and carefully poured a stream of coffee into his cup. "I don't want your money." The pot landed back on the burner with a thunk.

"Then what the heck do you want?"

"A second chance. I know I don't deserve it, and I know most men would kick me right out the door. But you're a decent guy. That's why I fell in love with you all those years ago. You're one of the good guys, Chuck." She sighed. "I mean, *Charles*. What I'm trying to say is, I'm hoping you'll let me stay."

He turned his full-on cop stare at her, wondering if she was giving him a line of bull. But her round face was contrite, the blue eyes open, without any trace of derision.

"Why, Bitsy? Why did you go?" It was the question he had asked himself over and over like some sort of tortuous mantra, until it seemed crazy to even wonder any more.

She bit her lip. It was not a habit he remembered, but he found it endearing, along with the punk-style blonde haircut, so different from the chin-length cut she'd sported fifteen years ago.

"I felt like I had a big pillow over my face and couldn't breathe," she whispered, the pink lips moving slowly. "You had your job, the kids were in school, and there was nothing for me to do on this dinky island. One day I imagined myself running away. After that, it was all I could think about. The idea started festering inside me, until finally I just took off." She looked down at her hands, twisted the little sparkly watch on her wrist. "I was wrong, and I knew it as soon as I left. I wanted to come back. But I was too proud. So I stayed, and the time went by. Before I knew it, fifteen years were gone." She bit her lip. "I figured that I needed to come back and make amends." She paused and looked away. "Before it was too late."

He gave a harsh chuckle. "What, do you know something I don't about my imminent demise?"

"No. I didn't mean it like that." Bitsy rose and crossed the vinyl floor, her slippers making little whooshing noises as she walked. An image of the chapel at the Nevada Cancer Center flitted through her mind. She saw the teak benches and chairs with their checkered cushions, including the one closest to the window where she had often sat. Bitsy willed the memory away.

She opened the refrigerator and took out an egg carton. "Is it so crazy for two people who were once in love to give it another shot?" She began cracking eggs into a bowl, the noise a staccato counterpoint to her question. "'Cause I don't think there's anything wrong with that."

She paused and turned toward him. "I'm making an omelet, if it's okay with you. I seem to recall it was one of your favorites?"

He nodded, thinking quickly of his cholesterol, and then not giving a damn. He'd tell her later, much later, about the fake eggs, low-fat cheese, and heart-healthy margarine dotting his refrigerator's shelves. In the meantime, he sat back in his chair and watched in amazement as his wayward wife cooked them both breakfast.

With Tina gone, hopefully to patch things up with Donny, Darby found herself ready to tackle some much needed repairs to the old farmhouse. The previous tenant, a single mom with a young daughter, had heard "scratching" sounds coming from the attic, and Darby suspected that some enterprising squirrels were making the empty space their home.

Dressed in her new down coat with a snug wool hat over her head and thick gloves on her hands, Darby climbed the wooden stairs to the attic. Although the temperature was numbing, the scent of the dusty old space was familiar. As a young child, she'd found the uppermost reaches of the farmhouse fascinating. Filled with boxes of her father's high school memorabilia, stacks of vinyl record albums, holiday decorations, discarded toys, paperbacks, and a steamer trunk from her grandparents, the attic was a silent haven of interesting items, a place where the young girl could explore and escape.

Now the space was empty. Any treasures from the past had disappeared, banished to the landfill, no doubt, by Jane Farr. She'd sold the house during her niece Darby's self-imposed exile from the island, and then, in a fit of remorse that still surprised Darby, bought it back again years later.

Darby switched on a powerful flashlight and peered into the eaves. Her gaze swept with the beam over the cracked floorboards, searching for signs of rodent activity. A little pile of debris below the window caught her eye, and she moved toward it cautiously, the old boards creaking under her weight.

It was a small mound of broken acorns. Darby noted a nearby window, missing a half a pane of glass, and the oak branch just a jump away from the sill. So a squirrel had been stashing food for the winter within the attic. Had he also moved in?

Crouching to see into the corner, Darby let the beam of light move slowly along the eaves. She saw nothing at first, and then a shape emerged, tucked way back and practically out of sight.

Darby took in a quick breath, wondering whether she was about to encounter a rabid roommate?

She removed her new coat, lay down on her stomach, and began belly crawling into the space, careful not to lift her head. The attic roof was studded with ancient nails, and Darby remembered their prick from childhood encounters.

She reached out with a gloved hand, gingerly touching the object, hoping it was not a squirrel, dead or alive. Her fingers probed something hard, and rectangular shaped—some sort of box. Darby pulled it toward her and began scooting backward, out of the eaves.

Ouch! Something sharp grazed her scalp. She winced, thankful that her tetanus shots were up to date, and backed up slowly. Finally she stood.

Coated with a thick layer of dust, the box in her hands was approximately ten inches wide and five inches high, and weighed several pounds. It was painted a bright red, with small brass hinges.

Darby wiped away some of the layered dust. Charming scenes of snow-capped mountains, trees, and blue-roofed temples emerged from the grime. *Japan.* She felt a glimmer of excitement. This little box was Japanese.

Darby bent down and picked up her coat, cradling the box and the flashlight as well. She shivered, the single-digit temperatures of the attic finally having an effect.

She shuffled on stiff, cold, legs toward the stairs. Taking them slowly, she descended, closed the attic door, and headed for the bathroom. She placed the lacquered box on the countertop and turned on hot water for a shower. She wanted to open the box—just for a quick peek—and yet she was frozen to her core.

And then she saw the blood.

FIVE

Whoosh!

Bitsy Carmichael raised the patchwork quilt up into the air and let it fall neatly onto the freshly made bed. She fluffed the two king-sized pillows, placed them at the headboard, picked up an empty water glass from a bedside table, and surveyed the room with satisfaction. As soon as Charles had left for the office, she'd scurried up the stairs to his room, tidied his closet and floor, and hung up several shirts and trousers. A quick pass with the vacuum cleaner and the space looked neat and orderly.

She placed the glass on a table by the stairs and entered the guest room. Bitsy was staying here (temporarily, she was sure) and the room was barely big enough for the twin bed, never mind her two suitcases. She took one and tried to shove it under the bed. No dice. She wheeled it into the hallway and jammed it into the linen closet, beneath a shelf piled with sets of frayed sheets. The other she took into Charles's room where it slid easily under his bed.

She finished applying her makeup in the guest bathroom. Running her fingers through the spiky blonde haircut she'd adopted in Las Vegas, Bitsy thought about the day. She'd straighten up the kitchen, make a shopping list, and then go to the grocery store for a few items. She frowned. There was a problem with that scenario. She did not have a car.

A knock on the downstairs door made her jump. She swept her lips with a dusky plum shade, dabbed on a little perfume, and scrutinized her image in the glass. She looked good, especially for a woman in her mid—okay, it was actually *late*—fifties.

Bitsy heard another knock as she descended the stairs, drinking glass in hand. She peered out the living room window. A truck was in the driveway, the same truck that had transported her from the ferry dock to the house.

Donny Pease.

She flung open the door and there he was, wearing a red plaid woolen coat and a sheepish grin. She gave him a bright smile. "Come in, come in, Donny. Brrr! It feels even colder than yesterday."

"Storm coming," Donny noted. He gave a shy nod. "Be your first since you've been back in Maine."

"You're right," she said, helping him out of his coat. "Let me fix you a cup of coffee and you can tell me all about your wedding plans."

Donny frowned. Tina had called and said she wanted to talk, but Donny wasn't ready to capitulate to the strong-willed redhead. Let her think about it a few more hours, he thought. Let her imagine what it would be like to call off this wedding.

Bitsy made a little noise with her throat, bringing him back to the present.

"Here you go, sir," she chirped. She was quite a bit cheerier than when he'd picked up her and her two zebra suitcases the day before.

"Thanks." He sat down with the coffee and took a sip. Coming here had seemed like a good idea a few minutes ago, but now he wasn't exactly sure what his plan had been.

"Did you work out there in Vegas?" His voice wavered a little and he blushed.

She did not seem to notice. "Waitressing. I had a few health problems and my nursing license lapsed, but I think I might see what I can do to get current again here." She took a sip of coffee. "What about you, Donny? How do you stay busy?"

"Caretaking, mostly. I worked at the old Trimble place for years. Now there's an Institute that owns the property and I work for them twice a week, keeping the old place up. The Inn has me do some maintenance work too, and then I have a water taxi business in the summer, bringing people back and forth who don't want to bother with the ferry."

"Good for you. And what about Tina?"

His face hardened a little. "She sells houses. I think this was one of the ones she was working on."

"Really? I didn't know Charles was going to sell."

Donny squirmed. "I don't know."

"It doesn't matter. Tell me about your wedding. Chuck—I mean, Charles—is looking forward to it."

"It's going to be a good time." *Provided we go through with it.* He felt a surge of bravery. "Why don't you come, Bitsy? Tina and I talked about it and she'd love to have you there."

A total lie, as he and Tina had barely spoken since their argument, and she'd certainly never suggested inviting Bitsy. But what the heck? Tina had all kinds of people coming to the wedding, relatives plus new real estate clients, many of whom he'd never even met. Not that he cared to.

He gave Bitsy an expectant look. "Well? It's tomorrow at one o' clock at the Congregational Church."

Bitsy smiled. She looked a lot like the young freshman girl he'd kissed after the homecoming dance, kissed and then cuddled, and then …

She tilted her head to the side like a curious seagull. "I'd love to come to your wedding, Donny. Just so happens I'm free."

Darby's oval face was streaked with red rivulets of blood.

I'm ready for a Halloween party, she thought, parting her sticky black hair with her fingers. *Or the title role in* Carrie. She touched her scalp. There it was: a gash just long and deep enough to bleed copiously. Nothing serious, but she would apply some antibiotic ointment after she showered.

She looked at the box, wanting to take one peek before she warmed up her core temperature. It was obviously Japanese, and whatever was inside most likely had belonged to her mother. Her heart beat faster. *I don't care how cold I am,* she thought. *I'm taking a quick look now.*

She lifted the small bronze clasp and tried to raise the lid, but it did not pull apart as she'd expected. Darby scrutinized the juncture of the box's top and bottom. It was sealed shut, glued together with some sort of hard, clear substance.

Darby put the box down and entered the shower. *So it's not going to be that easy,* she thought, as the warm water melted the chill in her bones. The box would need a sharp object to cut through the glue before it would yield its secrets. She let the water wash away the dried blood from her face and hair and applied a small amount of shampoo, careful to treat her scratch gently.

When she was finished, Darby toweled off and dressed in jeans and a warm sweater. She quickly blew dry her long black hair, grabbed the lacquered red box, and headed down to the farmhouse's kitchen.

A small paring knife cut through the glue easily. Moments later, Darby undid the brass clasp and eased the top up on its hinges.

She could tell right away that the box contained a number of different items. With trembling hands, Darby forced herself to go slowly, first exploring the beautiful box itself.

It was lined with bright pink satin. The inside cover was a mirror, upon which was painted a peaceful little scene. In the upper left was the edge of land, dotted with a few fir trees. In the mirror's lower right corner was a bridge, or perhaps a balcony, with a red railing. A geisha wearing a pink and black kimono stood contemplating the beauty of the water and distant shore. Overhead, several birds winged their way through the sky.

Darby set the box on the kitchen table. She put a log in the fireplace, replaced the screen, and sat down to examine the lacquered container's contents.

A length of straw rope with wisps of line attached was the first item. Darby pondered its significance, knowing it must have some sort of meaning, or else it would not have been saved. She shrugged and placed it on the table.

Next was a four-inch, cast-metal Buddha, depicted in a seated position. Darby turned it over and saw some Japanese characters. She placed it next to the straw rope and pulled out the next item, a beautiful piece of silk in a deep blue shade, decorated with butterflies.

She stood and held it up. It was the sash to what must have been an exquisite kimono. Had it belonged to her mother? Or her grandmother? Darby refolded it carefully and placed it on the table. The red lacquered box had given up nearly all of its secrets.

A small Polaroid snapshot, faded with age, showed a young girl with chin-length black hair, smiling and dressed in a tiny pink kimono. *My mother*, Darby realized. She gazed at the pert little face, searching for similarities with the mother she still vaguely remembered. A perfect little smile, and a pointed, almost impish face. Yes, those were the same qualities she remembered of Jada Farr.

Last was a small, leather-bound journal, full of writing that Darby could not understand. Although her mother had taught her a few words in Japanese, she had never discussed the alphabet with her American-born daughter. Darby turned the pages carefully, but it was a puzzle, as foreign to Darby as if it had been Egyptian hieroglyphics.

She replaced the contents of the box, letting the soft silk caress her hands. She was certain this sash had belonged to her mother, as had the other items. This box held mementoes of her Japanese heritage, a culture she had willingly relinquished as the wife of John Farr. How long had the box been tucked up in the attic? Had Jada been the one to seal it shut, and why?

Darby had little time to think as her door flew open and a breathless Tina Ames burst in.

"You'll never guess what I just saw," she wailed, collapsing onto one of Darby's kitchen chairs. "Donny was driving around that tramp Bitsy Carmichael! I saw her sitting there next to him, smiling like she was having a grand old time!"

"I'm sure there is a good reason why she was in his truck, Tina. Where did he take her?"

"To the police station. But they could have been all over town before that."

"Now come on, Tina. The Chief has only one car. Bitsy probably needed a ride and Donny helped her out."

"He shouldn't be taking women in his car, Darby! Give me a break."

"Wait a minute. Don't you drive men around all the time?"

"That's different! I'm taking them to see houses. I'm *working*." She sniffed. "I suppose Bitsy could have called him for a ride. After all, he was the one who picked her up yesterday."

"That's right. Did you talk to Donny yet? Are you two over your argument?"

"Kind of." Tina made a face. "Actually, no."

"Did you tell him you'd go on the trip?"

"Not exactly."

"Why not? Tina, it will be fun to go away together. Warm weather, sunny skies, strolling Mariachi bands... You'll absolutely love a break from this chilly island."

"I suppose." She walked to the fireplace and warmed her hands.

"As a co-owner of Near & Farr Realty, I'm telling you to take the time and go."

Tina turned with a smirk. "Okay, okay." She pointed at the lacquered red box on the table. "What's that?"

"I found it in the attic. It has some of my mother's things in it."

"The attic? What the heck was it doing up there? Jane sold this house ages ago. No personal property should have remained."

Darby nodded. "It was shoved in the back, under the eaves. I think it's gone undetected for all these years." She pulled out the piece of straw rope, the small Buddha, and the kimono sash. "I have no idea what the straw is for, nor do I know if this little guy is anything special. But look at this beautiful piece of silk."

"Gorgeous." Tina fingered the fabric, her eyes wide. "I can just see you in that color. You'd look like a goddess."

Darby laughed. "I don't know about that, but check out how cute my mom was as a little girl."

"Aww... she's adorable! I can see how you resemble her." She peered into the box. "What's in the notebook?"

"Nothing I can read," Darby said, pulling it out. "Maybe when I'm back in California I'll find someone who can translate it for me."

Tina snapped her fingers. "There's a guy up in Westerly who specializes in this kind of stuff," she said. "You know, Japanese art and history. The paper ran a story on him a few weeks ago." She fingered the kimono sash as she continued. "He's the assistant curator at the Westerly Art Museum. Eric Thompson. You ought to bring the box up there and see what he has to say."

"Good idea." Westerly was north of Manatuck, about a forty-five minute journey including the ferry to the mainland.

"Think you might go today?" Tina twirled her hair, waiting.

"Why, you need something?"

"Well, actually, yeah. My sister Terri lives in Westerly and she's got some shoes for me to try on." Tina gave a shy grin. "I know, I know, it's all about me and my wedding."

Darby laughed. "You're finally starting to sound like a bride! Sure, I'll head up the coast and see if Eric Thompson is in. Even if he's not, I'll get you those shoes."

Tina grinned more widely. "I'll tell Terri to meet you at the museum." She pulled on her pink coat and carefully did the enormous buttons. "Guess I better go find my groom. I've got to make sure he's still gonna marry me."

On the ferry ride from Hurricane Harbor to Manatuck, Darby telephoned her office in California. ET, her capable assistant, answered and assured her that everything was going fine. "Please, enjoy your weekend without worrying about us," he urged. "Claudia is showing some property, I'm entering listings—it's just another typical day at Pacific Coast Realty."

Darby laughed. "Fair enough. I'll check in with you on Monday." She then told ET about the red lacquered box and its treasures.

"What an amazing find," ET's resonant voice held wonder. "Almost as if your mother placed it there for you to discover, all these years later."

Darby agreed. "I can't wait for you to see it, ET." She pictured him, standing ramrod straight, dressed in an impeccably tailored suit, and realized that she missed him. "I'll speak to you soon. Be sure to thank Claudia for her good work."

"I will. And you—concentrate on your driving." His voice held a touch of concern.

"I'm still on the ferry!"

"Good. Remember your vow to take life a little slower."

Darby thought about ET's words as she cruised to Westerly. With the roads free of ice and very little traffic, she let the little Jeep's wheels hug the pavement, enjoying the sensation of zooming around the coastal road's corners. She remembered her promise, made in the fall after she was cited for speeding, to stop racing from thing to thing. *But I like driving fast,* she realized. *It's part of who I am.* She chuckled, picturing ET tsk-tsking and calling her "Speedy Gonzalez."

Her thoughts drifted to Miles's arrival from California, and whether he would find the old farmhouse comfortable. She imagined his lanky frame in the living room, a fire roaring away in the fireplace. It was going to be a fun, romantic visit, and she was counting the hours until his arrival that evening.

She turned off the highway. The road curved east and Darby followed it, catching glimpses of the bay as she wound around and down into Westerly village. Galleries, cafés, and small restaurants dotted the quaint streets, although many were closed for the season. Anchoring the small shopping district was an imposing brick building that Darby knew housed the art museum. A banner stretched across the front announced a portrait exhibition just getting underway.

She pulled into a parking lot, scooped up the red box, and headed for the entrance.

A slight redheaded woman with a warm smile was waiting just inside.

"Darby? Tina told me you'd be wearing a long red coat. I'm Terri Ames Dodge."

She stuck out her hand and Darby shook it, smiling. Terri was a slightly shorter version of her sister, with the same inquisitive expression and long fingers ending in bright red nails. She wore cream-colored wool pants and a soft blue cashmere sweater, and tan loafers with little tassels.

"I see the family resemblance, Terri. It's nice to meet you."

"Yes, we Ames girls are all made from the same mold. You'll see when you meet Trixie." She handed Darby a plastic shopping bag. "Here are the shoes. Thanks for being our delivery service."

"My pleasure. I'm hoping to see one of the curators."

"Yes, Tina told me. Eric's office is around the corner."

Darby followed Terri through a small maze of offices until they came to an empty one. "I'm sure he'll be right back," Terri said. "I saw him when I first arrived and told him you were planning to meet me." She cocked her head to the side. "Want to see the portrait exhibition while you wait?"

"Sure." Terri led the way to the gallery and the two viewed the portraits in silence. All were by Maine artists, including several names Darby recognized.

"Alcott Bridges," she read, stopping before a framed painting of an elderly man that seemed to loom over the room.

"Yes, probably his most famous work." The two gazed up at the painting. Terri pointed to the man's gnarled hands, clutching a wooden gavel. "Bridges is able to create such intricate details. The veins, the way the fingers curl… and look at the depth of emotion in the eyes. Just amazing."

Darby read the printed description of the portrait. "This man was a judge in Manatuck—Edwin Collins. It says there was some controversy when the work was first exhibited."

Terri nodded. "A few collectors claimed it was a forgery. The story went that Bridges had this big commission, but that his wife was gravely ill. Supposedly he paid another artist to complete the judge's portrait."

"Is that truly forgery?" Darby asked. She scrutinized the work once more, as if the answer lay in the judge's stony countenance.

"You raise an excellent point." A trim man with a silver goatee and blue-rimmed glasses had come up behind them. He extended his hand. "Eric Thompson, assistant curator."

Darby juggled the bag of shoes and red box. "Darby Farr. And this is Terri—"

Eric Thompson laughed and gave Terri a hug. "We go back a long way. How are you, my dear?"

"Very well, Eric. Now back to Darby's question. Assuming Alcott Bridges did have help in creating this work, does that make it a forgery?"

He shook his head. "Forgery is a type of fraud in which the artist claims his work was created by another person. That's not the case here. If indeed Bridges had a helper—someone to fill in the minor details, for instance—he would be part of a long history, the tradition of the workshop. For example, Peter Paul Rubens used workshop assistants to complete his paintings. In modern times, look no further than Andy Warhol or Jeff Koons, both of whom had a studio approach to the creation of their art." He leaned back on the heels of his shiny black loafers. "In my professional opinion, even if Bridges painted only a portion of this work, it would not be a forgery. Perhaps one could claim it isn't as authentic as his other portraits, but for all we know, the story could merely be malicious gossip." He turned and smiled at Darby. "My personal belief is that

Alcott Bridges painted this portrait—the whole thing. It's what he himself has always maintained. If you ask me, the man is unstoppable as an artist. Recently he's relinquished portraiture and taken up landscapes. He's in his early eighties but just keeps on creating."

Darby took a last look at the judge before following Eric Thompson and Terri Ames Dodge back toward the offices.

"I'll say goodbye here," Terri said. "Give my sister a hug and tell her to relax. I'll drive down this afternoon, before the worst of the storm."

She waved and left Darby with the curator.

"Talk about your powerhouse women," Eric Thompson commented, indicating Tina's sister with a nod of his head. "Terri Dodge has done more for this community than anyone I know. She's an avid fundraiser and networker—someone who cares about Westerly and the future of this museum." He clapped his hands. "Well. Let's see what treasures you have in that beautiful red box of yours. Come right into my office."

He opened the door to a comfortable room with two leather chairs and a wide antique desk. Books lined one wall of the office, while exquisite paintings hung on the other. Eric followed Darby's gaze as she beheld each of the artworks.

"A little perk of my job, I'm afraid," he chuckled. "I enjoy a rotating display of our smaller works. My own private gallery, if you will." He took a velvet cloth out of a desk drawer and spread it over the surface of the desk. "Let's see what you've brought."

Darby placed the box on one corner of the velvet and watched as Eric ran his fingers over the red lacquered surface, smiling.

"This is a jewelry box, as I'm sure you've surmised, made in the mid-1940s or so. These scenes of Mt. Fuji, the rice fields—they are all hand painted." He undid the small brass clasp and opened the box. "Hand painted on the inside, on this mirrored glass, as well." He nodded and pulled out the first item, the straw rope with its wisps of line.

"Yes, I remember this. It's called *shimenawa*. You find it at the entrances of holy Shinto places to ward off evil spirits, or marking the boundaries of sacred grounds or shrines. In Japan's small towns and cities, merchants and businesses, as well as private individuals, often hang the *shimenawa* on their front doors at special times of the year. Similar to our tradition of a Christmas wreath." He reached inside the box for the seated Buddha and grinned.

"Don't you just love him?" He smiled fondly at the little statue.

"There is writing on the underside."

"Oh, I know," Eric Thompson said, chuckling. "And I can predict what it says: Great Western Buddha." He flipped it over, peered through his blue-rimmed glasses, and nodded. "Bingo!" His voice dropped to a conspiratorial level. "These little guys are sold at temples throughout the country as souvenirs. Nowadays they are made of plastic. The fact that this one is metal means it is probably from the 1950s or '60s."

Darby nodded. She pulled the photo of her mother in the kimono out of the box and gazed down at the smiling little girl.

"May I?" Eric took the image in his hands. "What a lovely child. Your mother, am I correct?"

"Yes. I'm sure these were her things. She must have brought them with her from Japan."

He looked from the photo to Darby's face. "You bear a marked resemblance."

Darby pulled the blue sash from the box. "I think this belonged to my mother as well, but I'm not sure."

Eric Thompson fingered the soft silk of the sash. "This is a handmade *obi*. The butterflies are actually sewn into the fabric, not printed." He folded the blue material gently. "The kimono that this belonged to was probably worth thousands of dollars. The *obi* itself is quite a treasure."

Darby took the folded blue silk from Eric Thompson with care, thinking of Jada Farr's graceful beauty and adventuresome personality. She'd nodded eagerly on the day her husband proposed an afternoon sail, laughed and climbed into the sleek vessel without any sense that the wave she'd tossed to her young daughter would be her last.

Darby was about to set the *obi* back in the box when she spotted the notebook.

"I nearly forgot—there's a journal as well," she said, handing it to Eric Thompson.

He opened the leather cover and scanned the contents. "I read Japanese fairly well, but I'm having a hard time deciphering these characters." He turned a few pages. "It's a diary, I can tell that much, although I think it predates your mother. Perhaps it belonged to her parents?"

"I suppose it could have. My mom was their only child."

Eric Thompson shook his head. "There appears to be a lot of numbers in the back of the book." He handed the notebook to Darby. "I'm afraid I can't be of much assistance."

"That's fine. You've been so helpful with the other items." She packed up the box, her gaze lingering on the photograph. "I'm sure I can find someone in Southern California who can translate the journal."

"Yes, I suppose you can. Let me know what you find out, will you?"

"I'd be happy to. Thank you, Eric."

"My pleasure."

Darby tucked the small box under her arm and started out of his office. A snapping of fingers made her pause.

"I nearly forgot. I met a Japanese man at a cocktail party just a few nights ago. He seemed like a smart young guy, said he was going to be in Maine for a bit. Perhaps he might shed some light on your journal." He fished around on his desktop. "I've got his business card right here." He lifted a few papers, pushed his glasses back on his nose. "Someplace..." Finally he gave a sigh. "How about if I call you with his name?"

"Sure." Darby scribbled down her number and handed it to Eric. "Thanks again."

Clutching the box and the bag of shoes, Darby headed out of the museum and back to her Jeep.

The blueberry muffin was soft and moist, with a sugar-crusted top that crunched as Donny bit into it. He sighed with pleasure. Of course, these were frozen blueberries from last July, and yet they retained a hint of summer, a tang enhanced by the cinnamon sprinkled liberally on the top.

Tina stared at him with an expectant face.

"Well, are you going to accept my apology or not?" She twirled her hair with her index finger—a dead giveaway that she was uncomfortable.

Good, Donny thought. *Let her squirm a little*. He chewed carefully and seemed to ponder her question.

"Let me just make sure I've got it straight. You'll come with me to Mexico?" He took another bite as she considered.

"Yes, for two weeks."

He shook his head. "Four."

She bit her lip. "Three?"

He gave a long sigh. "Fine. We'll go for three weeks." She didn't need to know that the owner of Beach Lady had called that very morning and said the fourth week was unavailable.

"And you'll think about what I said? That selling houses shouldn't come between us and the things we want to do?"

Tina nodded contritely. She touched his arm with a red-painted fingernail. "I'm glad we've survived our first fight." She scrunched up her nose. "Do you have time to kiss and make up?"

Donny blushed to the roots of what remained of his hair. "Lord, girl, you are something. I'll make an honest woman out of you yet."

She laughed. "I know. But until then ... "

He put down the blueberry muffin and followed his bride from the kitchen to his bedroom.

SIX

A WRINKLED COPY OF the *Manatuck Gazette* lay next to Darby. She was seated on the ferry, on her way back to Hurricane Harbor, and had decided to come out of her car and into the ferry's warm cabin for the half-hour voyage. Holding a cardboard cup of coffee more for warmth than sustenance, she scanned the front page. Sure enough, a long story about Lorraine Delvecchio's death dominated the news.

Ms. Delvecchio was employed by the Hurricane Harbor Police Department before leaving to join the Manatuck Police Department, where colleagues say she was dedicated to her job. "She was well suited to our department," said Manatuck Chief of Police Lawrence Eisner. "Attention to detail and confidentiality were the hallmarks of Lorraine's demeanor."

Darby continued reading. The article described how the avid walker had apparently slipped at the end of the Manatuck Breakwater and plunged to her death. It quoted the state medical examiner as saying she'd died from drowning, although hypothermia had also been a factor. *"It's almost impossible to survive in water this cold,"* the doctor was quoted as saying.

Darby refolded the paper and frowned. The story did not mention anyone else on the Breakwater, nor did it ask for information to identify the unknown walker. Perhaps the police were still working out the details of Alison Dyer's account? She glanced out the window, streaked with sea spray. The island loomed before her, its seaweed-choked rocks gray and forbidding. *Time to head back to the Jeep.*

The ferry docked and Darby started her engine. It chugged a little in the cold and Darby shivered as she blasted the heat. *Perhaps Chief Dupont knows the status of the investigation,* she thought. *I'll stop by the police department and see what he can tell me.*

Darby resisted the temptation to bring the Chief a pastry from the Hurricane Harbor Café, remembering his love of sweets and his newly trim waistline. *If I give him anything, it should be a Tarte Aux Pommes,* she thought, smiling at his fondness for the apple pie. Instead, she drove by the restaurant, bar, and The Hurricane Harbor Inn. After heading up the hill, she followed the winding island road to the town's municipal building.

A tall, reed-thin man with a toothy smile introduced himself when she entered. "I'm Deputy Tom Allen," he said. "Chief Dupont's here, but he's not alone." He grinned and rapped loudly on the Chief's office door.

"Chief Dupont? Someone here to see you."

"Come in."

A compact woman with frosted blonde hair stood by the Chief's cluttered desk. She turned an expectant face their way, and Darby felt a stab of recognition. *The traveler with the zebra suitcases.* Could this be Bitsy Carmichael?

As if reading her mind, Charles Dupont waved his hand in the blonde's direction. "Hi Darby, this is Bitsy, my, er, wife." He blushed and looked down at his desk.

Darby felt for the guy. He was obviously uncomfortable with the whole situation. She smiled at Bitsy and shook her small hand. "Welcome back to Maine."

"Why, thank you," Bitsy said, seeming genuinely pleased by the welcome. She lowered her voice as if sharing a secret. "I understand you're the island's *other* famous runaway." She waggled her eyebrows in a suggestive manner.

"I suppose so," Darby said, knowing that Bitsy was right, that the story of her teenage escape from Hurricane Harbor was a local legend. Old-timers loved to describe how she'd stolen her Aunt Jane's truck and driven it clear across the country, blasting through the miles of highway until there was no more pavement left to drive. Her home for the past ten years had been the laid-back surf town of Mission Beach, California; her ocean, the Pacific.

"I'm glad you came by, Darby," the Chief said, assuming his customary attitude of control. "I need to speak with you. Bitsy, honey, can you skedaddle for a minute while I talk to Darby? Then we'll go out for lunch, I promise."

"Okay, Charlie. I'll be in the hallway, waiting on you." She rose and flounced out of the room, wearing a mischievous little smile.

The Chief chuckled uncomfortably as Bitsy closed the door. "Kind of a strange situation," he muttered.

Darby kept her face neutral. "I'm sure." She resisted the urge to shake him by the shoulder. Had he actually just called Bitsy "honey"? And since when was Charles Dupont nicknamed "Charlie"?

Instead she sat down in one of the plastic chairs in front of his cluttered desk. "Any news on the investigation into Lorraine Delvecchio's death?"

"That's exactly what I wanted to talk to you about." He shook his head. "I had a call this morning from Detective Dave Robichaud. He said they interviewed that woman Dyer, the one you spoke to, and didn't find her story compelling enough to rule that Lorraine's death was anything but an accident."

"Didn't they believe Alison?"

"No problems with her credibility, but her story's not as solid as it seemed. She did leave the window to answer the phone and use her washroom. Apparently they checked her telephone record and she was on the line with the telemarketer much longer than the few minutes she described. In fact, she must have been intrigued by the idea of a stay in a timeshare, 'cause she spoke to the guy for ten minutes." He frowned. "And there's no telling how long she was in the washroom."

"But that doesn't change the fact that she saw a person in a ski mask walking down the Breakwater."

"No, but as Detective Robichaud pointed out, people are allowed to walk there wearing any damn thing they want."

Darby nodded. "Because Alison didn't actually see someone push Lorraine, they're unwilling to go down that path, is that right?"

"Correct." He ran a hand through his short gray hair, even more thinly distributed than Darby recalled from the summer. "Listen, Robichaud is a good detective, but I know that girl didn't slip off that seawall. There's no way on this earth she fell accidentally. She was pushed, Darby. Every cop instinct I've got tells me that."

"I believe you, Chief. But what I keep wondering is this: why would anyone want Lorraine dead? Who in the world had a motive to kill her?"

Charles Dupont gave an unhappy grunt. "More than one person, for all I know." He scribbled something on a piece of yellow legal paper and tore it from the pad. "Here's some homework for you."

Darby read the single word. "*Hyperthymesia*. What is it?"

"I believe it's what got poor Lorraine Delvecchio killed," he said, and his voice had the sound of total certitude. "I've gotta go have lunch with the prodigal wife, but you see what you can find out about that condition. Mark my words, Darby. That word right there is what signed her death warrant."

Darby walked back to the Jeep, thinking about her conversation with the Chief. Could something called hyperthymesia have led to a woman's death? Before starting her car, she pulled out her phone and punched in the term.

A superior type of memory, she read. She thought a moment. Had Lorraine been burdened—or blessed—with such a condition?

There was much more information, but she'd look into it later. Instead, she called Near & Farr Realty and heard Tina's brisk voice say hello.

"Shoe delivery for Ms. Ames," Darby intoned.

"Wahoo! Are they just spectacular, or what?"

"Truthfully, I haven't even looked at them. They're heavier than flip-flops, I can tell you that."

"Those shoes are Manolo Blahnik! They probably cost Terri close to a thousand bucks. Do you want me to come pick them up?"

"No, I thought I'd stop by the office. Can I bring you a sandwich from the Café?"

"Nah. I'm watching my waistline until after the wedding. But any kind of soup is great, as long as it isn't chowder."

"Gotcha." Darby hung up and drove to the center of town. She parked beside the Café, leaving the shoes and box on the passenger seat.

The Jeep's thermometer said the temperature had risen to twenty-five degrees, but Darby shivered as she walked. The air was cold, cold and damp. Above the tops of Hurricane Harbor's wooden buildings, large gray clouds were massing together. *It's the moisture bound up in those clouds that's causing the bone-penetrating chill,* Darby thought.

The Café bustled with a hungry lunchtime crowd. Darby waited several minutes before ordering two bowls of curried butternut squash soup. The restaurant's owner, a fifty-something banker from Boston, chatted as he rang up the sale. "Looks like we're in for a good dumping," he commented. He saw Darby's puzzled face and added, "Snow. Sounds like a blizzard, if you can believe what the weather people say. Of course, you can't always go by their predictions! Half the time they are dead wrong."

Darby took the bag with the two containers of soup and thanked the man. Was a blizzard truly forecast for the imminent future? What would that mean for Miles and his flight from California?

She walked to her car, thinking that the lack of a television at the old farmhouse had meant she was oblivious to the weather report. No wonder the air felt so damp. It was going to snow.

The compact office of Near & Farr Realty was located a quarter mile up the hill from town, with a slice of harbor just visible from the small parking lot. Darby parked, grabbed the soups, and headed down the icy path. Tina met her at the door and flung it open.

"Yum! I swear that I can smell that soup already. Curried squash, right? Can't wait."

Darby placed the containers on a scarred wooden conference table. "I forgot spoons, I'm afraid."

"No biggie, we've got some here. Jane insisted we have cutlery, wine glasses, and cocktail plates at the ready, just in case she needed to booze up some potential buyer." She grinned. "That aunt of yours was a character." She plunked two spoons, two napkins, and two glasses of sparkling water on the table. "I miss her."

"Thanks." Darby couldn't say whether she missed her Aunt Jane. Their relationship had been so fraught with complications that it was almost a relief having it over. *I miss the parts of her I didn't fully appreciate,* she thought. *If we'd had the chance to know each other as adults, we might have found common ground.*

The women enjoyed their lunch in silence. When Tina was finished, she pushed aside her cardboard container. "Okay . . . bring on the shoes!"

Darby laughed. "They're in the car. Be right back."

She dashed out and opened up the Jeep's passenger door. The red lacquered box was there, but the white plastic bag holding the shoes was not on the fabric seat. She looked in the back but found nothing. Finally, she looked under both of the seats and in the cargo compartment.

The Manolo Blahniks were gone.

Baffled, Darby trotted back to the building and gave her friend the news.

"What?" she gulped, her face turning an ashen gray. "Terri's going to kill me."

"They were in a bag on the front seat." She thought back, remembered leaving the box and the bag, and heading to the Café. She had not locked the Jeep. "Somebody must have stolen them when I picked up the soup. I feel terrible."

Tina jumped up from her chair. "I'll have to stall until I can find an identical pair." She paced the wooden floor of the office, clearly in her own world. "First I'll say they didn't fit, that's why I'm not wearing them for the ceremony. Then I'll pretend that I forgot to bring them for her to take home. In the meantime, I can probably find a pair online …"

Darby picked up the office phone and called the Hurricane Harbor Ferry Service. She explained the theft and asked if they would be on the lookout for anyone boarding the ferry carrying a white plastic bag. To her surprise, the person on the other line agreed.

"Sure." He took down Darby's number. "Hate to tell you, but there've been other thefts on the island: a lady's pocketbook from the Inn, and some guy's cashmere coat. Ripped right off the rack while he was drinking beer at The Eye. Can you believe that? He had to walk home in these temperatures without a coat."

"Does Chief Dupont know?"

"Sure, but do you think he's going to get much done now that Bitsy's back in town?" The man gave a hearty laugh as Darby thanked him and hung up. Poor Chief Dupont. He was now the subject of Hurricane Harbor's extremely active rumor mill.

She faced her friend, who had stopped her pacing.

"Tina, I'm so sorry. I should have locked the car when I went into the Café."

"Aw, honey, I don't care about the stupid shoes one bit. The ones I've got fit me fine and look great." Her face darkened. "It's Terri that I'm worried about. She takes these kinds of things—designer clothes, crap like that—very seriously." She snorted. "Trixie and I joke about her all the time. Not to her face, because she'd get so upset. But when we're alone, we call her Queen Name Drop. She's just a little too full of herself for our taste."

Darby recalled the curator's praise of Terri's fundraising prowess. "She seems to be pretty involved with what's happening in Westerly," she offered.

"Oh yeah. She was the same way when she lived here. But then she got tired of the island. One day she just packed up her husband and kids, and moved. She said it was because Westerly had a better school system, and maybe that was part of it. If you ask me, she wanted to reinvent herself in a town where she wouldn't be known as one of the Ames girls."

"What does Terri's husband do for work?"

Again a snort from Tina. "Not much. He runs some sort of consulting company. His family's filthy rich, so he spends most of the time doing things with the kids—coaching sports, driving them here and there. The guy's an absolutely doting father. I think if he'd had his way, they would have had a great big family." She sighed. "Don't worry about the damn shoes, okay? Just remember: Hurricane Harbor's not quite as safe as it used to be."

Darby nodded. She thought of her parents and their afternoon sail, an innocent outing that had ended in tragedy. As she logged onto a spare computer, her mind spun with one question: Had Hurricane Harbor ever really been safe?

Tina Ames pushed in her chair and grabbed her pink coat from the rack. "Headed off to meet Alcott Bridges," she announced, buttoning the coat's enormous black buttons. "I know you just came back from Westerly, but do you wanna come along?"

Darby looked up from the computer. Definitions of Lorraine Delvecchio's condition, *hyperthymesia,* filled the screen. "Sure. You driving?"

"Yep."

Darby pulled on her coat and grabbed her phone and a notebook. She followed Tina into the cold afternoon, shivering at the damp February air.

"Your vehicle locked now? You wouldn't want this thief stealing that cool box from Japan."

"It's locked. You know, you're right—it's strange that the box wasn't taken."

"Maybe the thief didn't think it was as valuable as a pair of fancy designer shoes."

"Good point. Those shoes are probably easier to get rid of, too."

"Exactly." Tina started her SUV and blasted the heat. "I'm betting this crook's a woman. Maybe that purse she stole was Gucci and the coat Pucci. This isn't some run-of-the-mill robber—this is a gal who likes quality."

"The Name Brand Bandit," Darby offered. She thought a moment. "That's the kind of thing you'd come up with."

"Ha! You're right. Some of my humor's rubbing off on you, and girl, that's a good thing." Tina steered onto the ferry and parked. "Isn't that Chief Dupont's car?"

Darby looked at the tan compact and nodded. "He and Bitsy were going someplace for lunch."

"Oh Lord," Tina groaned. "I suppose I'm going to have to talk to her sometime. Now's as good a time as any. Come on."

Together the women left Tina's car and headed into the ferry's cabin. Sure enough, Charles Dupont and Bitsy Carmichael were seated in the corner. Bitsy gave a little wave in their direction.

"See, Darby, I finally did get Charlie out of the office." She gave his arm a little punch. "Gotta eat, that's what I always say."

Chief Dupont's round face was crimson. He managed a small smile that was more of a grimace.

"Where are you headed for lunch?" Tina asked brightly. She extended her hand toward Bitsy, the red fingernails pointed like daggers. "I'm Tina Ames. Not sure if you remember me, but…"

"Of course I do, Tina! What a big week this is for you. Donny told me all about your wedding, and I hope you don't mind, but he invited me. I'll be going with Charlie, of course." Bitsy patted his arm and he sighed.

Darby slid her eyes toward Tina. If the redhead was surprised by the revelation that Bitsy Carmichael was to be a guest at her ceremony, she did an excellent job hiding it. "Of course we want you there, Bitsy." She turned to Darby. "Did I mention that our hair appointments are tomorrow morning at ten? We'll need to take the ferry across, but my sister Trixie's making cocktails." She glanced hastily at Chief Dupont. "Of course we'll be taking a taxi back and forth to the beauty parlor."

Chief Dupont nodded. "Smart move." He turned to Darby. "Any luck with your homework?"

"Yes. What a fascinating gift."

"I'm not sure Lorraine always saw it that way."

"What gift?" Bitsy's round face was in a pout. "What are you talking about?"

"Lorraine Delvecchio had a rare condition called hyperthymesia," Chief Dupont explained. "I asked Darby to look into it. What did you find out?"

"It's a kind of superior autobiographical memory. People with hyperthymesia can recall specific events from their personal past with extraordinary clarity."

"I remember things from my past," Bitsy sniffed. "Like the day I met Chuck—I mean—Charles. You were at the elementary school, picking up the kids, and I was subbing for the school nurse. Remember? Alana fell off the merry-go-round and scraped her knee, and I came running over with a bandage." She smiled fondly.

To Darby's surprise, Chief Dupont smiled too. "She still hates the sight of blood," he said.

Tina jabbed Darby with a pointy elbow. "Good Lord," she muttered. Out loud she asked, "So how is this memory thing special?"

"Lorraine described it once," Chief Dupont said. "She didn't like to talk about it, but we worked together so closely that she confided in me. I gave her a random date: May 29, 1999. She not only remembered that it was the day the Discovery Shuttle completed its first docking with the International Space Station, but she also described a story in the *Bangor Daily News* about a cold case murder investigation that was being reopened. I checked it out, and she was right." He paused. "Lorraine said it worked like this: she pictured a calendar in her head. She went to the date, May 29, and then could see, like a little movie, what had happened on that day. She knew what she was wearing, what she had for lunch, and who'd called her on the phone. All this personal stuff, in addition to world and local events she'd read or heard about back on that day."

Bitsy and Tina shook their heads in amazement.

"I don't know if I'd want to remember all that crap," Tina said.

"Me neither." Bitsy shuddered.

"Some people with superior autobiographical memory can recall events from twenty or thirty years back," Darby said. "Chief, did Lorraine ever say exactly what she could remember?"

Chief Dupont leaned forward. In a low voice he said, "She told me she could remember every single day of her life from the time she was a child of ten." His eyes met Darby's as the ferry prepared to dock. "My personal theory? I think she remembered some things other people wanted left forgotten."

Alcott Bridges lived on Manatuck Harbor in a shingled turn-of-the-century cottage with a ten-foot-wide porch that wrapped nearly around the house. A smaller, second-floor porch ran across the front, along with three jaunty gables topped by a small widow's walk. Views of the bay and a distant Hurricane Harbor were unbroken this time of year, but Darby noted that even in the summer there would be nothing save a few low-growing beach roses between the house and the spectacular view.

She and Tina walked up the frozen driveway, past the porch's round columns, to the door. "Some place, huh?" Tina asked as she rapped on the wide porch window.

"The setting is gorgeous and I love the exterior. Has the inside been updated?"

"We'll find out." Tina knocked again. "Mr. Bridges?"

They watched as the artist shuffled toward them. He wore a crimson silk dressing gown belted at the waist over what Darby assumed were his pajamas. His sparse hair was gray and disheveled; his face lined and sporting a week's worth of stubble. He yanked open the door with surprising force and jerked his balding head.

"Don't let all the heat out, ladies! Come in, come in." He pushed the door shut behind them and waved an arm in the direction of a room. "Go ahead into the parlor." Darby heard the swishing sounds of slippers on the wood floors. She glanced at his feet and saw elaborately beaded leather moccasins.

Alcott Bridges regarded his visitors with sunken eyes ringed by deep circles. "Well?"

Tina cleared her throat. "Mr. Bridges, I'm Tina Ames from Near & Farr Realty, and this is my associate, Darby Farr. You phoned us about selling your house."

He raised a bushy eyebrow. "So I did," he said gruffly. "I suppose I should show you around."

He proceeded to lead Tina and Darby through the house, stopping before a locked door off the kitchen. He produced a key and used it with practiced rapidity.

"My studio," he said, pushing open the door and allowing them to enter. Darby and Tina stepped inside.

It was a remarkable space: an old post and beam barn with large wooden timbers, and walls painted a clean white, reminiscent of a gallery. On the pristine surfaces hung paintings of every shape and size—portraits, mostly, bearing the unmistakable style of the great oil painter.

"Sweet Lord," said Tina. "You are one talented man."

Alcott Bridges managed a small grin. "One tries."

The center of the studio was dominated by a large easel, upon which rested a canvas half-painted with a modern landscape of varying geometric shapes. Darby edged closer to the work, deciphering the gray cubes and blocks, finally recognizing the subject.

"The Manatuck Breakwater," she breathed, remembering that the curator in Westerly had mentioned the artist's new direction.

"Yes." He inclined his head slightly, as if critiquing his own work, and then turned to Darby.

"You have a good eye. Not everyone sees what is not readily apparent."

"Thank you." She noticed shapes on the Breakwater and pointed to one. "Those are people, right?"

He nodded. "Strolling that thing is quite the local pursuit, I'm afraid."

Darby turned to him. "Can you see the Breakwater from your house?"

"From the upstairs bedrooms, of course. But I drive over there when I want to paint."

"Were you there on Wednesday?"

"No, I'm afraid not. Now that it is so cold I work from photographs." He shuffled to a table and handed her several prints. "This is what I use. The rest—" he tapped his head, "is up here."

Tina moved closer to look at the photographs. "Did you hear about the girl who fell off the Breakwater? Her body was found yesterday."

"No. How distressing." Alcott Bridges picked up a stray paint brush and placed it inside a glass jar holding dozens more. Absently he asked, "Not a local, I hope?"

"Actually, yes," Darby said. "She was a woman I went to high school with. She worked for the Manatuck Police Department. Her name was Lorraine Delvecchio."

Alcott Bridges's whole body stiffened. He turned jerkily toward a tattered armchair and stumbled slowly toward it. "You say she's dead?" The old man sank into the chair.

"Yes," Tina answered. She turned a puzzled face to Darby, her auburn eyebrows raised in surprise.

Darby was watching the artist intently. "I'm sorry for this shocking news. You must have known Lorraine."

He frowned, knitting the bushy brows together. "No, no. I didn't know the girl." He shook his head for emphasis. "I'm just—well, I'm horrified to hear such a terrible thing has happened. Negative emotions—someone causing harm to someone else—you see, I don't want them to be a part of my art."

He raised his head and gave Darby a pointed look. "As an artist, I feel things much more acutely than others." He looked down at the floor. "So distressing." A moment later he lifted his face, fixing Darby with a stare from his watery eyes. "Perhaps you'd better go."

Tina and Darby exchanged looks.

"Okay, Mr. Bridges," Tina said. "We'll see ourselves out. I'll check back with you next week to talk about a listing price, but if you have any questions, you can call me before that."

He nodded once. Darby and Tina moved quietly out of the studio, through the kitchen, and out the porch door.

"Did you see how he acted when you said Lorraine's name?" Tina pushed the porch door shut and faced her friend. "He sure as hell knew that girl. What a load of bull, saying he's an artist and feels things more than other people. He's not telling us the truth."

"I agree." Darby opened the car door and slid inside. "He definitely had an intense reaction to hearing she was dead, and he didn't assume it was an accident, either. I couldn't tell whether he was relieved or taken aback, could you?"

"Relieved," Tina said, with a firm nod of her head. "I'm good at reading body language, and that man welcomed the news. He did everything but jump up and down and shout 'Hallelujah!'"

"Okay, let's say you're right, Tina. The question then becomes, why?"

"Do you think it has anything to do with this super-duper memory thing?"

"Superior biographical memory? I don't know. The Chief certainly thinks it's what got Lorraine killed." She turned to her friend, now headed toward the ferry office. "I wish we could get into Lorraine's house and poke around. Any ideas?"

"Darby Farr!" Tina huffed. "I don't believe you need to ask that question." She swiveled toward Darby, her blue eyes piercing. "Let me remind you that we are real estate agents. Poking around in people's houses? That's what we do best."

SEVEN

Bitsy Carmichael sipped a diet soda and waited. The waitress had come by twice already, and both times she'd put her off. "I'm waiting for my husband," she'd replied. It had a comforting ring to it.

She looked at her nails and sighed. The polish was chipping and would look like hell for the wedding. She'd see if there was a beauty parlor on the island, or get back over here in the morning.

The waitress looked toward the restaurant's front door and smiled brightly. Sure enough, it was Charles, sliding into the booth and apologizing for making her wait.

"Give us just a minute," she said to the waitress. To Charles she gave an expectant look. "Did you find out what you needed?"

"No." He closed his menu. "Do you know what you want?"

She nodded. The waitress again materialized, pad and pen in hand. "Cheeseburger with coleslaw," Bitsy ordered. "And another diet soda."

"I'll have the low-fat special." He said it regretfully, and then sighed. "Here's the thing, Bitsy. Detective Robichaud is totally sympathetic to what I'm saying, but he thinks everything's got an explanation. The scrapes on Lorraine's hands, the trauma to her skull—all that could have happened when she first fell in. There is no evidence that anyone else had anything to do with her death."

"What about her memory?"

Another sigh. "He thinks it's interesting, but not a motive for murder." He sipped a glass of ice water. "Maybe it's time for me to let this go."

She waited a moment, and then shared an idea that had been percolating all morning.

"I have an idea. Let's get another puppy. Another Golden like Aggie."

"There's no dog like Aggie, you know that." He said it sharply, picturing the canine that had been his companion all those years he was alone. Suddenly his mood changed and he grinned. "Remember when she chewed Derek's math book? I had to call the school and convince them that yes, the dog really had eaten his homework."

Bitsy giggled. "What about that flowered armchair from your mother? I'll never forget when you sat in it and it just kind of collapsed. Aggie had eaten out all the stuffing from inside, right?"

He nodded. The waitress arrived with their lunches and plunked down the plates.

Charles surveyed his cottage cheese, sliced fruit, and shredded lettuce. The scent of Bitsy's burger was tantalizing, and he watched as she picked it up and took a juicy bite.

He sighed. Could he truly let this thing with Lorraine go? Accept that perhaps she had indeed suffered a fatal fall off the Breakwater, and that it had been entirely her own doing?

Resolutely he picked up his fork and scooped a bite of cottage cheese. He didn't like it, neither his lunch nor the conclusion about Lorraine's death, but it was just the way it was.

Lorraine Delvecchio had lived on a quiet, dead-end street in Manatuck, in an area that had once been attractive single-family homes and was now mostly dilapidated rentals. Of the six or so houses on the street, hers looked the most cared for, although several of the shutters were sagging and the exterior badly needed repainting.

Tina pulled into the driveway and parked the SUV. "Let's take a look."

"How are we getting in?"

"Leave it to me, my friend. Leave it to me." She scurried out of the car and approached a side door of the house. Darby watched as she tried the door, found it to be locked, and then pulled something from her pocket. After several moments, the door swung open.

Tina turned a triumphant face to Darby and beckoned with a gloved hand.

Darby hurried up to the house and joined Tina inside a small entryway with a steep back staircase. Coat hooks lined the floral-wallpapered walls. She thought briefly of asking her friend how she'd opened the door so quickly, but decided that she didn't really want to know.

"It's freezing in here," Tina said. "Her pipes are gonna burst, if they haven't already."

Darby nodded. "I'll check the oil gauge before we leave and make sure she didn't run out of fuel." She entered the living room and looked around. It was neat, with several framed photos of ocean scenes and a shelf of perfectly lined-up books, most of which were suspense and mystery paperbacks.

Tina had wandered to the front of the house. "Hey, look at this," she yelled.

Darby joined her before a pantry in the kitchen. Straight rows of canned goods were aligned in rigid formation, standing at attention like soldiers in a regiment. Boxes of cereal, dried fruit, and pasta were similarly arranged.

"A little bit of a neat freak, huh?" Tina closed the pantry door.

"I read that many people with Lorraine's memory condition have obsessive-compulsive disorder," Darby said. "I suppose it makes sense when you think of how highly organized their brains are."

"Not exactly like mine," Tina snorted, hugging her jacket around her thin frame. "Let's get a move on. I'm getting way too cold to hang out much longer."

Darby agreed. The two mounted the front stairs, peeking in Lorraine's blue and yellow bedroom, her tidy bathroom, and a small room used as an office containing a desk, laptop computer, and a small wooden chair.

"I wish we could take the computer," Tina said.

Darby opened one of the desk drawers and pulled out a small red spiral-bound notebook, no bigger than a deck of cards. She flipped through the pages and saw groups of words and numbers. Some of the numbers had dollar signs.

"Tina, take a look," Darby said. "She was keeping track of expenditures or something." There were dates in the upper margins.

"Stick it in your pocket," Tina said, shivering. "It's not like it's something of value like that computer, right? It's not gonna do Lorraine any good staying here in her desk and will just get tossed by whomever gets stuck cleaning this place out." She opened another drawer and exhaled. "Bingo!"

Darby was just about to ask what she had found when a door slammed downstairs. Both women froze, the same thought on their minds: someone was inside the house.

Alcott Bridges awoke with a start. *Gracie, Gracie*—she'd been in his dreams again, young and vibrant, laughing as they'd climbed Raven Hill for a picnic lunch. How pretty she'd looked, fresh and happy, her smile lighting up the whole hillside.

He felt a pang of loss. Gracie was gone. Only the guilt remained, eating away at him like acid corroding metal. He closed his eyes, ready to experience that pain, and felt instead unexpectedly light.

Lorraine Delvecchio was dead. Perhaps the news was in one of the papers littering the living room, or in the one waiting on his porch. He took a shaky breath. *I'm free*, he realized. *I'm finally free.*

He rose stiffly from the armchair in the corner of the studio and stretched gently, his limbs feeling more supple than they had in years. Hunger gnawed at his stomach but fixing food was far from his thoughts. The easel, with his latest canvas half completed, beckoned to him from the center of the room. Alcott Bridges felt it drawing him in, putting brushes in his hands and oils on his palette.

In a trance-like state, he began to paint.

Tina arched her eyebrows as they listened to the footsteps below.

"Hello?" A female voice, questioning.

"Hello, we're up here." Darby motioned to Tina and they went to the stairs. A heavyset woman wearing a man's plaid jacket stood below, an orange cap pulled over frizzy brown hair. She looked to be in her sixies, and wore a worried expression on her face.

"Glad to see it's you two," she said. "I was afraid some kids were in here rooting around."

"We're real estate agents from the island," Tina explained. "This is Darby Farr. She went to school with Lorraine. I'm Tina Ames."

"Esther Crandall, the neighbor next door." She looked around the house and shook her head. "Terrible shame about Lorraine. Falling off the Breakwater like that? I still can't believe she's dead."

"Had you known her a long time?" Darby asked.

"Five or six years. Ever since she bought the place." Esther Crandall stomped her feet against the cold. "She was a good neighbor, quiet and easy to talk with. She kept her house nice, especially the inside. I used to tease her about the peeling paint and such, and she'd say that the outside didn't matter, it was what was inside that counted."

"Did Lorraine have many visitors? Friends stopping by?"

The stout woman shook her head at Darby. "Nah. She kept to herself, which was fine with me. Not that she wasn't friendly." She gave a sad smile. "Every time she went on one of her trips, she'd bring me a little something. Special hand lotion, or dark chocolate. That was nice of her, I always thought."

Darby and Tina nodded.

"I didn't know she traveled so much," Tina said. "What kinds of places?"

"Oh, all over. Switzerland, Bermuda—you name it. Why, I think it was next week she was going off to the Hawaiian Islands! Guess someone will have to cancel those tickets." Esther Crandall made a concerned face. "You two are turning into icebergs. Better get out of here."

The three went back out the side door, with Esther closing and locking it. "Guess you know about the spare and all," she said, replacing a metal key on a small hook behind a little "welcome" sign. "I'll get the oil company over here and see why her furnace isn't working." She put a hand on an ample hip. "What'll you be asking?"

Darby and Tina exchanged blank looks.

"For the house. What'll be the asking price?"

Tina gave a quick smile. "We're working on that now, Mrs. Crandall. I'm going to look at what's sold recently and figure that out. You'll be the first person I call."

The older woman nodded as they climbed into Tina's car. They saw her wave, the sleeve of the plaid jacket fluttering like a flag, before she lumbered back across the frozen strip of grass between the houses.

"So little Lorraine Delvecchio was a world traveler," Tina commented, pushing buttons on her heater until it blasted hot air. "Where in the world did she get the money to take those kinds of trips on her salary?"

"I don't know, but I'm hoping this notebook can tell us," Darby said, tapping the book concealed under her coat. "I'll start analyzing it as soon as I thaw out."

"Good idea," Tina said, reaching into her coat pocket. "While you're at it, take a look at this."

Smirking, she placed a small computer thumb drive into Darby's gloved hand.

"Pretty good score, huh Detective Darby? I just knew she'd have something like this, and bam! There it was in her drawer."

"Impressive, Tina. How did you know?"

Tina steered toward the ferry and pulled into line. She put the car in park and turned to face her friend.

"You saw those soup cans, lined up like a firing squad? Anyone who's that crazy organized is gonna have backup for her computer." Tina gave a satisfied smile. "I'm getting pretty good at this, aren't I?"

"Tina, it's scary how good you are getting. I don't even want to know how you opened that locked door."

Tina feigned innocence. "It just opened right up itself," she said.

The two women chuckled as Darby took out her cell phone.

"Somebody left me a message," Darby noted, preparing to play it.

"I got one, too," said Tina. "It's Alcott Bridges." She listened a moment and then shut off her phone. "Darby, he's decided not to list his house after all. Why do I think the news of Lorraine's death had something to do with it?"

"Maybe her notes or the thumb drive will tell us." Darby listened to her phone and frowned. "My message is from a guy wanting to see that Japanese box I found. He said he can meet me at four o' clock today."

"Wow." Tina shifted into drive and climbed slowly onto the ferry. "Well, he'd better hurry it up." She glanced at the cloud-covered sky. "We're starting to get snow."

Darby looked at the surface of the adjacent cars, already thinly coated with thick white flakes. Miles was out there somewhere, sitting on a plane and headed to the island.

Straight into the path of a blizzard.

Darby stood under the shower's hot water, letting it melt the chill in her bones. Where in the world was Miles? She'd already tried to phone him, receiving only his message. Was he stranded in some airport? If so, why didn't he call?

She toweled off and dressed in jeans and a turtleneck. A fire was going in the farmhouse's fireplace, and Darby fed it until it roared. Outside the snow was coming down fast, and seeing through the flakes to the road was becoming difficult. It was not a night to be anywhere but home.

Darby took out her phone and called the number for the Portland Jetport. Her heart sank as a harried agent checked Miles's airline. "Cancelled," she barked. "No one's getting into this airport tonight."

The agent's terse message hit Darby harder than she'd expected. Along with the worry about Miles's whereabouts, there was something else … keen disappointment. *I was looking forward to seeing him. We would finally have had time alone.*

She walked into the kitchen and poured herself a glass of wine. It was not her habit to feel sorry for herself, but she poured it anyway. *One glass,* she promised, peering out the kitchen window.

Although it was not quite four o' clock, outside it was pitch black, the wind starting to howl like a living thing.

She ambled back to the living room, pulled a chair and lamp up close to the fire, and opened Lorraine's notebook. A series of pages appeared to be dated at the top, with two columns, one of numbers and one of letters.

The letters were grouped in twos, like initials.

FE, HX, VG.

Darby couldn't think of anyone with initials like that. She tried to come up with words, but not much made sense, especially when she contemplated the X.

She sipped the wine. It was a rich Barolo, and she set her glass by the fire to warm and looked again at the dates. They were each a month apart, going back about a year. Some sort of accounting, but for what?

She sighed and sipped the warmed wine. Tomorrow was Tina's wedding, and Darby knew, true to Maine form, it would happen, storm or no storm. "The hairdresser is coming to us," Tina had announced on the ferry. "One way or another, Donny will get her to the island." Darby smiled. *It will probably be a beautiful, snowbound ceremony. If only Miles could be here …*

A sharp rap on the door startled Darby out of her reverie. Could it be that Miles had found a way to the island despite the storm? She jumped up from the armchair and dashed to the entryway, flinging open the door with a welcoming smile.

Snow swirled around the figure before her, a tall, dark, handsome man who was most definitely not Miles Porter.

"Drink up, Pease!"

A beer was thrust in front of Donny, some of it sloshing over the rim of the glass onto the table. It was late afternoon at The Eye, and a larger-than-normal crowd had gathered to celebrate with their friend. "Let's go, drink 'er up!"

The man goading him on was Lester Ross, Carlene's younger brother. Unlike his sister, Lester held no grudges against Donny or any members of the Pease family. He was a merchant mariner, home for a month or so, and one of Donny's best friends.

"Come on, it's your last night of freedom!" The others at the table cheered, raising their glasses as Donny lifted the stein and drained his beer. No sooner was his glass empty, than Earl the bartender arrived with a fresh one.

"So—you ready for this, Pease?" Lester put an arm around his friend's shoulder.

"I guess I'm as ready as I'll ever be."

Lester chuckled. "Tina's a good woman. Kind of bossy, but a lot of fun, too. Can she cook at all?"

"Oh, yeah," Donny said, remembering Tina's famous fruit pies, stews, and chowders. She could cook alright—and he had the expanding waistline to prove it. "I expect that Tina's one of the best cooks on the island," he boasted. "We'll have you over for supper and you'll see for yourself."

"Okay by me," Lester said, draining his beer. He consulted his watch. "Speaking of wives, mine will be wondering where I am with a snowstorm raging. What do you say I drive you home?"

"Sure. Let me just visit the facilities." Donny rose unsteadily to his feet, holding on to the table until the room stopped spinning. *Good thing Lester's driving me home,* he thought, beginning to lurch toward the back of the bar. *I've had a few more than I'm used to.*

Earl grinned as Donny passed him. "You okay there, groom?"

Donny waved a hand in response. He needed that bathroom, and quick.

The back hallway of The Eye was crowded with boxes containing bottles of beer, mini pretzels, and toilet paper. Donny found the door of the restroom and yanked it open. He stumbled in, fumbling for the light switch. Where the heck had it gone to? Finally he located a pull cord and tugged, hard.

Shelves stuffed with more supplies surrounded him. This was not the restroom after all, but a jam-packed, walk-in closet. He grunted and was moving toward the door when a white plastic bag hanging from a nail caught his eye.

Written on the front in black Sharpie in fancy script was the word "Tina."

What the heck?

Donny reached for the bag, knocking down a whole case of party peanuts as he did so. The crash was loud, and before he could make his getaway, a handful of men had gathered outside, pointing at the prostrate Donny with glee.

"Just what in the world are you doing, Pease?" Earl pushed his way through the crowd of men, ruffling his hand through his hair. His feet were spread wide, and from Donny's vantage point he looked enormous. Earl shook his head, no doubt annoyed at the spilled snacks littering the closet floor.

Donny struggled to his feet, crunching several nuts as he did so. "What am I doing?" He was clutching the white plastic bag in one hand, and supporting himself against one of the closet walls with the other. "I'm the one who should be asking you that question, Earl." He fumbled in the bag and pulled out its contents. Holding two white stilettos with sparkly buckles before the rest of the men, he demanded, "Just what the heck are you doing with my girlfriend's sister's shoes?"

Darby stared at the dark-haired man for a good thirty seconds before he cleared his throat.

"Ms. Farr?" His English was perfect, with a hint of an accent that Darby couldn't place. "I'm Kenji Miyazaki. I'm sorry if I've startled you."

Kenji Miyazaki. Where had she heard that name before? Darby's thoughts swirled before her like the blizzard outside as she racked her brain to remember.

"Mr. Miyazaki, forgive me for not letting you in, but I don't know who you are, and I don't understand why you're here." Snow was collecting on the wood floor at Darby's feet, but she wasn't about to let a stranger enter without knowing just who he was.

"Eric Thompson, the curator at the Westerly Art Museum, suggested that I get in touch with you. He said that he told you I was in the area?"

Darby gave an inward groan. So this was the person Eric Thompson had met at a cocktail party, the one he thought could shed some light on the red lacquered box's journal.

"Yes, Eric did mention you. But he said he would call me with your contact information."

"I'm afraid that's my fault. I stopped into the museum shortly after you were there, and I persuaded Eric to let me get in touch with you." He paused. "I've been trying to reach you for a few months now."

A few months? Darby thought back to late summer. Hadn't her office told her of a Japanese man trying to contact her in California?

"I work with Hideki Kobayashi," he explained. "At Genkei Pharmaceuticals."

Another silent groan. Darby remembered glancing at a message from a senior vice-president of the mega-company headed by Mr. Kobayashi, a client she'd helped to purchase a large Florida estate. *I threw that message away…*

Finally she stepped aside. "Come in. It's a crazy night for anyone to be out."

Kenji Miyazaki gave a self-conscious laugh and dusted the snow off his shoulders. "You're right about that. I was foolish to go anywhere in this storm." He stomped off his boots and stepped into the house.

Darby closed the door behind him. "Let me take your jacket."

He was surprisingly tall—about six feet—with neatly cut black hair, an athlete's trim muscular physique, and an open, friendly face. "Thank you. I promise I won't stay long, and I'm so sorry for interrupting your evening."

Darby hung the dark blue jacket on a nearby hook. "Where are you going from here, Mr. Miyazaki?"

"I've got a room on the mainland." He glanced at his watch, a jet black timepiece with an etched black dial and luminous silver hands. "I'll catch the ferry at five."

"Have a seat by the fire. Can I get you anything to drink?"

"No, thanks, I'm fine." He gave a little nod and Darby was reminded of her mother. A small gesture, but one she used to do as well, here in this very house.

Darby took a seat. "Why have you been trying to reach me, Mr. Miyazaki?"

"Please, call me Ken." He gave a self-deprecating smile. "As I mentioned, I work closely with Hideki. He asked me to contact you, which is why I left messages at your office." He paused. "I'm in California quite often. On my last trip I stopped in at Pacific Coast Realty and tried to see you."

"And now you've tracked me to Maine?"

He laughed, showing straight white teeth. "Yes, that's right. I've been hunting you down, Darby Farr." His grin was boyishly attractive. "Actually, it's pure coincidence that I'm here at all. I was in a snowboarding competition over the weekend."

So Kenji Miyazaki was an athlete. Darby dimly recalled her new sales agent Claudia mentioning something about some sort of competition, but that had been months earlier. "Weren't you competing in an event in California, too?"

He nodded. "Hang gliding, out on Point Loma. I'm afraid I'm an extreme sports junkie. I like the adrenalin rush, so whenever I have time, I indulge."

"I see." She looked into his face, so open and guileless. "We're several hours from the mountains here on Hurricane Harbor. What brought you to the coast?"

"I have a retired friend in Westerly, and I decided to pay her a visit. She took me to a little cocktail party, and there I met Eric Thompson. We talked about Japanese translation. I gather from what he said that he told you about me."

"Yes." She'd forgotten about the contents of the red box. Was Kenji Miyazaki here because of the journal, the little Buddha, and the lovely kimono sash? Or did his visit have a darker intent, one having to do with Darby's grandfather's past?

As if reading her mind, Kenji Miyazaki said, "Hideki told me you were quite upset to learn about your grandfather's involvement in northeast China during the war. It must have been a terrible shock."

Darby flashed back to her time in Florida. She felt the same sinking feeling she'd experienced when kindly Mr. Kobayashi had laid out the fearful facts. Her grandfather Tokutaro Sugiyama, a scientific officer for Genkei Pharmaceuticals, had been sent by the Imperial Japanese Army to a remote part of China where secret experiments in biological and chemical warfare were conducted against civilians.

"Do you have information about him?"

A slow nod. "I have been trying to find you, to set the record straight."

"I'm not sure what you're talking about, but I'm listening." She looked down at her hands, steeling herself against whatever awful stories she was about to hear.

"I believe your grandfather was an innocent man, Darby." Kenji Miyazaki's eyes searched her face. "He knew that the so-called research was terribly wrong, and he risked his life trying to stop the experiments."

Darby's head jerked upward.

"How do you know this?"

"I discovered archives of the statements from scientists who were questioned. They admitted that there were a few men who refused to participate in the Unit's activities. I think that your grandfather, Tokutaro Sugiyama, was one of them."

"But you don't know for sure."

"No." He gave a small shrug. "It's more of an instinct at this point. But the answer may lie in the diary he kept, if that's indeed what you found."

Darby felt her heart pound. *Perhaps my grandfather wasn't complicit after all. Perhaps he'd tried to stop whatever human suffering he could.*

"I'll get the journal." She hurried to her bedroom, picked up the jewelry box, and brought it back into the living room. She swallowed, conscious that her mouth was dry. *I'm an emotional wreck*, she thought. *These events took place more than sixty years ago, and yet I am trembling.*

Kenji Miyazaki placed his hands on the lid, grazing her own as he did so. "May I?"

She nodded. "It's nearly four-thirty, and I know you need to make your ferry. How long are you staying in Maine?"

"I'm flying back on Sunday." He smiled as he removed the box's contents: the grinning Buddha, lustrous kimono sash, and the other items. "I tried to find a room on the island, but everything was booked. Some sort of wedding tomorrow."

"Yes. That's my friend Tina." Darby glanced out the window at the storm. The snow was piling up quickly, nearly drifting against the glass. Getting Kenji's car out of the driveway would mean starting to shovel immediately. And then when would she learn about the journal's secrets?

He opened the book and scanned the pages. "I can tell you right now, it's a daily record of his time at the camp. I wish I had time to read it. I believe these entries hold the answers we need concerning Tokutaro's involvement in China."

Darby exhaled. She hadn't appreciated how desperately she wanted to know of her grandfather's innocence until that moment. Should she give Kenji the journal to take with him and translate at a later time? She didn't like parting with such an important piece of her family's history. And yet she couldn't bear the thought of waiting to know of her grandfather's involvement any longer.

She took a breath. "Kenji, I have a very strange request." She felt her face flush as she continued. "Would you consider spending the night here so that you can translate the journal? I have a guest room, and I'd be happy to fix us both dinner."

She braced herself for some sort of lewd grin. Instead, Kenji lifted his gaze, his face serious and striking at the same time.

He held up the diary. His black watch caught the firelight, reflecting sparks that danced on his wrist. "This means that much to you?"

She nodded. "I need to know the truth, one way or another. If my grandfather's journal holds any information at all, I want to know what it is."

"I see." He rose from the chair, placing the book on the coffee table in a careful fashion. He thought for a moment. "I understand how you feel, but I do not think my staying here would be appropriate. Perhaps we can meet when I am on the West Coast for business?"

Darby rose as well, disappointment so palpable she could taste it. "Alright then. We'd better go shovel."

EIGHT

THE WHEELS OF DONNY'S truck gripped the snow-covered road as he turned slowly into Tina's driveway. He parked behind a big SUV with Massachusetts plates and climbed out and into two feet of fresh snow.

Tina's split-level ranch was lit up like a Christmas tree. Donny trudged through the drifts, making a narrow path to the front door that would be gone in ten minutes. Man, it was snowing hard, the flakes piling up so fast the plows were having trouble keeping up. The wind was howling, too, heaping piles that took an unsuspecting driver by surprise with their depth.

He knocked twice on the door and then entered. The twang of country music—most likely the Dixie Chicks—met his ears, along with the sound of lilting female voices floating just above the melody. He grinned. Tina was never happier than when she was with her kid sister, Trixie.

He found them in the kitchen, a huge, half-full bottle of white wine on the counter. Plates holding colorful salads waited to be eaten, but the women were too busy catching up to pay their dinner much mind.

Donny cleared his throat so as not to scare them, but both women shrieked just the same.

"Donald Duck Pease! You scared the living crap out of me!" Trixie Ames squealed. "Get yourself over here so I can give you a giant hug!"

"What the heck, Donny, are you trying to give us both heart attacks?" Tina was laughing as she asked the question, holding her sides as if she would burst. "What's that you've got in your hand?"

Donny bear-hugged Trixie and then turned a triumphant face to Tina. With a flourish he pulled an exquisite pair of white stilettos out of the plastic bag.

"Just some old shoes I happened to find."

More high-pitched squeals of delight from the women.

"You rascal! Where in the world did you get your hands on them?" Tina reached for the heels.

"The bartender at The Eye, the new guy, Earl. He says he came across them on the sidewalk but I don't believe him one bit. Deputy Allen's gone over there to search. I wouldn't be surprised if he finds a lot more stolen goods."

"Earl is the Name Brand Bandit?" Tina ran a hand over the stiletto heels and turned to Trixie. "Darby came up with that. Catchy, huh? Wait until she hears we got these babies back." Tina jumped up from the table, pulled off a pair of heavy wool socks, and slipped her feet into the shoes. "Oooh, Trixie! You can't believe how amazing these feel."

Donny shook his head at his wobbly bride to be. "Can you walk in them? You don't want to break an ankle for our trip to Beach Lady."

"Don't you worry, Donny Pease," Tina said, making her way to his side on unsteady legs. She towered over him in the heels and had to bend down to drape her hands over his sloping shoulders. "I will not let anything get in the way of having a wonderful time with you down in Mexico, not even my jitters over flying." Abruptly she did a little spin and faced Trixie. "Guess what? I'm starting to look forward to this trip!"

Her sister laughed. "Well of course you are, silly! Everyone likes a vacation, especially to a nice, warm, beach!" She pointed at Tina's feet. "Are those the ones that Terri gave you?"

Tina pulled away from Donny and yanked off the shoes. "Darn right. Don't let her know anything about them being stolen, okay?" She put the shoes on the kitchen table and turned to Donny. "Terri's getting her little one settled at the inn, then she'll head on over here. Your timing, Mr. Pease, is perfect."

Trixie lifted the shoes and scrunched up her nose. She was a shrunken-down, more voluptuous version of Tina, petite and curvy, with the same wild curls in a delicate strawberry blonde hue. "They are kind of pretty, aren't they? I like the sparkly buckles. But I can't believe they cost hundreds of dollars."

"Uh-huh." Tina snorted. "Like a thousand bucks. Believe me, I'm glad I don't have to replace them." She turned to Donny. "You are so amazing! Finding these for me, and catching a thief in the process! I'm going to have to give you a kiss."

She leaned forward and planted one on his lips, making a loud, smacking sound.

He blushed and shook his head. "You girls are a little tipsy, I can see that." He leaned back on his heels, trying to regain control of the situation. His own buzz had worn off after he'd crashed to the floor of Earl's stockroom. "Speaking of Darby, I thought she would be here?"

Tina waved a hand in the air. "A mysterious visitor stopped in, so she bagged out on us."

"Miles? I thought the airport was closed."

"No, not Miles. He's stuck in Chicago, poor thing." She shook her head. "This is some Japanese guy named Ken. Darby didn't go into details."

Donny frowned. For some reason he couldn't quite name, he did not like the sound of that.

The painting was finished. Alcott Bridges stood back and surveyed it with a critical eye. A decent composition, yes, anyone could see that, and his command of brush strokes and shading were superb. Technically this canvas was one of his best works. But did he feel the emotion?

Bridges disposed of his brushes, palette, and smock. Nearly ten-thirty—no wonder he felt exhausted. His burst of frenetic creativity had lasted several hours, and during that time he'd done nothing but paint. Now he was spent and starving.

He flicked a light on in the kitchen and pulled a stuffed chicken breast from the refrigerator. Into the microwave it went for several minutes. Sage-scented poultry filled the room, making Alcott's mouth water. Removing his entree with a fork, he transferred it to a chipped plate and sat down at the table.

The Breakwater was finished. He felt a sense of relief and gratitude, the same sensation he always experienced when completing a big work. He cut a piece of chicken, stabbed it, and chewed thoughtfully. This called for a drink of something special.

In the upper cabinet Alcott kept a half-full bottle of single malt whiskey. He stood on a step stool to reach the bottle and climbed down carefully. He then uncorked the bottle and took a long pull. A moment later, he'd found a small tumbler, filled it nearly full of the amber liquid, and sat down again.

The chicken was rubbery but Alcott was too hungry to notice. He ate nearly the whole portion, put his plate in the dishwasher, and headed back to the studio with his Scotch. He stood before the painting for a long time, sipping the whiskey and waiting.

Slowly a warm feeling crept over him, partly the result of the alcohol, but also a sensation from his study of his work. It was affecting him, yes, it was reaching him at the spirit level, lifting him to a higher place. He felt as if he were floating, hovering inside the landscape of the painting, experiencing the angles of the granite rocks, the spray of the foamy water, and the turbulence of the waves. He closed his eyes and whispered to the woman who remained, even in death, his muse.

We did it, Gracie. We did it again.

He set down the glass of whiskey and turned off the light. Gracie was pleased, he sensed that, and her spirit was at rest. He shuffled slowly to his bedroom, thinking back over the extraordinary day. The news he had longed to hear had finally come. His tormenter was gone. He had nothing to fear, no need to worry. He changed into a flannel nightshirt and eased his body into bed, feeling as light as the snow that fell steadily outside his bedroom window.

Darby let out a long, slow, breath. "My grandfather was a good man," she finally managed.

Kenji Miyazaki looked up from the journal. He dipped his head gently and closed the little book. After hours of reading, one thing seemed clear: Tokutaro Sugiyama had been an outspoken critic of all that had transpired at the notorious Unit 731. Whenever possible, he had worked to release the Chinese people under his care, had warned others about impending experiments, and even sabotaged the work of his superiors to end suffering. He had done the best he could do in a horrible situation, a situation he neither chose nor desired.

Darby realized her grandfather had been as much a prisoner as any one of the Unit's victims. And yet he had never given up trying to change the awful reality of the place.

Tears slid down her cheeks and she wiped them with her sweater. "Ken, I don't know how to thank you for tonight. I'm—I'm overwhelmed."

He stood and crossed the room, lowering himself so that he was kneeling beside her. Very gently he said, "It's a lot to take in. The things that went on there are nearly impossible to comprehend."

Darby nodded. She didn't quite trust herself to speak about the horrors her grandfather outlined in his entries. The testing of innocent Chinese men, women, and children at the hands of the Imperial Japanese Army's scientists and doctors had been horrific, an inhumane period in which all thoughts of decency and morality had been ignored.

She felt a tsunami of sadness. *All those victims,* she thought. *All those lives taken so horribly.* Darby closed her eyes, as if she could block out the images, and found herself leaning against Kenji's shoulder.

He moved next to her on the couch. She continued crying quietly against him, feeling his strongly muscled arms holding her tightly. It was grief, not only for those faceless victims she had never known, but also for her grandfather, who had spent years of his life in a living hell.

"Do you think my mother ever knew the truth?" Darby's voice was muffled against the soft flannel of Kenji's shirt.

"I do." He pulled away, gently, and looked into her eyes. "Your mother spoke and read Japanese. She may not have gotten the whole gist of the scientific language, but she understood enough to know that Tokutaro was not a willing participant in anything that happened."

Darby bit her lip. "I'm so glad." The mystery of how and when her mother had obtained the journal remained unsolved. *Perhaps it doesn't matter now,* she thought.

She wiped away her tears and looked into Kenji's face, seeing only compassion. Slowly, his hand reached up to stroke her glossy black hair.

"So much pain for someone so exquisite." He cupped her chin with his hands as if cradling a fragile teacup, leaned forward and kissed her.

She closed her eyes. Kenji was trying to erase her sadness, to replace the horror with hope. She kissed him back, felt his hands brush her slender neck. Little ripples of longing stirred somewhere inside her.

"Kenji …"

Seconds later he pulled away. "Forgive me. That was wrong." His voice was husky. "I'm going to go now."

"You can't. We tried shoveling you out, but it's snowing too hard."

"Yes, but …" he hesitated. "I'm not going to take advantage of the situation." He rose to his feet and bowed slightly. "I will go up to bed. Good night, Darby Farr."

Watching him walk up the stairs to the room she'd prepared earlier, Darby's overwhelming emotion was surprise: not just that he had kissed her, but that she hadn't wanted it to end.

"Rise and shine, beautiful bride!" Terri Dodge pushed open the door of her sister's bedroom with her knee. "It's a real winter wonderland out there."

Tina opened one eye and yawned. "Lordy, what time is it?"

"Eight-thirty," chirped Trixie Ames, entering the room with two mugs of coffee. She watched as Terri placed a tray atop her sister's lap. "Doesn't that look yummy, Tina? Your very own wedding day breakfast."

Tina gazed down at the perfectly poached egg, glass of orange juice, cup of coffee, and toast. "Delicious! But why aren't you two eating with me?"

"We already enjoyed ours," Terri explained. She took the proffered mug of coffee from Trixie's hand. "Trix and I are going to sit right here and watch you eat every last bite."

"That's not going to be hard," Tina said, munching the toast. "Naturally, I'm starved." She washed down the bread with a swig of juice. "I'm glad you guys put me to bed when you did. I feel nice and rested. How do I look?"

"Like you got your beauty sleep," Trixie said, smoothing her sister's curls with one hand and sipping her coffee with the other. "You are going to be a gorgeous bride."

"Speaking of gorgeous… How did my Manolos fit?" Terri straightened the edge of the comforter in an absentminded way.

Tina stole a quick glance at Trixie, who gave a tiny grin. "Just fine! Can't wait to wear them." She pierced a piece of poached egg with her fork. "So what's it look like outside? Did we get twelve feet of snow, or what?"

"Not that bad—only three. But it's piled up pretty high." Trixie grinned. "You're lucky that Donny's got his own plow. We'd be stuck in your driveway for the whole day if it wasn't for him."

Tina nodded. "He's a good catch." She pointed at an orange slice that was cut in the shape of a heart. "Aw… how cute. You guys are too much." She picked up the fruit and popped it in her mouth. "Florida sunshine, right?"

"More like Valentine's Day." Terri stood up and put her hands on her hips. "I'll go clean up the kitchen and get ready for the hairdresser. She's coming at ten, right?"

"Yes," Tina affirmed, popping another piece of orange in her mouth. "It's Connie Fisher from Manatuck. She's coming here because of the snow."

Terri cocked her head. "The DA's wife?"

"That's right." Tina had been faithful to Connie for years, and didn't trust anyone else to touch her curly red locks.

Terri shrugged. "Whatever. I'll be in the kitchen if you need me." She picked up her coffee cup and left the room.

"What, I didn't name drop enough for her?" Tina asked, giving her sister a playful nudge. "That was a close call with the stupid shoes."

"No kidding. I was pinching my thigh so I wouldn't start giggling." She reached down and lifted the tray. "Terri gets her hair done at some fancy place in Boston, doesn't she?" She tipped her head. "She means well, you know. It was her idea to fix you breakfast in bed."

"I know. I love her, but I'm thankful every day that you came along, little sister. I don't think our childhood would have been bearable without you."

Trixie smiled. "Glad to be of service. Now get yourself up and going, lazybones. You got a big day ahead."

Darby entered the farmhouse kitchen wearing jeans and a red sweater, heading straight for the coffee maker. She stopped short, spotting Kenji already awake and standing by the window. He was holding something in his hand and frowning.

"Good morning," she called. "What's the problem?"

He turned and gave a quick grin. "Not exactly a problem. I was trying to send a message on my phone and it appears there's no service."

Darby yawned. "I think the storm took out the tower. I tried to make a call last night with no luck." She peered out the window. "Looks like we got a couple of feet." She pointed at the coffeepot. "Are you a coffee drinker?"

"Yes—thanks." He was wearing a vintage ski sweater in a blue and red snowflake design and jeans that hugged his muscular torso. "Thanks for the room. I slept very well."

"You're welcome." Darby filled the pot with water and turned to face him. She'd decided not to mention the kiss. *It was late,* she reasoned, *and I was overwrought.* "It's me who should be thanking you. I feel like a giant weight has been lifted off my back. I'm so appreciative of your time, Kenji."

"Don't mention it." He pointed at a little red notebook on the kitchen table. It was the one Darby had found in Lorraine Delvecchio's desk. "I don't mean to snoop, but what are you doing with a book written in cipher?"

Darby put down the pot of water. "What do you mean?"

He grinned. "I'm like a little kid when it comes to codes and ciphers. Always fancied myself a secret agent or something." He picked up the notebook and flipped through the pages. "It's some sort of accounting—mostly numbers—but the letters are written in a classic Caesar cipher."

"Can you explain?"

"Sure. It's a simple shift of the alphabet, in this case, by four letters. Common enough, and easy to do, but still effective." He looked down at the notebook's inside cover, where a meaningless string of letters had been scribbled. "*This is the property of Lorraine Delvecchio,*" he read. "That's what it says."

Darby felt her mouth grow dry. She forced herself to fill the coffee filter with grounds, pour through the water, and start the coffee maker before turning to Kenji.

"Did you figure out the whole thing?" she asked.

"There's nothing really to decipher," he explained. "All that's here is a series of initials, and months. What's important is why this record was kept." He lowered his voice. "I may be wrong, but I think this Lorraine Delvecchio is an extortionist. These appear to be month-by-month records of payments from five people identified by their initials."

"How far does it go back?"

"Ten or eleven years."

Darby's mind whirled. Lorraine had been a secretive woman with an amazing memory. Had she also been a blackmailer? Was that how she financed her exotic trips?

She reached out and took the little notebook. "You may have just solved an important riddle. Can you show me the initials?"

"Sure. They translate to BA, ML, DT, AB, and RC."

Darby grabbed a piece of paper and jotted them down. "You're sure?"

"If she hadn't written this little sentence at the beginning of the book, it would have been a lot harder. Initials don't give you much to go on. But she's a show off, and that's why I figured it out."

A show off? Darby tried to reconcile her last memory of Lorraine: meek, mousy, and nondescript, with Kenji's characterization. It was difficult to picture the cowering woman as a brazen blackmailer. Her face became grim. Was one of Lorraine's victims her killer?

She remembered Lorraine's home. The exterior had screamed neglect, and yet the interior was confident and ordered. She thought back to Esther Crandall's words. The neighbor had quoted Lorraine as saying "the outside didn't matter; it was what was inside that counted."

Darby roused herself from her musings. Outside, the rumble of Donny Pease's truck as he plowed the driveway broke the serene stillness. She turned toward her houseguest. "How about some breakfast?"

"Darby Farr, meet my sister Trixie." Tina was beaming as she ushered Darby into her warm living room. Country and western tunes played from another area, the smell of something cinnamon-flavored wafted on the air, and three redheaded women smiled nearly identical smiles.

"Hi, Trixie," Darby said. She recognized Terri Dodge and gave her a quick hello.

The pint-sized version of Tina grinned. "Thank goodness for someone with another color hair! This wedding party was getting pretty ho-hum, if you ask me."

Darby smiled at Trixie. "I love seeing all of you with your gorgeous curls. Did one of your parents have red hair as well?"

Terri nodded. "Believe it or not, it was our Dad. Mom's a brunette, and so is our brother, Travis. But Dad was a carrot-top, and so pleased to have three redheaded little girls."

Tina grabbed a framed photo of the siblings sitting sideways, arranged by age. Tina, Terri, a dark-haired boy, and finally little Trixie all smiled obediently at the camera. "That's Travis," she said. "Afraid he's not going to make it to the wedding. He's stuck in an airport, just like Miles." She raised her eyebrows. "Speaking of Miles, what's up with this new guy? Donny said it looked like he spent the night?"

"Oooh," Trixie teased. "I don't even know you, and already I'm getting some juicy gossip."

"He stayed at my house, but it was purely platonic," Darby said. "He didn't have a choice, given the storm."

"What idiot goes out in a storm like that to begin with?" Tina huffed. She shook her head. "Oh, who cares. How about a Mimosa while we wait for Connie?"

Darby watched her friend bustle to the kitchen to retrieve the drinks. Tina had a valid point: it was definitely odd that Kenji Miyazaki had ventured out in a blizzard to visit a stranger on an island. Was his appearance in Maine as coincidental as he'd claimed?

He'd been trying to reach me for months, she reminded herself, hoping to ignore her nagging doubts. *I not only learned about my grandfather, but Kenji deciphered Lorraine's list of initials.* Surely those things were positive.

A knock on the door signaled the arrival of the hairdresser. "I'll get it," Trixie yelled, bouncing out of the room. Darby heard her greet the woman and moments later they had entered the room.

"Hello everyone, I'm Connie." The newcomer gave a little wave and smiled. "Look at all this beautiful red hair!"

"Except for Darby," Tina said, flouncing into the room with a tray full of orange drinks. "Care for a Mimosa, Connie?"

"Sure." The petite blonde took a glass from the tray and thanked Tina. She looked at Darby's glossy black mane and grinned. "You've got beautiful hair, but I can make you a redhead too, if you'd like."

The others laughed, and a moment later Terri was raising her glass in a toast.

"To our friend and sister Tina!"

The women smiled and sipped their drinks. Darby let the delicate flavor of the juice linger on her tongue. It was light, sweet, and flavorful.

"Ummm . . ." she said. "Natalie's Orchard."

Tina turned an astonished face to her friend. "Don't tell me you tasted this juice and knew where it came from!"

Darby looked away, embarrassed. She hadn't meant to say the words out loud. "I recognize the taste." She took another sip. "Remember, I spent some time in Florida a few months ago. That's where Natalie's Orchard is located."

Tina shook her head. Under her breath she said, "That's your little super power, girl. It's like Lorraine and her amazing memory."

"Lorraine who?" Trixie had finished her Mimosa and placed the glass back on the tray.

"Delvecchio. I don't know if you'll remember her. She used to work for Dr. Hotchkiss."

"Such a shame about what happened," Terri said. "Such a waste."

"What happened?"

"She fell off the Breakwater," Terri continued. "When was that? Wednesday? I'm losing track of time."

"Speaking of time, we'd better get you ladies started." Connie, holding a stack of clean towels and a purple laundry basket filled with equipment, gave a bright smile. "I've got what I need, so let's rock and roll. Your wedding is at one o' clock, right?"

A blur of blow-drying followed, punctuated by laughter, more Mimosas, and nibbles of a delicious cinnamon bread provided by Terri. Later, while they waited for their nails to dry, Tina turned to Darby and lowered her voice to a conspiratorial whisper.

"So tell me about this mysterious visitor. I'm dying to know what you did."

Darby laughed. "Nothing! His name is Ken—short for Kenji. He translated that journal that I found in the attic, and gave me good news about what it said."

"Yeah?"

"Basically my grandfather hated what was happening with the biological weapons and tried to prevent it." She smiled. "I'm so relieved. I'll tell you the whole story another time, but here's something else: this morning Ken got his hands on Lorraine's notebook. Turns out she was keeping track of payments from people, and those letters were in a kind of code or cipher. Ken cracked the code and now we know the initials of her blackmailing victims."

"No kidding. What are they?"

Darby thought a moment and recited the letters.

Tina snapped her fingers and then winced as she remembered the polish. "Crap, I think I just messed up my ring finger." She called out to Connie and then continued. "You said the initials AB, right? Why, that's gotta be Alcott Bridges! That explains why he seemed relieved to hear Lorraine was dead."

Darby nodded. "I think you're right, Tina. Lorraine must have had some kind of incriminating information on him."

"Dirt, isn't that what they call it? She had some dirt on him as well as other people in the notebook." Tina giggled, showing her ring finger to Connie. "I shouldn't be laughing—it must be the Mimosas."

The hairdresser made a tsk-tsk sound over Tina's smudged polish. She wiped it with a cloth and whipped a bottle out of a pocket to touch it up. The acrid smell of nail polish filled the air.

"Maybe it had to do with that scandal over who painted one of his famous portraits," mused Darby. "Whatever it is, I'll go and see him tomorrow. Who knows, maybe Alcott will want to come clean."

"Oh—I get it," Tina giggled, as Connie placed her right hand back under a small nail dryer. "Come clean from the dirt." She thought a moment. "What about the computer drive? Anything good on that?"

Darby widened her eyes. *The thumb drive from Lorraine's desk.* "Believe it or not, I forgot all about it!"

"Oh, I believe it. You were too busy hanging out with Talking Ken." She started giggling again.

Darby rolled her eyes. "Tina, you never quit." She looked at her friend, hopelessly laughing at her own joke, and then could not help but chuckle as well.

Donny Pease spotted Tina as she entered the back of the church and thought he had never seen anything more beautiful.

She wore a long, white, satin gown that hugged her body, and over it a long-sleeved lace jacket with flowing lacy sleeves. Around her neck was a pink ribbon holding a delicate gold heart, which glinted in the church's twinkling lights. The effect was magical, as if she were a Valentine confection come to life.

Donny grinned and saw Tina smiling back at him. He knew in an instant that they would be fine, that their marriage would be everything they both had hoped. He watched her glide up the aisle, escorted by her Uncle Titus, and surrounded by their friends and family in the cozy space. Now she had reached him. Her uncle hugged and kissed her, and then handed her toward Donny's outstretched hand.

They kissed gently and turned to their bridal party. Tina's sisters were pretty in their pink velvet dresses, and the men—Lester Ross, an old fishing buddy named Cal Holbrook, and Terri's husband Tripp Dodge—were handsome in their tuxedos, but it was Darby Farr, her black hair shining against the pink velvet, who looked spectacular. Not as lovely as Tina, Donny told himself, because no one could look better than a bride on her wedding day, but pretty darn close.

The minister, an elderly man whose booming voice filled the sacred space, began the service. Donny squeezed Tina's hand and gave a happy little sigh.

Darby had taken her first sip of celebratory champagne when she felt a tap on her bare shoulder.

"Give us a kiss?"

She whirled around. A tall man in an elegantly fitted tuxedo stood before her, his rugged face wearing a shy smile.

"Miles! You made it!" She sprang to her feet.

He pulled her close and she inhaled the faint bayberry scent of his skin. "Darby Farr, you look totally amazing. How is it that each time I see you, you're more beautiful than I remember?"

She blushed and looked into his warm eyes. "Where in the world have you been, and how did you get here? Sit down and tell me everything."

"It's a rather boring story. I'll tell you quickly, but only if you promise to dance with me."

"Miles Porter, you drive a hard bargain." She pretended to consider his request. "Deal."

He pulled up a chair and sat down, his long legs nearly touching the pink velvet of her dress. They were in the elegantly appointed ballroom of the Hurricane Harbor Inn, snug and safe against the tall snowdrifts outside.

"Okay, a brief telling of my travels. I spent Thursday night in O'Hare, huddled on some plastic seats with a whole horde of stranded people, many of whom tended to snore, and quite loudly, too. First thing the next morning, I rented one of the few remaining cars left in Chicago and began driving. I was at it all day yesterday, only stopping when I couldn't see the road anymore. I passed a fairly miserable night in a drafty little motel in New Hampshire. And now here I am."

"You drove through the blizzard?"

He nodded. "I'm sorry I didn't call. I lost my bloody cell phone at the airport, or believe me, I would have rang you up a few times. I hope you didn't worry too much?"

Darby bit her lip. The truth was, she'd been distracted by Kenji Miyazaki—although she had tried to phone.

"You're a big boy," she said lightly. "I figured anyone who could report from the world's worst war zones could handle a few flakes of snow." She raised her delicately arched eyebrows. "Besides, there's been some excitement around here."

Miles leaned in closer. "Aha! Lorraine Delvecchio? Do tell."

Darby related the new questions surrounding the woman's death, the suspicious person Alison Dyer had spotted on the Breakwater, and the strange notations in the little spiral notebook. She then told him about Kenji's arrival on the island and his cracking of the Caesar cipher.

"Whoa, who's this fellow?" Miles's brow was furrowed. "I don't think I like the idea of a strange man appearing out of nowhere."

Darby felt her cheeks flush. "He didn't exactly come out of nowhere," she said. "He works with a client of mine, Hideki Kobayashi. Kenji was here in Maine for a snowboarding competition, but he's been calling my office in San Diego for months. The curator of the art museum in Westerly gave him my number..."

Miles held up a hand, traffic policeman style. "As much as I want to hear about all this, I think I'd like to dance with you even more." He cocked his head in the direction of the music, where the band was starting to play a familiar tune. "Shall we have a toast first?"

He grinned and reached across the table for a glass of champagne and held it aloft.

"To wonderful surprises," Darby said.

"Indeed." He touched her glass with his and took a long swallow. "And to my beautiful Valentine on St. Valentine's Day." They drank again. "Now, Miss Farr, I'd like the pleasure of a dance."

"Oh?" Darby's face wore a mischievous look. "I have a better idea."

She leaned over him in the pink velvet dress, yanking his bow tie in a playful manner, until she had pulled a surprised but delighted Miles out of the hall to a small cloakroom. There, Darby closed and barricaded the doors.

"This isn't like you," he observed in a whisper.

"I know." She leaned in to kiss him, and then, all thoughts of the red lacquered box, the spiral notebook, and Kenji Miyazaki's boyish grin temporarily forgotten, she let go of all caution and gave Miles Porter a wonderful reason to come in from the storm.

NINE

At least the chocolate mousse cake is good, thought Bitsy Carmichael, spooning another bite of the decadent dessert into her pink lipsticked mouth. The rest of the dinner had been forgettable—a stuffed chicken breast, cold asparagus spears, and twice-baked potatoes that were so dry they might have been baked three or four times. She sighed and pushed the plate away, glancing to see if anyone was watching. Like the Queen, she hated mere commoners to see her eating.

Charles was speaking with a tall man, but she saw him glance in her direction and then conclude his conversation. He loped toward the table, a worried look on his lined face.

"What's the matter, Bitsy? Aren't you having fun?"

"I'd have more fun if you stuck around," she said, just a touch irritated. She twisted the band of her jewel-encrusted watch. "Who's that you were talking to?"

"Scott Fisher, the Manatuck DA. Wouldn't be surprised if he's the Attorney General some day."

Who cares, Bitsy thought. Instead she gave a coy smile. "Remember how we used to like to dance, Charlie? What do you say we give it a whirl?" She put a few fingers on the sleeve of his sport coat and tapped lightly. "Come on…"

He sighed and shook his head, helpless before her fluttering false eyelashes. "Bitsy, it's been years since I danced. Can't we just sit here a moment?"

She rose to her feet and took his hands. "Oh, Chuckie, it all comes back to you." She squeezed his fingers in a playful manner. She leaned in closer, allowing him a peek down the front of her gold-flecked cashmere sweater. "Just like I said to you the other night," she purred into his ear. "It all comes right back."

Chief Charles Dupont's face flushed scarlet. He rose to his feet and let her pull him toward the music. "One dance," he said weakly.

She widened her eyes, demurely, the smile still playing about her lips. "We'll see," she murmured.

Across the room, Trixie Dodge nudged her sister. "Terri, who's that adorable guy with Darby? They're just coming into the hall. That's not her husband, is it?"

Terri shrugged. "I don't think she's married," she said, accepting a glass of sparkling water from the bartender. Her own husband was dancing with their youngest child, a freckle-faced redhead named Tiffany. She looked over her glass at Trixie. "And what about you? Anything romantic that I should know about?"

The younger woman shook her head. "Nope. But you'll be the first to know." She jabbed Terri with an index finger. "Here comes Darby with her stud muffin now."

The sisters greeted Darby, giving Miles a curious look.

"Hello, stranger," Trixie said. "Who might you be?"

"This is Miles Porter." Darby presented him with a grin. "He had a terrible time getting here, but thankfully made it in one piece."

"Or so I think," Miles said, smiling. He stretched out a hand to the sisters. "It's a pleasure to meet you. I was lucky enough to meet Tina and Donny the first time I came to Maine. They make a wonderful couple."

The three women nodded as they watched Donny twirl Tina into a spin, her long satin gown fanning out in gentle waves.

"What is it you do for work, Miles?" Terri inquired, sipping her water. She patted her auburn curls with a graceful hand. A large diamond winked from one tapered finger.

"I'm an investigative journalist," he said, giving a self-deprecating smile. "Although at present I'm doing some consulting work in Northern California. What about you?"

"I'm a stay-at-home mom. My youngest is right over there dancing with my husband."

"You make yourself sound like you're such a homebody when that's not totally true," Trixie interjected. "What about all the fundraising you do for the Westerly art museum, the hospital, and the library?"

"Yes, but I think Mr. Porter is talking about paying work." Terri shrugged. "I'm looking forward to reentering the job market in the near future. But I have three kids, and my husband—well, *we*—didn't think it was a good idea for both of us to be away from our home so much." She gave an ironic smile. "The funny thing is that my husband ended up spending a lot of time parenting as well, so

I could have worked after all." She brightened. "But that day's fast approaching. Tiffy's almost seven, can you believe it?"

"You're kidding!" Trixie put down her beer with a thump.

"Trixie is in the Coast Guard," Darby offered. "Where did you say you're based? Martha's Vineyard, Massachusetts?"

"Nantucket. It's a beautiful island, much bigger than Hurricane Harbor, but just as desolate come winter." She grinned. "The good news is that spring comes a whole heck of a lot faster."

"Oh, rub it in," Terri said. She pointed at her husband. "Excuse me. I'm going to see if Tiffany will let someone else get a dance or two in."

"I'll come with you," Darby said. "I'd like to meet another of the redheaded 'T' girls."

When she and Terri were out of earshot, Darby touched Terri's arm. "Can I ask you something?"

The redhead paused and gave her a puzzled glance. "Yes?"

"Did Eric Thompson mention anything to you about a man named Kenji Miyazaki?"

"The snowboarder?" She thought a moment. "We didn't discuss him. Why?"

"I was just curious." Darby wasn't sure what she was after, but she had hoped Terri Dodge would be a source of information. "You didn't meet him, so …"

"I didn't say I didn't meet him," Terri corrected. "I said that Eric and I never discussed him. I was introduced to Kenji at a cocktail party—the same one where Eric met him."

"I see. Was he with his friend?"

"What friend?" She frowned. "He doesn't know anyone in Maine. At least that's what he said."

Darby thought back to Kenji's mention of a retired friend in Westerly. "He said that a friend had brought him to the party."

Terri shook her head. "I knew everyone there—except for Kenji, that is. Believe me, Darby, he came to that gathering alone." Terri motioned to Tiffany and a trim, tanned man. "Darby, meet my husband, Tripp Dodge, and my youngest child, Tiffany."

"It's great to meet you both." She shook Tripp's hand and smiled at the little girl, who was looking with frank curiosity at Darby's black hair.

"You have the shiniest hair ever," she said. "Can I touch it?"

"May I touch it," Terri corrected, rolling her eyes. "I'm sorry, Darby."

Darby laughed. "Sure." She knelt down. "Can you reach, Tiffany?"

The little girl stroked the dark strands and smiled. "It's smooth, like Harold's fur," she observed, adding, "Harold is my favorite cat."

"Well, I'm glad to hear that!"

"We have three kitties, right Tiffy?" Tripp Dodge's face lit up as he spoke. "Harold is the fattest and the laziest."

"He's not the laziest," Tiffany corrected, sounding a lot like her mother. "Not when it comes to getting fed!"

Everyone chuckled and Tiffany ran off to sneak some frosting from the wedding cake.

"Are your other children here?" Darby asked.

"No, both the boys are away at boarding school," Tripp said. He turned to his wife. "Gosh, I do miss them. I wonder if they can re-enroll in Westerly next year? That way they'd be home with us."

Terri shook her head. "We've been over this, Tripp honey. That would be a giant academic step backward." She turned to Darby. "Both Tommy and Tyler are doing so well at their private schools in Connecticut. It was a hard decision, sending them away like that, but totally the right one for both of them." She gazed toward the dessert table where Tiffany was licking her fingers. "When the time comes, I'm sure we'll do the same with Tiffy."

Darby slid her eyes to Tripp's face. He wore the dejected look of a boy who's lost his favorite baseball cap.

Terri smiled brightly, determined to change the mood.

"Come on, honey. Let's get in a dance or two at my big sister's wedding." She gave Darby a quick smile. "Excuse us."

Darby nodded and watched them glide to the dance floor. A moment later, Miles was at her side. "That's ginger-haired Terri, is it? And her husband?"

"Yes. Tripp Dodge is his name. Not sure what he does, but Tina hinted that he's pretty well off."

"I should say so," Miles said. "Charles Dodge, III is his full name, although even in the business world he goes by Tripp. I did a story on the family for the *Financial Times* awhile back. His grandfather was a chemical engineer who invented a canning process for condensed soup. Needless to say, he made a fortune."

"According to Tina, Tripp doesn't work much."

"I dare say he doesn't have to."

Darby thought of Tripp's face when he spoke of his sons. *He's a family man. I wonder why Terri doesn't seem to see that?*

The reception was winding down. Tina and Donny had waved goodbye, and now, wrapped in their winter coats and hats, they hurried, smiling, out the door of the inn and into Donny's pre-warmed truck.

Darby felt Miles squeeze her hand. "Where are the lucky newlyweds headed? Bermuda? Jamaica? Somewhere warm and toasty, I trust?"

"Nova Scotia."

"Canada? Surely you're joking!"

Darby laughed, seeing Miles's surprised look. "They both love it up there, plus they are going to Mexico for nearly the whole month of March." She nudged him. "Doesn't Nova Scotia sound romantic?"

"I think it sounds cold!" He leaned over and kissed her cheek. "Although I'd go to the Arctic if you asked."

"How about a little sleuthing instead? I'd like to pay a quick visit to Alcott Bridges, and see if he'll open up at all about Lorraine Delvecchio. I'm dying to know if the initials in the notebook are his."

"Sounds good to me. Do we stop at your house and change first?"

Darby knew that if she went back to the farmhouse with Miles, she'd have a tough time going back out again into the cold. "No, let's stop and see him right now. We're perfectly timed to get the next ferry, and who knows? Maybe our fancy duds will catch him off guard."

"Ah yes," Miles said. "The old, 'Dress for Duress.' Works like a charm every time."

She giggled, letting him slip her into the long down coat. "Miles Porter, you are a clever one," she said, zipping it up. "Let's see just how much information you can get out of Mr. Bridges."

"Remind me again of what we're trying to discover?" He had a long camel's hair coat, fur hat, and thick gloves.

"We need to know if Lorraine was blackmailing him," she said, linking her arm through his. "That and whether he killed her because of it."

"Oh, I see," he said lightly. "Just two easy questions. Lead the way, my dear Darby. Lead the way."

The roads in Manatuck were slick, covered with a thin layer of ice where traffic had melted the snow and it had refrozen. Miles had offered to drive his rental car, but Darby insisted that she take her Jeep. "You've got to be sick of driving," she reasoned. "And this is my home turf."

He grinned, watching her handle the slippery roads with ease. "You certainly are a pro," he said, leaning back on the seat. He sighed. "I hope our visit with Mr. Bridges doesn't take too long."

"It won't," Darby said cheerfully. "You'll see that he's not a forthcoming kind of guy."

"Artists don't tend to be chatty, now do they? Too many creative impulses rattling around in their brains." Miles paused. "Tell me more about the dead girl, Lorraine Delvecchio. What sort of person was she?"

Darby recounted her research of Lorraine's exceptional autobiographical memory, and Miles nodded slowly.

"Hyperthymesia," he said thoughtfully. "What an asset it would be for an extortionist."

"Exactly! All the little incriminating things we see but forget? Lorraine remembered those moments." She slowed as she approached a curve. "I wonder what the connection could be between Alcott and Lorraine?"

"Didn't you say that she worked for a doctor? Perhaps Alcott Bridges was a patient."

"Could be. Dr. Hotchkiss saw practically everyone in the area, so there's a good chance he took care of Alcott." She pulled up in front of the house's impressive porch. "Here we are," she said. She regarded the cottage and frowned. "Place looks awfully dark."

"Indeed." Miles climbed out of the Jeep and looked in the garage's side window. "Car's still here," he announced. "No tracks going in or out of the snow. Do you think our artist friend is asleep?"

"It's only six o' clock. Unless he's not feeling well, why would he be in bed this early? And if he was ill, wouldn't there be at least one light on?"

"Maybe he's one of those very thrifty Yanks."

"Perhaps, but I'm concerned. Let's try to get in."

Darby pulled on a pair of tall rubber boots and, tucking the pink velvet dress into them, waded through the unbroken snow to the front door. She jiggled the old brass knob, but it was locked.

Miles tried a side door that led to the kitchen, but it was locked as well. "I'll go round back," he announced, jogging around the corner. Darby waited a moment and then heard him yell her name.

She followed his trail through the snow to the back door. "Good work, Miles," she said, following him into the darkened house. They both felt the walls for light switches, with Darby finding one that illuminated the room. "Mr. Bridges?" she called out.

They were in a small room that Darby had glimpsed earlier with Tina. A low table with a sewing machine, baskets of fabric, yarn, and brocades was before them, along with a faded chintz chair and tall dressmaker's dummy. On the walls hung several portraits of a serene, smiling woman—the same woman—in various poses and at varying ages.

"That must be Grace Bridges," she whispered. "Alcott's wife. She died about five years ago, I think."

"Pretty lady," Miles observed. "I'll bet he misses her."

They crept quietly into a hallway and listened for sounds. Except for the ticking of a tall grandfather clock, it was quiet.

Darby called out again. "Mr. Bridges? Everything okay?" She indicated another door. "That leads to the studio. The kitchen's that way, and I imagine several bedrooms are upstairs. Alcott's room is off the kitchen so he doesn't have to climb stairs." She led the way with Miles following close behind.

The kitchen was dim in the dwindling light, but Darby and Miles discerned a small stack of dirty dishes, piles of unopened mail, and several empty, unwashed cans of condensed soup.

"This fellow's aiding and abetting Tripp Dodge's lifestyle with all these cans of soup," he commented, as Darby pushed open the bedroom door. "He seems to favor only one type: cream of…"

"Miles!" Darby's voice was an urgent whisper. "Come here. It's Alcott Bridges."

Miles spun on his heel and joined her at the threshold of the bedroom.

The elderly man lay sprawled across the double bed. He wore a faded dressing gown belted around his thin waist. Both arms were outstretched, the hands open as if in supplication. Bunched at his feet was a threadbare quilt and several thick wool blankets.

Darby saw a framed photograph on the floor and moved to look at it. Grace Bridges, her smile warm and inviting, beamed from behind the cracked glass.

"I take it he is dead?" Miles asked, his voice quiet.

"Looks that way." She felt his skin. "He's cold to the touch." Darby looked at Alcott's vacant eyes, staring toward the ceiling, and sighed. "Too late now for me to ask you about Lorraine Delvecchio," she said. She turned to Miles. "I'll call the Manatuck police."

He gave a nod of agreement and together they retraced their steps out of the room and through the kitchen. At the door to the sewing room, Darby stopped. She stared down at a small table upon which were a set of keys and a blue plastic case.

A checkbook. She picked it up and flipped through the register where the old man had kept track of his expenditures. "Here it is, Miles—L. Delvecchio." She flipped back. "And again here."

"How much did he pay her?"

"Looks like two hundred dollars a month."

"You don't take trips to Switzerland and Hawaii on that kind of money," Miles commented, peering over Darby's shoulder.

"No, but keep in mind Lorraine had four other sets of initials in that book. Perhaps Alcott Bridges was small potatoes. She could have had victims willing to pay a whole lot more."

"Right." He glanced around the dark room. "Darby, let's discuss this somewhere else."

She put the checkbook back on the table and spun, smiling, to face him. "Don't tell me my brave investigative reporter is frightened!"

"Not in the least," he answered. "I'm just thinking ahead. You're going to call the Manatuck police, and then Chief Dupont. Chances are he'll want to meet us at the house, and—" he paused. "I'm dead on my feet."

Darby considered the tall Brit's lopsided grin. She had whisked him from the wedding reception right to a dead man's home, after he'd barreled his way through a blizzard. And he was correct: the day was still young.

"You're right. Back to my house and a nice warm fire. I'll call 911 right now, and then phone Chief Dupont from the ferry."

She ushered Miles out the door, closed it firmly behind them, and watched as he crunched his way through the snow.

Bitsy Carmichael had a bad feeling about the phone call.

It had come just as they had entered their house after the wedding, and she could see from the look on Charles's face that it was important. He talked rapidly for a few minutes, and then hung up, replacing the receiver with a bang.

"What is it?" she asked, taking off her heels. Her feet were killing her, and she was already contemplating a half-hour soak in the master bathroom's large tub.

"It's Darby Farr," he said, taking off his suit coat. "She stopped in at a house in Manatuck and found the artist Alcott Bridges dead."

"That's the Manatuck police department's problem, isn't it?"

"Yes. I'm headed over to see her."

"Can't she wait until the morning?"

He climbed the stairs to their room to change. "I'll be back before you know it," he called over his shoulder.

Bitsy collapsed on the couch. *No use pouting*, she figured. He was going whether she pitched a hissy fit or not. Instead, she turned her thoughts to the wedding.

Except for the food, which she'd judged to be substandard, it was a quaint little ceremony. Nothing like the glitzy affairs she'd been to in Vegas, of course, but cute and cozy. Tina had seemed besotted, and although Bitsy wasn't super crazy about her, she was glad for Donny that he was happy.

She flipped through a magazine while she waited for Charles. How strange that he was heading out on police business on a Saturday night. Why didn't people consult the calendar when they decided to drop dead?

He descended the stairs hurriedly, strapping on his gun when he reached the bottom. She watched as he strode across the room and bent down to kiss her.

"See you later. I'll call if I'll be late getting home."

She nodded, watching as he went out the front door and into the darkness, the feel of his stubbly chin still lingering on her skin. *Home*, she thought, curling her feet under her bottom and thinking how much she liked the sound of that word. *I'm finally home.*

Darby answered the door and ushered Chief Dupont into the snug farmhouse.

"Thanks for coming by. I'm sure you're tired from the wedding."

"You're not kidding," he said. "That Bitsy kept me out on the dance floor all afternoon. I'm going to need a whole bottle of Advil just to be able to walk in the morning." He grinned. "But it was a fun time, and that redheaded friend of yours certainly looked happy."

"She did. Donny, too."

He bobbed his head, gave a questioning look. "Miles here?"

"Upstairs, having a little rest. He's exhausted from driving, poor guy. Can I get you something to drink? Glass of wine, cup of coffee?"

"Nah, I'm fine. Let's talk this thing through and then we both can call it a day." He pointed at the little kitchen table. "Should I sit down?"

"Let's go into the living room. I've got a fire going."

He followed her in and eased himself onto the couch. "Spoke to the Manatuck guys after they went over to Alcott's place. Sounds like he had a heart attack last night, but we'll see what the medical folks have to say." He paused a moment. "Wish I could have seen that checkbook you found, because I don't like what you're suggesting, Darby. I knew Lorraine, and I find it impossible to believe she could have been a blackmailer."

Darby was quiet.

"I mean, this was a woman I trusted for several years. It just doesn't fit."

Darby lifted the notebook from the coffee table and gave it to the Chief. "Tina and I found this in Lorraine's home office. There are columns with numbers and payments, and a bunch of initials that didn't make sense at first, but seem to be encrypted."

"Encrypted? What are you talking about?"

"I'm told it's written using a Caesar cipher."

"What the heck is that?"

"It's a simple substitution cipher in which each letter in the message is replaced by a letter several positions down the alphabet. When these initials are deciphered, they are BA, ML, DT, AB, and RC."

"And you think the 'AB' is Alcott Bridges?"

"Well, those are his initials, and he was writing regular checks to Lorraine. If we can show a correlation between the checks and this notebook…"

"Okay, okay. Let's say for a moment that you're right—that Lorraine was playing at extortion. Just what would she have on Alcott Bridges?"

"Miles suggested she could have known something from her employment with Dr. Hotchkiss, but I've been thinking about the scandal with his painting of the judge. Might Lorraine have had information about its authenticity?"

"Who knows? With her memory she may have known something about everything, when you think of it." He sighed and leaned back on the couch. "Give me those initials again. I want to write them down, see if I can come up with more names."

Darby read the letters as the Chief scribbled them on a piece of white paper. He folded it and pushed it into his pants pocket, giving her a frank look.

"What do you think about her slipping from the Breakwater now? Seems to me it's clearer all the time that she was murdered."

"Do you think the Manatuck police will start treating it like a homicide?"

Chief Dupont nodded. "Let's hope. You can bet I'll be in touch with them again." He glanced at his watch. "I'd better go. They're still trying to contact Alcott Bridges' family, so keep his death under your hat for the time being."

"You know I'll be discreet." She followed him to the door. "It was nice getting to know your wife."

He blushed. "Bitsy? Yes, well, thank you." He pulled on his coat and gave a shy grin. "I know the whole town thinks I'm crazy, but heck, I'm glad to have her back."

Darby smiled. "She's lucky to have you, Chief." On an impulse, she gave him a small hug. "We all are."

"Thanks." The voice was gruff, his cheeks slightly reddened. "I was thinking. Would you like to get together and swap stories about your parents? I have a lot of memories—not just about Jada, but your dad, too."

"I'd like that very much."

Darby watched as Charles Dupont departed, driving into the dark night with his police beacon off and siren quiet. When his taillights had disappeared around the corner, she shut the door against the cold.

Once I detested the very sight of that man. And now I feel fondly toward him, almost protective.

She knew that Hurricane Harbor's Chief of Police did not need her to worry about him. And yet he seemed newly vulnerable, thanks in part to the reappearance of Bitsy Carmichael.

Darby shook off her gloomy thoughts and prepared to head upstairs, when she remembered the thumb drive Tina had taken from Lorraine Delvecchio's desk. Would it reveal more about the identities of the dead woman's victims? She pushed it into the USB port in her laptop and waited. A password was requested, and Darby nearly groaned.

Undaunted, she began typing in permutations of Lorraine's name, then address, and finally random things she now associated with her furtive classmate. *Breakwater. Manatuck. Hawaii.* Finally, it was a word that she tried on a whim that worked.

Memory.

A second later, there were five scanned images on the drive.

Darby clicked on one and a close-up photograph of a couple embracing filled the screen. The man's back was to the camera, his countenance hidden, but the woman's face, framed by wavy brown hair that fell to her shoulders, was smiling and happy.

Darby did not recognize the woman, and when she clicked on the rest of the photos she saw that they were much the same: full, head-on views of her; obstructed, rear shots of the man. She frowned. They were pretty poor blackmail photos, if that's what they were.

Chief Dupont might recognize the woman, she thought. Sighing, she removed the thumb drive and turned off her computer. *Too bad I didn't think to show him when he was here.*

Miles Porter was still sleeping when Darby entered her bedroom. She changed into a silk teddy, smiling as she remembered her promise to Tina to "be a little bit braver." *The little cloakroom interlude at the wedding was pretty courageous,* she thought. Tina would no doubt approve.

She slipped into bed. Miles stirred and rolled over, his hand accidentally brushing the smooth fabric over her breasts. Instantly he opened his eyes.

"Well . . . this has to be the best wake-up call ever," he said softly. He reached for her hair and stroked it, while she sighed and snuggled into his broad chest. Their bodies curved together under the thick down comforter.

Miles kissed her forehead. "You have no idea how long I've waited for this moment."

"I have some idea," Darby murmured. She sought his lips with hers and they shared a long, lingering, passionate kiss. "I've been waiting, too."

"I have just one question for you," Miles whispered. "Do we need to discuss this Kenji chap?"

Darby ran a hand down his torso, lingering on his taut stomach and then tracing her fingers down and over his groin.

"It can wait until the morning."

"Right. Let's leave it for then, shall we?"

He rolled onto his side, pulling her close with powerful arms, a sudden urgency so unexpected that she gasped. His signature scent of bayberry was faint and yet the merest whiff was like an illicit drug. She breathed him in and let herself be carried away.

TEN

Bitsy Carmichael stirred in the warm king-sized bed. *Bacon.* It was the scent of Sunday mornings from her childhood, the boisterous band of young Carmichael girls clamoring around their father as he flipped blueberry pancakes on the electric griddle while a pound of bacon sizzled in the skillet. The big breakfast was followed by the whole family taking the ferry to Manatuck for Mass at St. Catherine's, because there was no Catholic church on the island. Bitsy smiled and stepped into her pink slippers.

Charles was humming a tune and stirring a pan of scrambled eggs when she entered.

"Good morning," he said, handing her a cup of coffee with cream. "Thought I'd make us a little breakfast."

"It smells delicious." She nibbled a piece of bacon. "I'll set the table."

She took plates from the cabinet and set them on the table, moving a piece of paper with initials and various names. "What's this?"

"Oh, something I'm working on," he said. "Put it on the counter."

"You seem to be in a good mood," she observed.

"Yes, well, I think I figured something out and I'm feeling like the most clever police chief in Maine."

"I see. Anything to do with Lorraine Delvecchio?"

"As a matter of fact, yes." He scooped eggs onto her plate and placed the platter of bacon between them. He'd decided that the low-fat diet was fine for weekdays, but on weekends he could splurge. "Orange juice?"

She nodded. "Have you told Darby Farr about your discovery?"

"Not yet. I was thinking we could take the ferry over to Manatuck this morning. There's someone I need to see, and then …" His smile was bashful.

"Yes?"

"Let's pick out a puppy. I called the shelter and they have some young dogs looking for homes. What do you think?"

"It won't be Aggie …"

"No dog can replace her," he said firmly.

"You're right. But it wouldn't hurt to just look and see what they have, right Charlie?"

He leaned across the table and kissed her cheek. "Never hurts to look," he agreed.

Weak sunlight struggled through the windows of Darby's bedroom, glinting off the brass hinges of the red lacquered box. Darby positioned it between them on the bed and opened it slowly, pulling out the silk kimono sash and draping it before Miles.

"Exquisite," he said, propping himself up with one elbow and fingering the fabric with his other hand. "This was your mum's?"

"Everything in this box belonged to her—at least that's what I think—except for this journal." She handed it to Miles and watched as he leafed through the pages.

"So this Kenji translated it for you?"

"Not totally. But he told me that it was a record of my grandfather's time in Manchukuo and that it showed he objected to what was happening."

"The experiments on the innocent Chinese villagers… is that what you mean?"

"Yes." She sighed. "Kenji was here for only a short time, but he gave me the gist of what it says."

"I understand. The important thing is that you now know your grandfather was a very unwilling participant." He glanced at the end of the journal. "These notations here," he pointed. "They look like formulas." He flipped through a few more of the pages. "Okay, time to tell me how you met him."

"Kenji? A series of strange coincidences, really. Hideki Kobayashi suggested he contact me, as did the curator of the art museum in Westerly who met him at a party." She thought back to Terri Dodge's words at the wedding. *Believe me, Darby, he came to that gathering alone.*

She bit her lip. "There is one strange thing. Kenji told me he had a friend in Westerly, but Tina's sister Terri insists he didn't know a soul. I'm wondering if he lied to me."

"Maybe he wanted to keep his friend's identity quiet." Miles gave her a little jab on the shoulder. "Maybe he's gay."

"You wish." Darby thought fleetingly of Kenji's kiss. She watched as Miles flipped to the back of the journal, studied the pages, then turned the book sideways and frowned.

"What is it?"

"I'm not sure." He pushed up on his forearms, his face taut. "Darby, did you look at this journal before you gave it to Kenji?"

"Yes. Why?"

He slid his finger against the binding. "At least one of the pages is gone."

"What?"

"Look." He pointed to a barely visible line. "That's a cut from an extremely sharp blade, probably a razor. I'm positive that a page—maybe more than one—has been removed."

Darby felt the blood draining from her face. "Are you sure?"

"Absolutely."

Darby got up and went into the tiny guest room. She opened a small medicine cabinet in the bathroom, remembering that there was an antique straight-edged razor on a shelf.

It was gone.

She swallowed and headed back to the bedroom.

"What is it?"

"Kenji. He may have taken part of my grandfather's journal." She told Miles about the missing razor and his face grew hard.

"I'm sure these are some sort of formulas, Darby." He pointed at the numbers. "Kenji not only speaks Japanese, but he works in pharmaceuticals. Perhaps he understood what these formulas mean."

Darby pictured Kenji standing at the window, frowning at his cell phone. Had he been attempting to send photographs of the journal before she'd entered the room? Had he then resorted to removing the pages with a razor?

"Miles, if these are formulas they could be extremely dangerous." She grabbed her jeans and pulled them on. Her stomach was flopping and she felt slightly sick. "We've got to find out what's going on, and fast."

———

Donny Pease sprinkled brown sugar atop his oatmeal, grabbed his spoon, and took a satisfying bite. What was it about getting hitched that could make a man famished? He polished off a few spoonfuls and took a swig of coffee. Tina was munching away on her Special K cereal, dialing Darby Farr with a long red fingernail.

"Tell her about the prime rib," he suggested, wishing he had a few raisins to vary the oatmeal's consistency. They'd eaten the night before at a family-run restaurant down the road where the special had been glistening hunks of prime rib, big as serving platters.

"I will," she promised, leaning back in the plastic chair.

Donny looked around the breakfast room, a beige box with a few fake ferns and a machine that dispensed milk and juice. Styrofoam bowls were heaped next to plastic drinking glasses and Styrofoam coffee cups, along with baskets containing sweeteners, fake creamer, and those little sticks for stirring. The only hot dish had been the oatmeal; the only other breakfast choices cold cereal and packaged donuts.

Okay, so this motel, located just over the border in Canada, wasn't anything to write home about, but Tina had assured him that it was just fine because the inn they were staying at in Nova Scotia was on the fancy side.

Donny heard her chirp a hello to Darby and relay the news they'd just received about Alcott Bridges's death.

"Well, I'll be darned," she said. She held her hand over the mouthpiece. "Darby and Miles already know about Alcott, because they were the ones who found him! Imagine that?"

Donny could imagine it, and didn't exactly want to. He'd had his share of finding dead bodies on Hurricane Harbor, thank you very much.

Tina asked Darby to call Alcott's lawyer. "He represents the estate, and says he wants to get the house on the market by March."

She listened to Darby, twirling a red curl as she waited. "I know it's kind of soon. But Alcott was eighty years old, so it's not like it's a surprise." She picked up her spoon. "Darby, I'll just die if that horrible Babette gets the listing. Will you scoot on over to see the lawyer as soon as you can?"

Darby must have said yes, because Tina sighed happily. She described the delicious prime rib while pushing her cereal around in her bowl in an absentminded way. Suddenly she sat bolt upright. "What? You mean the FBI guy?"

Donny waited, his heart beating a little harder, until Tina finally hung up the phone. "Donny, listen to this: that Kenji guy, the one who stayed overnight at Darby's house? He might be a crook." She told him about the journal and shuddered, her red curls bobbing with anger. "First those shoes and now this. What is this world coming to?"

He scooped the last of the oatmeal from the Styrofoam bowl and licked his plastic spoon. "Could'a told you he wasn't any Boy Scout," he said. After all, only two kinds of people went driving around in a Maine nor'easter: idiots, and desperate men who were up to no good.

"The jail?" Bitsy Carmichael squealed, half in disgust, and half in delight. "I've never set foot in a jail."

"Not even in your wild Vegas days?" Charles Dupont ruffled her spiky blonde hair, amused by her excitement at the prospect of visiting the Manatuck County Correctional Facility, otherwise known as the jail.

Bitsy thought back. One particularly wild night had taken her to the sheriff's office, but that was about it. "Nope—never."

"Then this will be a first." He parked the car and pointed at the door. "That's where we go in. We'll have to see how far you can come with me. The prisoner may or may not want to see both of us."

Bitsy raised her eyebrows. Surely a man hard up for female company was going to want to see her! She gave a sweet smile. "I'll be as charming as possible, Charlie."

They crossed the plowed parking lot, Bitsy stepping gingerly in her pink fur-lined boots. She wore her leopard coat and pink hoop earrings, frosty pink lipstick, and furry white gloves.

"Charlie?" She stopped in the middle of the lot, her hands on her leopard-lined hips. "Are you happy I came back to Maine?"

He pursed his lips. Why she was choosing to ask him this question now in the parking lot of the jail was a mystery. "Yeah, I am." He knew that she was the same woman who'd abandoned him before, and that she might take off again, without warning, just as she had fifteen years earlier. And yet he was still glad for the time, glad for her company, glad to watch her prance across the parking lot in her ridiculous, wonderful getup.

She thought for a moment, her brow furrowed. A small smile crept across her face.

"Me, too," she said, linking her arm with one of his. "I mean, when would I ever get to escort a handsome police chief into a jail?"

They'd reached the entrance, a big, metal door painted olive drab. Charles pulled it open. Inside, a uniformed guard sat at a table, flipping through a cooking magazine. He glanced up and quickly dipped his head in greeting. "Good to see you, Chief."

"Thanks. Evan, isn't it?"

"That's right." The man blushed. He was little more than a boy, really, maybe twenty or so years old. "Who are you here to see?"

"Leonard Marcus."

The man looked at a computer screen. "He's in B. You know how to get there?"

"Yeah, I remember." He placed a hand on the small of Bitsy's back and steered her toward a door. "Thanks, Evan."

A loud buzzer sounded, followed by a hollow clanking sound, and Chief Dupont pushed open the door. Bitsy trotted behind him, her heart beginning to pound.

The corridor was long and dim, devoid of any windows except for several small skylights at the top of the halls. Another uniformed man stood inside the corridor, rocking back and forth from the balls of his feet.

"Help you?" He seemed surprised to see them.

"I'm Charles Dupont, Chief of Police for Hurricane Harbor. This is my wife, Bitsy. We're here to see Leonard Marcus."

The guard nodded. "It's not visiting hours, Chief, but we can make an exception for you." He leafed through some papers on a clipboard and then looked up. "Marcus is right down the hallway. He doesn't get many visitors."

They walked down the corridor, following the guard, past cells where men sat on their bunks or at small desks. One man was doing one-handed push-ups, grunting with exertion every time he raised his amply-muscled body. Another stood by the cement block wall, book in hand, reciting poetry in calm, gentle tones, as if he were reading to a beloved grandchild.

"Hey, Walt." The guard waved at the next inmate who was reclining on his bed. "Going to watch the basketball game later on?"

"You bet."

"Augusta's going to take it, you'll see."

The guard's goading received a loud snort of derision from the prisoner. "No frickin' way. You'll see."

The guard smiled at the Chief. "You follow the tournaments?"

Chief Dupont shrugged. "Of course. Can't live in Maine and not pay attention to the February games."

Bitsy thought back, remembering the fervor of the semifinal and state high school basketball championships. Droves of people filled gymnasiums across the state throughout the season, but especially in February at tournament time. Was it the freezing temperatures, lack of daylight hours, or scarcity of other activities that made the sporting events so popular? To say basketball was big was like saying lobsters had claws. Both were obvious, undeniable facts.

The trio stopped short before a dark cell. "Hey, Marcus!" called out the guard. "You got company."

Bitsy peered into the cell, bracing herself for what she might see. The image of a thin, jittery drug addict with a murderous glint in his eye was what she expected; a vision conjured up from countless episodes of crime and courtroom dramas.

The prisoner rose from his bunk. He was tall and fit, with graying hair cut stylishly short. His face was lined, but handsome, with a trim mustache and well-groomed eyebrows. *He stole money from loads of people,* Bitsy reminded herself. And yet he was undeniably attractive.

Charles introduced her as well as himself, and explained they were there to ask some questions about Lorraine Delvecchio.

Leonard Marcus nodded gravely. "I heard she passed away," he said, his voice surprisingly sonorous. "Do your questions have anything to do with her death?"

"In fact they do," Charles Dupont said. He looked into the prisoner's eyes. "I believe she was murdered."

Leonard Marcus put a finger to his lips and seemed to ponder the statement. He reminded Bitsy of an English professor ensconced in a book-lined office at some ivy-walled college, not an inmate of the Manatuck County Correctional Facility.

The air was still, scented with the odor of dozens of incarcerated bodies. The murmur of other prisoners was background noise for the occasional heavy clank of the locking doors. Bitsy noticed she was holding her breath in anticipation of his response.

Leonard Marcus finally spoke. "Murdered," he said slowly, nodding again as if considering the concept. He looked up at Bitsy and then flicked his gray-green eyes to Charles Dupont. "You're saying someone shoved Lorraine Delvecchio off the Breakwater." He put his hands in the pockets of his orange jumpsuit, a gesture that looked somehow elegant "It's very likely that she was indeed murdered. The question, dear Chief, is by whom?"

Alcott Bridges's lawyer was the head of an old Manatuck family firm, Anderson & Anderson. He answered Darby's call with a hearty hello and then thanked her for responding so quickly.

"This is a somewhat unorthodox request," the lawyer began, "but I wonder if we couldn't meet this afternoon? I'm leaving town for a legal seminar in Miami, and I'd like to jet off to Florida knowing that this disposition of Alcott's property is underway."

Darby thought a moment. She and Miles were headed to a large estate on Hurricane Harbor to meet Ed Landis, a Special Agent with the Federal Bureau of Investigation. Darby had met Ed several months earlier, and had known he was the one to call with her questions regarding Tokutaro's journal.

"Can we meet just after noon?" she asked the lawyer.

"Terrific. Do you know where my office is?"

"Yes."

Darby finished the call and looked up, feeling Miles's eyes upon her.

"Are you okay?" His voice was gentle. "I know this whole thing with the journal is upsetting."

She nodded, struggling to contain her emotions. "It's just that I was so relieved to think my grandfather was above suspicion, that he hadn't played a part in the taking of so many innocent lives. What if Kenji Miyazaki lied to me about the translation? What if this journal proves incriminating to my family?" She bit her lip, keeping the tears at bay.

He pulled her close. He was wearing the Irish knit sweater he'd brought from San Francisco and Darby, despite her distress, was smitten.

"There, there," Miles cooed. "What did Ed Landis say on the phone? He'll have a translation typed up for you by tonight. I think it's going to turn out that your grandfather was innocent, but at least you'll know the truth, right?"

Darby moved her head in agreement, not trusting herself to speak.

He gave her a hug. "I'll go start the Jeep and get it nice and toasty for you. Okay?"

Again she nodded. Miles gave a reassuring smile, pulled on a hat, and headed outside.

Darby took a deep breath. Miles was right—the truth was what she needed. She picked up two coffee cups and carried them into the kitchen. She felt emotion welling up once more, but this time it was anger and she did not tamp it down.

Kenji Miyazaki invaded my home and quite possibly stole my property. She gritted her teeth. Had he been after whatever secrets the journal held all along?

She thought back to her conversation an hour earlier with Hideki Kobayashi, the president of the pharmaceutical company where Kenji also worked. During the dapper businessman's purchase of an estate in South Florida months earlier, the two had developed an easy friendship.

It had been difficult to call him with her suspicions regarding Kenji.

At first the older man had said nothing, and then he exhaled a long, slow breath.

"Your remarks sadden me, Darby. I have always thought of Kenji Miyazaki as a son. I have supported him in his climb up the ladder at Genkei, and yet..." he paused.

"What is it, Hideki? Tell me, please."

"And yet I have wondered if there is another side to him. If so, he keeps it well hidden, like a tiger shields his claws, and yet sometimes I sense it is there, dark, and possibly deceitful."

"What do you mean? Can you be more specific?"

Hideki Kobayashi sighed and Darby winced. This was causing the old man pain, and yet she had to know the truth.

"Kenji is ambitious."

"There's nothing wrong with that."

"No." He paused. "Desiring power in itself is not a crime."

Darby felt a twinge of impatience. "Do you trust him, Hideki?"

"Kenji has been helping me with a delicate situation, involving the theft of intellectual property from Genkei."

"Corporate espionage?"

"Yes. We have tried to conduct our own internal investigation, but at last I consulted an expert in these matters. He came back to me only days ago with painful news. The stealing has been from Kenji's division."

Darby swallowed. "Hideki, I'm not sure what these formulas in my grandfather's notebook are, but I'm worried enough that I'm going to the authorities." She waited a beat. "I've contacted the Federal Bureau of Investigation."

There was silence on the other end. At last Hideki Kobayashi spoke, his voice weary and yet resolute. "Darby, you must take whatever actions are necessary. I will continue to believe in Kenji

Miyazaki's character until there is proof to the contrary, but please let the FBI know that I am ready and willing to cooperate."

Darby brought herself back to the present. She pulled on her red down coat and grabbed her purse. Gone was her sadness, and even her anger, replaced by a determination to get the journal into the hands of a professional who could unlock its secrets.

Kenji Miyazaki was by now off the island. Darby pictured his boyish face, seemingly so open and friendly, felt again his passionate kiss, and gritted her teeth. *Thank goodness I'll never see him again. Unlike Lorraine Delvecchio, I don't have to be tortured by memory. I can happily forget all about him.*

She walked along the snowy path to the Jeep where Miles Porter waited.

ELEVEN

"So what did Leonard Marcus do that was so bad?" Bitsy asked as they walked across the snowy parking lot to the car. "He certainly doesn't look like a criminal."

Charles Dupont gave a wry grin. "No, he looks like a wealthy businessman, which is just what he was until he was indicted for money laundering and concealment of records in a federal investigation." He opened her door and waited until she was tucked inside. "Right now, he's serving time for driving under the influence. That's why he's here in Manatuck. Meanwhile, the Feds are building their case against him."

"For what?"

"It appears that Marcus masterminded a pretty successful insurance scam. The authorities think he and his partner bilked thousands of investors out of some $700 million."

"That's unbelievable! Did they rip off anyone around here?"

"All over the world. They convinced people to buy life insurance policies held mostly in the names of people dying of AIDS.

The proceeds were used to purchase several homes—including a $3 million waterfront place in Westerly."

"Who owns it now, the Feds?"

"Not yet, but if he's proven guilty, it's theirs."

"So he stole and Lorraine Delvecchio …"

"You're not to repeat a word of that conversation." Charles Dupont's voice bore a hard edge.

"Sorry." She put a finger to her pink lips, signifying that she would be discreet. "And what about Marcus's partner? Is he locked up, too?"

"Hanged himself in his cell last year. Guess he didn't like prison food."

Bitsy giggled. "Oh, Charles! Gallows humor, right?" She rested her hand on his thigh. "I love it when you make me laugh."

He shot her a look. "Then I'll have to do it more often."

The squawk of his police radio interrupted the quiet. Charles pulled over and put the car in park. "Chief Dupont." He listened intently. "I know where that is. I'll be there."

He hung up, his lined face flushed.

"What is it?"

"Police work. The Manatuck guys need me later today."

She frowned. "But it's Sunday!" She looked out the window at the winter white landscape. "I wish you were already retired."

"Soon enough," he said. He looked at his watch. "We still have time to go to the shelter …"

"Yes!" She clapped her hands, her mood transformed in an instant. "I almost forgot, and now I'm as excited as a kid. Let's head there right now, Charles! I can't wait to get my hands on those puppies."

The turn-of-the-century Merewether estate lay blanketed under several feet of snow. Darby and Miles kept the engine running while they peered across the white landscape of the estate's sweeping lawn, broken only by a snow-covered cedar playset. By now the storm had completely subsided, and slivers of blue sky were visible behind retreating clouds.

"Seems our friends are tardy," Miles commented, checking his watch. He frowned. "Remind me again of how you know this FBI fellow Landis."

"He was on the island in June," she said, putting her hands in front of the car's heater. "Undercover work having to do with organized crime and the Fairview transaction."

Miles thought back to the events that had led up to the sale of that property. "Why is it we're meeting here?"

"It's the only place on the island with a private airstrip," she explained.

"An airstrip! Whatever for?"

"The previous owner headed up a corporation and needed to be able to get back and forth for business meetings. And the current owner ..." She paused. "After last summer, I tried to find out who owns the Merewether estate. It's a little hush-hush, but it's definitely government property."

Miles regarded the hulking house and snow-covered lawn. "Whatever would the Feds want with this big place?" He tilted his head at a faint whirring sound. "Amazing how quickly these fellows work. You rang Landis up this morning and he's wasted no time getting here."

The noise grew louder. Darby scanned the sky and spotted a helicopter buzzing over the ocean and toward the estate. "There he is, Miles. This should be quite the grand entrance."

They peered out the Jeep's windows, watching as the blades of the helicopter whipped up loose snow into a blinding whiteout. Through the curtain of flakes a figure clad in a dark blue survival coat with a fur-lined hood emerged and ran toward them.

"He thinks he's in Alaska," murmured Miles.

The man motioned to the back seat as if wanting to enter, and Darby and Miles both nodded. The door beside Darby's was yanked open and a rush of cold air entered the vehicle.

The door slammed and the newcomer removed his hood and gloves. "Ed Landis, Special Agent, FBI," he said, extending a hand. "Good to see you folks for a second time, although I'm sorry it's once again under difficult circumstances."

Darby swiveled in her seat to see Ed Landis straight on. She remembered how his curly brown hair framed a classically Roman face, and watched as he rubbed his hands together, trying to warm them up.

The agent gave them an intent look. "I'm all ears."

"A man named Kenji Miyazaki arrived in Maine sometime earlier this week," Darby began. "Through what might or might not be coincidence, he came to see me on the island on Friday. He ended up staying as my guest overnight due to the blizzard. I showed him a journal, written by my Japanese grandfather during the Second World War, and Kenji gave me some idea of what it said. The next morning I saw him with his phone and the journal, and he remarked that he was not getting cell reception." She paused. "This morning,

Miles was looking at the journal and noticed some pages are missing. We think Kenji may have removed them with a razor, perhaps because he wasn't able to send photographs with his cell phone."

Ed Landis pointed at the journal. "May I?"

Darby handed it to him. "It's a record of my grandfather's time in China—or at least that's what we think."

Landis gave an emphatic nod. "I've got a translator on standby. We'll be sure you get a complete report of whatever material isn't classified."

"Classified? What do you mean?"

"I can't go into it, I'm afraid." He blew air out of his lips and seemed to reconsider. "Look, I spoke to Hideki Kobayashi. Some pretty serious corporate espionage is happening at Genkei Pharmaceuticals, and it's unclear whether this fellow Miyazaki is involved. He had a reason for tracking you down and reading this journal, I'm sure of that. We don't yet know what he was after, or why."

Darby looked at Miles, whose face was grim.

"Is Darby in any danger?" he asked.

"We can't be sure. At this point, we're still hoping Miyazaki's motives turn out to be good." He paused. "Did he sense you were suspicious of him in any way?"

She shook her head. "No. I didn't suspect him of anything. I saw nothing out of the ordinary, and we parted on good terms. I probably wouldn't have noticed the missing pages, if Miles hadn't pointed them out."

Landis slipped the journal into a plastic bag. "I doubt that you'll hear from him again. I hate to say this, but he got what he wanted."

She nodded, not trusting herself to speak.

"Okay, then." Ed Landis reached across the seat and shook their hands. "I'm headed back to Boston, and then on to Washington. We'll take good care of this journal, Darby. I'll be in touch."

Clutching the bag, Ed Landis trotted across the snowy expanse and into the waiting helicopter.

Anderson & Anderson, Attorneys at Law, was located by the Breakwater in an old Victorian home built by a Manatuck quarry owner in the late 1800s. The businessman had amassed a fortune shipping granite from Hurricane Harbor and other towns along the coast to America's wealthiest cities. Now, as Darby crossed a wide granite step leading into the law firm's entrance, she reflected that the speckled mineral—most likely quarried right here in Manatuck—still graced the likes of the Washington Monument and many of the buildings in the nation's capital. Little wonder that the office's foyer contained stained, leaded glass, parquet floors, and a wide, curving stairway with burnished maple stairs.

It had been a silent ferry ride for her and Miles, each of them thinking about the journal and Ed Landis's comments about Kenji Miyazaki. *He got what he wanted.* Darby shivered at the recollection of those words. To think she had allowed him to spend the night in her home, never mind console her with a kiss …

Beside her, Miles Porter gently squeezed her hand. "You're far, far, away, love." His eyes held concern and she looked into them gratefully.

"Not anymore," she whispered, gripping his hand in return.

The sound of a throat clearing caused them both to look up.

"Darby?" A smiling man with thinning gray hair and a short, rotund body crossed the polished floor toward them, his hand extended. "Attorney Bartholomew Anderson. Pleasure to meet you."

Darby introduced Miles and together they followed him to an ornate office with big bay windows affording a view of the Breakwater parking lot. She felt her eyes drawn to the view, wondering whether the attorney spent any time gazing out.

Bartholomew Anderson followed her gaze. "Wish I saw more of the water, and less of the asphalt, but we can't have everything, right?" He gave a hearty chuckle and glanced at his watch. "I don't want to keep you folks tied up on a Sunday, and I do have a plane to catch, so I'll be brief." He waved a hand in the direction of the snow piled outside and grinned at them. "Can't say I'm not pleased to be leaving for Miami. It's in the eighties down there and sunny."

"How long are you staying?" Miles's voice was polite.

"Only two nights. Wish it was longer. My wife's sister has a timeshare right on the beach. We've been before and just loved it." He seemed to be remembering the sand and surf, but pulled himself back to the business at hand. "Now then, let's talk about poor Alcott."

He shuffled some papers. "Here's what I will need you and Tina to complete before the estate releases the listing. I know Alcott had spoken to you before his untimely death, so you probably have much of this information already. Standard stuff, nothing complicated, although I should tell you that there is an agent from another brokerage firm we're considering."

"I see." Darby lifted her eyes. "Who would that be?"

"Rocky Coast Real Estate—Miss Applebaum."

This was the agent Tina had mentioned with such disdain. Darby gave Bartholomew Anderson a firm nod. "I'm sure when you see our sold figures, you'll know that Near & Farr is the right company to list Mr. Bridges's home. It will be you making the decision, is that right?"

"Absolutely. I'll be checking e-mails while I'm in Miami, and my paralegal Maureen will be in touch as well." He made a face. "Can't get away nowadays. Not like you used to." He rose and came around his massive desk toward them, ready to go home to his packed suitcases.

"Mr. Anderson, I have one or two quick questions about Alcott Bridges. Did he ever confide in you about making payments to keep something quiet?"

"Hush money?" The portly lawyer shook his head. "I don't recall a thing. Why would anyone wish to blackmail Alcott? He lived a pretty quiet life, you know. Most artists do."

Darby could think of one or two artists whose lives were far from quiet, but she kept her thoughts to herself. "What about the scandal surrounding his painting of Judge Collins?"

Bartholomew Anderson waved a hand dismissively. "That whole thing was ridiculous. Of course Alcott painted that work! Art historians from around the country spoke in support of him when that foolish claim came up." He made a harrumphing sound. "Now, if you're finished with your questions ..."

"Almost." She gave a sweet smile. "Can you tell me what happens to Alcott Bridges's assets? His paintings? The house?"

"Well, I'm not sure if it's any of your business, but proceeds will be given to the hospice association here in Manatuck. They took such excellent care of his wife, Grace. The paintings will go to the

Westerly Art Museum." He raised his eyebrows. "Are we finished, Miss Farr?"

"Yes, thank you." She and Miles walked toward the door, ready to leave his office, when Darby had another thought. She turned toward the lawyer. "Mr. Anderson, I see that your windows look out over the Breakwater parking lot. Did you notice the daily visits of Lorraine Delvecchio?"

His eyes flicked to the window and back. "She's the poor girl who fell to her death?" He shook his head regretfully. "Of course I've seen her picture in the newspaper, but no, I never knew her nor noticed her comings and goings." He gave a thin smile. "We may seem like a sleepy firm on the coast of Maine, but believe it or not, we're quite busy."

"I'm sure you are," Darby said. She felt Miles's hand on her waist giving her a gentle tug.

"Have a first-rate visit to Miami," he said. "And thank you for your time."

Darby let herself be steered out the door and down the granite steps.

"Tina is going to have your head," Miles chuckled.

"I know," Darby moaned. "That guy's never going to give us the listing after my barrage of questions. It's going to go to Tina's arch enemy, Babette Applebaum."

"May I make a suggestion? Call the fellow's wife, find out where their little timeshare is, and have a bottle of champagne waiting. Tell her it's a surprise for her wonderful husband."

Darby flashed Miles a wide grin. "Bribe him, you mean?"

"It's hardly a bribe! More of a thank-you gift."

"Whatever it is, it's a great idea. What is it you Brits say? Brilliant?"

He reached over and ruffled her glossy black hair. "Spot on," he said.

Miles stoked the fire in the farmhouse's cozy living room while Darby worked at her computer getting a sales analysis ready for Bartholomew Anderson. The day before she'd had an Internet connection installed so that she wouldn't need to make endless trips to the library. She clicked send and sat back with a sigh.

"That's done, although I have a strong suspicion it isn't going to do any good. I'm not looking forward to telling Tina the bad news."

Miles was on his haunches adjusting the logs with a poker. "You sent the champagne, right?"

"Sure did. An expensive bottle, too. I guess we'll just have to see what happens." She cocked her head to the side with a question. "Miles, who was it that Anderson said was the beneficiary of Alcott's estate?"

"The art museum, wasn't it?"

"Yes, they're getting the paintings, including that new one of the Breakwater. But remember he mentioned a nonprofit that had helped Alcott Bridges' wife. Was it the District Nurses Association?"

Miles snapped his fingers. "Hospice. He said the local hospice association was getting the proceeds from the sale."

"Good work." Darby bit her lip and did a quick search on the computer. "Here they are: Manatuck Home Care & Hospice." She scanned the website. "Sounds like a wonderful organization."

"I've told you about my friend Diana Whitby, haven't I?" Miles pushed a shock of dark hair out of his eyes. "Good friend of my mum's who lives in San Francisco? Kind of a surrogate auntie for me. I stayed with her until I found my own flat."

"Yes, I recall that, although I guess I didn't know her name."

"Well, Diana's older sister died a few weeks ago after a long illness. Cancer, I think. It was devastating for Diana as they were extremely close, but she said the hospice care her sister received made the whole thing much easier. She was able to die peacefully and without pain in her own home, surrounded by family."

Darby looked up from the computer. Her Aunt Jane had died in the hospital in Manatuck, connected to a variety of machines, but then she had been unconscious. Would it have made anything better if she had been at home?

She glanced at the website once more, reading through the list of community people connected with the hospice. Attorney Anderson was listed as a trustee, she noticed. So was Babette Applebaum.

Darby groaned.

"What is it, love?"

"Babette serves on the Board of Trustees for this Manatuck Home Care & Hospice along with Bart Anderson." She looked heavenward. "Champagne or no champagne, we're doomed." She sighed and scanned the other names. "This one rings a bell: Charles Dodge, III. That's Terri's husband, right?"

"Right. He goes by Tripp, remember?"

Miles rose from the fire and sat down on the couch next to Darby. He gently pulled the laptop from her arms and leaned in to kiss her. She felt the rough wool of his Irish knit sweater brush against her cheek.

"Now, if you had hyperthymesia like Lorraine Delvecchio, you wouldn't have to ask me so many questions." He nuzzled her ear as he spoke. "Then there would be more time for us to do other things."

Darby kissed Miles but then pulled away. "You've hit on the big question, Miles. What did Lorraine remember that somebody wanted forgotten? Who was she blackmailing?"

She thought back to the list of initials in the notebook. "One of the blackmailing victims was 'BA,' right? We now know two people with those initials: Babette Applebaum and Bartholomew Anderson. Is that just a coincidence, or could one of them have been paying money to Lorraine?"

"Anderson said he didn't know her, remember?"

"Yes, but he could have been lying. Or maybe he was telling the truth and it's Babette who was being blackmailed."

"Have you ever met this Babette?"

"She's new in town. Used to summer on the island, and now she works with a luxury firm out of southern Maine. I've never spoken with her—but I think it's high time I did."

Bitsy Carmichael watched her husband strap on his service revolver under a loose-fitting leather jacket. "You're wearing your gun? Is this something dangerous, Chuckie?"

Charles Dupont shook his head. "Routine, honey. Just a good idea for me to have it, that's all." He didn't tell her that the Manatuck guys had told him to be prepared for anything.

She rolled her eyes. "Can't you just tell them you're busy?" *I'm whining like a little kid,* she thought, but she didn't care. There was bad energy around this outing, she could feel it.

"Nope." He bent over, kissed her lightly on the forehead.

"Why can't Dozer go?" She was one of the few people who knew Tom Allen's nickname.

"Because *Deputy* Allen," his voice was sounding stern now, "isn't who they want." He stood up. "I'll be back for dinner. I pulled some beef stew out of the freezer."

"How long has it been in there?"

"Since you left for Vegas." He saw her shocked face and laughed. "No, I just made it two weeks ago. Pretty good, too." He backed away, grinning, and started for the door. "See you soon. Take good care of Rosie."

At the sound of her name, the furry Labrador-mix puppy they had found at the shelter raised a hopeful head.

"Wait." Bitsy rose from the chair where she had flopped and hurried to him. Wrapping her arms around his barrel chest, she hugged him tightly. "I love you, Charles. I always have."

He hugged her back, catching a whiff of her musky perfume. "What's all this? I'll be back before you know it." He smiled, opened the door, and headed into the darkening sky.

The number for Babette Applebaum rang twice before a brisk voice said hello. Darby introduced herself, and then asked if she would have time to meet the next day.

“What about?” The woman on the other end sounded harried. “I’m perfectly happy working with Todd Stockton and Rocky Coast Real Estate, you know.”

“I’m not trying to hire you, although I understand that you’re a good agent. I wanted to ask you some questions.”

“Look, I need to know what this is about. I’ve got a lot going on …”

“Okay.” Darby had wanted to speak to Babette face-to-face, but she was running the risk of alienating the woman, so she posed her question. “Did you know Lorraine Delvecchio?”

“The Breakwater accident victim? No. I mean, I recognized her face when I saw the picture, but I didn’t know her.” Her voice had the ring of sincerity. Unless she was an accomplished liar, it sounded as if Babette Applebaum was telling the truth.

In the background a child’s shriek preceded a bout of loud crying.

“I’ve got to go. My kid’s just knocked something off the counter.” Darby could hear her yelling to the child and then the click as the receiver went dead.

“Well?” Miles Porter held several logs that he stacked by the blazing fire. “Did you find anything out?”

“I don’t know. She said she didn’t know Lorraine, and I believed her.”

“So that leaves our friend Bart. Do you have a cell phone number for him?”

“Yes … what are you thinking?”

“Never you mind. Let me have the number.” Miles waited while Darby found the listing information for Alcott Bridges’ house and handed him Bartholomew Anderson’s number. He punched it in and listened intently. A moment later his face hardened. "Mr. Anderson? Why yes, hello, this is Mr. Porter calling on behalf of Lorraine Delvecchio. We are compiling a list of Ms. Delvecchio's friends and relatives…" He stopped, obviously interrupted mid-sentence. "Oh, I see. Well that's odd because she has you on a list that we found in her desk." He waited, saying nothing else for a few beats. "Yes, yes, let me write that down. Quarry Landing, you say? In Manatuck. Thank you very much, sir." He hung up and gave Darby a triumphant smile.

"So?"

"So, I'd say that your Mr. Anderson is not telling the truth. He does know Lorraine Delvecchio. When I mentioned a list with his name on it you could practically hear the wheels in his head turn. I wouldn't be surprised if he's our 'AB' set of initials."

She frowned. "But is he our killer, Miles? And if so, has he just disappeared for good?" She blew air out of her mouth. "I'm calling Chief Dupont. He needs to know what we're thinking."

Bitsy answered the phone with a languid hello. The clipped voice of Darby Farr apologized for interrupting her Sunday afternoon, and then asked for Charles.

"He's not here, Darby," Bitsy explained. "Went off on some mission with the Manatuck Police Department. I can have him call you when he gets back."

There was a pause at the other end. "Yes, if you could have him call me. Meanwhile, I'll see if he answers his cell phone."

"I doubt that. I get the feeling it was some sort of operation, if you know what I mean. Like a stakeout."

“Here on Hurricane Harbor?” The real estate agent’s voice was incredulous. “That’s odd.” She cleared her throat. “I’ll speak to him when he comes back, then. Thank you, Bitsy.”

Bitsy hung up the phone and padded in her pink slippers to the kitchen, Rosie trotting along behind her. *I want a glass of wine,* she thought. Just to take the edge off the anxiety she was feeling around Charles’s departure. *He’s a cop,* she reminded herself. *This is what cops do.* And yet she couldn’t shake the feeling that he was in some sort of danger.

When the knock on the door came an hour later, rousing the puppy from a nap on its corduroy dog bed, Bitsy had found and devoured half a bag of chocolate morsels. Even if she had discovered something stronger, it wouldn’t have helped to dull the pain from the devastating news she’d been dreading all day.

TWELVE

DONNY PEASE MADE THE phone call to Darby Farr with shaking hands. Tina was in the bedroom of their suite at the Halifax Inn, crying her eyes out as she jammed items into suitcases. Bitsy had phoned him, almost incoherent with grief, and he'd told her to sit still, that someone would be over to keep her company.

That someone had to be Darby.

The phone rang for several seconds and Donny nearly despaired, but a moment later he heard her voice, calm and competent as always.

"Chief Dupont is dead." He hadn't meant to blurt it out like that, but sometimes the best way to deliver bad news was to put it out there without any sugar coating.

"God, no." He heard the intake of breath on the other end. "What happened?"

"Shot in the head by a drug addict. He died instantly." Donny's voice quavered and he had to reach for the hotel's desk for support.

"Unbelievable."

It was unbelievable, Darby was right, and yet, damn it all, the news was also true. Deputy Tom Allen and Manatuck's Chief of Police had been to see Bitsy, delivered the awful facts, and were still with her now for all Donny knew.

"Bitsy needs someone. She's hurting pretty bad. Can you—?"

"Absolutely." She drew a deep breath. "Miles and I will head over there right now."

He sighed. "Tina's packing. We're leaving tonight. Call us if you get any more details."

"I will." Darby's voice was steady. She was once more in control. "Please, Donny, you and Tina drive carefully, okay?"

"I'll get Tina back to Hurricane Harbor safe and sound."

He hung up the phone, squared his shoulders, and went to console his wife.

Miles and Darby were surprised to see several cars in the driveway of Chief Dupont's ranch. "Word is out," muttered Miles, his boots crunching on the now-hardening snow. He put an arm around Darby. "You okay?"

She nodded, relieved to feel him close. "Thanks for being here, Miles."

He squeezed her gently in response. "You're welcome. I'm glad you're not alone."

They opened the door, feeling a warm blast of air as they entered the foyer. There was the sound of voices murmuring and over that, a woman's soft crying. Darby saw several women seated around Bitsy, as well as a trio of men, two of them in uniform. She smelled the dark aroma of coffee.

Miles helped her out of her red coat and placed it on a nearby chair. He took her hand in his and they walked into the room.

Bitsy looked up with a tear-stained face.

"Darby," she said, rising on unsteady feet. "It's just so horrible."

Darby reached out and hugged Bitsy, feeling tears welling in her own eyes. She let them fall as they embraced.

"I'm so sorry, Bitsy. He was such a good man."

The blonde woman waggled her head, her spiky hair bobbing up and down. "He was wonderful. Why I ever left him, I'll never know. I came back here to make it up to him, and now…" She sobbed softly, her shoulders heaving.

Darby saw two women on the couch share sympathetic looks. They each clutched coffee cups, and one of them had a plate of homemade chocolate chip cookies on the table before her. As Darby comforted Bitsy, she watched a small puppy emerge from the kitchen, run to the table, and knock the plate of cookies to the floor.

"Rosie, no!" Bitsy squealed, pulling away from Darby. The other women hurried to scoop up the cookies before the furry golden pup could wolf them down.

Bitsy held the little creature by a thin red collar. "No, no," she said softly. An instant later she had picked the puppy up and was burying her face in its coat.

"Charles and I just picked her out today," she said, her voice muffled by the fur. "We had so much fun looking at all the shelter dogs and settling on this little one. Charles was so excited to find a puppy, and one that was part retriever like our old dog, Aggie."

"She's adorable," Darby said, reaching out to stroke the dog. It seemed good that Bitsy was talking. "You got her in Manatuck?"

Bitsy bobbed her head. "We went over there after breakfast. First Charles had to see someone at the jail of all places, and then we went over to the pound."

A tall man wearing a sweater and pants appeared beside Bitsy. "How are you holding up, Mrs. Dupont?"

She shrugged. "I don't know." Turning to Darby, Bitsy introduced the man as Detective Robichaud from Manatuck. "This is Darby Farr. She was a good friend of Charles's."

"I'm Dave," he said, "and I'm sorry for your loss. Charles was a great guy and a heck of a good policeman."

Darby nodded. Detective Robichaud was clean-shaven, with neatly cut dark hair and a powerfully built body. "You were with Chief Dupont . . . ?" She couldn't quite complete the sentence.

He glanced in Bitsy's direction. "I was. I've explained to Mrs. Dupont that we were working together to arrest a suspect here on the island. The guy took us completely by surprise and fired shots. I returned fire, but not before Chief Dupont was hit."

Bitsy's eyes had grown glassy and she sank onto the couch where the women consoled her. Darby lowered her voice. "Did he die instantly?"

Robichaud gave a slow nod. "Yes."

Darby's head dropped. She didn't want to believe it; and yet the truth was sinking in. Charles Dupont was dead.

Miles appeared with a mug of coffee and handed it to Darby. She looked up, her eyes brimming.

Detective Robichaud introduced himself to Miles. The men waited quietly while Darby sipped the coffee and regained her composure.

After a few moments she spoke again.

"Detective Robichaud was just telling me how it happened," she told Miles. "He and the Chief had gone to arrest a suspect and they were taken by surprise."

"Was it just the two of you?" Miles asked.

"No," the detective said gravely. "Detective Paulsen from my department was at the back of the house, guarding that exit. He heard the whole thing, but couldn't help us out until it was too late."

Darby sighed. "Thank you for the explanation. It helps to know exactly what happened. I'm glad you weren't injured as well."

He gave a sad smile. "Thank you. And now if you'll excuse me, I'm going to see how Chief Dupont's deputy is doing."

Donny drove steadily through the dark afternoon. While Tina slept on the seat beside him, he watched the road, noting how the white farmhouses nearly blended into the snowy landscape, save for their tall red barns. He saw Christmas lights still adorning some town centers, and the sweep of crow's wings against the high banks. He thought about Chief Charles Dupont, a man he'd known his whole life, and about how crazy it was to think that he was now dead. He thought about Bitsy, about the way she had disappeared so long ago, and about the Chief's ability to accept her back.

That said a lot about the man, Donny thought. The Chief had been willing to forgive.

Forgiving wasn't the same as forgetting, Donny knew, although an awful lot of folks confused the two. If you could make yourself forget things, well then why not forgive? It was the pain of remembering that made forgiveness an almost extraordinary act. The fact that you would remember the injustice—the one you loved abandoning you and your children for more than a decade—and yet still chose to grant pardon.

And now it was up to the rest of the island to follow the Chief's example and show Bitsy compassion. She was a widow. Her plans for a life with Charles Dupont had been brutally dashed. If she chose to stay on Hurricane Harbor, she would need care and support.

He glanced over at his slumbering bride. "Be nice to Bitsy," he whispered. "She's gonna need all the help she can get."

A soft snore escaped Tina's lips and Donny Pease had to smile. *Well, that was something, anyway*. Not quite a yes, but he'd take it.

Darby and Miles carried coffee cups and plates from Bitsy's living room into the kitchen, loading them into the dishwasher and putting leftover food in the refrigerator. Chief Dupont's adult children had arrived and were talking with Bitsy.

Darby didn't want to interrupt the grieving family, but Bitsy looked up as she and Miles were putting on their coats and hurried over.

"Thank you for coming, Darby," Bitsy said. She ran a hand through her disheveled blonde hair. "You and Miles are so helpful, and I just want you to know how much I appreciate that you were here to keep me company."

Darby zipped her coat. "We're close by if you need us." She gently squeezed the other woman's arm. "You get some rest, okay?"

"I'll try." She made a brave attempt at a smile. "This morning we had breakfast together, and now he's gone..." She wiped her eyes. Suddenly her face hardened. "I wish he'd never gotten that call."

"Which call?" Miles's voice was gentle.

"The one for the stakeout. I told him not to go."

Darby heard the bitterness in Bitsy's tone. "When was this?"

"When we left the Manatuck jail." She sighed. "We went over there to talk to a man named Marcus. It was something about the woman who used to work for Charles."

Darby shot a look at Miles. "Lorraine Delvecchio?"

Bitsy nodded. "The one who slipped off the Breakwater."

"Did the Chief seem satisfied with what Marcus said?"

"I think so. He was pleased. Well, not really pleased, but content. Like whatever he heard made sense." She drew in a breath. "Charles was trying to help." She turned her face away, her voice shaking. "He always wanted to help. That's why he agreed to go with the Manatuck police. But why today, of all days?"

Darby shook her head and hugged Bitsy hard. She had no answers for the sobbing woman, and no way to make the truth any less painful.

The fabric of any small town is tightly woven, and when that town is an island, the threads are even more closely constructed. Chief Dupont's death in the line of duty shook every resident, from the postmistress who read about it in an e-mail, to the busboy waiting on a whispering couple at the Café. Stopping at the island's one convenience store to get gas for the car, Darby and Miles saw in the shocked faces of the storekeepers that the news of their police chief's passing was a bitter blow.

Miles thumped a carton of ice cream on the counter and pulled out his wallet. "It's good for what ails you," he said gently, in answer to Darby's raised eyebrows. He paid for his items, and then grabbed the carton and his change. "You ate next to nothing today. A little ice cream is not going to kill you."

Darby winced at his words but Miles didn't notice. Instead, he looked at her thoughtfully as they climbed into the Jeep.

"What about this Marcus fellow, the one the Chief was questioning?" Miles started the Jeep. "Seems like he could be our 'ML' from the list."

"I suppose." Darby gazed vacantly at the parking lot as Miles backed up. She felt his look of concern. "What?"

"You're utterly exhausted. I'm sorry I even brought up the whole thing. Tell you what, we're going back to the house, curling up on the couch with some Moose Tracks and an old movie. Everything else can wait until the morning."

"Moose Tracks?"

"Chocolate ice cream with marshmallow, fudge, peanut butter, and who knows what else. I hear it's absolutely smashing."

"Okay." She sighed and leaned against Miles's shoulder. Did she even care what the Chief had discovered at the jail? The man was dead. He had been her friend as well as a last link to her parents. She felt a deep grief, so profound that she could not imagine it ever disappearing.

Bitsy's stepson Derek gave her something to help her sleep. He was a doctor in New Hampshire, and explained that he'd call in a prescription the next day, but for now she should take a mild sedative so that she'd be able to rest.

He had been so kind, he and his wife, as well as Charles's daughter, Alana and her partner, Rosemary. Bitsy had been dreading their arrival, expecting them to somehow blame her for their father's death, but neither one had said an unkind word. Instead, they had treated her with compassion. And she, in turn, was trying to comfort them.

"He was a wonderful father," she blurted out at one point, quickly glancing to see how the kids would react.

"He was," agreed Alana. She glanced at her toddler son, careening around on the living room rug. "And a good grandfather." She smiled sadly at Bitsy. "I have some cute photos of Dad with Jonas. I'll send them to you."

Bitsy nodded numbly. Apparently Charles had phoned both his son and his daughter after Donny's wedding to tell them about her return. According to Alana, he'd also told them that he was taking their stepmother back, that he'd forgiven Bitsy, and wanted her company.

Bitsy hadn't dared ask what they had responded. She was brave, but not that brave.

Now she watched little Jonas crawl determinedly toward Rosie, a look of stern concentration on his round, ruddy face. Rosie greeted the baby with a furiously wagging tail and a huge lick of his drool-splattered chin. Alana looked on, amused.

Bitsy rose unsteadily to her feet, wondering if the sleeping pill was already taking effect. "I'm going upstairs," she announced. "The candlelight vigil ..."

"Don't worry about it," Alana said softly. "Derek and I will be here." Islanders would soon gather in front of the house to show sorrow over their Chief's death, but Bitsy didn't think she could bear it.

"Do you have everything that you need?"

"Yes, we're fine," assured Alana. She scooped up little Jonas and came to her, the baby clinging to an outthrust hip. "Goodnight," she said softly, leaning close to kiss Bitsy's cheek.

"'Night," Bitsy managed, the tears rolling slowly down her face.

Darby awoke on Monday morning before Miles and crawled quietly out of bed. She tossed on a robe and slid into her slippers, heading down to get a fire going and the coffee on.

Then she remembered.

Chief Dupont is dead.

Darby staggered on the last few stairs, grabbing the worn banister for support. All the strength drained from her legs and they buckled below her.

She lurched to the loveseat. It was too painful, too horrible, a gaping, fresh, and yet somehow familiar wound, as if a lance were ripping apart her very soul once again.

She buried her head in her hands. Her hair made a black curtain, closing her off from the rest of the room. Darby felt more alone than she had in a long time. Alone and afraid.

A moment later, she was amazed to hear something as ridiculous as the ring of her cell phone. Despite herself, she lifted her chin and glanced at the display.

Tina Ames.

"We're an hour from Westerly," the redhead said, ignoring the usual convention of saying good morning or hello. "Donny's done an amazing job of driving through the night, and I'm so grateful. I can't wait to be back on Hurricane Harbor." She paused. "How is she?"

Darby swallowed. "Bitsy can't believe it—no one can."

Tina's voice was grim. "Tell me about it. Try hearing the news when you're a gazillion miles away." Donny said something in the background, but Darby couldn't make it out. "You okay?"

Darby held her breath, unable to answer.

"Darby? You still there?"

"Tina—I want to sell this house."

"What? Why?"

"It was a mistake to think I could come back here."

"Darby, listen. You're in shock. We all are."

"I can't go through this again. I just can't."

"Look, you were close to Chief Dupont. His death's gonna hit you hard. Don't make any decisions right now." She paused. "Where's Miles?"

"Upstairs."

"Go be with him. You shouldn't be alone."

"I'm—I'm fine. I just realize that I don't belong on Hurricane Harbor. I never did."

"Darby…" This time it was Miles who spoke, Miles who was beside her, scooping her into his powerful arms, and muttering to Tina that he'd take it from there.

———

Cradling their coffee cups and bundled in their coats, Darby and Miles trudged through the snow and across the plowed road to the cove. They stood in silence on the smooth sand, the steam from their cups circling upward, the sounds of the morning muted as if in mourning.

"He asked me if I wanted to hear some stories about my parents," Darby said, her voice breaking. "Now I'll never get the chance." She pulled her eyes from the placid water and searched Miles's rugged face. "Listen to how selfish I sound. How can you even stand it?"

"It's not selfishness speaking. It's grief, darling." He put an arm around her shoulders. "It's damn difficult, this journey we're on. We love and we lose. And we think we'll never love again because it hurts so badly."

She moistened her lips. "I find myself thinking that if I avoid all this—" she swept her gloved hand around the cove—"then I can forget how sad it makes me feel."

"Hence your busy life in California."

She nodded. "The thing is, I was just starting to remember the good things about Hurricane Harbor. The times I spent here in this cove, hunting for beach glass."

"Did you find any?"

"Yes." She smiled sadly. "Is that it, Miles? Have I been living my life avoiding the pain, and in the process, shutting off all the happy memories, too?"

"You wouldn't be the first person to do that, Darby, and you probably won't be the last." He gave her a gentle hug and their coffee cups clacked together. "I'd like to find some of that beach glass myself, you know? When it's not quite so bloody cold."

Together they turned from the water. The low farmhouse with its twin maples rose before them, surrounded by snow, smoke curling from the chimney.

"Shall we go home?" Miles asked.

Darby nodded and moved forward.

A fresh cup of coffee in hand, Darby sat down to try calling the Manatuck County Correctional Facility.

The phone rang only once before a phone tree inviting her to press one for English met her ears. She pressed one and continued listening and pressing buttons until she finally reached a real person.

"Manatuck Correctional." The voice was flat and tired.

"Hello. I'm wondering if you have an inmate named Marcus? His last name would start with an 'L'."

"What is this, a treasure hunt?" he said. "We don't have anyone with a first name of Marcus. Sorry."

"Are you sure?"

"Lady, I've worked here for two years and I know all our guys. We've only got a couple hundred. Sorry."

She hung up and turned on her computer. Maybe Bitsy had been mistaken, and the name had not been Marcus at all.

A footfall made her look up. Miles, his arms full of wood, was heading toward the fireplace.

"What are you up to?"

"Trying to find this Marcus Somebody. I'm doing a search right now."

"Perhaps Marcus is the surname," Miles suggested, releasing the logs on the hearth.

"Hmmm … good idea." After a few moments, she leaned back, a triumphant grin on her face. "Miles, you're brilliant! Here's a story on Leonard Marcus. He's serving time for drunk driving but has been indicted by the federal government for money laundering and a long list of other offenses, all tied to a fraudulent insurance scheme."

"I like the idea of being brilliant," Miles joked. "Wonder what the connection with Lorraine is?"

"That I don't know," Darby admitted. "Feel like a trip to the jail with me later on to find out?"

He leaned in to kiss her. "Sure, if you will be the jail bait."

She put down her coffee mug. "I thought you British men were supposed to be so proper and correct."

He eased toward her on the couch. "A common misconception, I'm afraid."

She pushed the computer to the floor and pulled him closer. Kissing Miles felt good, as if it could make the pain of Charles Dupont's death disappear, at least for a while. Seconds later they both yanked off what little clothing they were wearing. As the fire crackled and hissed before them, Darby and Miles temporarily forgot their grief and engaged in some early morning exercise of the romantic kind.

The phone rang as both of them were toweling off from a shower.

"We're here," Tina announced, her voice sounding resigned, yet strong. "Just about to head over to see Bitsy."

Darby glanced at Miles's naked body. "We're not quite ready."

"Don't hurry over on my account. I've got Donny. He'll hold my hand." She paused. "You doing okay?"

"Much better."

"Good. Hey, what ended up happening with Alcott Bridges's house? When do we list it?"

Darby bit her lip. She wasn't looking forward to telling Tina that she'd likely alienated Bart Anderson with her pointed questions. "Haven't heard yet, but Tina, I'm afraid I—"

"Hang on, Donny is yelling something." Darby heard muffled voices. In an instant, she was back. "Darby, my cell is ringing. It might be Bart Anderson as we speak. Gotta go!"

Click.

Darby winced, wondering how annoyed Tina would be. She sighed and was about to brush her teeth when the phone rang again.

"Popular girl, aren't you?" Miles teased. He'd put on some clothes but still looked good to Darby. *Get a grip,* she told herself. *You're like a love-struck teenager...*

She checked the caller and groaned. *Tina.*

The redheaded agent wasted no time.

"Okay, I'm annoyed about Alcott Bridges's house!"

Darby steeled herself. The expensive champagne had obviously not done the trick.

"Tina, I know I screwed up. I—"

"You bet! I leave you in charge for two days and look what happens."

"Well, I—"

"I *never* take a commission of less than six percent, never, and you told this guy five and a half! For goodness sake, Darby, how are we supposed to make any money?"

"You mean we're getting the listing?"

"Of course we're getting the listing. Who else? Babette Applebaum? Give me a break." Tina snorted in disgust. "You'd better have given me a fabulous wedding present. I haven't opened them up yet, but it had better be good."

Darby thought about the dinner and dancing night she'd arranged for Donny and Tina in Mexico. "It is."

"Okay, then." Tina sounded mollified. "What are you and Miles planning to do today?"

Darby told Tina about Leonard Marcus and their intended trip to the jail.

"Only one problem with that," Tina said thoughtfully. "The initials in Lorraine's little ledger were 'ML', weren't they? Not 'LM'."

"You're right."

"Maybe they are all turned around, you know, like another encryption? The 'BA' is really 'AB', or Alcott. That would mean there's a 'CR', and a 'BA'."

"Who might be Bart Anderson," Darby interjected.

"No way! The lawyer?"

Darby described Miles's subterfuge and the attorney's reaction. "We aren't sure how they knew each other…"

"Oh, there's millions of ways that woman could have known him, especially if she never forgot anything! She worked for Doc Hotchkiss for all those years, and he could have been a patient. Then there's her job with Chief Dupont or the Manatuck police. She was on a few committees here and there, and she walked that darn Breakwater. Heck, I suppose he could have been her lawyer, right?"

“Right. This initials idea of yours is interesting. Miles and I will work on it while we sit on the ferry.” She paused. “If you’re okay with visiting Bitsy with Donny, I’m thinking Miles and I could go across now.”

“Sure, ditch your best buddy for the good-looking English guy. See if I care.” She chuckled. “Nah, I can handle Bitsy by myself. Good luck at the jail, and let me know what you find out.”

“I will,” Darby promised.

Donny was glad to see Tina back to her old self. The shock of the tragic death had lessened, and now, as she marched across Chief Dupont’s frozen driveway, a pound cake held in her outstretched hands, he recognized her trademark determination, grim as it was. She was once again the Tina who took charge.

“Let’s plan to stay about an hour, huh honey?” Tina’s eyebrows were raised with the question.

He felt himself blushing. He wasn’t used to being called “honey,” but he sure did enjoy it. “Sounds about right,” he said. He reached up and used the Chief’s door knocker, let it thunk down, and then opened the door.

Bitsy was on the living room couch, a puppy frolicking at her feet. A young woman—Chief Dupont’s daughter, most likely—stood sniffing the diaper of a rosy-cheeked toddler, and somewhere a television blared out a sitcom with a canned laugh track.

“Donny, Tina, come in,” Bitsy called out. “Do you know Alana? And this is little Jonas. And this …” she scooped up the puppy, “Is Rosie. Charles and I picked her up on Sunday, just before …” her voice trailed off.

Tina thrust down the pound cake and rushed to Bitsy's side, wrapping the woman in her arms. They hugged silently for a long time, with only the little boy's repeated "doggie, doggie," breaking the quiet. Donny felt his throat tightening at the scene. He glanced at the Chief's daughter, sobbing silently while the toddler struggled to get down.

"I'm sorry, Alana," Donny said haltingly. "Your dad—he was a good man."

She nodded and wiped her face with the back of a hand. "Can I get you both a cup of coffee?"

Tina and Bitsy separated. "Sure," Tina said. "Cream and two sugars."

"I'm set," Donny said. He watched Alana carry the toddler into the next room, the puppy careening along behind them.

"Sit down," said Bitsy, waving at the living room furniture. Her face brightened. "How was your trip to Nova Scotia?"

Tina told her about the inn in Halifax, and the wonderful bedroom with the nice, fluffy comforters. "We had tea in the afternoon with these flaky scones," she said. "They were just wonderful. Good thing they don't sell them at the Café, or I'd weigh twenty pounds more."

Bitsy managed a small chuckle. "Speaking of food, how about we have a little piece of your pound cake? It looks delicious."

"Sure. You sit a minute. I'll go and cut it up." Tina strode out of the living room, pound cake in hand.

"She's an awfully nice girl," Bitsy observed, watching as Tina disappeared. "I'm glad for you, Donny."

"Thanks." He looked down at the floor, unsure of what to say. "What do you think you'll do now, Bitsy? Will you stay in Hurricane Harbor?"

Bitsy cocked her head. "Yes, I think I will. At least that's my plan. I might do some work with the hospice organization, use my nursing training. I'm not sure. But I do know that it feels good to be here. Even if I don't have Charles..." She started to cry softly. "I'll still have his memory, and be around people who cared about him." She wiped her nose. "They had a vigil last night. Right in front of the house. Alana said it was beautiful to see all the flickering candles."

Donny shifted his weight from one leg to another. He wondered if he should go to Bitsy and comfort her. *I could rub her back or something,* he thought.

Tina returned with the coffee and cake, took in the weeping widow, and glared at Donny. She plunked down the plates and wrapped an arm around Bitsy's shoulders. "Aw, honey, I know it's hard. Donny and I are so, so, sorry."

Bitsy lifted a mascara-streaked face toward Tina. "You know the worst thing? Detective Robichaud told me this morning that Charles knew that guy who shot him."

"The drug dealer?" Tina's eyes narrowed. "Who was it?"

"Ross. Denny Ross. Did you know him?"

Tina shook her head. "Nope." She glanced at Donny. "Did you?"

He gave a slow nod. "Denny was Carlene and Lester's brother." He pictured Denny, a ne'er-do-well who'd been living for years in Rhode Island. He'd just come back to Maine at New Year's, and hadn't wasted any time in becoming a major family embarrassment. Now he was dead, killed during the shootout.

"Crazy Carlene? The one you were with when you found Lorraine's body?" Tina's voice squeaked. "Well, I'll be. And Lester! He was in our wedding..."

"Lester is a good man," Donny said firmly. "And Carlene... she's just kinda odd." Denny, however, had been another story—the rottenest apple in a family where several bore bruises.

He reached for his pound cake, determined to change the subject. "You need anything at all, Bitsy, you call Tina and me," he said. "Charles was our friend, and now you are, too."

To his surprise, Tina reached out and patted Bitsy's hand. "We mean it," she said softly. "We're here to help."

Bitsy gave a sad, brave smile. "I can't tell you how good it feels," she said, her voice breaking, "to finally have friends."

Tina gave a sympathetic smile, squeezed Bitsy's shoulder, and handed her a piece of pound cake. Donny watched the exchange, his heart swelling with love, thankful for the redheaded angel who was now his wife.

Darby and Miles were about to enter Manatuck County Correctional Facility when Darby's cell phone rang. She looked down at the display. "Miles, it's Ed Landis." She pushed a button. "Hello?"

"Darby, Ed Landis here, FBI. Are you somewhere we can talk?"

"Sure." She clicked the phone on speaker so that Miles could hear. "I'm listening, and so is Miles."

"Okay. I've got some bad news."

Darby glanced at Miles, whose face was grave. "What is it?" Darby asked.

"There is a formula here, for a highly toxic substance. This substance, if created in the lab, would be responsible for wide-ranging disease and death on a scale we can't even imagine."

Darby swallowed. Had her grandfather known of this formula? Worse still, had he tried to steal it? For what use?

She flicked her eyes to Miles. "What is it, Ed?"

"*Yersinia Pestis*, otherwise known as the Black Death."

"Bubonic plague?" Miles's voice was incredulous. "As in the disease that ravaged medieval Europe?"

"I'm afraid so." Ed Landis exhaled and continued. "The Japanese knew that the bacterium had three forms: bubonic, spread by fleas or other parasites; pneumonic, contracted by inhalation of the bacteria; and septicemic, caused by contact with a sick person's open sore or blood. I'm afraid that the scientists of Unit 731 succeeded in creating a fourth, synthetic form of this bacterium, one that would no doubt prove the deadliest of all."

Darby felt her skin grow clammy. She didn't want to know, but she had to ask. "What is it?"

"Waterborne," Ed Landis said, his voice grave. "They created a strain of the plague that would live in fresh water, contaminating aquifers, reservoirs, ponds, streams, and rivers."

"And now..." Darby's voice was small.

"And now that formula is in the hands of Kenji Miyazaki, and we don't know why."

"Do you think he plans to sell the formula?" Darby could hardly bear to ask the question.

"It's possible that he's in it for the money."

Another adrenalin rush, Darby thought, remembering the athlete's words.

Ed Landis sighed. "He's our top priority, Darby. If you hadn't contacted us, who knows what might have happened."

Darby felt a mix of emotions—fear, because of what the synthetic bacterium could do; anger, that she had been duped by Kenji and allowed him access to her home and the journal; and sorrow, because her grandfather had been a part of the whole evil mess.

It was Miles who asked the question she could not voice.

"Ed, why do you believe Darby's grandfather had the formula in his journal?"

Landis grunted. "Sorry—I thought I covered that in the beginning. From the translation of the journal, it's clear that Tokutaro Sugiyama abhorred what he saw happening. We believe he copied the formula before destroying it in the lab for one critical reason: in the event it was ever produced, he knew the formula could help create an antidote." He paused. "Hideki Kobayashi has suggested Miyazaki's motives may be the same."

Miles glanced at Darby. "And the translated journal?"

"We're sending a copy to Darby electronically. I'll warn you—it's pretty tough to read. The commander who ran that place was truly evil."

Darby pondered the journal and her grandfather's covert theft of the formula. She would read his words, maybe not right away, but eventually. "Thank you, Ed. I hope you catch Kenji soon."

"Don't worry." The FBI agent's voice held a touch of bravado which Darby prayed was well-founded. "We'll find this guy before he knows what hit him."

"Good." A cold breeze lashed her hair against her face. Darby Farr shuddered and clicked off her phone.

Bitsy cleaned up Rosie's kitchen floor "accident" in a kind of a fog. Detective Robichaud's words played again and again in her head, skipping like the vinyl records of her youth. *Denny Ross hated your husband, Mrs. Dupont. If I had known, I wouldn't have asked Charles to come…*

She remembered Denny and the whole Ross family—crazy Carlene who took to the sea as a teen, an older brother named Mitch who set someone's trailer on fire when he was just a kid. The fact that Denny had ended up a drug dealer was not a surprise. Only Lester, the youngest one in the family, had chosen a stable, normal way of life.

She sprayed ammonia on the linoleum, wiped it clean with paper towels, and carried the whole lot to the garage. Removing the lid from a plastic garbage can, she tossed the trash inside.

She was about to replace the cover when a piece of paper caught her eye. It was lined, ripped from one of the small steno pads Charles kept around the house. She peered at it, noticing a series of initials with scribbled notes next to them. It was Charles's writing. She recognized the loopy letters and the way he made long crosses on his "Ts." Her eyes filled up with tears.

She tugged the paper from the rest of the garbage and held it, crying softly, until she heard Rosie's whimper from the door.

"Everybody wants to see you," the guard said to the inmate. The prisoner was a lean man in an orange jumpsuit, and he sat on his bed reading a magazine. Hitching his thumb at Darby and Miles, the guard continued, "More visitors. Why is it you're suddenly hot, Marcus?"

Leonard Marcus lifted his eyes and slid his glance from the guard to Darby. He stroked a trim mustache with one hand. "To whom do I owe the pleasure?"

"I'm Darby Farr and this is Miles Porter. We're here to ask some questions about Chief Dupont's visit yesterday."

His face was shrewd. "I hear he's now dead. Doesn't bode well for you folks, I'm afraid." He chuckled softly. His gray hair was cut short and his lined face became pleasant and open. Darby could see why he'd be a successful con artist. Leonard Marcus looked warm and approachable, someone you would trust. *Like Kenji Miyazaki*, she thought.

She cleared her throat.

"Yes, Chief Dupont's gone." It was incredibly difficult to say those words, and Darby doubted it would ever get easier. "We're here to follow up on a conversation he had with you about Lorraine Delvecchio."

Marcus clenched his teeth. The movement was nearly imperceptible, but Darby spotted it nonetheless.

"What about it?" He rose from the bed and faced Darby and Miles.

"Was Lorraine blackmailing you?"

"Why is it you want to know?"

"Your name was in her ledger book, next to some sums," Miles explained. "Was she demanding money?"

He shrugged. "Perhaps." His face remained impassive, but his eyes were mocking.

"We have reason to believe Lorraine Delvecchio was murdered," Darby said evenly. "I'm sure Chief Dupont told you."

"He may have mentioned it."

"We're trying to determine who she was blackmailing. Maybe that will tell us who pushed her off that Breakwater."

Miles stared hard at Marcus. "What information did she have on you?"

Leonard Marcus gave a rueful laugh. "Not enough, it turns out." He shook his head. To Darby it seemed he was making a decision. Finally he flung down his magazine. "Oh, what the hell."

Darby held her breath, hoping Marcus was about to shed light on Lorraine Delvecchio's career as a blackmailer. *We need real confirmation that she committed a crime,* she thought. *That our suspicions are correct …*

"Lorraine worked for Dr. Hotchkiss," he began. "Back before all this happened, I saw her quite frequently—probably four times a month." He laced his fingers together, took a moment to think. "I managed the finances for several elderly island ladies, and they liked me to squire them around to their various appointments."

"How was Lorraine involved?"

"Somehow, she caught on to the fact that I was engaged in minor medical insurance fraud. You know, helping the ladies make claims on procedures they didn't actually have, depositing some of their checks in my account—that sort of thing." He cocked his head to the side. "I'm still not exactly sure how Lorraine figured it out. The old ladies certainly didn't have a clue. At any rate, she threatened to expose me, both to my clients and the police. I called her bluff because I didn't believe she had any proof." He looked at them with a frank stare. "Turns out she did have evidence, and quite a bit, too. Unbeknownst to me, I'd left a little paper trail that clever Lorraine had followed."

"What kind of proof?" Darby asked.

"Oh, copies of insurance claims from the women, that kind of thing. Suffice it to say that it was easier and cheaper for me to pay her off than to risk exposure with my clients. I didn't think the material would stand up in court, but one never knows." He cocked his head again. "Of course, it's never just one payment with a blackmailer. Before I knew it, she had me on a regular schedule. I was forced to accept her as another one of my expenses." He turned an expressionless face toward them, but Darby noted that his eyes were menacing and hard. "I thought of killing her once or twice. Hiring someone to stage a botched burglary or monkey with her car. But that's not my style. I'm not a murderer, although I've gotten to know one or two of them here." He rested his chin on his hand.

"Lorraine stopped collecting when the Feds indicted you?"

He nodded. "She realized that her threat of exposure was pointless when I was probably going to jail anyway." He looked back toward the cot. Suddenly, he whipped his head around, his expression dark, and slammed a fist against the bars. "The truth of it is, I've often asked myself if I'd have gone along with Kevin's scam if I hadn't been shelling out to Lorraine. She put me under a certain amount of pressure, you know?" Once more his features relaxed and his face became bland. "I'm glad she's dead, whether by accident or not. She was one devious little bitch."

Darby looked at Miles. At last they had proof of Lorraine's role as a conniving, manipulative crook. *Only her unfortunate victims saw her "Mr. Hyde" personality*, thought Darby.

She swallowed. "Were you aware that she was blackmailing other people?"

"Not really. She did make a comment once when I was late in sending her a payment. She said, 'Nobody else gets away with missing a deadline.' I asked her if she extorted money from everyone at the medical practice, and she actually laughed, said something like it had turned out to be a wise career move."

Miles raised his eyebrows at Darby, and then tilted his head toward the exit, non-verbally communicating that it was time to go.

"This has been helpful, Mr. Marcus." Darby met the prisoner's gaze. "Thank you for your candor."

Leonard Marcus shrugged. "Why not? Maybe helping catch Lorraine's murderer will carry some weight with the Feds." He turned toward his cot. "Really, when you think about it, what have I got to lose?"

Miles took Darby's elbow and steered her toward the exit. As they hurried down the dim corridor, they felt the cold eyes of the inmates boring into their backs.

The door of the Dupont home was unlocked, but Tina knocked loudly as she pushed it open so as not to startle anyone. The puppy, its tail wagging so much that its furry body quivered, greeted her with enthusiasm, and then quickly squatted on the floor.

"Rosie!" Bitsy, rounding the corner, gave an exasperated sigh and knelt down. "Tina, what am I doing wrong? This dog won't stop having accidents on the rugs." She produced a squirt bottle and paper towels and quickly cleaned up the urine. She rose to her feet. "I'm sorry—what a greeting." She spotted the large metal pot Tina was holding in her outstretched arms. "Whatever you have in there smells awfully good."

Tina smiled. "My famous chicken gumbo soup, Bitsy. Figured you could use something warm on the stove. I'll take it to the kitchen." She marched past Bitsy to the kitchen and plunked the pot down on an empty burner. "If you're not going to eat some soon, better put it in the fridge or freeze it," she called.

Bitsy entered the kitchen and threw away the soiled paper towels. She rinsed her hands at the sink. "Thanks. I think I'll have some right now, if you don't mind. I'm starving. Care to join me?"

Tina was about to decline when she surprised herself. "Yes, I'd love a little bit. Like a cupful, okay?" She eyed the small kitchen table. "Let's sit right here and have some."

Bitsy grabbed a bowl and small cup from the cabinet and a ladle from a drawer. She took the lid off the pot and scooped them each some of the fragrant soup.

"It smells delicious." Bitsy carried the bowl and cup to the table. "Want something to drink?"

"Nope. I'm all set. But spoons would be helpful." Tina pushed a piece of paper to the side. "What's this?" The paper was ripped from a small notebook and bore the same initials as in Lorraine's ledger, plus scribbled notes in a loopy handwriting.

Bitsy placed soup spoons at their places. "I found that in the garbage. Alana must have been cleaning up and tossed it away. I think it's something that Charles was working on, something to do with Lorraine Delvecchio?"

Tina gave Bitsy an appraising look. "Could be." She peered at the initials and the notes. Next to "BA" was written "Alcott," and then another word: Grace. Beside the initials "ML," Chief Dupont had written "Marcus," followed by "fraud." Beside "DT" he had reversed the letters and written "ab," along with a question mark. The rest of the letters—AB and RC—were reversed and had question marks.

"I wasn't sure what it was at first, but I figured you'd want to see it," Bitsy said in a small voice. "You and Darby."

Tina nodded. "Good work, Bitsy." She pursed her lips. "Any chance you found anything else in the actual notebook?"

Bitsy shook her head. "No."

Tina shrugged and spooned some of her soup into her mouth. The broth was rich and fragrant, with chunks of chicken, celery, pepper, and barley, and had been seasoned so that there was just a hint of heat. She glanced at Bitsy to see if she was eating. The blonde was attacking the soup as if she was famished. Tina smiled.

"You know, I do believe Donny's got a puppy training video at his house," she offered. "I could have him bring it over this afternoon if you'd like."

Bitsy looked up from her soup bowl, a bit of broth dribbling down her chin. "Oh, that would be super, Tina." She wiped her mouth with a napkin. "Can I ask another favor? I desperately need to get my hair cut. Charles's service is tomorrow, and I—"

"Say no more, I understand." Tina fished a little address book out of a voluminous red pocketbook and scrawled down a number. "Here you go. This is the woman who did my hair for the wedding." She patted her red curls.

"Your hair was beautiful for the wedding!" Bitsy gushed. "Thanks. I'll call her right away."

Tina rose from the table. She picked up her cup and took it to the kitchen sink. "I need to go, Bitsy, but maybe I can come back with Donny later on." She pointed at the paper on the table. "May I take that?"

"Sure." She handed the page to Tina. "That could be the last thing Charles wrote," she said sadly.

"I'll take good care of it."

Bitsy shrugged. "Doesn't matter. He probably ripped it out of the pad to show you guys." She gave a brave smile. "Thanks for the soup and the hairdresser."

Tina gave Bitsy a hug and headed for the door. The puppy, who was nowhere to be seen, was suspiciously quiet.

Miles carried a tray to the table and placed Darby's salad and half sandwich before her. "I got you a fizzy water. Will that do?"

"Perfect." Minutes before, the duo had driven off the ferry and realized that they were starving. Now, they were seated at the Hurricane Harbor Café, their lunches before them. A sign scrawled in the window announced that the restaurant would be closed the following day for Chief Charles Dupont's funeral.

Darby glanced down, her eyes taking in Miles's enormous submarine sandwich with pieces of lettuce, turkey, tomato, and sprouts sticking out the sides. "You're not hungry, are you, Miles?"

He grinned and picked up the long roll. "Nah—thought I'd have a little snack is all." He took a big bite and began chewing happily.

Darby uncapped her carbonated water and took a sip. "That jail was a depressing place."

"They aren't supposed to be walks in the park, love." Miles's voice was muffled by the thickness of the roll.

"True." She picked at her salad. "What makes somebody like him cheat people out of their life savings? Why does a quiet person like Lorraine Delvecchio threaten to spill someone's secrets if she doesn't get what she wants?"

Miles made a thoughtful face. "In Leonard Marcus's case, it's definitely greed, right? He sounds like he was an opportunistic thief who knew he could bilk those old ladies, and then thought he could scam all those investors."

"Right." She took a bite of her chicken salad on whole wheat and chewed thoughtfully. "What about Lorraine?"

"Greed must be playing a part with her, too. At least as far as Marcus was concerned."

"I get the feeling that Leonard Marcus thinks he is far superior to just about everyone. Maybe Lorraine felt that way, too. I mean, she had this unbelievable memory that nobody knew about. And yet I can't help but remember what I used to think of her—that she was mousy and..." she paused. "Weak." She turned her eyes up to meet Miles's. "Maybe that's why she did it, Miles. Everyone assumed she was meek and mild, yet here she was blackmailing at least five people. Perhaps the whole thing made her feel powerful."

"Like eating this enormous sandwich," Miles joked. "It's not actually even a sandwich, it's a beach-wich. I take that back. It's a whole coast-wich."

"Ugh." Darby groaned. She touched his arm lightly. "Despite your corny comments, I wish you didn't have to leave tomorrow."

"Me, too." He crinkled his nose. "I hate the thought of being without you."

She sighed. "Seems whenever we are together, it's never long enough." Her face brightened. "Your plane is late in the afternoon, right? So at least we can spend most of the day together."

"Yes. I'm wondering if we might catch our friend Bartholomew Anderson before I head for the airport. I'd like to question him about his involvement with Lorraine, too."

"Good idea. I'll call his paralegal and see if we can get an appointment." She pulled out her phone and looked at it, frowning. "Tina called. I missed it when we were at the prison." Cell phones had not been allowed and Darby had left hers at the main entrance. "I'm going to listen to her message."

Miles nodded and took another enormous bite.

A moment later, Darby was punching in Tina's number. "Miles, she has information on another one of Lorraine's victims." She bit her lip. "Tina?"

The redhead minced no words. "About time you called me back! You want to solve this mystery, or what?"

"Absolutely. Tell me what you found out."

"I'd rather show you," Tina said. "Are you and Miles in a compromising position?"

Darby felt her cheeks blush as she looked at Miles, contentedly chomping away on his sub. "No. We're at the Café, having a late lunch."

"Great. I'm at the office, working on Alcott Bridges's listing. Come on over." She clicked off and Darby put down her phone.

"Tina's got something she wants to show us," she explained. "Wrap up your coast-wich and let's go."

Miles grabbed a napkin and swaddled the sub. He helped Darby into her red coat and pulled on his own, then picked up the sub and his soda and followed her out the door.

Already the daylight was disappearing and the harbor looked cold and gray. The pair walked the short distance up the hill and around the corner to the Near & Farr office, but by the time they reached the door, they were both chilled.

"Let's take a warm tubby tonight," Miles suggested with a lewd grin.

Darby shushed him. "Quiet! Tina's already convinced all we do is fool around."

"Well ..." he opened the door. "Unless we're finding dead bodies or making prison visits, that's pretty accurate, right?"

Darby felt the warmth rise in her cheeks. "Tina! We came as fast as we could. What have you got?"

She pulled a piece of paper from a giant red pocketbook and placed it on a conference table. "Take a look. Chief Dupont was working out the initials. Somehow 'TD' and 'AB' are related. And he's got 'Grace' written next to Alcott." Tina paused. "Grace was Alcott Bridges's wife."

Darby and Miles exchanged glances. "She received care from the same hospice association that's getting the proceeds from the house," Darby mused.

"Uh-huh. And I called a friend of mine who volunteers for them, and she gave me somebody else's name. I called her and she told me that there'd been rumors years ago that Grace's death was hastened along a bit."

"Meaning?" Miles asked.

"Meaning Alcott may have poisoned her," said Tina triumphantly.

"A mercy killing," murmured Darby. "Let me guess: Was her primary care physician Dr. Hotchkiss?"

"You got it. I'm thinking that our quiet little Lorraine figured it out and made grieving Alcott pay so she'd keep quiet."

Darby recalled the old man's reaction when he'd heard of Lorraine Delvecchio's death. "No wonder the poor guy was relieved to hear she'd died."

"Right. I wonder if the whole reason he was going to list in the first place was to pay off Lorraine. He must have been living in such fear and guilt." Tina stomped a foot, making her red curls bob furiously.

"This is good work, Tina," Miles said. "Did Bitsy give you this paper?"

"Yes. She found it in the trash after the Chief's daughter was cleaning up. He never got a chance to tell us what he'd figured out."

Darby put a finger on the initials "TD" and the small "ab?" next to it. "You're thinking that the 'ab' refers to Alcott, right?"

Tina nodded her head, causing her red curls to jiggle. "Yep."

"Strange that they aren't capitalized like the rest," commented Miles, unwrapping his lunch and taking a bite. "Tina? Care for some sustenance?"

"No, thanks. I had some soup with Bitsy." She scrutinized the letters. "Well, what can they be if they aren't initials?"

"I don't know. Bitsy didn't have any ideas, did she?"

"No." Tina sighed and went to her computer to shut it down. "That poor woman. She's hurting, and then she's got this puppy making puddles all over the house. The Chief's kids have been great, but it can't be easy for any of them. I wonder what Bitsy will do when all this is over?"

"She probably doesn't know herself yet," offered Darby. She glanced at Miles. "Let's take a ride over there and visit. Do you think that's a good idea, Tina?"

Tina shook her head. "She's gone over to Manatuck to get her hair done, so she's all set for a while. I'm going to meet Donny when I finish this and we'll go up to see her." She paused. "Did you ever take a look at that thumb drive?"

Darby nodded. "A man and a woman, embracing, but only the woman's face is visible."

"Who is it?"

"I couldn't tell. You'll have to take a look."

"Okay." She frowned. "That's enough about all this. You two need to do something fun. Go out for dinner or something."

Darby thought about Miles's plan for a romantic bath. *That can always happen afterward . . .*

Miles took the last bite of his submarine sandwich, chewed it, and grinned. "Dinner? What a brilliant plan." He balled up his napkin and tossed it into a nearby wastebasket. "I'm absolutely starving."

Darby and Tina couldn't help but laugh.

Bitsy settled into one of the ferry's hard plastic seats and sighed. It had been nice to do some normal things in Manatuck—buy a few toys for the dog, flip through a magazine at the beauty salon—and not feel the crushing sadness of Charles's death, if only for a few moments. She fingered her hair, happy with the way the trim felt. The hairdresser had been tactful, allowing Bitsy to say as much or as little as she felt comfortable. She sighed again. It had been good to take a break from the island.

She closed her eyes. There was a dull throbbing behind her eyelids and she willed it to stop. Maybe if she got some coffee.

She rose and walked to the small snack bar. A heavyset woman waited for a coffee as well, a coarse wool hat on her head. She accepted her Styrofoam cup and turned toward Bitsy, her eyes ringed with dark circles.

"Hey Carlene," said the man who'd handed her the coffee. "Too bad about Denny."

Bitsy squinted at the woman's weather-beaten visage. Was this Carlene Ross?

A scowl filled the other woman's face. "What are you looking at?"

Bitsy paused. *What do I say now? Your brother was the one who killed Charles?* She felt anger well up inside her. *Because of your brother, my husband is dead…*

The woman's rough face puckered and she looked about to cry. Was she feeling the same anguish, having lost a sibling in the shootout?

Bitsy felt her anger cooling. "Sorry for your loss."

Carlene looked away and then back at Bitsy. It was obvious she had no idea who Bitsy was, but she gave a curt dunk of her head and pushed past her.

Bitsy reached out a hand for her own cup of coffee. The ferry employee met her eyes and gave a barely noticeable nod. His hand seemed to linger over hers, as if he were blessing the bestowing of the hot liquid.

She cradled the cup and returned to her plastic seat.

Two hours later, Donny and Tina sat in Bitsy's living room, watching a dog trainer discuss puppy behavior on Charles Dupont's enormous television.

"She makes it sound so simple," complained Bitsy, taking a forkful of macaroni and cheese. Rosie whimpered from her corduroy dog bed, in the middle of a canine bad dream.

"Well, it is simple. You're the one in charge, Bitsy. You're the alpha wolf." Tina sipped her wine and grinned. "Don't you feel like a wolf?"

"Not yet." She pushed away her dish. "I'm not sure what I feel like. I'm just hoping I can get through this service tomorrow without looking like an idiot." She sighed. "I want Charles's kids to be proud of me."

"Don't you worry, Bitsy," Donny said. "You'll do just fine."

"Who's in charge of the service, Bitsy?" Tina asked.

"The Manatuck Police Department. They have been so helpful. I never knew how much work Charles did with them." She asked in a soft voice, "Will you guys be there?"

"Of course, Bitsy. We'll both be there." Tina gave a pointed look in Donny's direction. "Would you like to come over with us? We can pick you up in the morning."

"No, I'm going with Alana and Derek." She gave a shy smile. "But thanks."

"Okay, well Donny and I are going to head off, let you get some sleep." Tina watched as Donny collected the dishes and took them into the kitchen.

"Thank you for the dinner, Tina. It was delicious."

"You're welcome. Get some rest, okay?" Tina gave the widow a quick hug while the dog trainer talked on about puppy socialization. "Oh! Almost forgot to tell you. Your hair looks fabulous."

Bitsy fingered her bristly hairstyle and nodded absently. "I think Charlie would have liked it," she said.

Miles and Darby lay opposite each other in the farmhouse's claw-foot tub, thinking their own thoughts and enjoying the steamy water. "Tell me again what Hideki Kobayashi said about the formula," said Miles thoughtfully, breaking the silence. The elderly Japanese man had sent Darby an e-mail just before they'd begun running the water.

"He thinks that Kenji may have 'appropriated' the formula for its positive applications."

"Appropriated, rather than stolen, eh? Did he say what those positive applications might be?"

"No, but he reminded me that many dangerous chemicals are now used in ways that turn out to be good. Take the *botulinum* toxin A, for example. It's one of the neurotoxins produced by *Clostridium botulinum*, commonly known as botulism, and yet now it's injected into people's foreheads to prevent wrinkles."

"Not mine, thank you very much! Still, there's a lot of money to be made with some of these accidental applications. Could that be why Kenji took the formula?"

"I'd rather believe it's because of good old-fashioned greed than because Kenji wants to cause mass extinction." She sank deeper until the water came up to her chin. "I wish Ed Landis would call and say he caught the guy."

"He will." Suddenly he splashed her playfully. "In the meantime, what's next?"

"We towel off, we have a drink before the fire ..."

"Oooh, I like where this is going, but that's not what I meant." His face grew more serious. "What's next with our relationship? Seems I'm always jetting in to visit you wherever you are. Then you pick my brain and ravage my body for a few days, and it's cheerio."

"Hey, the ravaging really just started," she said.

"True. I would have liked the ravaging to have begun months ago, but I do stand corrected." He rubbed her shin with his hand absentmindedly. "Tell me where we stand, Darby."

She thought a moment before answering, because it was an important question and she did not want to blurt something out.

"I know where I stand, Miles." She swallowed and looked into his rugged face. "I love you."

He gave a slow grin. "Funny you should say that, because I love you, too. In fact, I'd kiss you right now Darby Farr, but you're way at the other end of the tub." He lifted up her foot, carefully smoothed away the bubbles, and planted a kiss on her big toe. "There. That will have to do for now."

She smiled as he placed her foot back in the warm water. "Maybe I should make the next trip to see you. Fair is fair, right?"

"Fairness! Now that's a novel concept." His eyes twinkled like the bubbles dancing on the top of the water. "We don't have to figure it all out tonight, or tomorrow, or the day after that. Things will happen in their own good time. Besides, I know you, and I know you don't like to be rushed in these matters."

She bit her lip. He was right—she'd been skittish about commitment, so afraid to accept Miles's love that she'd very nearly lost him. "What do you say we get our robes and move to the fire?"

He sat up slowly, giving her a long, level look that was full of desire. "Sure. Put on your robe, but I promise you won't be wearing it for long."

He eased himself to a standing position and climbed out of the bathtub, water streaming from his muscular thighs and broad back. Darby felt a pleasant stirring. She stayed in the tub for a moment more, enjoying the view.

THIRTEEN

THE NEXT MORNING DAWNED clear and cold. Darby and Miles joined the contingent of islanders boarding ferries bound for Manatuck and the funeral of fallen Police Chief Charles Dupont. The passengers were silent, huddled in their winter coats and hats, with only the shrieking of the gulls overhead to break the unnatural quiet. Miles clutched Darby's gloved hand, squeezing gently as she fought to stay composed.

In the Manatuck ferry terminal's parking lot, garishly yellow school busses waited with engines idling, ready to bring mourners to St. Catherine's for the service. Darby and Miles climbed onto a bus, catching the eye of the Café's new owner as they crowded onto a seat. He acknowledged them sadly and looked away.

Inside the church's hushed sanctuary, row upon row of uniformed police officers stood at attention, ready to pay their respects to a fellow officer, whether they had known Charles Dupont or not. The resonant strains of a bagpipe played as the pews filled and then overflowed with those waiting to say a final goodbye to Hurricane Harbor's Chief of Police.

Bitsy, flanked by Charles's grown children, sat in the front row. She seemed very small in a basic black dress with long sleeves, her blonde hair more subdued than usual, a grim expression on her face. Every few minutes she dabbed a white tissue at her eyes, and cried openly at the tributes from Charles's colleagues, especially the poignant words of Deputy Tom Allen.

"The Chief was a like a father to me," the gangly man said, looking down at the Dupont children and Bitsy. "No words can tell you how very much I will miss him."

When the echoes of the twenty-one gun salute died away, refreshments were served in the church's parish hall. Darby and Miles mingled with the other mourners, paying their respects to Alana and Derek, and giving Bitsy big hugs.

"She looks numb," Darby whispered to Miles.

"I suppose she is," he said. "But the healing has begun. I think she will be okay." He looked into her almond-shaped eyes. "What about you? I know this death has hit you especially hard."

Darby thought back to her conversations with Chief Dupont and his memories of her mother, Jada Farr. *That's what I'll miss the most.* He'd been a bond to her family. And now that link was gone.

"I'll heal as well," she said softly. "I guess we all will."

Tina and Donny approached, their arms linked. Tina's eyes were rimmed with red and she sniffled and bit back tears.

Darby put a hand on the redhead's shoulder and the two exchanged looks.

"Makes you realize how fragile life is," Tina said, her voice breaking. "One day you're here, and the next—gone."

Darby, Miles, and Donny nodded. They were silent as Tina sobbed quietly, her thin shoulders moving under Donny's draped arm. Suddenly she stopped. "What the—"

A streak of golden fur raced by them, headed for one of the tables laden with luncheon meats.

"Rosie!" Bitsy's wail pierced the mourners' quiet murmurs. "Rosie, come!"

Darby held her breath as the puppy stopped short and turned in the direction of Bitsy, who stood in the middle of the room with her hands on her hips. "Come!"

The dog wagged her tail and trotted to Bitsy.

"Sit!"

Rosie acquiesced. The crowd watched as Bitsy reached down and grasped the puppy's collar. "Good dog," she cooed, stroking its head.

Spontaneous clapping broke out as Donny rushed to help Bitsy take Rosie to another room. Bitsy blushed and gave a tiny smile. "She was Charles's idea," she said, to general laughter. "I just couldn't leave her at home." She bit her lip and wiped her eyes. "I bet he's up there right now, chuckling away."

Darby looked at Tina. "I can picture that so clearly, can't you? Chief Dupont would have found this funny."

Tina agreed. "That man had a wonderful sense of humor." She glanced toward Donny and the puppy and shook her head. "Why the heck would anyone bring a dog to a funeral? Oh, well, I suppose anything goes nowadays."

The mood of the room underwent a subtle change, thanks to Rosie's intervention. Mourners were now telling stories about Charles Dupont in a lighthearted, almost celebratory, manner.

Tina pulled her friend close. "I do think it's gonna be okay."

Darby nodded. Miles was right—the healing had begun.

Deputy Tom Allen wasn't sure what to say when people praised him for the words he'd uttered about Chief Dupont. He'd said what was on his mind, that was all, and it felt strange to accept thanks for that. He picked up a soft finger roll, ripped it in half, and took a bite. Perhaps if he were eating, he could just wag his head and that would be enough. He wouldn't have to talk anymore.

The words of Detective Dave Robichaud had been especially hard to hear. "I know what you meant," he'd said, "about the Chief being your family. It was the same for me when I was your age." Dave Robichaud had paused, looked him straight in the eye. "Growing up, I was always the one watching out for everyone. When I joined the force, someone finally cared about me." He'd scanned the room; put a hand on his shoulder and squeezed. "The rest of us are here for you, Dozer."

Deputy Allen had wanted to cringe at the use of his old nickname, but instead he'd thanked the detective and watched him lope away. Now, as he chewed on the roll and thought about Charles Dupont, he sent a silent prayer heavenward.

Rest in peace, Chief. Rest in peace.

Darby felt a tapping on her shoulder as she was pulling on her red coat. She turned, coming inches from the concerned face of Alison Dyer.

"I was hoping to speak with you before you left, Darby." The older woman glanced toward Miles and lowered her voice. "Any luck on finding the person who killed that poor girl?"

"No. The only official who seems to have thought she was murdered was Chief Dupont, and now that he's dead . . ." Darby paused. "I haven't found anyone who saw anything, and there is no physical evidence. Perhaps it was an accident after all."

The woman's lined face grew dark. "No, Darby. It could not have been an accident! That woman knew what she was doing on that Breakwater. She didn't fall into that water. I saw the person who pushed her, I know I did." She scanned the crowd of mourners, just beginning to dissipate. "Chief Dupont knew it, too."

Darby looked down at her hands. The words of Charles Dupont came back to her in a rush: *I knew that woman and I know there is no chance in hell that she slipped. We are talking about someone who did this every stinking day, in weather way worse than this. She wore the right kind of clothes for this kind of thing, heavy boots with good soles. She didn't slip, Darby. I know that.*

She glanced up. "I'll keep looking," she said simply.

Alison Dyer closed her eyes and nodded. "I know you will," she said. She peered at Darby through her round glasses. "I just know it."

Darby watched as Alison hustled away and out of the church.

"What was that all about?" Miles asked, pulling on his coat. He frowned in the direction of the retreating figure.

Darby explained. "She's right, Miles. I owe it to Chief Dupont to figure this thing out."

"Maybe Bartholomew Anderson will give us the answers we need," Miles said. "Maybe he's our guilty guy."

Darby zipped up her red coat, her face beautiful yet determined. "If he attended the service, he's already left. Let's go find out."

A pink sunburn made Bartholomew Anderson's nose and cheeks look as tender as raw beef. Darby watched him register fleeting disappointment as they entered his office, and then quickly cover it with a superficial grin.

"You're still here," he commented, shaking their hands. "I would have thought you'd have left this Maine weather for the West Coast by now." His joviality was so forced that Darby wanted to laugh. Instead she raised an eyebrow.

"Speaking of weather, I take it the sun was shining in Miami?"

"Oh, yes. Lovely little getaway, but never long enough." He put his fingers together in the shape of a tent. "Now, what can I do for you?"

"I want to thank you for your confidence in Near & Farr Realty," Darby began. "I know Tina Ames will do a great job selling Alcott Bridges's property."

"Yes, yes, I'm sure of that." The portly attorney pursed his lips. "Surely you didn't come here to tell me that?"

Miles glanced at Darby.

"We're here about Lorraine Delvecchio."

"Ah, yes, the girl who fell off the Breakwater. I told you, I didn't know her ..."

"She knew you, Mr. Anderson. Well enough to blackmail you."

"What are you talking about?" He stood up and ran a hand over his thinning hair. "Blackmail? Don't be ridiculous."

"Your name was found on a ledger in Lorraine's home," said Miles calmly. "She knew something about you, didn't she?"

"That's ludicrous! You don't have any proof."

"In fact, we do," Darby said. "We have evidence that you were making payments to her ..."

"Impossible! I only paid her in cash ..." he stopped, put a hand to his sunburned nose, and looked stunned. "I mean ..."

"Why was she blackmailing you?" Darby's voice was insistent.

He raised his head, his face forlorn. "She took advantage of a stupid mistake."

Miles glanced at Darby. This was what they'd been hoping for.

"She had photos," Bartholomew Anderson said, his voice weary. "Of me and another woman. I don't know how she got them, but she threatened to take them to my wife."

"Unless you paid up," Miles offered.

The attorney gave a resigned nod. He opened a file drawer and pulled out a folder, tossing it to Darby. "It doesn't matter who it was, or that it was five years ago. Dolores would have been crushed."

She opened the folder. Inside were several glossy full page prints of a man and woman embracing, the same images Darby had seen on the drive. She placed the photos back in the folder.

"How did you get these?"

"From Lorraine's house. As soon as I heard she was dead, I went over there and searched for them." He looked up. "They weren't even hard to find. Right in her desk, as if they were a file of recipes." His face darkened. "You can't imagine how difficult it was for me to see that woman every single day prancing down that pier."

He pointed out the window with a shaking hand. “I had to watch her park her car and give that smug little smile…”

He turned to face them. “I hated her, of course I did. In case you’re wondering.”

“Why didn’t you just tell your wife?” Darby asked. “These photos would have had no power if she’d known.”

“Have you ever been married, Darby?” He glanced from her to Miles. “You think things like affairs are easy in a marriage?” He shook his head. “I couldn’t tell Dolores. It would have destroyed us—our family, my career…” he gave a harsh sigh. “I have a reputation in this city. These stupid photos would have ruined me.”

“But your face isn’t even recognizable.” Darby pointed at one of the images.

“It doesn’t have to be,” Bartholomew Anderson said darkly. “They would still have shattered my life.”

There was a pause before Miles spoke again, his voice clear and firm.

“Where were you on the day Lorraine died?”

“What? You can’t think I did anything to harm her!” His face showed shock. “She fell off that Breakwater, everyone knows that.”

Darby gave the attorney a piercing gaze. “Someone pushed Lorraine Delvecchio,” she said quietly. “Another figure was seen on the Breakwater. Was it you?”

“No! You’ve got to believe me. I’m not that kind of person.”

“Then where were you?”

Darby tensed as Bartholomew Anderson opened a desk drawer and pulled something out. She pictured a heavy revolver…

He lifted an appointment book. “Wednesday? Why, I was here, at my desk, working.” He squinted. “Billed some clients by the name of Wilson, if you must know." He closed the book with a thump, looking pleased. "There!"

"Can anyone corroborate your whereabouts?" Miles queried.

"My secretary, of course. She's here when I'm here, naturally."

Darby glanced at Miles. "Does she take a lunch break?"

"Of course. But I don't see why that matters."

"If she left at noon, she wasn't here when Lorraine was killed. You could have seen Lorraine coming and met her at the end of the pier."

"Are you saying that I ran out there and pushed her off? Excuse me, but I'm not exactly an Olympic athlete." He rose to his feet as if displaying his generously proportioned physique. "Look, I did not kill that girl. I don't think anyone did. I think she simply fell off the end of the Breakwater and drowned." He fingered the file with the photographs. "And do you know what else I think? I think she got exactly what she deserved."

"One more question," Darby said. "Who is the woman in the photographs?"

The look he gave her was resigned, all the bluster seemingly gone. "Someone I met many summers ago," he said softly. He licked his lips. "Babette Applebaum."

Darby and Miles shared a quick glance. "Was Lorraine blackmailing her as well?"

The attorney shook his head. "No. That's the one part of this whole sordid mess that doesn't cause me shame. For some reason, Lorraine left her alone."

Miles and Darby rose from their chairs, leaving the lawyer staring out the window at the Manatuck Breakwater lot.

"So?" Miles asked Darby as they waited for her ferry. "Do you think he pushed that girl?"

She shook her head. "No, I don't. I think he hated Lorraine with a passion, but I just don't see him running a mile out there, shoving her, and running back. Physically I don't think he could have done it. What about you?"

"I agree." He sighed. "If Lorraine didn't know Babette, it's unlikely she had anything to do with her murder. That leaves 'TD' and 'CR,' right?"

Darby nodded. She glanced in the direction of the water and saw that the ferry was chugging into view. "You know what, Miles? It's not easy to care about Lorraine Delvecchio's killer. The woman was vile."

"Even vile people deserve justice, don't they? Besides, you aren't doing it for her. You're doing it because Chief Dupont asked for your help."

"Correct." She reached for Miles and gave him a fierce hug. "Remind me of that when you call, okay? I'm liable to lose sight of my motives here without you."

"You won't lose sight of anything," Miles assured her. "Just promise me one thing: you'll keep yourself safe."

"I will." She kissed him, long and hard, inhaling the bayberry scent she loved.

He grinned.

"You've got the next visit, remember?"

"I'm already looking forward to it." She grabbed her pocketbook and turned to board the ferry. Overhead a gull shrieked in the cold sky. "I love you."

He grinned again, his rugged face becoming boyish. "Ditto," he said.

Darby watched as Miles steered his rental car out of the ferry parking lot. Already she missed the tall Brit's comforting presence, but she pushed aside her thoughts to focus on what she knew about Lorraine Delvecchio's death.

She was a blackmailer of at least five people. Three of them—Alcott Bridges, Leonard Marcus, and Bartholomew Anderson—had been eliminated as suspects. Darby thought about the two other victims. What connections could she make with Lorraine and the initials? Was there anyone who might have had an inkling about the woman's acquaintances?

Two of her employers—Dr. Hotchkiss and Chief Dupont—were now deceased, but presumably whoever she worked for at the Manatuck Police Department was still there. She popped up from her seat. "I've changed my mind," she explained to the dockhand. "I'm getting off."

He shrugged. "Suit yourself. Couple of minutes later and you would have been swimming."

Darby hustled off the ferry and made her way through the snowy parking lot. Ahead of her loomed Manatuck Community Hospital where her Aunt Jane Farr had been a patient. Darby thrust her hands deep in her pockets and kept walking. The police station was only a few blocks away.

The imposing brick building was modern, with large glass windows and a sophisticated video surveillance system at the revolving front door. In a nod to the past, there was a large granite block with an engraved dedication thanking Manatuck's veterans of past wars. Darby glanced at it and hurried in.

The building was open, but largely deserted, in deference to the memory of Charles Dupont. A peek at a directory indicated the offices for several departments, including homicide. Darby noted Detective Robichaud's name. *Perhaps this is where I should start,* she thought.

The tall man looked up as she knocked on his open door.

"Darby? Come on in." He pushed a pile of papers to the floor. "Beautiful service for Chief Dupont, wasn't it?"

"I think his family was very touched."

"Good." He sighed. "It's tough on all of us. He'll be missed on the island and in Manatuck, too." He shook his head. "I figured that my place was here, let some of the younger officers take the afternoon off. What's up?"

"I'm sorry to just barge in like this, but I wanted to talk about Lorraine Delvecchio's death, and I wasn't sure who's handling the investigation."

"Darby," he said gently. "There is no investigation. That poor woman slipped to her death."

"I think you know that Chief Dupont did not believe it was accidental."

"Yeah, Charles and I discussed it a few times. She had this superior memory condition that he felt might have made her some enemies."

"That's right. In fact, at least five people had motives to kill her."

"Really?" He raised his eyebrows in surprise. "What are you talking about?"

"A ledger in her home showed that Lorraine was blackmailing five people. We've identified three of them: Alcott Bridges, Leonard Marcus, and Bartholomew Anderson."

"No way. I can see Marcus, but Bridges and Attorney Anderson?"

Darby nodded. "Bridges couldn't have killed her. He was too frail, and I don't think Anderson has the physical stamina, either. The other two ..." she hesitated.

"Yes? Who are they?"

"I'm not sure. One's initials are 'TD', and the other is 'CR'."

"Initials? Their full names weren't mentioned?"

"That's right." She paused, hoping her explanation did not sound silly. "She referred to all of her blackmailing victims by initials."

"I see." He thought a few moments. "This is the first time I've heard about a ledger. I assume it's with Chief Dupont's things?"

"No," Darby said. "I have it."

He frowned. "To think that she was blackmailing people, right under our noses ..."

"Do you think this means she might have been murdered?"

"I have to say, no, it doesn't change my opinion of how she died. Did some people have motives to kill her? Apparently so. No one who gets blackmailed is happy about it, I'll tell you that. Did they kill her? No, because this was not a homicide. She lost her footing, hit her head, and drowned, with hypothermia as a contributing factor. No one pushed her, Darby. She slipped and died, end of story. Her death was ruled accidental. Charles Dupont didn't want to accept it, but it's the truth."

She remained silent.

"Listen," his voice was gentle. "I think Chief Dupont felt a little guilty…"

"Guilty? Why?"

"Because of how he terminated Lorraine."

"You mean he fired her?"

"Basically, yes. He lined her up with this job, but I know the Chief was worried that she knew the real reason."

"But he was satisfied with her work, at least that's what he always said."

Detective Robichaud gave a tiny smile. "There was another reason, Darby. She made a pass at him."

"Lorraine?"

"Yeah. When he lost all that weight, she came on to him, and it freaked him out. He told her she needed to transfer."

Darby shook her head. Had guilt over Lorraine's change of jobs been at the root of Chief Dupont's insistence that Lorraine had been murdered? She swallowed. Why hadn't he mentioned the real reason she'd transferred?

"I don't know what to say. Chief Dupont was convinced her death was no accident."

Dave Robichaud tapped a finger on a file. "I know. Sometimes we all pursue wild goose chases." He stood up. "Tell you what, I'm going to follow up on this blackmailing angle anyway. I'll want to see that ledger, too. Any idea who 'TD' and 'CR' might be?"

"No." She rose to her feet, her head spinning with the new information. "Thanks for listening, Detective Robichaud. I'm sorry if I wasted your time."

"Please don't feel like that," he said, walking her to the door. "Charles was your friend. I hope he knew how lucky he was."

"You need to get some exercise," Tina said, when Darby called her from the Hurricane Harbor dock and relayed her conversation with the detective. "You're starting to sound overwhelmed, and I'm worried about you. When was the last time you went for a run, or even a walk for that matter?"

Tina had a point. Back in Mission Beach, Darby was a devoted runner, logging several miles a day. But in the frozen landscape that was Hurricane Harbor in February, she had barely moved a muscle.

"I danced at your wedding." She didn't mention her other forms of exercise with Miles.

Tina snorted. "Whoop-de-do. Give that girl a medal." She paused. "Seriously—there's about two hours left of daylight. How 'bout you borrow my snowshoes and go for a little hike? Good way to get rid of stress, and God knows we've all had enough of that."

Darby considered. The sun was still warm on her cheeks, even though the air was freezing. Perhaps some time outdoors would clear the thoughts rattling through her brain. The Chief, Lorraine Delvecchio, Miles's departure … it was all too much at once.

"Good idea. Where do I find them?"

"They're just inside the front door," Tina said. "Key's under the mat. You can go right up that hill behind the house, if you want. Donny hikes up there all the time. Says it keeps him limber."

"Juniper Ridge?"

"Nah, the easy one in front of it . . . Raven Hill."

Darby pictured the broad mound behind Tina's split-level ranch. "My parents and I used to picnic up there. Should I take Rosie, give Bitsy a little break?"

"Nope. I've got her with me here at Donny's house, and she's out like a light. Played fetch with a tennis ball for about an hour at lunchtime." Tina sighed. "Hey, Terri's coming over for dinner later on, Bitsy too, hopefully. Donny's going to be at The Eye for a dart tournament, so it's just us girls. Want to come? You can thaw out from your snowshoe with a glass of wine."

"Sure. I'll bring some."

"Great. Have a good walk and I'll see you around six."

Darby drove to Tina's little ranch. The house was modest, but Tina had taken good care of it, and it would make the young family purchasing the property at the end of the month a nice home. She found the key, unlocked the door, and grabbed the snowshoes. Right away she saw that her long red coat was too bulky to move comfortably in. She took it off and found a lighter jacket in a powder blue shade in her friend's neat closet.

Darby zipped the jacket and pulled her wool hat over her ears. She locked the door, hid the key, and stepped into the snowshoes. After adjusting them to fit her feet, she began trudging across the lawn to the back yard.

The sun was still bright off the white expanse of snow and Darby wished she'd remembered her sunglasses. She walked with an easy gait, the snowshoes plunking softly in the snow, her arms swinging loosely at her sides. There was only a faint trail to follow, but Darby wasn't concerned. It was impossible to get lost on Raven Hill.

The climb was gentle. When Darby reached the top fifteen minutes later, she stopped and considered Juniper Ridge. A craggy series of peaks with sheer granite faces, the Ridge was an extremely challenging climb in the summer. Now, however, those same smooth surfaces were coated with several feet of snow, changing the landscape so drastically that Darby decided to give it a try.

She began the ascent. Right away it was evident that this climb would get her heart pumping. She smiled, feeling the burn in her thighs. Shoeing up the rugged face of Juniper Ridge—or however far she made it—would be an accomplishment.

The snow was the perfect consistency under her feet—firm, but yielding, cold enough that it did not clump on her snowshoes nor so powdery that it flew into her face. She let out a long sigh of pleasure as she took a big step and hoisted herself up a snow-covered rock. It felt good to be exercising in the cold, so different from her early morning runs in Mission Beach, California, where it was almost always a sunny seventy degrees or so.

The sun was dropping lower in the sky and Darby stopped and glanced at her watch. Nearly four p.m. Darkness was coming later to Maine—finally—as winter's grip on the northeastern state lessened. *I've got about an hour before it starts getting dark*, she reasoned, wondering if she should turn back toward Tina's house now.

She allowed herself a few minutes of stillness to admire the view. The ocean was just visible, a thin ribbon of blue stretching over the tops of the scrub pines. Up ahead there was a considerable climb to a spot where the view would be spectacular. *I'll go up, take a look, and then hustle down. It will be totally worth it.*

The ascent up the knobby face took ten minutes, but Darby had been correct about the vista. The ocean, a cold, dark blue dotted with whitecaps, surrounded the rocky island's perimeter of spruces. It was breathtaking, and Darby said a silent prayer for the majesty that surrounded her.

She took a deep breath and smelled the pine-scented air. This was what she missed most about living in San Diego, this easy access to unpopulated nature. In California there were plenty of trails, but they were always dotted with people. She missed Maine's wildness, the many miles of untamed spaces that were the norm, not the exception. She longed for rolling hills without fancy ranch homes scarring the land, or cell phone towers, or billboards. *I miss Maine,* she realized. *I miss home.*

Darby gave a quick shiver. Her body was cooling down, and the light blue jacket felt thin and insubstantial against the lowering temperatures. It was time to get moving before she got a serious chill. She took one more look at the ocean, and then turned to glance down at her path up the hill.

A shape was moving toward her. A man.

He was moving quickly, running at a fast clip, closing the gap of maybe one hundred yards with rapid speed. He wore a bulky dark jacket, dark pants, and something black on his face.

Darby's breath caught in her throat. *A ski mask.*

She let out a cry of alarm and then turned immediately up the hill. Without a moment's hesitation she began stepping as quickly as she could up the face, thinking nothing except that she had to escape. Her breath came out in jagged little puffs, and her lungs burned with exertion, but still she pushed herself higher, higher, faster and faster, in an effort to flee the masked man. *Who is he? Why is he after me?* Her brain asked the questions, and her body gave only one answer: run.

FOURTEEN

Bitsy hung up the phone and felt the first smile in days tugging at the corners of her mouth. She'd just received a dinner invitation from Tina Ames, and it was exactly what she felt like doing—relaxing with a few women over wine and a casserole. Tears welled up in her eyes. Tina, her high school boyfriend's new wife, had become a friend. Who would have thought it possible?

She walked across the kitchen and pulled open the refrigerator. There was a new container of smoked mussels, a few olives, and a good wedge of Brie. She'd put it all on a platter, add some crackers, and voila! An appetizer for Tina's party, along with a big bottle of wine, of course.

She closed the refrigerator door. The house was silent, and she recognized with a pang that she missed Rosie. The rambunctious puppy was not only a welcome distraction, but she was good company. Bitsy sighed. It was pretty pathetic when you started thinking of a young yellow retriever as your companion, she thought.

She wondered who else would be at Tina's little party. Terri, Tina's sister from up the coast in Westerly, and definitely Darby. *Maybe I can get a ride with Darby.* She trotted to the phone and punched in her number.

The phone rang and rang, and Bitsy was about to hang up when Darby's message came on. "Give me a call about carpooling to Tina's," Bitsy said, adding a "thanks," just before she hung up.

There was about forty-five minutes before it was time to go to Tina's. Bitsy hated empty time, because it made her think of Charles. If Rosie were here, she'd kill some time by playing with her, giving her a treat, or cleaning up whatever mess the dog managed to make.

She glanced at her reflection in the hall mirror. Dark circles under her eyes, no makeup, and hair that looked decidedly dirty. She ran a finger through the spiky hairdo. Charles had liked it. He'd said it was cute…

He would have loved me when I was bald, too, she thought. *When I was getting all those treatments at the Nevada Cancer Center…*

Sadness washed through her. Before it could carry her away completely, Bitsy took a deep breath and climbed the stairs to the master bathroom, turning on the water for a long, hot shower.

Darby didn't dare glance backward to see the man's position. Instead, she crested the top of Juniper Ridge and began running across the narrow edge. She heard a scraping sound and panicked, but it was only the teeth of Tina's snowshoes grating against bare rock.

A large boulder loomed before her. Should she descend the ridge in the other direction? She whipped her head back the way she had come. There was no one there.

Her heart pounding, Darby looked wildly around the ridge. It was empty and silent, the only sound the drone of a faraway plane. She swung her head to the side and caught a fist as it jammed into her face.

"Where is the box?"

Kenji Miyazaki stood before her, the mask removed to reveal his once handsome features, now contorted into an ugly sneer. Steam rose from his matted black hair, and his eyes flashed in a cold fury. "Answer me! Where is the box?"

Darby put a hand to her cheek where his punch had connected. She pointed at the ski mask. "You killed Lorraine Delvecchio?"

"I don't know what you're talking about. I want the box."

"The box?" Her voice sounded dazed. *Get a grip,* she told herself. *Remember your training...*

He raised an arm to hit her again, this time from the other direction, but she swiftly blocked the move.

His face remained impassive. If he was impressed, he wasn't about to show it. "The red lacquered box!" he hissed.

"It's at my house..."

"*It's at my house,*" he jeered. "Don't you think that's the first place I looked? Where the hell is it in your house?"

Darby moved her jaw. It was sore, but still working. "Why do you need it? You got the formula."

His black eyes bored into hers. "I ask you again, Darby Farr. Where is the box?"

An image of her grandfather flashed before her eyes. Had he imagined this very scenario?

Suddenly she knew.

"Something is missing," Darby said calmly. "A part of the formula. And you think it's in the box?"

His eyes narrowed. "You listen to me. You're going to take me back there and get me the damn box." He gave her a rough shove and she stumbled, nearly falling into the snow. "Get moving!"

Darby took a step down the embankment. His volatility was dangerous. He was a thief and a spy at the very least, and there was no way she could trust that he'd simply take the box and go.

She bolted down the ridge.

Kenji Miyazaki shouted an obscenity. Darby heard him grunting as he pounded in his snowshoes behind her. An instant later he'd grabbed her arm and yanked it back, hard, so viciously that she felt it disconnect from her shoulder socket.

"You think you can outrun me?" He spat out the question. "I'm a world-class athlete, and you're a little skinny nothing. I'm fitter and smarter, and the sooner you accept that, the easier this will be."

"What are you going to do with the formula?" She was panting, hard, and trying to figure out her next move.

He gave an arrogant snicker. "That's the least of your worries. Now, this is what we're going to do…"

A popping sound made Darby look up to where Kenji was standing, or at least where he had been standing just a moment earlier. For some reason, he was no longer there.

She glanced down. Kenji Miyazaki was face up against the white hillside, his arms extended as if he were making a snow angel, a crimson liquid pouring from his neck and staining the ground blood red.

Darby gasped. It took only two seconds for her to comprehend that Kenji was dead and that the popping sound had been a gunshot. She pulled her eyes from the widening crimson pool toward the direction from which she guessed the shot had come.

Detective Dave Robichaud was sprinting toward her. "Darby, are you okay?" he yelled.

She thought a moment. Her feet seemed stuck in the snow, her body was becoming dangerously chilled, and her left arm hung slackly from her shoulder. One side of her face was numb thanks to Kenji's fist, but she was alive.

He was suddenly before her, panting, the gun in his right hand now pointed down toward the snow. "You okay?" he repeated.

She moved her head slowly.

He glanced at the body and back at Darby. "Looks like your shoulder is dislocated," he said. "Can you walk?"

"Yes," she managed, not moving at all.

"Here," he reached gently for her uninjured arm and led her away from Kenji. "You don't have to worry about him anymore."

"How did you find us?" Her tongue felt thick in her mouth. "How did you know?"

"The FBI called and said he was headed this way. Tina told me you were here."

He scanned the snow in front and behind them. Their slow trudging had brought them to the spot where Darby had stood and admired the view only minutes before Kenji had appeared.

"Did you come up here alone?" Dave Robichaud asked.

"Yes." She shook her head, feeling as if she were in a dream. "He must have followed my tracks."

Detective Robichaud nodded. "What about your phone? Did you make any calls?"

"No." She reached in the jacket's pocket, the one she could access with her uninjured arm. "It's not here. I must have dropped it."

"That's okay. You won't need it."

Darby's heart made a quick constriction. *Won't need it?* What an odd thing to say…

Suddenly all of her faculties were back, sharp and clear. She was a deer in the forest, the fraction after a twig snaps. *I'm in danger.*

Her mind ran through the options while her face stayed expressionless and her feet trudged on. Out run, out maneuver, out smart? In a flash, she had made her decision.

Darby wheeled on Detective Robichaud, going for his gun, using an Aikido disarming technique she'd learned in the martial arts academy back in San Diego. Her eyes on his, she brought both of her hands down hard on the wrist holding the gun, ignoring the shooting pain from her shoulder. Driving it in a swift counterclockwise move, she grasped the handle of the gun and trained it toward his heart.

"What the hell are you doing?" His voice was surprised. Then it hardened.

"Give me my weapon." He spread his hands palms out in the characteristic gesture of submission. "Come on, Darby, this isn't funny. I know you're scared from your encounter with the Japanese guy, but you need to give me the gun. Now." He took a step toward her.

"Don't come any closer or I'll shoot." Her voice was strong and clear.

His eyes became two narrow slits. "What are you talking about? Why in the world would you want to harm a police officer?"

Darby saw the anger in his face. This man was dangerous, she knew it with every pore of her body, and yet she did not quite know why. "Tell me about Lorraine Delvecchio."

"What? Oh, come on, Darby. She fell off that pier. What more is there to say?"

"She was blackmailing at least five people."

"Yeah, well, she wasn't blackmailing me. Why in the world would I kill her?" He brought his hand up to his face and Darby started.

"Don't move—"

Detective Robichaud's leg contracted and then thrust out in a forward kick, knocking the gun from Darby's grasp. Another kick dealt a resounding blow to her injured shoulder, sending her collapsing to the ground in pain.

"Hopefully it's broken," he spat, keeping a wary eye on her as he bent to grab his gun. "What in the world did you think you were doing?"

Darby's whole left side screamed in pain.

"Get up!" he ordered, kicking her ribs with the toe of a winter boot. "Get the hell up right now!"

"Why? You're going to kill me anyway. Why not here?"

He gave a soft laugh that raised the hair along her spine. "You're something else, Darby Farr." He knelt down to her level, the gun aimed at her brain. "So beautiful and so smart."

He let out a loud breath. "You're correct—I am going to kill you, but not right here. You, my little amateur detective, are going over the side of this pretty ridge. That way, I can blame it on your eager friend Mr. Miyazaki."

Darby lifted her head, slowly and painfully, and stared into the barrel of the gun. "You killed Lorraine," she said. "You hid behind the lighthouse, and pushed her off the Breakwater."

"Yes," he purred. "I did."

"Why?"

"Because she was a conniving blackmailing bitch, that's why."

"What did she do to you?"

He stood. "Get up!" he snarled. "Now!"

Darby used her good arm to push herself off the snow, wincing in pain as she moved. "I can't," she said, sinking back to the cold comfort of the ground. "You'll have to kill me here."

"That's not the way it's going to happen," he spat, yanking her roughly to her feet. She moaned, but he ignored her cry. "We are following my plan, dear Darby." He shoved her toward the edge of Juniper Ridge. "And my plan involves you breaking your neck after a fall from this lofty peak." He grabbed her roughly by the waist. "Any last words?"

"Yeah," she said softly. In a lightning move that took every ounce of energy, she swung her powerful right leg up, around, and toward Detective Robichaud's head.

The metal of Tina's snowshoe connected with Robichaud's skull with a satisfying ker-thunk. He thudded to the ground, the gun spurting from his hand. Darby scrambled to pick it up, keeping her eyes on the motionless man, the beneficiary of one of the best roundhouse kicks Darby had ever executed.

A moment later she used her last reserve of energy to shoot him in the foot, just in case.

Armed with hiking poles and wearing a powerful headlamp, Donny Pease moved swiftly in his snowshoes up the side of Raven Hill, following the oval-shaped tracks of Darby Farr. Donny had heard the crack of gunfire echoing across the island, had seen Darby's red coat hanging on a hook inside the doorway of Tina's house, and now his heart pounded with dread for the young real estate agent. What the hell had happened? Was she okay? Did all this have anything to do with the other deaths on the island?

"Probably just some kid shooting turkeys," Deputy Tom Allen had drawled when Donny reached him from the truck. "Nothin' to be worried about, Pease."

That was the trouble with the man Donny knew by his middle-school nickname, Dozer. He was both unimaginative and lazy, a dangerous combination for anyone, but especially someone in law enforcement. No wonder the Manatuck police were "helping out" Deputy Allen while Hurricane Harbor's town officials searched for Chief Dupont's replacement. Thank goodness everyone on the island had enough sense to know that Dozer himself was basically inept, that he could never be Chief material.

"Why can't she just stick to selling houses?" Donny said aloud, speaking of Darby, but thinking about Tina, too. Even though his new wife was at home with a just-baked tuna noodle casserole, wringing her hands with worry over Darby's whereabouts, she was just as crazy when it came to embroiling herself in dangerous situations. "Lord, keep them all safe," he prayed, hustling even faster up the knoll.

When he crested Raven Hill and faced Juniper Ridge, the moon had risen enough to give him some additional light. He scanned the sides of the snowdrifts, searching for anything that moved. "This is nuts," he intoned, yanking out his cell phone and calling Dozer's mobile. He left a terse message for him to get his butt in gear, hung up, and shoved the phone back in his pocket.

A shrill whistle cut through the night. Donny knew that whistle, and responded with a high-pitched call of his own. *Tina.* So much for her being safe with a casserole at home! Sure enough, he saw a small group of flickering lights making their way up the hillside. He shook his head, trying to be annoyed.

"Whew," the tall redhead exhaled when she'd reached his side. "That's the fastest I ever hauled my sorry rear up that incline." Her sister Terri appeared, breathing hard, wearing a too-big parka that he recognized as one of his. Behind her, the stout figure of Bitsy Carmichael continued trudging, a look of dogged determination on her red-splotched face.

"Hey!" she shouted. "This isn't some church picnic! Keep moving!"

"Hang on, Bitsy. Donny's going to tell us where to go so we're an efficient search party." Tina cocked her head like a heron hunting fish and fixed her questioning eyes on Donny.

He swallowed.

"Er, right." Thoughts of his days in scouting flitted across his mind as he quickly surveyed the ridge. "Think of this as a grid. Tina, you do the quadrant to the far left, Terri, you head thataway, and Bitsy, you go right. Try to walk in a pattern so you don't miss anything. I'll take the top of the ridge." He paused. "We don't stop until we find Darby. Even if you locate somebody else, we're not done until we find Darby. Clear?"

The women nodded somberly and turned to start the search.

Huddled under a small outcropping about twenty yards from the unconscious Dave Robichaud, Darby did not hear Donny give the search party their instructions, nor did she see the dancing lights of their headlamps. She was lying on her uninjured shoulder, throbbing face against the snow, with her legs tucked up as close as possible. She'd stumbled upon the cave-like space by sheer luck, collapsed on the ground, and in her confused hypothermic state imagined there was a large heat lamp—the kind used in Southern California's outdoor cafes—directly overhead. So warm was the imaginary air blowing from the phantom lamp that Darby tried removing Tina's blue jacket, but her dislocated shoulder prevented any action.

She could feel her body slowing down. Her heart struggled to keep beating, her breathing was languorous and shallow, and her thoughts seemed to come slowly from very far away. Mustering the energy to care about her condition was no longer an option for Darby. She was sleepy, incredibly sleepy, and ready to surrender to a fatal slumber.

She felt herself slipping toward the intense heat of the lamp, felt the throbbing in her face start to subside, and sensed that this would be her welcome end. She closed her eyes, glimpsing the smiling faces of her long-dead parents. Her father whispered, “Hang on, Little Loon,” and her mother gave an encouraging nod, but Darby began drifting off to sleep.

It was Bitsy who found the body of Kenji Miyazaki, nearly tripping over him as he lay spread-eagled on the snow. She screamed, a piercing sound that ripped through the still night, and then knelt to find a pulse.

“He’s dead,” she muttered to Terri, who had run to her side despite Donny’s instructions. “Never seen him before, have you?”

“Yes,” said Terri. “He was a friend of Darby’s, I think.”

Another shriek made the hair on their necks stand up straight.

“That’s Tina!” Terri cried, jumping to her feet and sprinting toward the sound of the scream.

Bitsy hustled behind her. At the crest of the hill she could just make out a tall man lumbering toward them, groaning and dragging his right leg. He reminded Bitsy of the Frankenstein monster, or one of those Sasquatch things, and he was babbling incoherently.

Bitsy was just about to yell when Donny’s voice boomed through the darkness.

“I’ve found her! I’ve found Darby!”

Bitsy abandoned the dazed man and raced with the Ames sisters across the snow.

“Is she … alright?” whispered Tina. They’d reached Donny, and the tiny cave, and were now holding their collective breath as he answered.

"Her pulse is weak, but it's there." Donny lifted her up. "She needs to get warm as soon as possible."

"Here." Tina unzipped her furry black jacket and yanked it off her thin frame. "Wrap this around her. I'll call the ambulance and tell them what we've got." She pointed in the direction of the limping man. "That's Robichaud, and he's gone out of his mind."

Donny wrapped the fur around the unconscious woman and began carrying her as quickly as he dared down Juniper Ridge. "He'll be okay," he yelled over his shoulder. "It's Darby we've got to worry about."

FIFTEEN

Deputy Tom Allen claimed he would sit outside of the Coveside Clinic room for the entire night.

"There's something fishy going on here," he confided to Donny. "Why in the world would Darby shoot Detective Robichaud, unless..." he shook his head and looked up at Donny. "I gotta say, this is outta my league. I called the Staties and they'll be here just as soon as they can."

"Good idea." Donny wasn't sure what had happened on that ridge, and he wasn't about to spout theories to Dozer, but he knew one thing: Darby Farr was innocent. And given that she was innocent, that meant that Dave Robichaud was not telling the truth. She'd no more tried to kill him than the man in the moon, and if she had shot him in the ankle as he kept insisting, why then she'd had an awfully good reason to do so.

Detective Dave Robichaud was lying. The fact that his hospital bed was only two doors away from Darby's did not give Donny any comfort, either.

"I'll keep you company," he told Dozer, who gave a grateful grin. "Lemme just go and find myself a chair."

Donny ambled to the waiting room where the half dozen chairs were all occupied, two of them by Terri and Tina.

"She's going to be alright, isn't she?" Tina asked anxiously.

"She's stable, and her core temperature's nearly normal." Donny managed a weak smile. "She's gonna be fine." He saw the dark circles etched under both the redheads' eyes, their nearly identical grimaces of worry. "Why don't you both go home and get some rest?" His voice was kind. "That way, you can visit Darby in the morning, when she'll be able to talk."

The sisters nodded wearily. "Okay," Tina said, rising to her feet. "I'll find Miles's number and let him know what happened." She turned a concerned face back to Donny. "You'll call me if there's any change in her condition, right?"

"You know I will," he said, reaching out to tousle Tina's hair.

She gave a shy smile and turned toward Terri. "Let's go, sis."

Terri gave a grave nod, her eyes downcast. Donny watched her somber expression. *My new sister-in-law's got something on her mind*, he thought. Just like Tina, she wore her emotions right out front like a darn billboard.

Sedated, warm, and as comfortable as she could be, Darby lay on the clean sheets of a bed at Hurricane Harbor's Coveside Clinic and slept. Her Aunt Jane Farr had donated a large chunk of money for the efficient medical building, and then had spearheaded efforts to purchase expensive diagnostic equipment, but Darby was in no condition to remember any of that now.

A young male nurse took her pulse and temperature, listened to her heart, and made notations on her chart. He adjusted the intravenous fluids that were hanging from a pole by her bed, and tucked the sheets and blankets around her thin body, being careful not to jostle the sling around her injured shoulder. She was beginning to recover from whatever had happened on that ridge, and he was pleased.

He left Darby's bedside, opened her door, and slid past the two men sitting outside the room. They were arguing quietly about baseball, their voices low and insistent. "Of course the Sox have a good shot at the Series," one of them was saying. The nurse smiled and headed down the clinic's narrow corridor.

Bitsy didn't have the heart to yell at Rosie for her latest transgression—chewing the passenger side seat belt in Tina's truck. The puppy had been bored, after all, bored and lonely, and now as she dozed next to Bitsy on the living room sofa, Bitsy felt a kinship bordering on love for the warm, fuzzy creature.

"Nobody's perfect," she whispered to the puppy, stroking her muzzle and the top of her head. The dog let out a satisfied little whimper in her sleep.

Bitsy thought back to Sunday, when she and Charles had chosen the puppy. She remembered the call coming in from Dave Robichaud, and Charles's pride at being asked to help the Manatuck department. What if Detective Robichaud had been up to no good on that day, as well? What did it mean that he and Darby had had some kind of serious, to-the-death struggle on Juniper Ridge?

She pulled a knitted shawl, one they had given her at the treatment center back in Vegas, around her body and snuggled next to the puppy. Darby was going to be okay, that was what Tina had said when she'd phoned ten minutes earlier. Darby would survive and explain the whole thing.

———

Deputy Tom Allen grinned and accepted the Styrofoam cup of coffee. "Where'd you find this, Pease?"

"Nurse's office. They've got a Mr. Coffee in there, and I brewed some up."

"So that's what you were up to. I passed by on my way to use the facilities. Didn't know you were a regular Suzy Homemaker."

Donny shrugged. "That's me alright." He took a sip of the coffee. "You want to go and stretch your legs a little, Dozer, go ahead."

"Maybe after I finish this fine cup of java." Tom Allen took a sip and sighed. "Have you ever tried those international coffees, the kinds that are flavored? I gotta say, I really love the one—"

A shot rang out and both men started, then jumped to their feet.

"What the—?" Deputy Allen sprang toward Robichaud's door, drawing his revolver as he moved.

"Stand away, Pease," he ordered.

Both men listened by the doorway, hearing nothing but the squeak of the nurse's sneakers as he raced down the corridor.

"What happened?" The young man's face was as white as the paper on his clipboard.

"Keep back!" Deputy Allen turned the handle of the door and pushed it open with his foot, pointing the gun straight ahead. "Robichaud?"

The detective lay motionless on the hospital bed, his revolver on the floor, a bright fountain of blood spurting from a bullet hole to his heart.

The outside temperature was several degrees colder the next morning, the sun struggling to climb into the sky. Darby awoke from a dreamless sleep to a stout nurse with short silver hair taking her vitals and asking if she'd like the window shade up. "The doctor mentioned moving you to Manatuck Hospital," she confided, smoothing the bed sheets. "But I have a feeling you'd rather stay here on the island."

Darby nodded. "I'd actually like to go home." Her throat was dry and the nurse handed her a cup of water to sip.

"I totally understand. How's that shoulder feeling?" The nurse raised her eyebrows, waiting as Darby wiggled it the tiniest bit.

She winced. "It's sore. But nothing a few painkillers can't take care of."

"That's the spirit," the nurse said, grinning. She lowered her voice. "I'm going to take you off the IV and get you some breakfast. The doctor will be in shortly, and that will be your chance to get out of here." She shuddered. "Can't say that I blame you for wanting to go, what with the shooting and all..."

"Shooting?" Darby felt her stomach constrict with anxiety.

"I shouldn't be saying anything, but heck, you'll find out soon enough." She paused. "The guy in the room right over there," she hitched a thumb to the left. "Detective Robichaud. He shot himself last night. Why he had access to his gun, I'll never understand, but I'm certainly not the one who makes the rules."

Darby swallowed. "Was it fatal?"

The nurse busied herself with the IV before responding. "Yes. I'm afraid it was."

A weight seemed to lift off Darby's chest and she felt as if breathing was suddenly easier. Dave Robichaud had tried to kill her, right after he'd confessed to shoving Lorraine Delvecchio off the Breakwater. Now he had turned that same murderous rage on himself. Darby's overriding feeling was of relief.

The nurse gave her a bright smile. "All set," she said. "I'll be back with some breakfast in a few minutes." She bustled out of the room, closing the door with a click behind her.

Donny trotted up the walkway to Darby's farmhouse and let himself in. Just as he'd feared, the inside temperature was decidedly chilly, the windows frosted up from the cold. He glanced around the normally neat kitchen, now a war zone. Pots and pans were pulled out of cabinets, drawers lay yanked out with dishtowels, utensils, and serving spoons scattered nearby, and the oven door yawned open, an enameled roasting pan overturned on the floor. "What in the name of heaven?" Donny shook his head and entered the living room.

There, the scene was much the same. Pillows pulled from the couch, logs dragged from the fireplace, and the contents of desk drawers spilled all over the floor. The house had been ransacked, and as Donny looked at the mess in Darby's bedroom, he remembered her incoherent ramblings on the ridge. She'd said the Japanese guy, the one Dave Robichaud had shot, was searching for some kind of box.

Donny called Tina. "Come on over and help me clean," he said, explaining the situation. He then hung up, lit a big fire in the living room, and started putting Darby Farr's house back in order.

Two hours later, Tina held Darby's good arm and led her from the door of the Coveside Clinic to the waiting SUV. "You're going to have to sit in the back, I'm afraid," she said with a grimace. "Bitsy's darn dog, Rosie, ate the front seat belt. Chewed it right up like it was a piece of licorice."

Darby giggled, and then winced. "Ouch! Laughing jiggles my shoulder," she said. "But boy, it is funny."

Tina tried to frown, but then grinned. "It is kind of funny. You should have seen Bitsy's face when I told her. She turned white as a ghost and started stammering something about insurance. I told her not to worry about it, but she's insisting on paying for it."

Tina helped Darby into the back of the SUV and fastened her seat belt as if she were a child. "If you're feeling better tomorrow, I'm taking you with me up to Westerly. There's a new spa up there with the works. We're getting manicures, pedicures, taking a sauna, and just plain relaxing."

"Sounds heavenly," Darby said. Spas weren't her thing, but the idea of decompressing in a warm place with a friend struck her as perfect.

"Good. Right now I'm taking you home and then letting Donny know what he can pick up for you at the grocery store, okay?"

"That's awfully nice of Donny."

"He wants to help," Tina said. "We all do." She didn't tell her friend that she and Donny had just cleaned up a monumental mess at the farmhouse. She started the truck, glancing at her phone before beginning to drive. "Huh. I've got a missed call from Terri. Wonder what that's all about?"

"Try her and see. I'm not exactly in any hurry."

Tina dialed her sister, said hello, and listened. She glanced at Darby. "We'll be there in ten minutes," she said. She listened for a few seconds more, and then hung up.

"Terri wants to meet us at your house," she said.

"Any idea why?"

"None whatsoever. I thought she'd taken the ferry back to Manatuck this morning, but I guess she stuck around." She thought a moment. "She was definitely moody last night, but we all felt unsettled after that idiot—or should I say those idiots—tried to kill you." She paused. "Have you talked to anyone about it? You know, like the police?"

"I was questioned this morning. They're launching an investigation today into Detective Robichaud's actions."

Tina whistled softly. "Even though he killed himself?"

Darby nodded.

"Will they investigate Lorraine Delvecchio's death?"

"Yes, and the raid that killed Chief Dupont."

"They don't think Detective Robichaud had anything to do with that, do they?" Tina's face was horrified. "Why would he have wanted the Chief dead?"

"I don't know. Maybe Chief Dupont knew something that Robichaud didn't want getting out."

Tina set her mouth in a grimace. "Guess there's only one thing we do know," she said as she pulled into Darby's driveway. She shut off the engine and swiveled toward Darby in the back seat, her face hard. "Dave Robichaud was one dirty cop. To think he pretended to be saving you from that Japanese guy." She shook her head and exited the SUV. A moment later she had eased Darby out of the back seat.

"Watch your footing on this ice," she warned, as a Mercedes pulled in the driveway. "Here's Terri. Crap! She looks like she hasn't slept a wink."

Darby stole a glance to see if Tina's assessment of her sister was correct. Sure enough, dark circles hung under Terri's eyes and her normally calm face was puckered with anxiety. "Hello, Terri," Darby called out.

"Hey." She walked up to them hesitantly. "How are you feeling? I know this isn't a good time, but—"

"It's fine," Darby said. "I'm glad to see you. Please, come on in."

Tina opened the door and held it for Darby.

The scent of burning wood welcomed them. The fireplace was stoked and burning, the temperature a cozy contrast to the frigid outside air.

"It's nice and warm in here," Darby said gratefully. She turned and smiled at Tina. "Do I have Donny to thank for that yet again?"

"I suppose so," she said, her cheeks pink with pride. "He's a good catch, that one."

The women shrugged off their coats and Darby heated water for tea. Tina carried cups into the living room, looking at her sister inquisitively. Once they were all sipping their beverages, Tina could no longer contain her curiosity. "Well?" she finally asked. "What's up, Terri?"

Her sister carefully placed cup and saucer on the coffee table. "I have something to tell you both." She looked from Darby to Tina. "And I hope I can trust you to keep it a secret."

"That depends, Terri," Tina sniffed. "What did you do?"

Terri shook her head and took a deep breath. "It's a long story—one I've never told anyone." She rose and walked slowly toward the fire, her back to the other women, and gazed at the flames for a few minutes. Finally she sighed and turned toward them slowly. "It happened back when Tripp and I were first married." She looked down at her hands, keeping her eyes downcast. "I got pregnant."

Tina snorted and slapped her thigh. "Well, of course you did! That's how I got my nephew Tommy. And then later you had Tyler, and Tiffy..."

"I mean before Tommy," Terri said quietly. "I found out just before the wedding."

"Oh! Did you lose the baby? You know, miscarry? That happens to lots of women." Tina looked at Darby to back her up.

"No, I didn't have a miscarriage."

"You decided not to have the baby?" Darby asked gently.

Terri gave a slow nod.

"I couldn't. I wasn't ready to be a mother. I'd just started a new job, and..." She closed her eyes. "An infant didn't fit into my plans. I know how bad that makes me sound! I just wasn't ready for the responsibility."

"Was it Tripp's baby?" Tina asked.

Terri's eyes flashed. "Of course it was Tripp's baby! That's why I've felt so guilty all these years. He absolutely adores children, and if he ever knew what I did ..."

"You were young, Terri," said Darby quietly. "You weren't prepared to be a parent."

Terri nodded miserably. "I wasn't, I know that, but still, I couldn't bear him knowing the truth. And so I've hid it from him all these years."

"Until someone found out?"

"That's right."

"Lorraine Delvecchio."

Terri gave a heavy sigh. "My doctor was Theodore Hotchkiss, and Lorraine was his secretary. She saw my records and knew what the procedure was." She rolled her eyes. "I suppose she figured out that Tripp was well-off, too. The first blackmail letter arrived a few months later."

"What a horrible thing to do!" Tina sprang from her seat on the couch and went to her sister, giving her a tight hug. "You must have wanted to kill her!" The comment hung in the air for several moments. Tina released her grip on her sister. "Not that you would have, of course—"

Terri managed a shaky smile. "I never thought of killing Lorraine, but I was angry." She came back to the couch and sat down. "Although, when I think about it now, the anger came gradually. At first I was just afraid. I knew my secret would devastate Tripp, and I thought that maybe he wouldn't love me anymore. I kept thinking that once I had a child, things would be different."

"And then you had Tommy." Tina's face was kind.

"Yes. He was born two years later. You remember, Tina—we were so overjoyed. I told Lorraine that I wasn't paying her anymore, that she would have to find somebody else to torment."

Darby gave Terri a level gaze. "And what happened?"

"She told me that the whole island would know what I'd done. That I was a baby killer, and that no one would want me—not my husband, not his family, and not little Tommy."

Terri had started to quietly cry. "So I kept paying her. I didn't know what else to do."

Darby thought fleetingly of Terri's move off the island. "Did you relocate to Westerly because of Lorraine?"

She nodded. "I thought that if we were farther away, she might leave me alone. But she wasn't about to let me stop making those monthly payments. In fact, she demanded even more as time went on. By then I'd built up a good reputation in the community. I had friends, and responsibilities … I couldn't let her destroy that."

Tina reached out and patted Terri's arm. "Honey, you could have told Tripp. You still can. That man loves you, and I know he'd understand."

She wiped her cheek. "Maybe. But I don't think I want to take that chance."

Darby pictured Lorraine's little ledger. The column for "TD" was the longest one in her book, going back more than a decade. "I'm glad for your sake that this all stopped."

Terri sniffed. "Thank you. You have no idea how relieved I've been to think that she can't blackmail me anymore. I could never have harmed Lorraine, but I wasn't sorry that she died. I know that sounds terrible."

"After what that woman did to you, all those years!" Tina ran a hand through her red curls. "Of all the deceitful, money-grabbing schemes!" She huffed out a breath and made a face at Darby. "You know, I'm starting to think that Robichaud did us all a big favor when he shoved Lorraine into the water."

Darby flashed on his description of Lorraine as a "conniving bitch." Certainly it seemed he had despised the woman. *But why had he killed her?*

———

"Do you think someone paid him?" Miles asked Darby an hour later. She'd called the British journalist as soon as Terri and Tina left, assured him that she was healing fine, and now they were discussing Dave Robichaud's possible motives for murder.

"I hadn't thought of that, Miles. I suppose that's an option, isn't it?" She was propped up in bed with several pillows taking any pressure off her shoulder, a legal pad and pen on the comforter next to her.

"I remember a case back in London in which a metropolitan policeman was pulling in several hundred thousand pounds a year doing 'favors' for business associates," Miles said. "Perhaps someone contracted with Robichaud to get rid of Lorraine."

"Maybe one of her blackmail victims," Darby mused, picking up the pad.

"Right." Miles paused. "Now let's see, you've got AB—that's Alcott Bridges, right? Not likely that he paid Robichaud, is it?"

"No. For one thing, he was completely surprised to hear of Lorraine's death, so it's unlikely that he arranged it."

"Good point," Miles conceded. "Leonard Marcus was incarcerated at the time, and although that doesn't seem to stop people from making deals with those on the street, he'd stopped making payments to Lorraine by the time of her death, right?"

"Yes." She jotted down more initials. "It's not Terri Dodge—she doesn't have the heart for murder."

"You're sure about that? She would only have had to arrange it, not pull the trigger herself."

"Miles, I looked into her eyes as she told us about being blackmailed by Lorraine for the past ten years. She's not a killer." Darby remembered the scribbled "ab" next to Terri's initials on Chief Dupont's notes. How had the Chief guessed Terri's secret?

"Okay. So that leaves Bartholomew Anderson, and 'CR', right?"

"Yes." She underlined Anderson's name and pursed her lips. "I can definitely see Bart arranging a hit on Lorraine, can't you? After all, she had that file of compromising photos, and he was terrified that she'd go to his wife."

"Right. When did he start making payments to Lorraine?"

Darby consulted her notepad. "Five years ago."

"What about 'CR'?"

"Two years ago."

"Interesting. 'CR' was Lorraine's newest victim, correct?"

"That's right, Miles. Maybe he or she knew early on that they weren't going to take it, and convinced Detective Robichaud to help them out with a well-placed shove."

"That would mean that whoever 'CR' is, he or she would also have known that Robichaud was operating on the wrong side of the law," Miles commented.

"Yes." Darby groaned. Her shoulder was aching, and she suspected it was time for another pain pill.

"Are you okay, love?" Miles voice was full of concern.

"Just sore." She tried adjusting the pillows again, but one would not go flat against the headboard. She pulled on it, and spotted something red wedged in between the mattress and the wall.

The lacquered jewelry box.

"Miles! I've found the red box, the one that belonged to my mother!"

"Wonderful, darling, but I didn't know it had gone astray."

Quickly she told him about Kenji's search for the object and his questions to her on the ridge. "Tina told me that he'd torn this place apart looking for it," she explained. "The only reason he tracked me down was because he couldn't find it." She ran a finger over the jewelry box's smooth surface, touching the tip of Mount Fuji and the intricate blue-tile roofed temples. She undid the little brass latch and opened it up.

"Miles, if Kenji had found this box, not only would I have lost this link to my mother, but he would have located whatever missing piece of the formula he needed." She took a shaky breath. "I need to call Ed Landis and let him know."

"I agree. Ring him up first thing in the morning." His tone changed. "You also need to get some rest, Darby. After all, you did just get out of hospital. You must be right knackered."

Darby smiled. Privately she'd begun to call Miles's delightfully odd expressions "Briticisms." "By that do you mean that I'm tired?"

He chuckled. "The word I was going for is exhausted, actually."

She yawned, as if proving his point. "I'm knackered all right, but I'm also relieved to have this little box." She touched the silk of the *obi* and bit her lip, overcome with gratitude. "I almost feel as if my mother were watching over me."

"Perhaps she is." Miles's voice was soft. He waited a second, before telling her he loved her, and then added gently, "Now go to sleep."

Not even the prescription painkillers could keep Darby from having nightmares about her recent ordeal. She dreamt she was on a snow-capped peak resembling Mount Fuji. On her feet were enormous snowshoes. Behind her, a man in a ski mask and silk *obi* was fast approaching, but she could not lift even one of her legs ...

She awoke in a cold sweat. Lying under the comforter, her heart racing, she took deep breaths and thought about the events on Juniper Ridge.

Kenji Miyazaki, wearing a ski mask, had hunted her down because he could not locate the lacquered red box. He'd had nothing to do with Lorraine's death, and yet Kenji had worn the very item of clothing Alison Dyer had seen through her scope. Had it been a coincidence, and nothing more?

Darby pushed herself up with her good shoulder. She reached for the glass of water she kept on the nightstand and took a sip. Dave Robichaud had confessed to pushing Lorraine to her death, but he had not given any reason why. *Robichaud shot Kenji*, Darby recalled. *Not to protect me, but to give himself an alibi. If he had succeeded in breaking my neck on the ridge, he would have blamed Kenji for my death, and no one would have known the truth.*

Darby swallowed. There was absolutely no sleeping for her now. Slowly she climbed out of bed and pulled on her robe. The bedside clock read three-thirty in the morning, but Darby was wide awake.

She picked up the lacquered jewelry box and cradled it carefully as she walked downstairs. In a few minutes she had a small fire going in the hearth, and she'd put on a pot of water to boil. The familiar routines of tending the fire and preparing tea soothed her jangled nerves, and soon the haunting ski-masked man of her nightmare was forgotten.

Once the water had boiled and her tea was ready, Darby glanced out the kitchen window, toward the cove. The winter sky sparkled with stars, and out of habit she looked for the constellation of her youth.

There he was: King Cepheus, the promise breaker, sitting on his throne with his pointy crown. She imagined her father retelling the story, heard him describing heroic Perseus, and felt a warm rush of gratitude. *I have wonderful memories,* she realized. *If I let myself recall them, I keep the people I love alive.*

Tearing herself from the array of bright stars, Darby settled on the faded couch with her Constant Comment and the red box. She sipped the hot beverage and opened the brass clasp, pulling out the jewelry box's treasures. Now the presence of Jada Farr was with her, both in the contents of the box and in the scent and taste of her mother's favorite tea. She smiled. Here was the dark blue *obi* that her mother might have worn fastened around a kimono that had no doubt been exquisite. She gazed at the photo of her mother as a child and then fingered the wisps of straw from some faraway temple. What was it Eric Thompson at the Westerly Art Museum had called them? *Shimenawa.* She smiled at her recall of the Japanese word. *Lorraine Delvecchio's got nothing on my memory,* she thought.

Abruptly she pushed the lacquered box aside. Her off-handed statement cut to the core of the dead woman's murder. What had she "had" on the mysterious 'CR'? Was that the person who had persuaded Detective Robichaud to take action?

I need a link between the detective and people from Lorraine's past, she thought. But how could she find anything on Lorraine, when she'd had so few friends, no family, and few admirers?

Darby grabbed her computer and found the website for the *Manatuck Gazette*. Perhaps a search of Lorraine's name would yield something interesting.

Only one news entry surfaced, an announcement of Lorraine's appointment to the staff of the Manatuck Police Department. Had she been blackmailing someone there, Darby wondered? Had she encountered something that would have embarrassed Detective Robichaud, and prompted him to take her life?

She took a sip of the soothing tea, tasting the spicy scented orange flavor, and tried to think. Someone had hated Lorraine enough to want her dead, and had arranged for a dirty cop to do the deed. Who?

Frustrated, she pushed the computer aside and picked up the jewelry box again. Now that the notebook was in the hands of the FBI, the only item remaining was the little metal Buddha. Darby picked him up and looked into his placid, plump face. Her mother had acquired him at a tourist site—or at least that had been Eric Thompson's explanation.

Darby held the chubby deity in her hand, remembering the curator's comment that today's versions were made of plastic. They were undoubtedly quite a bit lighter, Darby thought, although it was surprising that this one, made of solid metal, should not feel heavier in her grasp.

She pulled the little Buddha closer and scrutinized its image. A grinning face with a wide body smiled back at her. The Buddha wore a flowing robe and little sandals. She flipped him over. A belt encircled the Buddha's waist, upon which appeared to be a small crack in the metal.

Darby inspected the crack. *A coin slot*? How had she not seen this before? Why hadn't Eric Thompson noticed it? She peered at the opening, realizing that the little man was actually a piggy bank. She rattled the Buddha, but there were no coins inside.

And yet … there was something inside of the opening. *Perhaps a bill*, Darby thought. She went into the kitchen for something long and skinny, but found only a toothpick. *Tweezers*. She had a set in her makeup bag upstairs.

The tweezers pinched the piece of paper and gingerly Darby started pulling it out. Once it fell back inside the bank, but she managed to grab it again and move it slowly toward the slot. At last the item was free, and Darby saw that it was not currency, but a piece of white paper that had been intricately folded to fit inside the Buddha.

She opened it up. Japanese writing, with a string of numbers, met her eyes.

Darby bit her lip and leaned back on the sofa. In her hands she felt sure was the key to preparing one of the world's worst biotoxins, a strain of bubonic plague capable of contaminating fresh water sources around the globe. She swallowed, her hands gripping the paper.

The missing piece of the formula.

SIXTEEN

THE WHIR OF THE helicopter blocked out all other noise at the Merewether estate, its blades once again creating a blinding storm of snow. From the warmth of her vehicle, Darby watched Ed Landis emerge from the cockpit and run toward the car.

He opened the door and climbed in beside her, pulling off a thick glove so that he could shake her hand.

"Good morning! Boy, it's cold up here. How do you all take it?" He shivered inside his thick survival coat. "What have you got for me, Darby?"

She reached in her pocket and pulled out a plastic zipper bag with the folded paper inside it. "I'm not sure, but I think it's what Kenji Miyazaki was after when he attacked me on the ridge." She handed him the bag.

"Christ, that's right! How are you doing?" Landis's handsome face showed concern.

"My shoulder was dislocated and I have some lovely bruising on my face, but nothing a little foundation can't cover," she said.

"Bet you're glad Miyazaki's dead," the FBI agent said bluntly.

"I'm relieved, put it that way. You probably heard about the other guy that tried to kill me."

"Robichaud, right? Sounds like one of law enforcement's finest. Why was he after you?"

Darby thought a moment. "You know, I'm not exactly sure. Obviously he felt threatened by something having to do with a local murder, but I don't know what that something is."

"You were getting too close to the truth."

"I suppose, but it's all still a puzzle." She pointed at the plastic bag. "What about the formula Kenji tore from the journal? Do you know where it is?"

Ed Landis raised his eyebrows. "We think we have it. Keep in mind it isn't much good without this missing piece."

Darby nodded. "So what happens now?"

"I take this back to Washington and it gets locked away where no one can get to it."

Darby thought about the little Buddha. The metal bank had kept the secret safe for decades. "I guess I'll never know why my grandfather put that slip of paper in a separate place."

"I think I know why," Landis said, tucking the plastic bag into the large pocket of his survival coat and zipping it securely shut. "Your grandfather understood human nature. He was afraid that someone would get their hands on the formula, and if that happened, he wanted a failsafe." He pulled on his gloves and regarded the real estate agent. "Take it easy for a while. No more encounters with maniacs, alright?"

Ed Landis opened the car door, slammed it shut with a little wave, and trotted across the snow to the waiting chopper.

"So what is the latest news from Maine?" The smooth voice of ET was like a warm hug cutting through the chilly late-morning air as Darby walked to the Hurricane Harbor Café.

"Oh, this and that," Darby said, not wanting to alarm her assistant with the story of her near escape at the hands of two deadly men. "I'm helping Tina with a few properties, and still working on my own house when I can."

"Why is it I feel you're not telling me everything?" His voice was concerned.

"What, do you think you're clairvoyant or something?" Darby tried to sound irritated, when actually she was asking herself whether her associate truly was psychic. "I'll be back in San Diego next week, don't worry. Meanwhile, what's happening there?"

"I'm extremely impressed with Claudia. She's managing to get some deals underway, even though it's the dead of winter."

Darby smiled. The "dead of winter" in San Diego meant seventy degree temperatures, the return of the whales, and fields of wildflowers, not heaps of crusted snow like she was climbing around now on her way to the Café.

"That's great. Please tell Claudia that I appreciate her hard work and that I'm looking forward to catching up." Claudia Jones was a new member of Darby's team, working as a sales agent while raising several young children. "And ET? I hope you know how grateful I am for all that you do."

"I know. Now you'd better let me get ready for work, or that boss of mine will have my head."

She laughed. "Goodbye, and thanks."

He hung up with a chuckle and Darby pulled open the door of the restaurant, ready to sit by the woodstove with a big bowl of chowder.

———

Donny Pease swiveled on his barstool and spotted Darby Farr entering the Café. She sunk gratefully into a chair by the woodstove, and began unzipping her red coat, wincing a little in pain.

In an instant he was by her side.

"Whaddya trying to do, Darby, dislocate that shoulder again?" Donny reached over, gently easing off her puffy coat. He draped it on an empty chair, his face crinkling into a look of fatherly concern. "Are you supposed to be up and gallivanting around?"

"A girl needs to eat lunch, Donny," she smiled. "Care to join me?"

The older man considered her invitation. "Only if it's my treat," he said. "I insist."

"Okay, then. Grab a chair."

They both ordered bowls of chowder—Donny the haddock, and Darby the clam—and sat back and waited for them to arrive. Darby asked him whether he'd purchased flights for Mexico, and Donny gave a shy grin.

"I bought them an hour or so ago," he said. "We head right out of Portland."

"Where exactly are you going?"

"The Yucatan peninsula, to a little village near Tulum." He pointed at the mounds of snow piled outside the Café's window. "Sure won't miss shoveling the white stuff for a few weeks."

"I'll bet you won't," said Darby, taking a sip of water. "I know I'm not going to miss it, either."

"When are you flying back to California?"

"Sometime next week. First I have to get a little more work done on that house of mine."

"Like what?"

"Get some cracked windows fixed, paint the upstairs bedroom, replace the old dishwasher—that type of thing."

"Make a list," Donny advised, as their bowls of steaming soup arrived, "and leave it for me. You do recall I've been a caretaker for close to forty years, right?"

"How could I forget?" The spry man had managed one of the island's biggest estates, Fairview, until the property had changed owners. "How is the old place doing?"

"Looks great. Lots of people having meetings there, that kind of thing. 'Course it's different from when the Trimble family owned it, but in a good way. You should stop by and see what they've done."

Darby knew that the new owner of the rambling property, the nonprofit Maine Island Association, was putting Fairview's size to good use, making it a campus for all kinds of groups working to preserve working waterfronts and island life. Recently the association's director, Ryan Oakes, had held a symposium on fisheries that had drawn experts from the whole Atlantic coast. She picked up her spoon. "Maybe I can get Tina to take me over there before we head to the spa."

"That's right!" Donny grinned and wiped his mouth with a napkin. "She's got you going with her to that new place up in Westerly." He whistled under his breath. "Sounds hoity-toity to me, but you girls will probably have fun."

Darby took a spoonful of the rich clam chowder and let the creamy warmth rest on her tongue. The taste was marvelous, the briny taste of the mollusks mingling with the buttery cream. *I've got to get Miles to taste this chowder,* she thought. *He will totally love it.*

To Donny she smiled. "Yes, Tina and I will enjoy ourselves," she assured him. "Can you think of a time when we haven't?"

The old man could think of several times the pair had been in danger, and those hadn't been side-splitting laughfests, but he pushed those thoughts away, bit his lip, and gave Darby a grin. After all, what harm could come to anyone in some high-falutin' beauty parlor?

———

Tina was dressed for a day in the city with her tight black pants and faux-fur cream-colored jacket. "I'm sick of wearing my same old winter clothes," she complained, as Darby hoisted herself into the SUV. "Tell me, do I look like Bitsy in this getup?"

Darby took in her friend's tall frame, mass of curly red hair, and razor-sharp expression. "Tina, you could not look like Bitsy if you tried," she laughed. She pointed at the plastic sack on the seat between them. "What's in the bag?"

"Those darn shoes of Terri's," she explained. "Forgot to give them to her yesterday, and she said she might stop by the spa while we're there so she can check it out."

She gazed at her friend, sitting next to her in the front seat. "If you want a seat belt, you've got to sit in the back," she said. "Remember, Bitsy's puppy..."

"I know, I know, she chewed the belt. After what I've been through the last day or two, I think I'll take my chances and live dangerously for an afternoon."

Tina started the SUV. "We can make the two o' clock ferry if we have a quick stop at Fairview, but it's got to be a short visit, okay?"

"Sure." She leaned back on the seat, relaxing her injured shoulder. "I'm curious to see what the Maine Island Association has done with the place. Ryan Oakes had big plans."

"I do see him around here and there," Tina said. "Ryan always seems to be in an upbeat mood, so my guess is that things are going well." She turned the SUV off the road and onto the long winding driveway to the estate.

Fairview was built in the fashion of the sprawling, shingle-style mansions from the turn of the twentieth century, and featured a giant, wraparound porch and several jutting, symmetrical eaves. The main house, perched as it was on the edge of a rocky cliff, never failed to take Darby's breath away.

A new parking lot had been created to the left of the property, and several cars bearing Island Association decals were parked there. Tina swung into a space and grabbed her turquoise pocketbook. "Remember, only fifteen minutes or so."

"Gotcha." Darby extricated herself from the SUV and closed the door. Pulling her red coat more tightly around her, she marveled that Fairview looked friendlier on a freezing February day than it had the last time she'd visited during the height of summer. The difference was that the house was now being loved.

"I can see they've sunk some money into this place," Tina muttered. "New paint job, for one. Wasn't the old garden shed over there when they bought it?" She pointed at a small outbuilding that was now closer to the main house.

"Yes, it was," Darby said. "I wonder what it's being used for?"

"That's our children's activities center," explained a trim man with a ready smile. He stood waiting for them in the brisk air without a coat, a big grin on his face. "Good to see you again, Darby!"

"Ryan! I was hoping you'd be here if we stopped by. You remember Tina, right?"

"I sure do. Come on in, ladies, and let me show you around."

The extravagant entryway seemed much the same, although an antique desk with flyers describing the organization's activities, mission, and projects was positioned right at the entrance. "We have a receptionist here most of the time," Ryan explained. "It's been a little slow this winter but we expected that."

He pointed at the ornate dining room where generations of Trimbles had dined. "This summer we'll have a café that's open to the public for lunch, featuring the best of Maine seafood. The formal living room is available for small receptions and parties, and we'll be able to cater them from our kitchen."

"Awfully pretty place to get married," Tina said, nudging Darby, who shot her an exasperated look.

"Our offices are back here," Ryan continued, "and upstairs. We also have a small library and gallery up there." He punched the button on an elevator. "The main stairway's still an option, but we put this in to meet code and so that we could use the upstairs for whatever we needed."

They entered the elevator and emerged on the second floor. "This is the gallery," Ryan explained, his face shining with pride.

Darby took in the gorgeous paintings and pointed at one. "That's by Lucy Trimble, isn't it?"

He nodded. "She gave it to us when we opened." He pointed at another painting, this one of the Manatuck Breakwater. "Alcott

Bridges. This is the first landscape he'd painted in years. I understand he was working on a larger version when he died."

Tina and Darby shared a quick glance, thinking of the elderly man and his studio.

"Goes on the market next week," Tina whispered.

"Can we poke our heads in the library?" Darby asked. "And then we'll let you get back to work."

"Certainly." Ryan Oakes led them to a cozy room with floor to ceiling shelves lined with books. "People have been so generous. When we explained to our donors what we were doing here, so many of them came forward with their personal collections. It's truly been overwhelming."

"Do you find that being on Hurricane Harbor has made it more difficult for your conference participants to get to meetings?" Tina was thinking of the ferry, and its inflexible schedule. She glanced at her watch.

"I suppose it's challenging, but I think the fact that we are on an island is what's making our conferences so attractive to groups around New England. We're the real deal, so to speak." He pushed the button for the elevator.

"Sounds like you are well on your way," Darby said to Ryan as he ushered them into the elevator. "I'm so pleased that this property is proving to be such a good home for the Island Association."

"Thank you. We couldn't have done it without you Darby, nor the generosity of Mark and Lucy. By the way, I just spoke to Mark this morning. He's in the Bahamas, visiting friends, but will be so glad to know you both stopped by."

They had reached the ground floor and were back in Fairview's impressive entryway. Darby took a brochure and gave Ryan a light hug. "Thanks so much for the tour."

"My pleasure. Come by this summer for lunch, okay?"

"We will," Darby promised, waving as she and Tina went out the door.

Bitsy Carmichael pushed away her plate of a half-eaten Cobb salad and sighed. Beside her, Rosie whimpered, as if sensing the sadness threatening to swamp her owner. "Here you go," Bitsy said, giving the dog a chunk of ham from the salad. She sighed again and knew it was time to get up and do something.

There were piles of Charles's things everywhere, but Bitsy didn't feel strong enough to sort through them just yet. Instead she moved little stacks of items to the dining room table, feeling as if she was at least accomplishing something by consolidating. Now she gathered up his date book and a duck hunting magazine and carried them both to the table, Rosie trotting along, hoping another chunk of ham would materialize. The dog sprang up and put both front paws on the table, pulling down the pile, and Bitsy scolded her.

"No! No jumping!" The dog looked mortified and dropped quickly to the floor.

Bitsy bent to pick up the address book and magazine, along with several pieces of paper that had fallen out of the book. One was a reminder slip from the drycleaner's in Manatuck. *Probably his uniform*, Bitsy thought. Another was a black and white photograph and caption, which looked to have been copied from a newspaper clipping. And the last was a coupon for a discount on an oil change.

She put the papers on the table. The photograph had writing on it, two letters along with a question mark, and a date. Curious, Bitsy pulled a pair of reading glasses from her pocket and scrutinized the image.

It was a typical donation photo of a community member handing a check to a charitable organization. A man in a suit was smiling as he proffered the donation, while the recipients—two women and a man—smiled as well. She read the caption.

James Williams of Manatuck Savings presents a check for one thousand dollars to Board Members of the Manatuck Area Battered Women's Shelter. Bitsy had seen flyers and posters for the organization, and knew it was still operating in a ramshackle old home in Manatuck.

She pulled the photograph closer and peered at the faces. She did not recognize James Williams, nor did she know the other man, but the two women looked familiar. One, she was sure, was the poor girl who'd worked for Charles and had been pushed off the Breakwater. She thought a moment. *Lorraine Delvecchio.* Her picture had been all over the *Manatuck Gazette* and it was easy to recognize her wan little face. The other woman reminded Bitsy of someone, but she couldn't think who. She squinted her eyes at the female features. It was someone she had seen since being back in Maine. But who?

If the date written at the top of the paper was correct, the photograph had been snapped five years earlier. She looked at the scribbled letters. *CR.* Was there a question mark next to them because

Charles hadn't been sure? Were they the unidentified woman or man's initials?

Bitsy shrugged and put the photograph on the dining room table. She looked about for Rosie, heard her whimpering at the back door, and hurried to get her coat and a leash.

SEVENTEEN

"Wasn't it nice of Terri to get me this gift certificate?" Tina asked. She and Darby had made the ferry to Manatuck in plenty of time, and were now cruising up the coast to Westerly and the spa. "She knew I'd want to check it out as soon as it opened."

"I'm thrilled to be going with you, Tina, but why didn't you ask Terri?"

"Because I wanted to do something fun with you. Besides, she's always getting facials and stuff at this resort right in town."

Darby smiled. She wasn't sure pampering sessions at spas were her thing, but nonetheless she was looking forward to a relaxing afternoon with Tina. "Have you spoken to Terri since she told us about her abortion?"

"Yes. She's relieved to have finally told her secret. I keep saying she should tell Tripp, so hopefully she'll get the guts to do that." Her face brightened. "Terri said for us to call her when we got to the spa. If she can, she's gonna stop by to say hello, and grab her fancy shoes."

"Great."

Tina pulled into a parking lot before a restored antique home. "Here we are," she said, shutting off the engine.

"What a lovely old place," Darby said, admiring the ornate bric-a-brac reminiscent of the Eastlake style.

Tina grabbed her pocketbook and opened the car door. "There's a well-to-do guy here in Westerly who has bought a bunch of older homes and fixed them up incredibly well. I mean, like top-notch. He just finished working on this one last fall, and then Connie bought it."

"Connie? You mean your hairdresser?"

Tina helped Darby out of the SUV. "Yeah. Didn't I tell you that this was her new place? She's going to keep her salon in Manatuck, but I'm not sure how long she'll cut hair there. She'd have to drive back and forth, but who knows? She's quite the businesswoman."

Even with piles of snow surrounding the building, Darby could see that it was impeccably restored. All of the outside trim had been freshly painted; a new, handicapped accessible walkway led to the entrance; and healthy evergreen bushes lined the front façade. Every detail bespoke quality.

Tina pulled open the door for Darby and ushered her into a soothing entryway with a coat rack and mat for their shoes. Soft music played in the background and the light scent of sandalwood freshened the air. A moment later a pretty young woman dressed in a clean white smock appeared with two pairs of slippers.

"Hello ladies," she said in a hushed voice. "Welcome to Evergreen Day Spa. I'm Liza. May I offer you some slippers?"

"Thank you," said Tina, easing them on to her feet. She turned to Darby. "So cozy!"

Her companion nodded. It *was* cozy, and not just because the slippers were sheepskin, but because the rooms were pleasantly warm, and illuminated with soft, low, lights.

"Come this way," said Liza, leading them into a hushed living room where a gas fire burned in a beautiful fireplace. "Do you know what services you would like today?"

"I think when I spoke to Connie we discussed the facial and massage package," Tina said.

Liza glanced discreetly at a card in her hand. "Yes, I see it right here. She suggests that you start with a sauna." She smiled at them both. "You're in for a treat."

"I can see that already," Tina said. "Connie has done a wonderful job. I can't wait to tell her."

Liza frowned. "I'm afraid she won't be in today." Her voice was apologetic. "She had some family stuff going on and needed to be home."

Tina scrunched up her nose. "That's a shame. I'll just have to tell her another time, I guess."

"Let's get you both a locker," Liza continued brightly. "You can place your valuables and change your clothes. I've got the sauna fired up and ready to go, and the heat feels especially nice on a raw day like today."

Darby and Tina followed the young woman to a pleasant room lined with pastel-colored lockers.

"You'll find a robe and several towels inside your locker. Help yourself to any beverages from the mini-bar before or after your sauna." She pointed to a door.

"There's the entrance. We recommend a visit of no more than fifteen minutes, so I'll be sure to come and get you should you lose track of time. As soon as you're through, I'll take you for your massages." Liza smiled. "Any questions?"

The women shook their heads and Liza departed. Tina opened her locker and pulled out a pristine white robe.

"This is going to be fun," she whispered. She crossed the room to the mini-bar. "Wonder what they've got in here?" She pulled it open and surveyed an array of bottles. "Fruit juices, flavored waters, green tea—want something, Darby?"

"Sure. How about a green tea?"

"Coming right up." Tina pulled two bottles from the mini-bar and handed one to Darby. "I'm impressed with this place so far. It's like a little oasis. I hope Connie ends up doing a good business."

"I'm sure it will be hopping come the summer." Darby opened her tea and took a sip.

"Hopefully." Tina pulled off her black pants and hung them in her locker. "I've always admired Connie and her drive. She once told me that she grew up poor but that she knew from an early age she wanted to have a better life. She went to hairdressing school and started her own little place. She married her high school sweetheart, Scott Fisher, once he got out of law school. His career kind of took off, you know? He's a District Attorney, and in the running for some other big state position. Anyway, I'm sure Connie could just quit working and relax. Instead she decided to open this place."

"Do you think that her difficult childhood has something to do with her drive?" Darby asked.

"Oh yeah." Tina's red curls bounced as she bobbed her head in agreement. "She once told me she'd grown up in a 'hovel.' That's not something you hear every day, now is it? I mean, lots of people might say their parents' homes were messy, or cluttered, or even crazy, but nobody describes their childhood home as a 'hovel.'"

"You're right." Darby had wriggled out of her jeans, pleased to note that her shoulder was healing and undressing was not as painful as it had been. She tied her robe around her waist and grabbed a towel. "Ready for the sauna?"

"*Sow*-na," Tina corrected. "That's the way they pronounce it in Finland."

"I see," Darby giggled, opening the heavy wooden door. "Come in to the *sow*-na, then."

The air was dry and hot and felt wonderful. Darby spread her towel on a low cedar bench and eased herself down. She and Tina took off their robes once they were seated.

"This is heaven," Tina breathed, settling back against the cedar. "Maybe I should get Donny to build me one of these in the back yard. He could power it with one of the old woodstoves he's got rattling around in his barn."

"Good idea," Darby said. "You can heat up and then roll around in the snow, just like they do in Scandinavia."

"Exactly." Tina sighed. "Wish I had brought in my fruit juice. I'm thirsty already."

"Here, take a sip of my tea." Darby handed the bottle to Tina, who accepted it gratefully.

"Thanks." She took a swig and gave it back. "So tell me, my little friend, what's going to happen with you and Miles?"

"Who knows? Neither one of us is sure where we want to live. He's got his job in San Francisco, and I'm in San Diego. Whether we can figure out where we both want to be remains to be seen."

"What about here? Miles seems to like Maine."

"He does. I guess I don't know if I want to give up my life in Mission Beach."

"You only went there because you were running away from here," Tina pointed out.

She's right, Darby thought. "There isn't room on Hurricane Harbor for two high-powered real estate agents," she joked.

"Ha! You know darn well that's not true." Tina took a deep breath. "You think Bitsy's going to stick around?"

"Seems like it. Didn't she say she was going to look for a nursing job?"

"Yeah." Tina cocked her head. "There has to be an explanation for why she came back here, don't you think?"

"She'll tell you when the time is right, Tina." Darby exhaled. "Whew, I'm getting hot. How long has it been?"

"Not quite ten minutes. But go ahead out if you're baking."

Darby stood up carefully, feeling a little dizzy. She took a sip of her green tea and waited until the little cedar room stopped spinning. "I'll meet you out there," she said.

"I'll only be a few more minutes myself." Tina lay back and sighed. "Feels so good. Maybe I'm going to like Mexico after all."

Darby chuckled and pulled on the door. It was heavy and did not budge. She tried again.

"What's going on?" Tina asked, opening one eye. "Your shoulder hurting?"

"No, I'm using my good shoulder. The door is stuck." Darby yanked on it again, using more force.

"Let me try." Tina rose and pulled on her robe. She tugged on the door but could not make it open. "That's strange. Do you think Liza locks it until the fifteen minutes are up?"

"I would hope not. What if you needed to get out for some reason? That wouldn't make sense."

"I guess not." Tina yanked on the door again. "Not getting this door open doesn't make sense either. Let's both pull it."

Together they tugged on the door but it did not give an inch.

Tina pounded on the wood with her fist. "Liza? We're ready to come out now." She stopped and listened but there was no noise over the soothing strains of the piped-in music.

Darby took a breath of the hot air and felt her lightheadedness returning. "I'm going to see if we can shut the heater off," she said, approaching the red hot box in the corner of the cedar room.

"Careful you don't get burned," Tina warned. She pounded on the door again. "Liza!" Her voice held a hint of panic.

The heater was an upright metal rectangle in the corner of the room. A small bed of glowing rocks covered with a wire cage was on the top, and at the bottom were two round circles that Darby assumed were vents.

"Do you see an off switch?" Tina asked.

Darby licked her lips. They were bone dry. "No. It's mounted to the wall and appears to be controlled from a remote location."

"Like Liza's rear end!" Tina fumed, pounding on the door again. "Connie had better fire her ass, that's for sure." She gave Darby a wild look. "Fifteen minutes is surely up by now. Where the hell is that girl?"

A scratchy sound came over the speakers, interrupting the music. "Tina? It's Connie."

"Oh, thank God!" Tina exclaimed. "Connie, we're stuck in the sauna. Liza was supposed to come, but we don't know where she is."

"She's right here, Tina." Connie's voice was very calm.

Tina's features grew puzzled. "Great. Send her over here to let us out. The darn door is stuck."

"It's not stuck," she explained in a patient tone.

"Yes, it is," Tina insisted. "We're getting too hot in here and it's stuck."

"It isn't stuck, it's locked."

There was silence as Tina regarded Darby with a look of disbelief on her face.

"Listen, Connie. This is Darby Farr. We need you to come and unlock this door right now."

There was a chuckle over the speaker. "I'm afraid I can't do that, Darby."

"Then send Liza," Tina pleaded.

"That's not possible. Poor Liza, you see, is heavily drugged. She can't hear a thing and won't have the slightest idea of what happens."

Darby's throat tightened at the sound of Connie's words.

She looked at her friend. The tall redhead's face was flushed a bright pink and she was panting slightly.

"What do we do now?" Tina whispered.

"I'm afraid you're going to die," Connie Fisher said. "It won't take too long."

"What are you talking about? I'm one of your best clients!" Tina shook her head. "If you think this is funny, Connie, it's gone way too far. Get over here and let us out."

"It's your little friend, Tina. She won't stop poking her nose into Lorraine Delvecchio's death. I can't take the chance that she'll figure things out."

Darby's mind was suddenly crystal clear. She had to get Tina out of the sauna, and to do that, she hoped her friend would keep Connie talking.

"Figure what out?" Tina drawled, her voice becoming weaker. Darby handed her the rest of the green tea and the tall woman gulped it down.

"Figure out that I arranged for Lorraine to die." There was a sigh. "I might as well tell you while you sit there and fry. Sort of a bedtime story, I guess."

Darby examined the door's hinges while over the loudspeaker Connie Fisher snickered.

"Lorraine Delvecchio was blackmailing me. She started demanding more money when news of Scott's possible appointment as Attorney General came out. I couldn't take the chance that she would destroy his career with my little indiscretion from five years ago."

"What did you do?" Tina put her hand to her head.

"It's more like what I didn't do," Connie explained. "I was on the board for a battered woman's shelter, and I diverted a few funds my way. It wasn't a big deal, and I planned to pay it back as soon as my finances improved. Anyway, somehow sneaky little Lorraine noticed. Years later she's got the nerve to approach me with a proposition. Either I start paying her, or she exposes me."

"Did you pay her?"

"What choice did I have? I couldn't let her ruin Scott's reputation by tarnishing mine. But then she upped her demands, as people like that always do."

"So you hired the detective…"

"Hired him?" Connie's voice was hard. "All I had to do was ask."

"Huh?" Tina was swooning and Darby was feeling faint. If she didn't think of a solution very soon, they would both be dead. A line Aunt Jane Farr used to say popped into her head, a saying that had always seemed ridiculous. "If your dreams have failed you, look up and dream again." She tilted her head upward and felt a faint rush of hope.

A metal grate of some kind was screwed into the ceiling.

"Dave was my brother," Connie said softly. "One of the few reasons I survived my messed-up childhood."

CR, Darby thought. *Connie Robichaud*. She glanced over at Tina, just in time to see the woman collapse onto the cedar bench.

EIGHTEEN

With Rosie asleep on her lap, Bitsy picked up the photograph once more. Lorraine Delvecchio receiving a check from the banker, another man, and a woman who looked familiar. Charles's scrawled writing: *CR?*

She thought back to the morning of the day he had died, when they'd visited the prison in Manatuck. Leonard Marcus had been in Lorraine's little ledger, one of her unfortunate blackmailing victims. Another had been someone with the initials "CR".

Was this what the scribbled letters meant? Was Charles suggesting that one of the people in the photo—either the unidentified man or woman—was the mysterious CR? Bitsy looked again at the faces, but she could not come up with any names.

Tina, she thought. Tina knew loads of people on the island. She picked up the phone and called Donny's house, and a gruff-sounding male voice answered.

"Did I wake you up from a nap?" Bitsy teased. She pictured the old caretaker blushing to the roots of his graying hair.

"Nah, I was just watching a little football, that's all."

Sure, Bitsy thought. Instead she asked if Tina was home.

"She's gone up to Westerly with Darby to some new spa or something," he explained. "They'll be back in a couple of hours." He paused. "Do you need something, Bitsy?"

She felt a pang of sadness, felt like saying *Yes, I do need something. I need Charles back, I need not to be alone, I need to get this forty-pound puppy off my thigh …*

"No, Donny. I'm just looking at a photo and trying to figure out who some of the people are. It was in the *Manatuck Gazette* five years ago, and Charles has some writing on it. I wondered if Tina might recognize anybody, that's all."

"Hmmm. Want me to have a gander? I'm headed over to check on the Merewether place and I can stop in and have a look if you'd like."

"That would be great. I'll put a pot of coffee on."

She hung up, pushed the puppy off her lap, and placed the photo on the top of the hutch, a nice high spot where Rosie couldn't chew it. The newspaper clipping and Charles's scribbles were little clues he'd left for her to mull over, and she wasn't about to let important police evidence get destroyed.

Darby rushed to her friend's side and shook her, hard. *No,* she wanted to scream in defiance. *We are not going to die!* She thought of how foolish she'd been to think everything was fine, when all along a murderer lurked in the shadows, just waiting to strike. *Who am I to think I can solve crimes? I don't know what I'm doing and now it's going to get us killed.*

Please, Tina, she prayed. *You can't die.*

To her amazement, Tina opened her eyes, focused on Darby's fierce look, and gave an imperceptible nod. Darby pointed to a duct at the top of the ceiling. Wearily Tina lifted her head and gazed upward, her eyes glassy.

Darby put a finger to her lips. She then indicated that Tina should lift her up so that she could reach the duct.

The two women were soundless, knowing that Connie was listening in.

Tina boosted Darby up with a little puff of exertion. Darby touched the grate and to her amazement, it moved. Only one of the screws was in place, the result of a hurried—or lazy—worker.

She rotated the grate outward so that there was a small opening into the ductwork, barely sixteen by sixteen inches. She glanced down at Tina.

The redhead's thin face was nearly scarlet and she was huffing like a marathoner. Darby ignored these signs and looked into her friend's eyes. There she saw determination—the same emotion that made Tina a tough agent. She wasn't going to let the crazed Connie win—at least not without a fight.

A moment later Darby felt Tina straining to lift her higher and she scrambled to gain a purchase on the opening. With every ounce of strength she could muster, Darby contorted her naked body and slid into the heating duct.

At the same time the metal scraped Darby's hot skin, the voice of Connie crackled over the speaker. "Hey! You ladies dead yet?"

"Well, I'll be damned," Donny said, gazing at the photo with interest. He was too engrossed to be embarrassed that he'd sworn in front of Bitsy. "That's Lucas Turner, the Catholic priest from Manatuck. He's in a nursing home now, poor fellow. Kind of lost his marbles."

"Father Turner! I remember him from St. Catherine's." Bitsy pointed at the photo. "And the woman?"

He squinted his eyes. "That's Tina's hairdresser. She's the one with the new spa up in Westerly." He put the photo down.

"Connie?"

"That's right. Connie Fisher. Her husband is the DA in Manatuck."

"Oh." Bitsy felt disappointed. She could now see the resemblance. The photo depicted a younger Connie, alright, but it didn't seem to matter in terms of Charles's notes. "Why do you think Charles wrote in 'CR'?"

"He must have been thinking of her name before she got married."

Bitsy felt a shiver that made her spiky hair stand even more on end. "What do you mean?"

"She was a Robichaud."

Robichaud? Bitsy's palms were suddenly damp. "Is Connie related to the detective who killed himself?"

Donny cocked his head. "Guess I never thought about it, but yeah, I think so."

There was a silence as Bitsy contemplated the implications of Donny's words. A moment later she looked into the caretaker's worried face.

"Tina and Darby are in danger."

Darby wriggled up the duct about a foot and spotted another metal grate opening. She inched toward it, her sweaty skin rubbing hard against the rough metal. It was some sort of a fan, probably for exhaust. Darby put her face against the grate and could feel the cold air of the February afternoon.

If the grate was bolted from the outside, she was out of luck. The most she could hope for was to stay alive until someone found her. But Tina, trapped in the hot sauna itself, would have no chance of escaping. Darby hoped it was not already too late.

She pushed with her good shoulder against the grate. The metal bit into her flesh, but did not move. She tried again, this time trying to ram it with her shoulder blade. Again, nothing happened.

Darby felt desperation rising and she fought to keep it down. What was it her Aikido master always said? *Do not overlook the truth that is right before you*. She examined the exhaust fan for the key to its truth, and saw it in the form of two bolts.

The bolts were lying across the grate, evidence of more laziness on the part of Connie's team of builders. Although in her real estate practice she had cursed them, she was now thankful for slipshod contractors. She butted against the grate with her head, and this time it budged.

Seconds later Darby had wriggled out of the opening and was standing stark naked on the roof of the spa.

Bitsy and Donny called Deputy Allen, who promised he would contact the Westerly police immediately. They then grabbed their coats and headed for the door.

"What about Rosie?" Bitsy asked, frantic.

"Bring 'er," Donny commanded. "Let's go."

They sped toward town, down the hill, past the Hurricane Harbor Inn and the Café, but the ferry was easing away from the shore as Donny and Bitsy pulled up. "Wait," Bitsy screamed. "Wait!"

"It's no use," Donny said. "They can't hear you, and even if they did, they don't stop that thing ever." He gave her a strange look. "Okay, listen. I know what we gotta do, but I tell you, it's going to be cold."

"Who cares? We've got to get to Westerly as fast as we can."

Donny grunted and threw the truck into reverse. He whipped around in a circle and headed toward the public landing. There he jabbed a finger at the dark ocean water. "My boat. Let's hope she starts in this bitter weather."

Bitsy gulped and grabbed Rosie's leash. She felt freezing cold already.

NINETEEN

Darby crawled across the slippery roof, her feet numb from the icy shingles. Whatever emotions she might have felt at being unclothed in broad daylight on a low roof in Westerly were obliterated by her worry at Tina's condition. She knew, in rough terms, what must be happening to her friend's weakened body. By now, Tina's system was sorely low on fluids, hindering her skin's ability to sweat and stressing her heart to the point where she was extremely vulnerable to an attack. Proteins in other organs, such as Tina's kidneys, had most likely become denatured, causing a complete shut down of those systems. And poor Tina's brain…

Darby knew that the human brain was super sensitive to high temperatures, and that excessive heat caused high-clarity thinking to vanish. Was Tina in a stupor on the floor of the sauna? Was she even still alive? As Darby jumped from the eave of the roof six feet down onto a crusty mound of snow, she prayed that the brain in her redheaded friend's skull had not yet fried.

“Darby?” Terri Dodge’s voice was horrified. “What are you doing?” She glanced up and down the street, pulled off her svelte mink coat, and wrapped it around the real estate agent, who was pounding on the door of the Evergreen Day Spa.

“Tina’s in danger,” Darby screamed, her body shivering under the fur. “We’ve got to get in there.”

“I’ve been trying. It’s locked.” She peered into her face. “What do you mean she’s in danger?”

“Connie Fisher tried to kill us. Tina is trapped in the sauna.” She looked wildly at the side of the building. “That window—we’ve got to break it.”

“But...” Suddenly Terri seemed to understand the severity of the situation. “You say she’s got my sister in there?”

“Yes!” Darby’s feet were numb as she tried to walk. “She’s trying to kill her.”

The next thing Darby knew, Terri had picked up a large chunk of ice and hurled it against the glass.

Donny tied a quick half-hitch to secure his boat and he, Bitsy, and Rosie scrambled out.

“I think the place is just over there.” Donny pointed less than a block away and began running. Bitsy followed, the dog pulling her like a water-skier over the snow. They dashed across the road. The streets of Westerly were quiet, the light starting to wane as the winter sun sunk lower in the sky.

Tina’s SUV was parked in the spa lot. Terri Dodge’s Mercedes was beside it.

"Right here." Bitsy, out of breath, indicated the Evergreen Day Spa's gracious front entrance.

A moment later, Donny yanked on the door.

"Closed up tighter than a drum," he said.

"Over here," Bitsy yelled, "There's a smashed window!"

Donny sprang to the side of the building and took in the gaping hole in the glass. He reached up with his gloved hands and hoisted himself into the space.

There was a moment of quiet before the silence was shattered with an ear-piercing scream.

Terri Dodge's hand was over her mouth, her eyes wide and unblinking. "Good Lord, is she alive?" She looked as if she would scream again, but Darby, bent over the body of Tina Ames, spoke first.

"Just barely. Help me carry her out of this heat and let's find some fluids."

Terri stood stock still, frozen at the door of the sauna.

"Terri!" Darby yelled. "Every second counts!" She grabbed Tina's legs and the towel. "Get her head!"

Woodenly Terri stepped to her sister's prostrate form and bent down. She cradled the curly head as tenderly as if it were a baby.

"Into the lobby," Darby ordered. Together they placed Tina on a white leather couch and Darby ran to find water. She returned seconds later with a paper cupful and put it between Tina's cracked lips.

"This isn't going to work," she exclaimed, trying to moisten the inside of Tina's mouth. She spread the fluffy towel over Tina's naked torso. "She needs an IV, and fast."

Terri pulled out her phone. "What's taking the ambulance so long?" she wailed.

A blur of motion in Darby's peripheral vision made her tense, but it was Donny Pease, his weather-beaten face a mask of anxiety.

"Oh my God," he moaned. "Please don't say…"

"Donny, she's alive, but very weak. If we don't get her some emergency treatment soon…"

Terri whipped her head toward the front door where Bitsy was banging forcefully. She jumped up, played with the locking mechanism, and finally swung the heavy door open to let Bitsy in.

Bitsy was panting, her blonde hair standing straight up. "The ambulance," she breathed. "It's coming around the corner."

Only after Tina was loaded on to the emergency vehicle did Darby come across a motionless Liza. She called for an attendant, felt for a pulse, and knew the situation was serious. The girl was barely breathing, slumped over a calendar, a glass of lemon-scented water by her outstretched hand.

"Unbelievable," Bitsy breathed, as the paramedics went to work. "Connie did this, too?"

Darby nodded. "Drugged her so that she wouldn't know what was happening."

"Where is Connie now?" Bitsy looked furtively around the waiting room.

"I don't know, but my guess is that she took off when she saw that I'd escaped. I think she helped herself to Liza's car so that she wouldn't be recognized."

"That's exactly right." Deputy Allen stood, legs akimbo, watching the stretcher leave the spa. He'd been on the mainland and heard the Westerly police responding to an emergency, and had driven over to lend a hand. "Connie Fisher's own car is out back, and I've got the authorities notified as to what she's driving." He turned a somber face to Darby. "We'll catch her."

Darby exhaled. "I'm getting my clothes and Tina's." She turned to Bitsy. "Let's head on down to the hospital."

"Donny took Tina's car and followed the ambulance," Bitsy said. "I'm afraid Rosie and I came with Donny in his boat."

"I'll take you to Manatuck," Deputy Allen offered. "I'm heading that way myself. Get ready and we'll go."

Darby found the little locker room where she and Tina had changed earlier and quickly put on her clothes. She grabbed Tina's clothing, Terri's fur, and Tina's pocketbook and headed back to the lobby. On the way, she passed the sauna room where she and Tina had been held captive.

The door was wide open, the room considerably cooler now that the heater was off. Darby looked up to where the grate hung from the ceiling. She thought she could feel the whoosh of cold air from the roof.

Bitsy approached the sauna and pointed toward the ceiling. "Is that how you got out?" Bitsy asked, her voice doubtful.

"Yes," said Darby. She remembered the dizzying sensation of standing naked on top of the icy roof. "Lucky for me I'm not afraid of heights."

Tina's curly red hair was a bright contrast to the white hospital bed's sheets. Donny sat beside her, holding her hand, a tender look on his face. He looked up as Darby opened the door and smiled.

Moments earlier, Darby had conferred with Tina's doctor.

"I don't think I'm betraying any confidentiality by telling you she's responding well to intravenous fluids and is resting comfortably," he'd said. "I don't expect her to have any lasting effects." He tapped on his clipboard with a gold pen as if to emphasize his words. "She's an extremely lucky and resilient woman."

Now Darby edged toward the bed and Donny. "She looks so much better," she whispered.

He nodded. "Did you talk to Dr. Vishnu?"

"Yes. She's going to be fine."

Donny's face softened with relief. "That's what he told me, too. One night here and then she can come home tomorrow morning." He frowned. "I hope she'll still want to go on vacation after all this."

Tina stirred, her eyes fluttering and finally opening. "Don't you dare cancel that trip to Mexico, Donny Pease," she croaked. "I'm looking forward to Beach Lady now more than ever."

"Okay, then, don't you worry. We'll have ourselves a real relaxing time." He grinned at Darby. "Same old Tina," he said under his breath.

"Yeah, and I'm not deaf, either." She swallowed. "Got anything to drink out there? Whiskey, bourbon?"

"Coming right up." Darby eased a plastic cup of water to Tina's lips and watched as she took several sips. "Is that better?"

"Much." She cocked an eyebrow. "What's the latest on psycho Connie? Have they caught her yet?"

Darby shook her head. "Not that I've heard." The story was all over the news: the attempted murder at the Evergreen Day Spa, the serious condition of one of the spa's employees, and the hunt for its owner, who happened to be the wife of the Manatuck District Attorney.

Darby placed a reassuring hand on her friend's bony shoulder. "It won't be long, you'll see. The authorities will catch Connie."

"What about Liza?"

"She's out of danger."

Tina motioned to the plastic cup of water. "I'll drink to that," she said, as Darby again raised it to her lips.

Tom Allen was happy to let other police departments take over the investigation of the attack on Darby Farr. He knew his own limits, knew also that the events of the past few days had traumatized him way beyond anything he'd dealt with thus far. The loss of Charles Dupont—his Chief, his idol—left him with an empty feeling of dread, as if he were trapped in a long, black tunnel without any way out.

Sure, the funeral had been magnificent. The uniforms, the music, the squad cars with their flashing lights—but none of it had really helped to soothe his grief. None of it would.

He'd sought out Pete Paulsen, who'd been at the stakeout, guarding the rear exit. Paulsen had told him Robichaud had ordered him to stay outside. "When I heard him yell 'Officer down!' that was the worst thing ever," Paulsen confessed. "I'll never forget those words."

And now Robichaud was dead, too. He'd tried to kill Darby Farr on that ridge, but why? Then he'd committed suicide. So he wouldn't have to face the music? And how did the hairdresser at the Westerly spa fit in? Deputy Allen shook his head, trying to make some sense out of the whole thing. Somehow it all tied back to Lorraine Delvecchio and her death on the Breakwater.

The gangly man sighed and rose from the leather chair where he'd been sitting. A dog barked in the yard next door, but it was a half-hearted kind of yelp for attention, nothing more. He went to the window and watched his neighbor's kid pick up a stick. He threw it over a mound of snow and the dog raced to retrieve it.

It was mid-afternoon, he figured, somewhere around three o' clock. School was out, and the sun still shone in the winter sky. He couldn't face going back to work today. Instead, he headed to the kitchen for a snack.

The ring of her cell phone brought Darby down from a step stool where she'd been spackling a bedroom wall. Her shoulder was better, the pain now a dull ache, but her bruised face still bore an angry purple cast in one spot. Tina would be released from the hospital in the morning, and Bitsy had suggested they hold a small welcome home party—a brunch—for her at Donny's house. Darby had agreed. Not only would it be nice for Tina, but it gave the grieving widow something positive to do.

She glanced at the display on her phone, noting it was a local call. Her breath caught. Perhaps Connie Fisher had been found.

She answered and heard the clipped voice of Deputy Tom Allen.

"Darby? I have some pretty bad news."

She reached out for an armchair, held on for dear life. *Not Tina. No…*

"There was an accident, in Boston," he gulped. "I only just found out about it. The helicopter, carrying the FBI agent from the island? It crashed on landing." He paused. "I know you knew the guy. I'm sorry."

Darby's head spun. She heard the spackle and putty knife fall to the floor. *Ed Landis*. What in the world had happened?

Miles's voice was direct. "A preliminary investigation is already underway but it shows no indication of what caused the accident," he said. She'd called him, crying, as soon as she'd been able to think. Minutes later he had found the grisly story.

"The air safety investigators took the wreckage to a secure area for more detailed examination," he continued. "They'll have a preliminary report in five to seven days."

"The pilot?"

"An experienced and lifelong aviator." He sighed. "I e-mailed one of my buddies at the National Transportation Safety Board and he's already responded. He's guessing mechanical failure. Even though these machines are inspected all the time, things happen." His voice softened. "I'm sorry, Darby. I know this is a shock."

"It's just so random, Miles. I can understand crime—it's the work of some pretty sick minds—but an accident like this? Out of the blue?"

"Yes, love, an accident." He was quiet, knowing she was thinking of another accident, so many years ago …

"What about the formula? The missing piece?"

"Burned in the explosion. With Kenji's death, this puts an end to the specter of a waterborne bubonic plague. That's one blessing, at least."

"My God." Darby bent over and put her head in her hands, still cradling the cell phone with one hand. It felt like her lifeline to Miles and his soothing voice. "I can't get Ed's face out of my mind. His family—and the pilot's—they must be devastated."

"I expect so. Losing the ones you love is hell."

Darby swallowed. The pain of her parents' death at sea came back in a rush, the sensation deep, piercing, like a knife stabbing her very soul. She sat in the same kitchen where she had laughed with them so many times and felt the tears slide down her face. Her soft sobs were for Ed Landis, John and Jada Farr, Charles Dupont, and for the stark, cruel, unfairness of life.

And while she cried, Miles was there, at the other end of the line. Listening, comforting, and letting it all pour out.

Bitsy balanced an egg and sausage casserole on her hip as she opened the door of Donny's farmhouse. "Good morning," she called, drawing it out into a sing-songy cry. She inhaled deeply. The air smelled of delicious brunch offerings—cinnamon, apple, and something else—lobster.

Darby Farr, wearing an apron emblazoned with the logo of the Hurricane Harbor Inn, came around the corner, a wooden spoon in hand. "Hey, Bitsy. Thanks for coming early to help. Bring that right on in here."

Bitsy slid out of her boots and followed Darby to the kitchen. She noted the granite counters and gleaming new appliances. "Wow. This is a bachelor's kitchen?"

"I know," Darby said, peeking under the tin foil at Bitsy's casserole. "Donny renovated last month as a surprise for Tina. He knows she loves to cook." She pointed at the egg and sausage dish. "That looks delicious."

"Thanks. Whatever you've got baking smells wonderful. Some sort of coffee cake?"

"Cinnamon apple cake," she said, checking the oven. "I've made lobster crepes as well. I don't know if you've ever met Alison Dyer, but she's coming and bringing a fresh fruit salad. Terri Dodge and her husband are on their way with a big green salad and some blueberry muffins." She thought a moment. "Donny's on tap to make Bloody Marys."

"This should be a wonderful welcome home party for Tina." Bitsy's face quickly clouded. "I still can't believe what you and she went through. To think that crazy Connie almost killed you both." She shuddered. "I brought that photograph if you want to see it."

"Yes," Darby said, keeping her thoughts focused on the brunch and not on Ed Landis's death. "This is the perfect time."

Bitsy found the black and white photograph on which Charles had scribbled "CR."

Darby looked into the faces of Lorraine Delvecchio and Connie Fisher, whose name had then been Connie Robichaud. "So this is when it all started," she said softly. "Connie stole money from the Battered Women's group. Lorraine found out about the theft and stored it away in that superior memory. Connie married Scott

Fisher, and when his star began rising, Lorraine began the blackmail."

"All the others paid up and shut up, right?" Bitsy asked. "But not Connie. She got her brother to push Lorraine off the Breakwater."

Darby put the photo down. "Yes, but that wasn't enough. She convinced him to kill Chief Dupont, too." She looked into Bitsy's eyes, now clouding with sadness.

"You think it was Robichaud who shot Charlie, not the drug dealer." The words came out slowly, painfully. She swallowed.

Darby nodded. "I'm afraid so, Bitsy." She paused, looked into the widow's troubled eyes. "Connie and her brother realized the Chief was determined to figure out the whole thing."

Darby watched while the distraught widow took it in. She continued softly, "Robichaud tried to kill me on the ridge for the same reason. When he botched that, he killed himself. I wonder if we'll discover Connie had a hand in that, too?"

"No!" Bitsy's face was now horrified. "She wouldn't kill her own brother?"

"I don't know. Could she have slipped into the room, placed the gun in her brother's hand, and pulled the trigger?"

"That would mean she was a cold-blooded murderer," Bitsy breathed.

"Unfortunately we can't use the past tense yet, Bitsy." Darby's face was grim. "Nobody's caught her yet."

The doorbell rang and Alison Dyer entered with a brightly colored fruit salad and a basket of fragrant muffins. Darby introduced Bitsy and the two women began chatting. A moment later, the oven's timer sounded and Darby removed her cake, filling the whole house with the scent of cinnamon and apples.

The doorbell rang. "I'll get it," Bitsy offered, moving toward the door.

"Thought these might cheer Tina up," Deputy Allen said, entering and holding out a bouquet of flowers and a bunch of balloons. "Something bright and cheerful, plus the latest report: Connie Fisher has been captured."

"That's the best news anyone could bring," Darby said, wiping her hands on her apron as she came out of the kitchen. "Where was she?"

"Down in Massachusetts, trying to get on a plane for who knows where." He smirked. "You know, I almost feel badly for her husband. He seems to have had no clue about any of this."

"That's love for you," Bitsy said, taking the flowers. "I'll find a vase for these and maybe you can tie the balloons on some of the chairs?"

Deputy Allen nodded. "Sure."

Darby put on some music and set out her apple cinnamon cake. She'd no sooner backed away from the table than the door opened and Donny stood smiling with Tina on his arm.

"Hooray!" Bitsy yelled, clapping her hands.

Tina looked around the warm home. "Well, I can tell you one thing: it sure smells delicious. And after eating Manatuck Hospital's food, I'm starved!"

The others laughed and helped the couple in. Donny set to work mixing Bloody Marys, and before long the little house was full of well-wishers. The atmosphere was light, although there was an undercurrent of disbelief around the actions of Connie Fisher, a woman they had all known and trusted, and for Darby, shock and sadness over the news of the helicopter crash. She'd tell Tina and Donny, but not today.

"To think all this stemmed from Lorraine," Alison Dyer commented. "When I think of all the times I watched her walk on that Breakwater, never knowing that she was such a schemer. The news report said she was blackmailing several people. Imagine!"

Terri Dodge glanced up quickly. "Lorraine Delvecchio was like a spider, preying upon her victims' weaknesses."

"All of those people, stuck in her little web," said Bitsy. "But Connie didn't cooperate." She sighed. "If only Charles hadn't gotten involved."

"He needed to know the truth." Darby's voice was gentle. "That's the kind of man he was."

"A good man," Bitsy said. She swallowed, her eyes brimming with tears. "I'm not going to let this town forget that."

"Won't be easy to find someone to replace him," Deputy Allen said. "I've heard there's a lady detective from out west who's interested in the job. She says she knows you, Darby."

"Me?" She thought a moment. There was a detective in Northern California, a woman named Nancy Nardone, whom she'd met only a few months earlier. "If we're thinking about the same person, she'd be a terrific candidate. Only one problem: I don't think she's ever been to Maine."

Donny Pease lifted a forkful of sweet lobster meat wrapped in a crepe. He dabbed it in a creamy white sauce and grinned. "She tastes one of these and it'll be a done deal."

Tina took a long swig of her Bloody Mary. "Lobster's all well and good, but I truly don't see what some big-city cop from California's gonna do on a little island like Hurricane Harbor."

Darby tucked her long black hair behind an ear and gave a rueful laugh. "You don't think she'd find enough to keep herself busy?"

Tina shook her head, sending her red curls bobbing back and forth. She met her friend's almond eyes with a mocking half-smile. "Heck no, Darby. You know as well as I do, nothing much *ever* happens around here."

THE END

© William von Wenzel

Top-producing Realtor Vicki Doudera uses a world she knows well as the setting for her series starring crime-solving, deal-making real estate agent Darby Farr. A broker with a busy coastal firm since 2003 and 2009 Realtor of the Year, Vicki is also the author of several nonfiction guides to her home state of Maine.

When she's not writing or selling houses, Vicki enjoys cycling, hiking, and sailing, as well as volunteering for her favorite charitable cause, Habitat for Humanity. She has pounded nails from Maine to Florida, helping to build simple, affordable Habitat homes, and is currently president of her local affiliate.

Vicki belongs to Mystery Writers of America, Sisters in Crime, and the National Association of Realtors. Sign up for her newsletter, find signing events, book club questions, Darby Farr recipes, and much more at www.vickidoudera.com, or drop her a line at vicki@vickidoudera.com.